HOMEWARD BOUND

HJ WELCH

Homeward Bound
Pine Cove Book Three

Copyright © 2019 by HJ Welch

This book is a work of fiction. Names, places, and incidents are either products of the author's imagination or are used fictitiously. Any resemblance to actual events, locales, or persons, living or dead, is entirely coincidental.

All rights reserved. No part of this book may be used or reproduced in any manner whatsoever without written permission, except in the case of brief quotations embodied in critical articles and reviews.

PERKINS FAMILY LIST

Sunny married **Tyee**. Their adopted children are:
- **Logan**
- **Darcy**
- **Hudson**
- **Rhett**
- **Micha**

Logan married **Nell**. Their children are:
- **Saul**
- **Rona**
- **Carlee**

Darcy married **Leon**. Their children are:
- **Pepper**
- **Charles**

Hudson is currently single.

Rhett married **Louella**. Their adopted children are:

PERKINS FAMILY LIST

Mateo and **Luis**

Micha is currently single.

COAL FAMILY LIST

Deb married **Joe**. Their children are:
    Swift
    Robin and **Jay**
    Ava
    Kestrel

Swift met **Amy**. Their daughter is:
    Imogen

PROLOGUE

Two Months Ago
Micha

This was all wrong.

Micha Perkins gripped the steering wheel of Dale's banged-up Kia Rio and glanced out the window for the tenth time in a minute. Dale had said he'd just needed to pick something up from one of the stores near the waterfront and that he'd needed Brie's help and for Micha to drive.

He'd also told Micha to keep the engine running.

Micha had tried listening to the radio, but the music had set his nerves on edge. It was late, even for this neck of Seattle. What stores were actually open? And why had Dale waited until now to collect whatever it was he'd ordered?

It was no secret that Micha and Dale rubbed each other the wrong way, but Dale had taken a chance on Micha when no one else seemed to care. Given him a place to stay, a home. Micha didn't need anyone to tell him he owed Dale many times over.

So why were all his nerves on edge?

This was how the house worked. Most of them were LGBT waifs and strays who'd come to the city searching for a new start. The house was a kind of family, and family looked out for one another.

Micha knew that, even if he'd been a pretty lousy son.

He wanted to do better with this family, and that meant listening to Dale. But Micha's gut was gnawing at him.

He knew Dale's business wasn't always on the level. *Fuck.* Why hadn't he gone with him? Brie was old enough to drive. He was pretty sure she had a license, if not a learner's permit. He knew better than to leave the two of them alone.

He angrily bit his ragged thumbnail and glanced in the rearview mirror again. Not that he could see much when half the streetlights were busted. But there was nothing to indicate Dale and Brie were coming back along the alley between the warehouses where he was parked.

What the hell did Micha know? Nothing. He needed to remember he was grateful for having somewhere to stay, somewhere that didn't eat all his meager pay from the dive bar he bussed tables at.

He needed to be mindful of his place.

So what if Dale was kind of a control freak? He kept the house together and didn't ask too many questions, not really. Was it too much to do what he wanted every now and again in return? It wasn't like he'd dragged Micha out for a mysterious pickup before.

What about Rich?

Micha tutted and chewed on another hangnail. Rich had always been trouble. The house was better off without him, wherever he'd gone. But he and Dale had certainly gone on their fair share of late-night expeditions.

Micha was being dumb, as usual. Dale and Rich had probably just been fucking. Micha was simply jealous, he was sure. He needed to face it. There was nothing weird going on here tonight. However…he couldn't quite shake the idea that it was bad to leave Brie alone with Dale at any time. Dale wasn't usually interested in women, but still…

Shit. What was that? It was too dark to really tell, so he cracked the window a fraction, letting in the August night air with a tang of exhaust fumes. Micha strained his ears.

That was an alarm.

He sat up straighter and wrapped his fingers around the cracked plastic of the wheel, the engine grumbling. It was fine. Alarms went off all the time in the city. It could have been the wind off the water. Or a fox, looking for dumpster scraps that could have bumped into something. Or kids with spray cans who had picked the wrong shutters to tag.

Except…were those people running?

Micha turned around in his seat, his heart thumping in his chest as he squinted through the gloom. *Fuck.* That was definitely Dale's muscular form and Brie's skinny legs pounding down the alleyway.

"GO!" Dale roared.

What? Surely he didn't mean for Micha to leave? They were only twenty feet away from the car. It was in drive, ready to move as soon as they were inside. What the hell were they carrying in their arms?

And was that a siren?

Dale yanked the passenger side door open, throwing himself inside. *"Drive!"*

"But-" Micha spluttered. Brie was still a couple of feet away from the back door.

"Go, you fucking moron!" Dale screamed in Micha's ear. It was the couple of seconds Brie needed to haul her door open and jump inside, scattering several white boxes over the back seat.

Micha floored it, Brie's door slamming shut as he tore down the alley.

"Dale? What the shit?" Micha screeched. "What's going on?"

"Shut the fuck up and get us the hell out of here!" Dale's eyes were blown wide and frantically darting around, looking in all the car's mirrors and out the rear window as they sped along the road. "God, you had *one* job, Perkins!"

"I'm driving, I'm driving," Micha snapped back, hurt that this was somehow his fault. He'd done everything Dale had asked, except for leaving Brie behind, but there was no way Micha would have done that. Dale must just not have realized she hadn't been in the car.

They hurtled around a corner, the late August air blowing through Micha's open window. Those were definitely sirens he could hear.

And they were getting louder.

"Dale, is that the cops?" he cried in disbelief. Glancing in the rearview mirror, he saw Brie's terrified face, stark white against her red hair scraped into a messy bun. For a brief moment, rage outweighed Micha's panic that he'd put her in danger. "Did you *steal* something?"

"None of that will matter if you just put your fucking foot down, you fucktard!" Dale was shoving the white boxes into a backpack he'd pulled from under his seat.

He was wearing gloves.

So was Brie.

In the middle of summer…

Holy fuck! "Dale, are those iPads?"

"Perkins, just – *watch out!*"

Micha slammed the brakes and pulled the wheel with everything he had, only just making the turn into another alleyway.

Away from the cop car that had been coming toward them with flashing lights and wailing siren.

Bile rose in Micha's throat. What was happening? How

had they gotten here? Everything had moved too fast. He'd just been waiting in the car, and then...

He didn't know these roads well enough. The flashing lights were behind them again, and he didn't know why they were running from them, anyway. Except he absolutely did. He just didn't want to admit it.

"Dale?" Brie asked anxiously from the back seat. Micha glanced in his mirror to see her twisting back and forth between looking at the cops and the road ahead.

"Take a left!" Dale barked.

Micha threw him a confused look. "But that's a dead end-?"

"Left!" Dale snatched the wheel and almost careened the car into the wall. Micha just managed to regain control and keep them on the road. Not that it would do them much good. They were headed toward another warehouse, but this alley led to the chained front gates, nowhere else.

"Dale, we can't-"

Dale cut Micha off, clicking his fingers aggressively in front of his face. "Pull in! There!"

This time Micha didn't hesitate. He just did as he was told.

But as the car swerved into the alcove, he must have missed a part of the plan. Because the second the car slowed, Dale had the door already open and was bolting back out into the night with his backpack and Brie right on his heels.

"Micha! Come on!" she screeched. Her ratty sneakers scrabbled to find purchase on the pebbled ground. Her young face was filled with fear in the harsh light from the car's interior. Then she spun around and was gone, while Micha was still fumbling with his seat belt.

The sirens were howling. It wasn't just one cop car behind them now but two. Micha couldn't tell his left from his right as he let his feet just run, adrenaline taking over.

Where was Brie? Was she okay? God, she was so young-

He should have been paying more attention. His feet tripped over something in the darkness, making him stumble. He pinwheeled his arms, catching his balance, but it had slowed him down enough.

"Freeze! Seattle PD!"

He turned as a flashlight swung over his face, temporarily blinding him. But he'd seen enough to realize the cop had a gun pointed at him.

Terror like he'd never known flooded his body. His legs locked as his hands flew up over his head. "I'm not armed!" he screamed. "I'm not armed, I swear!"

There were more lights dancing in front of his eyes, dazzling him. He heard footsteps pounding and people shouting, but his feet were rooted to the spot. That was until hands grabbed him, turning and shoving him against the chain link fencing.

His hands were wrenched behind his back as the air whooshed from his lungs. Tears stung his eyes, but he tried to blink them back while his cheek was pressed against the fence.

"You have the right to remain silent," the faceless cop was reciting. Micha bit back a sob. *No, no, no.* This wasn't his life! How was this happening?

Then he saw her, crouching on the other side of the fence, behind a truck. Brie. Micha wasn't sure how she'd gotten through, but she had. She was far enough away and in enough darkness that it didn't seem like the cops had spotted her, but he had. Then he saw Dale looming behind her, placing a hand on her shoulder.

Micha wasn't going to ruin her life too. He stared right at her. She looked like she wanted to run to him.

He shook his head.

"No."

She'd be able to read his lips from where she was. He hoped it was enough to stop her. Sure enough, Dale pulled on her shoulder. Then they both melted into the shadows.

"Sorry, kid," the cop said, presumably in response to him saying 'no.' "Do you understand your rights or not?"

Oh, Micha understood plenty.

He had just fucked up his entire life in the space of less than ten minutes. The question was, was there anyone else out there who even cared?

1

SWIFT

"There must be some mistake."

Mrs. Bowman from Child Protection Services looked sympathetically over her bifocals from the other side of her desk. It was crammed with piles and piles of manila folders, several old coffee mugs, a dusty but well-watered money plant, and numerous picture frames that were all pointed toward her. She was in her mid-fifties with a round figure and a scarf around her neck with a pattern of swallows on it.

Those details felt easier for Swift to absorb in that moment. Even throughout the two-hour drive across the state to Olympia he hadn't really believed what she'd told him over the phone. But now the evidence was undeniable.

It was in the very next room.

No, not it. She.

Swift's daughter.

He covered his mouth and leaned his elbows on his knees. His mom rubbed his back. It was a very long time since he'd asked her to come with him to do anything, but there was no way he could have done this alone, and he was extremely grateful to have her there. He could feel her looking between him and Mrs. Bowman, for once at a loss for words. Mrs. Bowman gave them another tired smile and pushed a box of tissues closer to him through the manila folder towers.

"Mr. Coal," she said kindly. "No one is questioning your ignorance in this matter. Ms. Dillard confirmed that she never informed you of Imogen's existence. But you are named as the father on the birth certificate. Would you like to run a paternity test?"

Swift leaned back, the old chair creaking under him. He blinked and rubbed his face before dropping his hands and glancing at his mom. "I mean, yeah, for legal purposes that probably sounds like a good idea. But it does make sense. The math works out for when we were dating. But then she broke up with me and moved out of town. I never heard another thing. She blocked me on Facebook…"

He trailed off as a lump rose in his throat. He realized his eyes were damp, so he hastily rubbed them while he tried to figure out what he was trying to say.

"I would have helped," he continued eventually, feeling his brow crease. "I would have paid child support. I know we didn't work out in the end – as a couple. But I swear, I would have done everything I could if I'd have known-"

Mrs. Bowman held her hand up, and Swift's mom squeezed his hand. "She knows, sweetie," his mom said. "You wouldn't have left Amy high and dry."

"Actually, I see a lot of unfit parents in here on a daily basis, Mrs. Coal," said Mrs. Bowman. "It's refreshing to see such passion from your son. Don't worry, Mr. Coal, you're not in trouble here. But with Ms. Dillard's change in circumstances, you can understand this means a lot for young Imogen."

Swift bit his lip and glanced again at the interconnecting

door between Mrs. Bowman's office and the private waiting room beyond. She'd said Imogen was through there, being looked after by a coworker. Faint, happy voices could be heard through the wood and frosted glass panel.

It was as if he'd woken up in someone else's body. He'd gone for his run before work, as usual, blending a protein shake after a shower and picking up one of his prepared Tupperware boxes for lunch. Just as he'd gone to open the door, his phone had rung.

And now here he was.

He reached out and touched the edge of the table, focusing on the dull wood grain as it was easier than meeting Mrs. Bowman's matter-of-fact gaze. "But Amy's okay, right? She's going to be okay?"

Mrs. Bowman sighed. "A DUI is a serious offense. She's been ordered by the court to submit for thirty days in rehab. But it is my professional opinion that as it stands, she is not fit to retain custody of Imogen. If you feel you are also not fit to take on the responsibility, I'm afraid there aren't other next-of-kin options on Ms. Dillard's side, so we would have to look into entering Imogen into the system-"

"No!" Swift surprised even himself with how loud he was. He sat back in his chair and tried to compose himself. "No," he said, calmer. He took a moment to choose his words carefully. "I can't say this isn't one hell of a shock, but I'm okay. I'll get over it. The last thing I want is for Imogen to think she's not wanted. I just…I suppose I thought that when I was going to become a dad, I'd have at least nine months to get used to the idea. Not three hours."

Mrs. Bowman nodded and sighed. "I completely understand. Do you need some more time before we bring her in, Mr. Coal?"

Swift looked at his mom. She beamed when she realized

he was looking, then nodded enthusiastically. "It's okay, pumpkin," she said with forced happiness. She'd hadn't called him that since he'd gone to high school. "You've got this. Piece of cake."

Swift felt they both knew that parenting was anything but a piece of cake, but with her steadfast support, he felt slightly less terrified.

He was going to be responsible for a whole tiny person! A human being with half his DNA! In thirty-two years, it was fair to say this was by far the most monumental thing that had ever happened to him. What if he screwed up? A mistake at work meant a scheduling conflict or someone injuring themselves on a rowing machine. Those kinds of things could be fixed with a phone call or an ice pack.

He now had a responsibility that was going to last the rest of his life. It didn't end when she was going to turn eighteen – he knew from his parents that he'd probably never stop worrying and trying to do what was best for her. Even if Amy got clean and wanted custody again, Swift's conscience told him he'd want to ask her to make it joint. A kid needed their father around, if possible. He wasn't going to let Imogen down, no way. No matter how scary the prospect of being a dad was.

So he needed to start right now.

He blew his cheeks out and mustered his best smile. "Yeah, piece of cake. Poor little thing's probably been through a rough few days already. Let's not keep her hanging on any longer."

He nodded at Mrs. Bowman, but she considered him for a moment. It was her job to put Imogen's interests first and foremost, so he didn't blame her for taking a second to weigh him up. But he was a practical sort of guy. It was always best to jump in and learn on the job, he found. He wouldn't know how to be a dad until he actually started *being* a dad.

It seemed Mrs. Bowman agreed. She smiled and nodded, brushing down her swallow scarf and blouse. Then she stood from her desk and crossed her office to tap lightly on the adjoining door. "Miss Dillard? Would you like to come join us?"

There was a scrambling from the other side. After a couple of seconds, a young woman opened the door. Then a small girl peeked her head around the wood.

Swift's breath caught in his throat, and his hand involuntarily flew to his chest. That was her. His daughter.

She blinked owlishly, then took another step, creeping into the office. Her light blonde hair was in a messy braid that almost reached her waist. It was the same color as Swift's hair, more or less, and he felt a pang.

Wow. This really was his little girl.

She surveyed the room, pushing her glasses up her nose. They were pink with winged tips and diamanté sparkles all over. "Hello," she said to Mrs. Bowman, pulling at her fingers. "Someone said my name."

Mrs. Bowman smiled affectionately down at her, gesturing over to Swift while her colleague disappeared back into the waiting room but didn't close the door. Imogen looked between Mrs. Bowman and Swift and his mom, both still sitting in their chairs. Swift knew he was pretty large and didn't want to scare her or anything, so he stayed still.

"Yes, Imogen. This is your daddy. Would you like to say 'hello'?"

Daddy. Christ on a cracker, Swift needed to get a grip. He swallowed the lump that threatened to rise again in his throat. He was excited and terrified, but that had to be nothing compared to how Imogen was feeling.

"Hi, Imogen." He waved, immediately feeling like a dork. Hopefully, she wouldn't judge him too harshly.

Unfortunately, she did indeed frown and push her glasses

up again. "I don't have a daddy," she announced, looking back up at Mrs. Bowman. "Mommy says some kids just don't have daddies, and that's okay. Emmet and Nicola don't have daddies either, and Juan doesn't have a mommy *or* a daddy because he lives with his *abuela.*"

Swift's gut twisted. He knew it wasn't his fault. For whatever reason, Amy hadn't wanted him to be a part of Imogen's life. But he was in it now, so there was no sense in wasting time on guilt. They needed to move forward in whatever way was best for Imogen.

"You're right," Mrs. Bowman said sagely. "Some kids don't have daddies. But you do. It was just a surprise! Your daddy heard about you today, and he drove *all* the way here because he was so excited to meet you."

Imogen was still frowning. "A surprise?" she said dubiously. Swift didn't blame her. There wasn't really an easy way to navigate a tricky topic like this.

He smiled and nodded. "Your mommy has done a great job raising you all by herself. But now she's told me how great you are, and I can help too! Isn't that neat?" He cringed. Did you say 'neat' to kids, or was that lame?

Imogen tilted her head and swished her long braid. "Are you a *good* daddy, though?"

Swift's mom let a laugh escape, then clapped her hand over her mouth. "She's a firecracker," she said after she lowered it again.

Swift glanced at Mrs. Bowman, who nodded at him. It was like she was saying, 'You can do this!'

So he leaned forward and clasped his hands together in what he hoped was a friendly manner. "I'm going to be the very *best* daddy I can be, if that's okay with you?"

Imogen wrinkled her nose, making the pink glasses slip again. "Okay," she said warily. "But when is Mommy coming home?"

Swift had gotten the lowdown on the long phone call before he had jumped into his car, picked up his mom, and driven as fast as he could to Olympia. Apparently, Amy had been doing her damnedest to look after Imogen, and that was why CPS hadn't stepped in sooner. But it seemed her alcoholism had gotten the better of her and she wasn't able to hide it any longer. Imogen's clothes were okay, and she didn't look underfed, but apparently the apartment she'd been living in with Amy was tiny, filthy, and devoid of any real comfort.

Mrs. Bowman had decided it was time for Imogen to have a new home, at least for the meantime while Amy did her stint in rehab.

"Mommy had to go away for a while," Swift said with a carefully positive tone. "So would you like to come and live with Daddy for a little bit?" He felt a surge of joy calling himself 'Daddy' for the first time, but it didn't last.

Imogen's lip wobbled. "I want Mommy."

Swift didn't think. He moved from the chair to crouch on one knee, opening out his arms. "I know, sweetheart. She'll be back in a few weeks. I promise I'll be a good daddy while she's gone."

Imogen sniffed, her glasses perching precariously on the tip of her nose. Cautiously, like he was approaching a skittish animal, Swift reached over and gently pushed them back up in front of her eyes.

With a sob, Imogen flung herself into Swift's arms. "You promise?" she said with a hiccup.

He stroked her hair, biting his lip as that overwhelmed feeling threatened to return. But he had this. It would be okay. "Pinky promise," he swore, hoping kids still said that.

Luckily, she seemed to understand and nodded against his neck. "Okay."

He stood, easily lifting her in his arms so she could sit on his hip. "And look," he said happily, jutting his chin toward his mom. "This is your new grandma. She's gonna spoil you *so* bad. Do you want to say 'hi'?"

Imogen sniffed and assessed Swift's mom. "Hi, Grandma," she said cautiously.

Swift's mom bounced on her toes, clasping her hands together as tears pooled in her eyes. She was clearly doing her best not to spook Imogen by lunging forward for her own cuddles. "My first grandbaby," she gushed in little more than a whisper. "And aren't you just *perfect*? It's so wonderful to meet you, Imogen."

Imogen rubbed her nose and nodded. "Okay," she said again. Hopefully she would become less wary with time. But at least she wasn't running away screaming. She was obviously a tough cookie. This was a lot for a five-year-old to handle.

"Okay, then," said Mrs. Bowman, evidently relieved as she sat back at her desk. "Let's get you to sign some things, Mr. Coal. Then you can be on your way."

"Does Imogen have any stuff?" Swift's mom asked. "Clothes, toys?"

"Oh, yeah, good question," said Swift. He should have thought of that.

Mrs. Bowman nodded. "Yes, right. Jenny? Can you bring through Miss Dillard's belongings?" Jenny must have been the coworker who had been watching Imogen before. Sure enough, within a minute she came through the adjoining door she hadn't closed before. In one hand was a small, slightly tattered pink suitcase with a mermaid key ring.

In her other hand was a cat carrier.

"Oh," Mrs. Bowman said, sounding slightly guilty. "There is just *one* other matter we probably should have discussed."

Imogen lit up like the Fourth of July, twisting in Swift's

arms and making grabby hands for the cat carrier. "Butter! Come here, Butter baby!!"

Swift raised his eyebrows and looked back at Mrs. Bowman, who sighed.

"Make sure you have Band-Aids," was all she said.

2

MICHA

The tire swing hadn't changed. Micha hoped it never would.

The edges dug into his legs through his jeans, but he didn't care as he swung gently back and forth in his folks' back yard. Even after close to fifteen years, Micha couldn't *quite* think of it as his back yard. It didn't help that'd he'd been away for the past seven of those years.

He hugged the top of the tire and scraped the tips of his sneakers in the dirt, shivering slightly. He should have put a jacket on over his sweater, but he couldn't summon the strength to go get one now. Instead, he looked over the orange leaves strewn over the yard and the ones still clinging to their branches. It would be Halloween soon, and Pops would no doubt decorate the place to the nines, as usual.

Micha desperately wished he felt at home here. There was no reason he shouldn't. It wasn't like Dad and Pops had done anything other than try to make him feel welcome alongside his older adopted brothers and sister. Micha wished he wasn't so damn *broken*.

He knew he never belonged anywhere.

Except maybe the house in Seattle. For a year or so, that had actually begun to feel all right. So long as Micha followed Dale's rules, which he had…

Fuck Dale, a voice snarled in his head. *Fuck him and his rules to hell and back.* Micha's fingers curled against the cold, hard rubber of the tire as he blinked away bitter tears. Dale had set him up that night and left him to take the fall. He'd damned near gotten Brie in trouble too, and that Micha really couldn't forgive. Micha wasn't exactly much, but Brie had her whole life ahead of her. She wanted to be a singer. She was *something.*

Micha knew he was beyond lucky to have gotten off with only a year's suspended sentence. Well, ten months considering time served. But try as he might, he couldn't really see that as a victory.

He wondered if the sting of such painful humiliation would ever fade. The moment he'd used his phone call to reach out to his folks was seared into his memory, flooding him with guilt and shame every time he relived it. Which, right now, was constantly. The heavy disappointment in Pops' voice when he'd answered the phone had been unbearable.

But he'd believed Micha when he'd told him what had happened. The whole family had. Of course they had. Why, Micha was sure he'd never know. No matter how much he tried to push them and their perfect lives away where they couldn't remind him of his failures, the harder it seemed they tried to bring him back into the fold.

He huffed, tears burning the back of his eyes again, but he refused to let them fall. He'd only been home a few days, and he was already itching to leave. He knew they were all doing their best to be kind and thoughtful. They were dancing around the arrest as much as his absence the past seven years when Micha had struggled in Seattle. He was the black sheep, the one who hadn't gone to college and never seemed to hold down a job for long. Their forgiveness and understanding just made him feel worse, and then he'd feel even worse again for being so ungrateful. It was a vicious cycle.

But he was also realistic. He couldn't go back to the Seattle house and was going to struggle even harder to get a job now that he had a criminal record. Staying rent-free with his parents made total sense, except for the part where Micha's depression was crushing him down.

He couldn't help but feel a small pang for the house. It had been the only place in his life where's he'd been openly gay, other than the guys he'd hooked up with. But a string of one-night stands didn't mean anything when he wouldn't see them again. In the house, everyone had been openly queer, and it had just been so refreshing.

There was no way he was going back to Dale, though. As desperate as Micha was, he at least knew that. He'd been honest with the cops when he'd said all he'd known that night was that he'd been asked to drive. But he'd had to admit he knew Dale, so why else would he have been there? He'd sworn he didn't know what they were doing or what had been in the backpacks, and he'd lied his ass off saying he'd had no idea who Brie was.

He knew he was incredibly lucky that they hadn't pushed him further on that, because Micha would have gone to prison rather than see her behind bars. Her mom had kicked her out the second she'd discovered she was a lesbian, not even giving her time to take anything more than what was in her purse and the clothes on her back. As much as he felt like the worst kind of sore thumb back here in Pine Cove, this house had never once stopped being his home.

Things would get better. They had to. Micha was so much older now, after all. Perhaps he'd stop feeling so desperately awkward and would relax around his family. Dad might have been a bit gruff since Micha had been released and returned back to Pine Cove. But Pops was cheerful as always, catching him up on local gossip and sending his enormous Great Pyrenees dog Peri in every morning to fetch Micha for breakfast. He was confident Micha would be able to get a job soon, as folks around here would actually listen to the fact that he was innocent.

Micha wasn't so sure, but he had to admit that hearing Pops say it so many times eased the knot of worry in his gut, if only slightly.

The best thing about being back home was getting to see all his nieces and nephews again. Adults had always scared Micha. Too many of them had treated him like dirt as a child, and even after his adoption, he'd encountered crappy teachers, power-hungry bosses, and friends who turned out to be back-stabbing users. But kids? You knew where you stood with them. They didn't play mind games. Who they were shone through like sunshine on a summer's day. Micha respected honesty, probably because he struggled so badly with it himself. But kids were just themselves, that was it.

Best of all was that since he'd been gone, his brother Rhett had adopted kids of his own. Twin boys all the way from Puerto Rico. That alone was worth Micha coming home. He'd spent yesterday managing to avoid most conversations by hugging either of the one-year-olds.

However, he was extremely surprised by the child who suddenly appeared from around the other side of the massive oak tree. She wasn't part of the extended Perkins clan, as far as he was aware.

He dug his toes into the dirt and stopped himself from swinging, staring down at the blonde girl. He'd guess she was about five, maybe six years old. Around kindergarten age, he was sure. Her long hair was kind of a mess, like it had been braided days ago, then not touched since. Her glasses overshadowed most of her other features. They were hot pink with sparkles and winged tips at the top, like ladies wore in the sixties. Her jeans were baggy and faded, and her T-shirt had My Little Pony on it – the old style. The design was faded and cracked, making him think the shirt might actually have been printed back in the 80s.

The girl pushed the sleeves up of the cardigan she had on over the T-shirt, squinting up at Micha on his swing. "Who are you?"

Micha's eyebrows crawled up his forehead. "Micha," he said. "This is my parents' house. Who are you?"

"Oh," the blonde girl said, nodding. "Okay. I'm Imogen. This isn't my house."

"Yeah," said Micha slowly as he grinned. This kid had attitude. He appreciated that. "I guessed. Are you here with someone?"

Imogen broke into a smile, showing off all the baby teeth she still had. "Yeah. My daddy. He said we were going to visit Uncle Brett, but grown-ups talking is *bor-ing*. So I snuck out. Can I try your swing?"

Brett. She must have meant Rhett. He was always so social, making friends left, right, and center. Micha couldn't really begrudge him, though, as he was the closest thing Micha could count as a friend.

Rhett was the youngest of the four biological siblings who Dad and Pops had adopted. Rhett had just been a toddler and didn't remember his birth parents. Maybe that was why he and Micha had bonded so strongly. Plus, he'd shared his PlayStation with Micha on his very first day. Micha hadn't been used to people sharing anything with him. He still wasn't, really.

In the end, it had been Rhett who'd convinced Micha to come back to Pine Cove upon his release. Micha hoped that if he tried really hard this time around, he might be able to feel as at ease with the rest of his family as he did with Rhett.

If her dad was friends with Rhett, then Micha didn't feel so weird about her sudden appearance. He glanced over the yard. and sure enough, there looked to be several people he could see outlined through the kitchen window.

He was always careful when it came to other people's kids, but Imogen just wanted a turn on the swing. So Micha hauled himself out of the tire to let her on. She eagerly scampered over and attempted to jump up, but she was too little.

"Do you want a hand?" Micha asked, rolling up his sleeves.

Imogen huffed and pushed her glasses up her nose. "Yes, please. I like your drawings."

Micha paused as he reached for her. Then he realized she meant his tattoos. He had plenty on his forearms that she could see. He was slowly joining them together into sleeves and intended to expand out onto his back. He might have been pretty scrawny, but his ink made him feel so much less of a small, skinny kid. The tattoos were his armor, protecting him from a world that had left him cold and hungry far too often. He'd even helped design a couple.

"Thanks," he said, turning his arms to show her more. "Do you have a favorite?"

Imogen gasped and covered her mouth, then danced on her toes. "Mermaid! Mermaid!"

Micha grinned, holding the inside of his wrist closer so she could inspect the pretty design properly. "And look," he said, offering his other arm out too. "There's a pirate ship. Do you think she makes friends with them?"

Imogen nodded emphatically. "She's gonna sing songs to them and save them when their ship crashes. Then she'll marry the prince."

Micha smiled ruefully. "There's always got to be a prince, hasn't there?" he murmured.

Maybe one day, his prince would come, too.

In the meantime, he pointed back at the tire. "Shall I help you up? Then I can give you a push."

"Yes, yes!" Imogen reached up, allowing him to carefully pick her up by the waist and hold her while she kicked her legs clumsily through the middle of the ring. "Now push me to the moon!"

"Wow," said Micha. "All the way to the moon, huh? That's really far."

"I'm an explorer," Imogen said proudly. "I'm going to go 'round the whole world, twice, then go to the moon, and then the sea. The bottom of the sea. Where the mermaids are."

"That's an awesome plan," said Micha. "Can I come too?"

Imogen nodded, using her whole body as he pushed her gently on the swing. She looked over her shoulder at him. "But we gotta pack first. You always gotta have your toothbrush and spare socks. Mommy said so. She's gone on a trip, but she'll be back soon."

Micha stifled a laugh. "Spare socks, got it."

"Higher!" Imogen cried, throwing up her arms and kicking her legs. She almost toppled out of the tire, but Micha caught her back with just one hand, and she didn't even seem to notice.

"Only if you hold tight," Micha told her. "How else will you get to the moon if you're not strapped into your rocket?"

Imogen saluted him, then reached up to hold the top of the tire. "Aye, aye, Captain!"

Micha laughed and pushed her just a bit higher. It was like this kid had melted away all his worries. Yeah, his life wasn't the best, but it could be *so much* worse. He was home, he had avoided prison time, and as far as he knew, Brie was safe. His family still loved him, even if he felt out of place around him.

But then this little angel had arrived and reminded him that he had his whole life ahead of him. He could still go exploring if he wanted. But for now, he was just going to enjoy making a kid happy by swinging her back and forth on an old tire. She was so optimistic. He wondered who her dad was. He was probably a pretty great guy.

Tomorrow might suck again, but right now, life wasn't so bad.

3

SWIFT

Swift had been pretty sure going to see his best friend would be a good idea. He'd been right.

Rhett was adopted. Rhett had just adopted his *own* kids. Rhett was always the guy Swift turned to when his neat and tidy life hit a bump in the road.

This wasn't so much a bump as an entirely new route he'd never expected to take.

"I don't know anything!" Swift cried as he paced in the older Perkins' kitchen. "What time does she go to bed? What does she eat? How do I do that thing with her hair? There's only so much I can YouTube!"

Rhett's place was fine, but it was nowhere near as big as his dad and pops' place, so they'd decided to meet there seeing as Tyee – Pops – wasn't at the diner today. Besides, it felt like a few more of the Perkins family wanted to help with the current situation, namely Tyee Perkins himself.

He reached out and patted Swift's shoulder, stopping him from walking around in circles. "You'll be fine, son. You just learn these things as you go along, I promise."

Swift nodded and shook his hands out, trying to dispel

the tension. He wasn't used to driving so much, and he'd had a hell of a lot on his mind while he'd been getting them all back to Pine Cove.

His mom smiled at Tyee, then sipped her coffee where she was sitting at the kitchen table. "This is a lot, Swift, but you've got a great support network. Your brothers and sisters are over the moon, as are your father and I."

Swift shook his head and ran his fingers through his hair before slumping into one of the wooden chairs. "I knocked a girl up, Mom. I had no idea. I haven't been looking after my own daughter."

Rhett scoffed and traded glances with his older sister, both of whom were also at the table. "Dude, you didn't know."

"And it's not your fault Amy kept this from you," Darcy added.

Tyee placed a fresh mug of coffee in front of Swift. "What matters is what you do now. You want to be in this kid's life, right?"

Swift sat up in his chair and nodded earnestly. "Definitely. But…what about work? I'm at the gym all kinds of hours."

His mom reached out and patted the back of his hand. "Yeah, you know…maybe you could cut back a little? It's great you work so hard, but this is an opportunity to enrich your life in other ways."

Swift toyed with the mug handle. She'd been saying he was working too much lately. "Yeah," he admitted slowly. "I could probably reduce my hours for when she's at school. Maybe. But that'll mean a pay cut, and I have to get her so much *stuff…*"

Darcy waved her hands and shook her head. "Nope, stop there. We kept a bunch of stuff from my two, and I know Logan and Nell packed a whole load of boxes into their basement from their three. We all assumed there would be more kids – especially with Rhett and Louella working on their adoption for so long, and Micha and Hudson might meet someone and each have their own. Not to mention grandkids-"

"Hey, not yet, slow down," Tyee grumbled good-naturedly. "I'm still not convinced I'm old enough to be a grandpa, let alone a great-grandpa."

Rhett rolled his eyes. "Saul is *eighteen,* Pops. You've been a grandpa for a while."

Tyee chuckled. "I'm stubborn."

From the floor, his massive Great Pyrenees dog gave a small sigh, rolling onto his side like a giant white cloud tumbling over in the sky. Swift smiled and reached down to give him a belly rub while looking warily at the carrier they had placed carefully on the side counter.

A scowly ginger face glared back at him from behind the bars.

"And I've *never* had a cat. No one has in our family has. Why couldn't she have had a dog?"

Suddenly anxious, Swift checked over his shoulder. But Imogen had scampered off to play outside. He could see her on the swing. He wasn't sure who was pushing her, but it had to be one of the Perkinses, so he wasn't too worried as long as he still had his eyes on her.

The last thing he'd want was for her to think he was complaining about her. That wasn't it at all.

It had only been a few hours and he was exhausted thinking about whether she'd had enough to eat, if she was going to start crying again, and, worst of all, if she was safe? It suddenly felt like every single tiny thing that had been perfectly fine was now a terrifying hazard. Door knobs, seat belts, even walking on the damn sidewalk. If she tripped, she could graze her knees or hands, and it would be Swift's fault.

He'd need a booster seat for the car and maybe the rubber corner things to put on his tables and cupboard handles…

"Pumpkin, breathe." His mom was rubbing his back again. Embarrassed, Swift realized he'd been gasping in his oncoming panic. So he inhaled deeply and slowly, massaging his temples.

"Okay," he said, putting on his game face. "This is fine. Just one thing at a time, right?"

Rhett grinned and slapped Swift's thigh. "One thing at a time."

"So, what needs doing?" Darcy asked practically. She wheeled herself over to the coffee pot, getting herself a top-up and holding up the pot to ask if anyone else needed one. When they said they were good, she took a sip from her own mug and came back to the table. "Let's start with the essentials. Both the kiddo and the kitty cat need food and somewhere to sleep. Can you swing by the store and stock up?"

"Sure. On what?" Swift pulled out his phone to make notes.

Darcy and Rhett shared a look with Tyee and Swift's mom. "Keep it simple," Darcy suggested. "Maybe ask her what her favorite food is? Seeing as it's a big day and she's been so well behaved, I'd say that deserves a treat."

Swift's mom nodded. "She can take your guest room, can't she? Grandma can buy her some jammies, oh, and maybe slippers!" She looked to be in seventh heaven, and Swift couldn't help but forget his many worries for a moment and be happy for her.

Imogen was the first grandchild in the family, the first niece or nephew. It was a pretty big deal, and as much as he was wrestling with his guilt at not knowing, he was pretty jazzed his family was very much seeing the cup as half full. In fact, everyone he'd spoken to so far had been crazy happy to discover Imogen's existence.

Swift was sorry it had taken Amy going into rehab to bring them together, but he really hoped she was on the path to sobriety now and they could work on co-parenting Imogen.

If he survived the next few weeks.

Right. Kid food. Cat food. Jammies. That didn't sound so terrifying. Imogen had come with a small assortment of things in her pink case that would tide her over for a few days, such as toiletries and a few items of clothing. And about twenty pairs of socks, for some reason. His spare room was always kept with fresh linen in case any of his siblings dropped around for an evening and decided to crash, so at least Imogen had a bed waiting for her.

But…that was it. What was Swift supposed to *do* with her? He'd managed to talk a bit with her, but day in, day out, what did five-year-olds get up to?

"I might need to get some toys and games – do kids still play board games, or should I just download some stuff on the iPad?"

Rhett and his sister shrugged. "Both would probably be good," said Rhett.

"I have a bunch of Pepper's old dolls I'm sure she'd love to donate," Darcy said. Fifteen-year-old Pepper was best friends with Swift's youngest sister, Kestrel. It was funny how small the town was, sometimes.

Swift swirled his coffee. "This isn't like how I planned it, though. You know?" He looked around the room, aware he'd blurted out this particular thought that had been gnawing at him. "I thought I'd meet a great woman, get married, have a baby…this is all backward."

Rhett snorted and kicked Swift's foot. "You're talking to

the wrong family, dude. None of us are normal. We all did it the 'wrong' way."

"Normal is so overrated," Darcy chimed in.

"What *is* normal, anyway?" added Tyee. Then he pointed a crooked finger toward Swift. "They told us that the only way was the white picket fence. Man and wife. Stay-at-home mom with two or more kids."

"All the ironing done," Swift's mom interjected, shaking her head. "With a fresh-baked apple pie."

"Sunny and I?" Tyee poked his chest. "We said no, that's not the only way. We knew we were married, four decades before the law let us have that piece of paper. We knew we'd have kids, even when no one wanted to let us foster, never mind adopt. Now look at us."

"I think what Tyee is trying to say," Swift's mom told him, "is that this is the twenty-first century. There is no one set way to be a dad or have a family. We'll find a way. The important thing is that you want to be in Imogen's life. Everything else will work itself out."

Swift nodded and rolled his shoulders. "Yeah, you're right," he said, finally starting to believe them. Just because none of this was planned didn't make it wrong. It was just one of those curveballs life liked to throw. He needed to let go of his doubts and hesitations and jump in with both feet and start learning by doing.

What was the worst that could happen? So long as he kept Imogen safe, he could weather tantrums or whatever else he'd have to navigate.

Suddenly, it was very clear to him. Imogen was the most important thing in his life now. All else came second. When he thought of it like that, it was pretty simple, really.

"Daddy, Daddy!" Imogen's voice came from the back porch, followed by the stomping of little feet.

"In here, sweetie," Swift called back, pleased with how natural the pet name felt. His mom beamed at him.

"See, you're getting it already," she said, squeezing his arm.

"Whoa, there," another voice said from the porch, although Swift couldn't see them. It must have been whichever Perkins had been pushing her on the swing. He sounded male. Maybe Saul, Logan's oldest kid?

Imogen came racing into the kitchen, her little cheeks rosy red from running around in the cool fall air, a few more strands loose from her messy braid. Swift made a note to also buy one of those detangling brushes Kestrel used.

While he mentally added to his shopping list, Imogen spun around, then yanked up her slipping socks. "Daddy, we went to the moon and found mermaids, and now we're looking for buried treasure!"

Swift grinned and invited her to sit on his lap. "That's fantastic, hon! Who were you playing with?"

"My new friend," Imogen said proudly as she scrambled up onto his legs. "He has nice drawings."

"New friend?" Imogen nodded as Swift looked up at the guy walking into the room with Imogen's small sneakers in his hands.

'Simple' went out the window.

For a second, Swift didn't register who he was looking at. He was so different, after all. Gone was the scrawny kid with the haunted brown eyes. In his place stood a grinning man who'd filled out from boy to adult in the past few years. His arms were decorated with various tattoos, and his once short dark hair was now thick and swept in bangs across his forehead.

But Swift would recognize Micha Perkins anywhere.

Suddenly his mouth was dry, which was ridiculous. Swift had always gotten along well with Rhett's kid brother, even going so far as to enjoy his company when Micha let his guard down for long enough and chilled out. Micha's eyes were on Imogen as he walked into the kitchen, his manner carefree and happy.

"Did you find that map, shipmate?" he asked with a grin, putting his hands on his hips.

Then he came up short, taking in all the people in the room he'd entered.

And just like that, all his walls went right back up before Swift's eyes. Micha dropped his hands and took a step back. There was the anxious teenager Swift remembered, flinching as people looked back at him.

"S-sorry," he said guiltily to his pops. "We were just playing."

Swift had never known what Micha had been through before his adoption to make him so untrusting of adults. But he'd always been incredible with his younger nieces and nephews. It was as if around kids, he could be his true self. Mixed in with the shock of seeing him again after all these years was a sadness that he was obviously exactly the same in that regard.

But physically, he was very different. So much so, Swift's heart did something it hadn't done in a fair while when looking at another man or even a woman these days.

It flipped.

Micha was gorgeous, even as he looked apprehensively at his pops and siblings.

Then he turned his gaze, and something worse passed across his face. If Swift had to guess, he'd say it was horror.

And it was directed squarely at him.

4

MICHA

"Swift?"

Micha had been convinced his return to Pine Cove couldn't get any more humiliating.

He'd been wrong.

Once he'd snapped out of playtime mode, he was able to observe his surroundings in less than a second, taking in his pops, brother Rhett, and sister Darcy, some women he vaguely remembered from years ago, and…

Swift fucking Coal.

Of all the people who could possibly have swung by for a visit when Micha was still reeling from his time served, the court date, and then the sheepish return to Pine Cove, why did it have to be gorgeous, perfect Swift?

He'd always been a saint. A star athlete with good grades and perfect manners. The kind of man Micha had wished he'd become but knew he never would. Swift and Rhett had become friends in their senior year, stayed in touch while they'd both gone off to separate colleges, then become BFFs when they'd both settled back down in Pine Cove.

Right around the time Micha was in his mid-teens,

hitting his sexual awakening with gusto. Then Swift Coal had started hanging around the house all the time, and Micha had gone from idly speculating that he was gay to falling into a total lust coma.

He could never think straight when Swift walked into a room, literally. Swift had golden skin, sunshine-blond hair, sculpted muscles, and a smile that lit up both Micha's heart and his cock at the same time. He'd practically trip over on the spot just by catching sight of the god-like Swift.

And now here he was.

Wait – *why* was he here? As Micha's brain scrambled to catch up, the reality hit him like a wrecking ball.

Imogen was in his lap. Swift was her daddy. That meant Mommy was either his wife or girlfriend.

It was ridiculous that Micha's reaction was crushing disappointment. He'd always known Swift was straight, and even if by some miracle he was bi or something, he was never going to look twice at his best friend's fuckup kid brother. There was nothing to be jealous of. Micha needed to be happy that Swift was happy and settled down.

He hoped these multitude of thoughts had flown through his mind as fast as it felt they had. Otherwise, everyone had been staring at him an uncomfortably long time.

He very nearly did that thing where he tripped over his own feet despite being stock-still. But he hugged himself and managed a smile that hopefully wasn't too much of a grimace. Oh, god, Swift had probably heard all about how the youngest Perkins was a felon now. Humiliation threatened to engulf him.

Swift's eyebrows rose, but his face morphed with a light half-smile. "Micha, wow. Long time no see. Glad to have you home."

Micha glanced at Rhett. That wasn't the reaction he would have expected. Had Rhett told him about getting busted, or had he been too ashamed? In any case, at least Micha was spared the embarrassment of Swift freaking out that his little girl had just been playing with a 'criminal.'

"Thanks," Micha managed to utter with a twitch of a smile.

His stomach was in knots, and his dick ached just seeing Swift again in person. Micha kept off things like Facebook – it wasn't really his thing, so he hadn't seen any recent photos of Swift. *Damn*. He was even hotter than he'd been before. Micha wondered if he was still a personal trainer.

Imogen twisted in Swift's lap, looking earnestly up at him with brown eyes she must have gotten from her mom. Swift's were blue, like the sky.

"Is Micha your friend, too?" she asked.

Swift blinked like he was surprised. Then he smiled at his kid. "Yeah," he answered, certainly surprising Micha.

He couldn't help a small flutter of warm pride that filled his heart. Did Swift really think they'd been friends all those years ago? Micha had hung out with him and Rhett a lot, sure, but he'd kind of assumed he'd been the annoying kid brother, getting in the way.

But then Swift looked back at Micha, offering him a genuine smile, and Micha's heart really did flutter. He couldn't remember the last time anyone had beamed at him like that who wasn't part of his adopted family. Maybe Brie, when he'd bought her ice cream and remembered her favorite flavor. God, Micha hoped she was okay.

Swift pointed at Micha's siblings. "You remember Uncle Rhett and Auntie Darcy who you met just now? Well, Micha is their brother, so he's your uncle, too."

Imogen gasped and snapped her head back around to Micha. "So that means I can see him again? Can we play again, Uncle Micha?"

Micha was sincerely touched, but he didn't want to overstep any boundaries. "Well, if your daddy says it's okay?"

For a second, Micha met Swift's gaze. It felt like electricity rushed over every inch of his skin, leaving him tingling. Then he remembered how to breathe again, offering Swift a shaky smile. He was amazed Swift returned it.

"Oh, sure," said Swift, nodding back at Imogen. "You can meet all the kids, too. But we should probably head home soon. I need to show you your new room, and Grandma said she'd take you shopping for some nice new jammies. Does that sound good?"

Imogen looked at the woman, who Micha now remembered was Swift's mom, Deb. Imogen considered for a moment, then nodded. "Okay. Thank you very much, Grandma."

Wait a second – new room? That didn't make much sense. Maybe Swift had just moved to a new house? Maybe he and Imogen's mom had split up and Swift had moved out? He seemed too cheerful for that, though.

Not that Micha would wish a breakup on anyone, especially not someone as nice as Swift. Micha smiled, remembering how Swift had always been so protective of his younger siblings, who were all LGBT. Micha supposed he'd always nurtured the hope that Swift might be bi or something, too. He might very well still be. But the point was that if he was happy and settled, Micha was pleased for him.

That didn't mean he wanted Swift finding out about his latest troubles, though, not if by some miracle he hadn't heard about them already. The easiest way to avoid that was to scram.

"Well, it was nice seeing you again, Swift," Micha said. "And lovely meeting you, Imogen. You seem busy, so I'll just-"

"Yes, very busy," Pops said, sitting up in his seat like he'd just had an idea. Uh-oh. Even the big fluff giant, Peri, stirred on the floor, interested in what Pops had to say. Sure enough, Pops clicked his fingers at Micha. "Darcy, didn't we store a bunch of your baby boxes up in the attic?"

Darcy frowned, then nodded. "Yeah, I think so. It was easier than trying to have them in our house."

Pops grinned and nodded back. "Excellent. Micha, why don't you help Swift with that?"

Micha raised his eyebrows and shared a look with Rhett. He didn't mind helping, but wasn't that kind of weird? Rhett was Swift's BFF, not Micha. "Sure, but Rhett-"

"Has to get back to those babies, don't you, Rhett?" Pops shook his head solemnly. "Louella can't be expected to manage the terrible two alone, can she?"

"Oh, no," Rhett spluttered. "God, I forgot the time. Of course not!" He hastily jumped up from the kitchen table.

He'd told Micha he was still wrapping his head around the whole fatherhood thing, which made sense as the adoption had only been completed about a month ago. As much as Micha loved kids, he wasn't sure he'd be able to cope with being responsible for one for the rest of their life, let alone two. He could barely take care of himself, after all.

"See you later?" Rhett said as he waved and dashed out of the kitchen. Pops looked back at Micha, reminding him of what he'd said.

"Oh, yes, so, uh, of course I'll help you, um, Swift." It was clumsy, but he meant it. Just because his dumb crush had apparently not dulled over the last several years didn't mean that Micha couldn't try and act like a normal human being around Swift. If he needed a hand, then Micha was there for him.

"Thanks, kiddo," said Darcy, clapping him on the arm. She'd always done that, ever since he'd arrived at the house as a scared ten-year-old. But for possibly the first time, the 'kiddo' and physical contact didn't make him wince. It actually felt kind of nice. Maybe Micha *was* starting to get over some of his childhood hang-ups?

"No problem," he said brightly, hoping if he faked it, everything would seem normal. "What are we looking for?"

Darcy tapped the side of her coffee mug. "If memory serves, there's a big white box labeled 'Pepper's clothes' and another brown one labeled 'Pepper's toys.' That's unless Leon boxed them up. In which case, they'll probably be marked with Dungeons and Dragons riddles, so in that case, Cthulhu help you."

That got a laugh from the room. Then Swift asked Imogen if she'd like a cuddle with her grandma. Deb looked so excited she might pee, almost as if she'd never held her grandkid before. Micha didn't judge her, though. Far better for someone to be a little too enthusiastic about showing a kid love rather than not giving a fuck beyond a welfare check.

He'd been so eager to help and show Pops he was grateful to be here and a team player he hadn't realized the implications of the task until Swift handed Imogen to her grandma, then rose from the table.

"Do you want to lead the way?" he asked Micha.

Ah. He and Swift were going to be alone. That was kind of the *opposite* of what Micha had hoped to achieve. But if he backed out now, he might look work-shy, which he definitely wasn't. He was going to show Pops he could do something and not screw it up.

Although he was possibly trying to prove that to himself more than Pops.

In any case, this was happening. So he needed to try and not embarrass himself and, if at all possible, not mention Seattle, his recent brush with the law, or generally do anything dorky.

If only he wasn't his own worst enemy.

"Oh my god, a kitty!" he cried as he passed the gray box that was perched on the kitchen counter. He hadn't given it a second thought when he'd entered the room. His attention had been so focused on seeing Swift for the first time in years. But he absolutely loved cats, and when he saw the little fluffer's ginger face peering out, he swooped down to look through the bars.

And he almost lost an eye for his trouble.

The cat hissed and swiped with his claws so fast Micha very nearly didn't jump back in time. But when he did, it was straight into Swift's strong arms and his rock-hard chest.

Micha froze, screaming *fuuuuuck* in his mind as he slowly looked up. Swift was looking down at him with a rueful smile.

"Sorry. Apparently, he's a bit of a menace."

Imogen giggled and bounced in Deb's lap. "Funny Butter Bee!" she cried.

Micha wondered if it was too late for the ground to go ahead and swallow him up. As embarrassed as he was, his cock was still excited at having Swift's hands on him. *Get a grip!* he chastised himself, slipping out of Swift's grasp.

"Stay away from the cat," he said, nodding with a small salute. "Duly noted. Shall we, uh, go get the things?"

Swift beamed, glanced at the rest of the people in the room, then held out a hand. "After you."

There were those perfect manners Micha remembered, just as devastating as they'd always been.

Because as much as he was undone by Swift's hotness, Micha was far more infatuated by his kindness. Anyone could be hot – like say, Dale. Objectively speaking, that asshole was good looking. However, he was also a prick, so as much as Micha had been besotted with him at the start, that had worn off pretty quickly. But someone like Swift, who protected the people around him and was always so thoughtful, was as hot as any porn Micha could think of.

So it was a good thing he was about to crawl into a cramped, dark space with him and try not to mortify himself.

Again.

"Fuck my life," Micha mumbled under his breath, leading the way to the attic.

5

SWIFT

"So the cat's name is Butter?" Micha asked as Swift followed him up the stairs toward the attic.

Swift laughed and shrugged. "It seems so. No idea why. All I keep thinking is 'butter wouldn't melt.' However, I'm not sure that's right. He pretty much looks as mean as he is." He lifted his hand to show Micha the couple of Band-Aids he'd had to use already, and he hadn't even let the damn cat out of his carry case yet.

Micha paused as he reached the landing, watching Swift as he caught up. "Did you just adopt him or something?"

Oh, shit. Micha didn't know. Swift barely knew what had happened that morning, let alone anyone else. He'd kind of assumed Rhett might have filled him in, but Rhett was respectful like that. He probably didn't want to go around blabbing, preferring to let Swift tell his own story.

"Yeah, so…" he said, trying to think where to start. He put his hands on his hips and nodded to himself. "You haven't been in town, so I guess you don't know. I just found out Imogen was my daughter *today.* The cat came with her. Her mom's in some trouble, so Child Protection Services called me, and well, here she is."

Micha's eyes had gone really wide, and he was gaping at Swift. "Are you serious?" he whispered.

Swift nodded, trying not to stare as Micha licked his lips. He'd never had that problem before, but Micha had been a kid back then. God, this was awkward timing, awkward person, awkward everything. But no matter how much Swift tried to inform his dick this was pretty poor timing to wake up and develop a crush, his dick wasn't listening.

He shifted his weight and tried to subtly adjust his jeans. He was glad he'd quickly changed before driving out earlier. He'd wanted to look presentable to meet CPS, but now he had the added bonus of a little extra coverage in the crotch area.

He mentally slapped himself. He was probably just tired from the round trip and emotional shock, but now was not the time to be thinking about a hot guy. He'd never acted on any bi feelings in the past, and he wasn't about to start. Not with Rhett's younger brother and certainly not when his one and only concern right now was supposed to be Imogen.

Thinking of his daughter managed to calm him down. She *was* his only concern, and a pretty face wasn't going to distract him from that.

"Yeah," he said in response to Micha's question. "Her mom's an old girlfriend who moved away and never told me she was pregnant. Now here we are, five years later."

"Because CPS took her from her mom?" Micha clarified.

Swift nodded but didn't want to go into too much detail, and he certainly didn't want to bad-mouth his daughter's mom. That didn't feel classy. "Just for now. But I'm hoping that when she's back on her feet, we can talk about joint custody. I-" His voice caught in his throat, and he smiled to try and hide the emotion that had welled up in him unexpectedly. "I didn't realize I was a dad. But I'm going to be now, for sure."

Micha considered him for a moment, then offered him a small smile back. "I bet you'll make a great dad," he said softly.

Swift let out a shuddery laugh. "I don't know. I'm pretty terrified," he admitted.

Micha raised an eyebrow. "You saved Imogen from going into the system, right?" Swift nodded. "Then you're already doing a great job," said Micha firmly. He then spun on his heels and marched determinedly toward the attic hatch.

Swift let out a breath. He supposed Micha was right; that was a good start. The trouble was, Swift couldn't even imagine what problems he might have to face, let alone come up with potential solutions. But at least Imogen didn't have to be afraid of where she was going to sleep tonight, and if Swift had his way, she never would.

Unlike Micha had.

Swift followed him down the hall to where he had popped open the hatch in the ceiling and pulled down the ladder that they would climb to get in there. "It's funny," Micha said, shaking his head, "I haven't done that for years and years, but somehow, it feels like I did it just yesterday."

He glanced at Swift as if he'd realized he'd said too much. But Swift knew he'd moved to the city, and he also knew he had gotten himself into a bit of a situation a couple of months ago. Seeing him here and now, Swift had to admit that he was glad to have Micha home again. As much as he'd grown and the tattoos made him look tough, there was still a delicateness there that made Swift want to wrap him in his arms and protect him from all harm.

That wasn't Swift's place, though. So instead he smiled at Micha and placed a hand on one of the ladder rungs.

"That's the thing about home," he told Micha. "It's always there waiting for you to come back."

Micha hummed and gave Swift a smile that didn't reach his eyes. Then he stepped onto the ladder and began to climb.

Swift watched Micha ascend, waiting until he swung his legs into the attic before following him. Swift didn't want to feel like he was invading his personal space right then. As he climbed, he tried to imagine what that would be like, growing up like Micha did. He'd been all alone until the Perkinses had taken him in when he was ten.

Rhett had once told Swift the whole story, how Micha had been left on the steps of a police station of a nearby town early one morning, mere hours after his birth. He had been wrapped in a sweater with a note that read 'My name is Micha, please take care of me.' Swift had previously thought that was awful. Who could do that to a baby? But as he'd grown up, he had been forced to consider that perhaps Micha's biological mom had tried to give him the best chance she could.

Unfortunately, Micha hadn't had much luck with his first few foster homes. Rhett hadn't known the details, only repeating what his parents had presumably said: some people just fostered for the government checks.

Thank god the Perkinses had finally found Micha and taken him in. They had fostered a lot of kids over the years, but only adopted Rhett and his sibs, then Micha.

The kids no one else wanted.

Swift was tempted to indulge in a fresh wave of anger on Micha's past, but really there was no sense dwelling on it. He would rather focus on the future. Because the truth was, on such an intense and bizarre day, Swift was pretty thrilled that Micha had walked back into his life.

He probably wouldn't stay long, Swift thought sadly as he

poked his head up into the attic. No doubt he'd be off again, back to the big city. So Swift was happy to spend a few minutes with him while he could.

"Imogen seemed to enjoy your game outside." Swift rested his elbows on the edge of the hatch, watching as Micha nimbly worked his way around boxes of holiday decorations, dress mannequins, kids' bikes, and sets of golf clubs.

Micha looked up with those wide eyes again. "Oh, um, I hope that was okay."

Swift frowned. "What was?"

Micha shifted and fiddled with the edge of a box that read 'Hudson's school reports.' "I should have asked your permission first. That was thoughtless."

Swift blinked. "Well, I assumed it was someone from your family pushing her on the swing…"

Micha gave him a sad smile. "You're going to need eyes in the back of your head. Don't be too trusting. Stranger danger and all that."

Swift chewed on his lip. "Oh god." He covered his face with one hand. "I'm already fucking this up."

He was surprised when Micha gently pulled his hand back down. He was dexterous the way he moved silently around. "No, you're not," he said firmly as he squeezed Swift's hands. "Fucking up would have been letting her be someone else's problem. You could have left her there."

Swift looked at him in horror. "No, I couldn't."

Micha smiled and blinked rapidly, releasing his hands. Swift felt the loss of his comforting touch immediately. "See?" Micha cleared his throat and rose to start looking at the boxes again. "You're doing fine. No one expects you to know everything right away."

Swift let out a sigh and managed his own smile. Everyone was telling him he could do this, so he needed to start believing it. He pulled himself all the way into the attic so he could help search. "Thank you," he said sincerely, then shook his head. "You were always so good with the kids, even though you were only really a kid yourself."

Micha gave him a curious look. "What do you mean?"

Swift paused. Surely he knew? "Your nieces and nephews. They all adored you. It was like you had magic powers to know how to talk to them and get them to eat their broccoli." Swift whistled and shook his head. "And Carlee? No one else learned to sign faster than you. Logan and Nell were so worried she would feel left out, but she wasn't, because of you."

Micha was looking at him even more strangely. Swift wondered if he'd said something wrong. But then Micha licked his lips as they twitched with half a smile. "You remember that?"

"Are you serious? Of course." Swift laughed. "You were a memorable kid, trust me."

Micha's smile was bashful this time. He touched his fingers to his chin, then arched them out, which Swift recognized as ASL for 'thank you.'

"You're welcome," Swift replied softly.

For a second, Micha held his gaze. Then he cleared his throat and rubbed the back of his neck. "I still can't seem to see the damn Barbies."

"Here, let me help." Swift began picking his way through the Perkins' family's keepsakes.

He definitely wasn't as agile moving through all the boxes as Micha was, as Swift was a fair bit bigger than him. Luckily, he managed not to put his foot through the ceiling, and soon enough, Micha let out an excited little squeak. Swift kind of liked the fact that he was trying to look all tough, but deep down, he was still that cute kid Swift remembered.

"I think this is it?" Micha looked over, his face animated

and happy. Much better than the closed-off, slightly haunted expression Swift remembered from before and had seen again in the kitchen just now.

Sure enough, Micha had come across his niece Pepper's boxes of childhood paraphernalia, which included clothes, toys, and even blankets, finger paintings, and locks of hair.

"Are you sure your sister doesn't mind me having some of these things?" Swift asked.

Micha scoffed. "No way. She's the least sentimental person I know. Leon only convinced her to keep all this stuff in case Rhett or Hudson had girls of their own. Or grandkids, I guess."

"Or you," Swift said. Micha blinked in confusion at him, which Swift didn't get. "If you have kids. Sorry, I assumed because of how great you are with them you'd want children. But, uh, it's not for everyone."

Why did he feel like he'd just totally put his foot in it?

Micha's expression had dropped, becoming sad. "I don't think I'll be a dad," he said as he picked up one of the boxes.

It must have been heavier than he'd thought, as it almost slipped back out of his grasp. But Swift snapped his arms out, catching it without thinking.

Suddenly, Micha's face was only a few inches from his own, his hands over Micha's.

For a second, they stared at one another. Then Micha laughed awkwardly and stepped away. "Thanks," he mumbled.

Swift looked down at the box. He didn't want to pry, but why did Micha think he wouldn't have kids? Especially when he was clearly a natural with them? Swift shifted the box in his arms, trying to find a way to say that without upsetting him further.

But the moment passed, and Micha turned away, looking

for the second box. It didn't take him long. Then he straightened back up and offered Swift a sad smile.

"That's it. Shall we head back down?"

Swift hesitated. The obvious answer was 'yes.' But his feet didn't seem to move.

He didn't want this moment to end. Why did it have to, though?

"So…are you staying in town for a while?"

Micha seemed thrown by the question. "Uh, yeah. I'm not really sure what my plans are. But I was going to look for work and stick around for a bit."

Swift grinned. "Great! I was thinking – if you wanted – we could maybe spend some time together and talk kid stuff?"

He felt a bit stupid as Micha still looked confused. "I mean," Micha said slowly, "I'd be happy to help, if I can. But Rhett, Logan, Darcy – they're all actual parents."

Hmm. Why *did* Swift feel like he wanted Micha's help above theirs, though? He was being a dork, trying to make friends with everyone again. Micha was younger than him. He wanted to be living his life and having fun, dating, that sort of thing. Swift needed to remember that not everyone was an extrovert looking to add every person they met on Facebook.

"Yeah, you've got a point," he said with a laugh. "I suppose I just want to be the best dad I can. Well, now you're back in town, you're welcome to come over whenever you like."

He turned, planning on taking his box back down into the house.

"But-"

Swift turned around again at Micha's voice, raising his eyebrows. Micha looked torn.

"Everything okay?"

Micha readjusted his box against his hip, then opened and closed his mouth a couple of times. His eyes looked glassy.

Shit. Swift got that feeling again that he'd put his foot in it.

"Micha, what's wrong?"

"Why would you invite me over?" Micha blurted. His face was flushed, and he sniffed. "Why would you want my advice? I'm a fuckup. Rhett must have told you."

Swift's heart clenched. He carefully balanced his box on top of another one, then stepped back over to Micha. He felt Micha watching him as he also took the second box to place down. Then he gently took hold of Micha's shoulders. He looked up at Swift with shining brown eyes.

"If I'm not allowed to call myself a fuckup, then neither are you, okay?" Swift said.

Micha swallowed and pursed his lips in a grimace before speaking again. "Swift, I – I was *arrested.*"

Swift felt his eyebrows rise. "Yes," he said carefully. "But Rhett said it was a misunderstanding. You had no idea what was going to happen, and you were tricked into it by that guy."

Micha blinked a couple of times. "You already knew?"

Swift rubbed his shoulders with his thumbs. "Yeah. And I'm so sorry that happened to you, but I understand. We all trust you still. I judge people by what they do in the here and now." He smiled. "And what I saw just now was someone being kind and patient to the person who has suddenly become the most precious thing in my life. So yes. You're welcome anytime to visit me and Imogen. She's had a lot of changes in her life. I'm sure a familiar face would be more than welcome."

Micha rubbed his eyes and nodded. Swift stepped away before it could get too awkward. But holding Micha's shoulders had felt like the right thing to do.

He hoped he was right. Micha offered him a small, encouraging smile. "Thank you."

"No problem," Swift assured him. He felt good, opening up with Micha. He was still holding a lot of pain, that much was obvious. But it was good to see his defenses lower just a little. "Shall we go find Imogen?"

It melted his heart to see the way Micha's face lit up. "Yeah," he said, picking his box back up. "She's going to love all her new stuff!" He paused, looking around. "I know Darcy said you could have some of Pepper's things…but Imogen likes pirates and exploring and space and stuff. Did you want to check out some of Charles's boxes too? Just because she's a girl doesn't mean she's not into dinosaurs or whatever."

Swift exhaled. "Wow," he said, that lump of worry rising in his throat again. "You already know her better than me. Jesus."

"Sorry," said Micha quickly.

"No, don't apologize," Swift insisted, puffing out his cheeks. "I must have told myself to stop panicking and take each thing as it comes twenty-five times since this morning. But I'm a planner – I plan everything! It takes me time to wrap my head around things, but I don't have any time. Imogen is here, right now. She needs me."

Micha smiled sympathetically. "Would it help if I told you once more that you're already doing great? And" -he chewed his lip- "if I *can* help out, I'd be honored. I'm between jobs right now, so if you need a babysitter or just someone to vent to, I'd…well, I'd love to lend a hand."

Something bubbled in Swift's stomach. The way Micha looked at him…he wasn't sure exactly how to read it, but his heart did that flippy thing again.

"Thank you," Swift said sincerely. "I might just take you up on that."

6

MICHA

Micha was just about coping. At least that was what he kept telling himself. He took a long slow breath and gripped the underside of the server's desk, looking at the cash register and reminding himself again that it was not the enemy.

He was used to this. He'd mostly done bar work out in Seattle. But covering a shift at his parents' diner suddenly felt like juggling brain surgery with rocket science. He couldn't fuck it up and let them down.

But he'd done this so many times as a teenager, just like everyone else in the family. Whether it was just for a summer or as a part-time job for years, all the Perkinses chipped in and helped Sunny Side Up run smoothly. As Micha breathed deeply again, he took a second to taste the buttery smell of frying potatoes wafting from where Dad was cooking in the kitchen. He let the gentle chatter from the patrons wash over him and looked at all their happy faces.

The diner was the heart of this town. People came here on dates and business meetings and to catch up with friends.

It had welcomed the townsfolk for over two generations just as warmly as it did newcomers and those merely passing by. Micha might have struggled to feel at home in this town as much as the rest of his family did, but he was immensely proud of what his parents had built.

So he flexed his fingers and carefully jabbed the correct buttons to input the order. He was almost at the end of the shift. He just needed to hang on a few more minutes.

"Are you okay, Uncle Micha?"

He looked up to see his niece, Rona, smiling at him. She'd just started her junior year at the high school and often took half-shifts a couple of times a week. She had Logan's chestnut hair and freckles but her mom's crooked, happy smile. She stuffed a few notes into her tip jar and pulled a couple of menus out of the stack.

It wasn't that she or her family needed the money per se, but she was a people person like Swift and Rhett. She liked this sort of job, and the Perkinses were all about instilling a good work ethic while young.

Micha had to say he kind of liked people, too. He just struggled to stop himself from worrying what they were thinking about him sometimes, especially back in Sunny Side Up. He couldn't tarnish his folks' reputation by getting an order wrong or accidentally upsetting a customer.

But he hadn't. He'd covered a whole shift, and in a few minutes, he could say he'd done an honest day's work for an honest buck. It had been a couple of months since he could be proud of anything like that.

He shook his head and managed a smile. "I'm good. Thanks, kid."

She winked and signed, *'You're welcome.'*

Carlee, her younger sister, had been born with a hearing impairment, and the whole family had rallied to learn as much ASL as possible. They often switched back and forth between speaking and signing, sometimes doing both, even when Carlee wasn't around.

Thinking of that made Micha think of Swift, and his heart ached.

It had been a couple of days since the loft incident, but Micha couldn't really stop thinking about it. He'd replay moments – good and bad – over and over in his head, like he was watching a film on TV. Swift had…confused him.

Micha understood his jitters about suddenly becoming a dad, even though he'd meant every word he'd said about Swift nailing parenthood. He cared, so everything else would fall into place. But the way he'd talked about Micha had come as a genuine shock.

Those were the words Micha kept playing again and again in particular. Swift had seemed so impressed with Micha. Like learning ASL was a big deal. Micha knew exactly what it felt like to feel all alone with no one to talk to. No way he was going to let his niece go through anything like that if he could help it.

Micha liked the way he'd felt when Swift had praised him, though.

The other words that were stuck in Micha's brain had been the most surprising and difficult to get his head around.

"I understand. We all trust you still."

How could Swift so easily dismiss the shit Micha had caused? Didn't he understand he'd only escaped being charged as an accessory after the fact because this was his first offense? Had Rhett not explained it properly?

Really, what it boiled down to was that Micha was perplexed and perhaps even a little threatened as to why someone so nice as Swift would want anything to do with him. Because before Swift, his mom, and Imogen had left the house the other day, Swift had insisted on swapping numbers with Micha.

And then he'd been texting.

It was ridiculous, but even though they'd only shared a few superficial messages, Micha couldn't stop rereading them. They warmed his heart and calmed his nerves when he thought about his total lack of future and how his life had spun out of control. Reading Swift's words anchored him in the here and now. They almost gave him hope.

Which was why when he'd hugged his dad goodbye in the kitchen, the first thing Micha did when he stepped out from Sunny Side Up into the cool evening air was to unlock his phone and read over the last few texts again.

Except when he looked down at the screen, he realized he had a brand-new message waiting for him from Swift.

Micha's heart leaped at the sight of Swift's name. They'd *never* swapped numbers back in the day. It was strangely validating now. Like Micha was a real adult with adult friends who had kids and careers.

Hey, dude. You're not free, are you?

That was kind of cryptic. It had only been sent in the last half hour. Micha had been working and therefore couldn't really have answered any sooner, so he tried not to fret he'd let Swift down already.

I am now! Just finished a cover shift at SSU. Everything okay?

He hovered awkwardly on the sidewalk as the sun dipped down past the horizon. He tried not to stare obsessively at his phone, but he couldn't lock the screen for more than a few seconds without opening it again, looking to see if the dots started dancing to indicate Swift was typing.

After a few minutes of this frankly exhausting routine that frayed Micha's nerves within the first thirty seconds, the dots began to move. He gasped so hard he almost choked on his own spit and had to wave off a concerned passerby. He was so hopeless, but he couldn't help the thrill he felt knowing that Swift was taking time to write to him.

We've gone into meltdown. I'm freaking out. I could really use some backup.

Micha stopped breathing as he stared at the screen. His first emotion was deep sympathy. He knew full well how traumatic kids' tantrums could be. They were basically screaming because they didn't know how to articulate themselves otherwise. But for all Micha had impressed the fact that his siblings were the actual, qualified parents, he was elated that Swift was reaching out to him. Micha didn't even care if he was his second, third, even fourth choice. If no one else was around in this precise moment, Micha was available. Pops had been beyond kind in insuring him on his car, so he even had his own transportation to drive across town.

Micha never 'rescued' anyone. He was always burdening other people. The idea he could be useful right then was intoxicating.

And surprising. Because Micha didn't question if he could help or not. Maybe deep down, he knew what Swift had said was true. He was pretty good with kids.

I'll be right there. What's your address? Do you need me to grab anything?

Micha was broke as fuck, but somehow spending money on Swift or Imogen felt like it wasn't real money. He'd splash out if it would help in these early days of fatherhood.

No, just you being here would be incredible. I could scream!

Micha's heart skipped.

Swift wanted him.

Not like that, he scolded himself. But for a second, it was nice to indulge in the fantasy.

Swift sent through his address right after that, so Micha

began walking hurriedly toward his borrowed car, typing in the address so his phone could give him directions. According to the route, he had four minutes to chill out and get over the fact that Swift Coal was paying attention to him. It was kind of pathetic, after all, to get that excited. The main focus here was whatever explosion of emotion Imogen had thrown at Swift.

Micha restrained himself by only ringing the bell of Swift's house once. It was a cute single-story place with steps leading up to a small covered porch. The wooden slats of the walls and roof were painted duck egg blue with white trimmings on the sides and windows. Wood chips covered the small front yard with circular stone steps to walk up, and from what he could see, there was a lush green lawn out back.

It felt like a home. It didn't matter it was a bit small. It had heart. Imogen was lucky to come live here. Micha would jump at the chance.

He was lost in thought when the front door flew open. But his mind quickly cleared as he took in the panic on Swift's face, the smell of something burning, and the wailing currently emanating from somewhere within the house.

"Oh, thank god," Swift croaked. He was dressed in sweatpants and an old, faded Pine Cove Lumberjacks T-shirt. His blond hair looked damp and was curling slightly around his ears. He swallowed and glanced anxiously back into the house. "It keeps getting worse."

Micha knew there was only one thing that made him feel better when he was spiraling. Brie was great at it, and it was the first thing Pops had done when he'd picked Micha up from prison last week.

So Micha didn't think. He just stepped forward and hugged Swift like he was one of his brothers.

"It's okay," he said earnestly, rubbing his back, not

minding that Swift didn't return the hug. "You'll get through this. Kids throw tantrums." He let go of Swift, who blinked owlishly at him. "Do you want to tell me what happened?"

Swift took a shaky breath. It was odd to see a big, tough guy like him so shaken. But this was what Micha had been talking about. Swift was already tied up in knots, worrying about Imogen. That was what *good* parents did.

Swift nodded. "Come in," he said as he stepped back from the door. Micha made sure to wipe his feet on the welcome mat.

Then he paused.

Oh, wow. He could identify one problem right away.

He was in a hallway that ran down to the kitchen. To the right was a living room then what looked like a bathroom. Then on the left were the two bedrooms. The outside of the house might have been rustic and log-cabiny like most of the town was, but inside, Swift had really made his mark.

The walls were duck egg blue too and all the finishes white. Then there were sleek silver knickknacks on tables, modern looking mirrors, bowls with glass pebbles, framed artwork. From the looks of the little speakers and dials by the light switches (also chrome) the place was wired for home automation and media access in every room.

This was a *grown up's* house. It was so neat and tidy Micha almost wondered if Swift laid everything out, using a tape measure. There wasn't a speck of dust. It almost felt a little chilly.

And a five-year-old and her ginger cat had just been deposited in this pristine home. It was more like a fancy hotel than somewhere a person actually lived. Not that Micha had seen anything like that in real life, only on TV.

As if on cue, Butter the cat appeared from nowhere, materializing like a ninja and leaping onto one of the small tables in the hall.

The one with a crystal vase on it.

The horror must have shown on Micha's face because Swift's eyes went wide, and he spun on the wooden floor… just in time to see Butter bat at the vase.

"No!" Swift rasped. "Bad cat!" He made to step forward, but Butter batted the vase twice, making it wobble. Then he looked at Swift as if to say 'What are you going to do about it?' "Butter," Swift growled. "Don't you dare – no!"

He lunged forward, just as Butter bounced his weight off the vase in order to jump from the table, sending the vase crashing to the floor and smashing into a hundred pieces.

Micha slapped his hands on his cheeks and gasped. Imogen's crying stopped, and the silence was deafening. "I'm so sorry," Micha whispered. "Was it expensive?"

Swift let out a deep, guttural moan and rubbed his eyes with a hand that had several more Band-Aids on, presumably courtesy of Butter's claws. "I don't care about that," Swift said sadly. "I care about the fact that there's now glass all over the floor, that cat hates me, and my daughter is crying uncontrollably. Or at least, she was?"

Unfortunately, another pitiful sob and frustrated scream came from the living room. Micha's heart dropped. "Look, don't worry about the glass. We'll vacuum it up in a second." He jutted his head toward the sound of Imogen wailing. "Any idea what caused that?"

Swift rubbed the back of his neck. "I was trying to cook dinner for her, but she doesn't want anything besides something called 'gettios.' Then she started saying her" -he bit back whatever emotion tried to escape- "her mom would make her 'gettios' and wouldn't make her go to school." He chewed his lip and frowned. "It's her first day tomorrow."

Micha ached for him. He'd really been thrown in at the deep end. "A tantrum is totally normal, considering all she's been through. Is this the first time she's acted out?"

Swift nodded. "I didn't know if I should put her in time-out or what? I know she's processing a lot, but she has to eat and she has to go to school tomorrow."

Micha nodded sympathetically. "Shall we go talk to her?"

Swift's eyes widened as he looked between the glass and the living room, but he also nodded. Micha wanted to clap him on the shoulder and assure him they weren't going into battle. But whatever confidence had led Micha to hug Swift on the porch had faded, leaving him with his usual shyness. Instead, he offered Swift a small smile.

"We got this. Come on."

They tentatively approached the living room. Micha glanced toward the kitchen, but nothing seemed to be on. He guessed that whatever had made the burning smell had been turned off for now. That was one less thing to worry about, at least.

Like the hallway, the living room was more like an art gallery or hotel lobby than a home. Everything was monochrome and hard looking with sharp edges. Or at least it had been until the toy explosion that was now all over the hardwood floor. There were dolls and dinosaurs and coloring books and jump ropes, all strewn out like a bomb had gone off. Micha glanced at Swift, who grimaced.

"Sorry for the mess," he whispered.

"Dude," Micha said, feeling some of his boldness returning. "You've got a kid now. This is nothing." Swift blinked as if that thought had only just occurred to him.

Imogen was curled up on the couch, sniffling. Her glasses had fallen off her blotchy red face and onto the floor. Pressed up to her tummy and wrapped in her arms was Butter, who must have run in here after his vandalism. He turned to glare at Micha and Swift as if to say 'how *dare* you make my princess cry like this?' Maybe that was why he'd trashed the vase, to punish Swift because Imogen was upset.

Micha held up his hands in a peace offering as he approached, not wishing to upset cat or child. "Hey, there, Imogen," he said softly. He rolled up his sleeves on his Sunny Side Up shirt, showing off his tattoos. "Do you remember me?"

Imogen sniffed, taking a shuddery breath as she peered at his ink. "Uncle Micha," she said thickly. "Hello."

He smiled warmly. Even when she was upset, she still had good manners. "Hello." He knelt down to her level, carefully picking up her sparkly glasses and slipping them back over her red nose. He made sure not to get too close to Butter, whose tail was swishing and ears were back dangerously.

"Now, what's all this fuss about?"

"I want gettios!" Imogen cried, her lip wobbling and tears threatening to spill again.

But Micha wasn't scared of her. Kids didn't mean it when they cried. They were helpless to their emotions. Not like adults, with ulterior motives.

"'I want' won't get you anything, I'm afraid," Micha said, raising his eyebrows. "How about we try 'Daddy, please may I have SpaghettiOs?'"

Behind Micha, Swift said a soft "Ohh" of understanding. Micha smiled. It was only when he'd heard Imogen said the word had he figured it out himself.

Imogen inhaled shakily and bit her lip. "Daddy, please may I have gettios? Thank you." Her voice was small but much calmer.

Swift didn't answer, though, so Micha glanced back at him, giving a subtle nod. He could tell in his pretty blue eyes that Swift didn't have any SpaghettiOs, but they could improvise or quickly head down the store.

Normally, Micha wouldn't advise giving a kid what they wanted when they threw a fit. But Imogen wanted something familiar when her life had been turned upside down, and had asked nicely as soon as Micha had requested her to. In his book, that deserved a bit of a reward.

Swift held his gaze for a second. Then his lips twitched with a small smile, and he exhaled. "Hey, little bit," he said, crouching down next to Micha to address Imogen. "I haven't got SpaghettiOs like Mommy. But that's Imogen and Mommy's special dinner, isn't it? Can Daddy make you a different kind of spaghetti, one with cheese?"

Imogen's brown eyes widened. "I like cheese," she said earnestly.

"Great," said Swift, sounding thoroughly relieved.

Imogen hiccuped and stroked Butter's head, making him purr. Apparently, he could tell his mistress was no longer distraught, although he was still scowling at Micha and Swift. "I'm sorry I cried, Daddy," said Imogen, sounding genuinely remorseful.

Swift sighed and pushed some of her wayward blonde hair back. It was in a ponytail today rather than a braid. "That's okay, little bit," he said. Micha liked the new nickname. So did Imogen, by the way she beamed. "It helps Daddy if you use your words like a big girl. I'm proud of you."

Imogen looked down at the floor for a second. "Mommy cried a lot," she mumbled. "And threw things. Not my things. Then she'd be sad if things got broken."

Micha felt a lump rise in his throat. He hadn't pried into Swift's ex's issues, but Rhett had speculated she'd been suffering from depression as well as alcoholism. He was glad she hadn't taken it out on Imogen from the sounds of it, but that was still tough on a kid. Butter shattering that vase probably didn't help if she was already sensitive to things being thrown.

Swift licked his lips, apparently considering his words. "Mommy's in a place with lots of kind doctors and nurses, hon. She's working very hard to feel better. Then she can come back to you." Imogen blinked behind her pink glasses, then nodded solemnly. Swift smiled. He was so beautiful when he was happy and relaxed. "Would you like a hug?" he asked her.

Imogen gasped and scrambled off the sofa into her dad's arms.

Unfortunately, that dislodged Butter and left him in a standoff with Micha.

Micha froze, staring the cat in the eye, not daring to move as he swished his tail and gave a low rumbling growl. *"Gooooood kitty,"* Micha muttered.

Butter obviously decided today was Micha's lucky day and jumped off the sofa…only to start scratching the upholstery.

"Oh, no, Butter!" Swift cried and clapped his hands, startling Micha and Imogen and sending Butter racing into the hall.

"Dude, you need a scratching post, stat," Micha said, shaking his head.

Swift rose his eyebrows. "Oh, that's a good idea."

Bless him. He didn't have a clue about any of this, which was funny, considering he had so many younger siblings that he'd been so protective over – and still was, in many ways. Maybe he was just oblivious to the more practical stuff?

"Do you want to tidy some of your toys while Daddy and Uncle Micha make some dinner?" Micha suggested as Imogen rubbed her face and smiled again. It was probably best if she stayed well away from the glass until they'd vacuumed it. Hopefully Butter hadn't gone anywhere near it, either. She nodded, but Micha held up his hands then tapped his forehead. "Wait," he cried like he was a dummy. "You gotta show me your favorite toy first!"

Imogen bunched her little hands and spun on the spot

before lurching forward and seizing a chunky plastic pirate ship. "This one! I'm the captain, and we sail on the sea and discover new plants and talk to aliens. Look! It's like your drawing!" She pointed proudly at Micha's tattoo, making him smile.

"Just like it," he agreed warmly. "Okay, how fast do you think you can tidy all this up?"

"Super-fast!"

Micha gasped. *"Super*-fast? Okay, then. Daddy and Micha will be in the kitchen if you need us, all right?"

She nodded, clutching her pirate ship as she hopped about, lining up some Barbies with her free hand.

Micha looked up as Swift caught his eye, smiling in relief as he stood. Swift fetched a vacuum cleaner from the hall closet as well as a dustpan and brush, which Micha took charge of. In minutes, the glass was all gone, leaving the table bare, but at least the hallway was no longer a hazard. They emptied the glass into the trash outside, then Micha followed Swift back into the house and the kitchen…

…where a knot suddenly twisted in his stomach. It was easy talking to Imogen, but now they were alone. Even Butter had made himself scarce. Micha had no idea what the hell to say to Swift.

Swift flopped against the counter, though, and ran his hands through his blond hair, letting out a relieved laugh. "Holy fuck," he whispered so quietly it was almost inaudible. "That was incredible," he said slightly louder. "You're a genius. How did you do that?"

Micha smiled shyly and shoved his hands into his pockets. "Um, practice. I'm glad I could help. I guess Rhett and the others were busy?"

Swift looked confused for a moment. "What? No." He laughed. "Dude, I called you first. I hope you don't mind. But everyone else is just all, 'You can do this, champ!' They don't seem to listen when I'm freaking out. You listen, though."

He leaned over and touched Micha's elbow. Where Micha's shirt was rolled up, meaning his fingers connected with bare skin, and it was almost like electricity shot between them, flying all over Micha's body. He bit his lip and suppressed a shudder while also trying not to freak out.

Swift had just wanted *his* help? No one else's?

Wow.

"Can I get you a beer?" Swift asked as he dove into the fridge, pulling out ingredients.

Micha blinked. It was his turn to be confused. "Oh, well… I was going to head off?"

Swift reappeared from the other side of the fridge door, looking alarmed and maybe even a little hurt. "Oh," he nodded and fiddled with the wrapper on a stick of butter. "I guess you have plans."

Micha almost snorted. Him? Plans? Not in this town. No one wanted him around.

Except…maybe someone did?

"Uh, no," he admitted. "I just didn't want to intrude."

The smile that burst to life on Swift's face took Micha's breath away. *"Dude,"* Swift admonished. "Don't be ridiculous. I'd love you to stay. We both would. That kid adores you. Like I said, you have magic powers. Come on, let me cook you some carbonara as thanks." He chuckled to himself. "I usually only make this on cheat day, but maybe Imogen might like it."

Micha watched with his heart in his throat as Swift opened, then passed him a beer. When he had one as well, they clinked bottles in a cheers. Wow. In what reality was he, Micha Perkins, having dinner with Swift Coal at his house? Crazy.

"Thank you." Micha cleared his throat and glanced at the burnt lima beans on the stove. Swift sighed and picked up the pan to toss the ruined veggies into the trash.

"Those went over like a lead balloon," he said, shaking his head.

Micha laughed sympathetically as Swift dropped the pan in the sink to wash later. Then he retrieved a pot to fill with water for the pasta.

"Um," Micha began.

Heat rose under his collar as he fiddled with the beer label, not sure if he should be telling Swift what to do. But he argued with himself that Swift had asked him there precisely for parenting advice. Not as a buddy. So it was actually better to talk about Imogen than anything else. Especially when Swift glanced over at him with an encouraging smile.

"You might want to do some research into healthy kid-friendly recipes," Micha said. "They eat much smaller portions than adults, particularly you who literally lives at the gym, and they have a sweeter palate. Oh! You can buy these cute plates that have portion sizes drawn on them for protein, carbs, and veggies…"

He realized he'd started rambling, so he trailed off and bit his lip, looking down at the beer label he was picking again. But Swift laughed.

"Those are all really great suggestions. Thanks, man. I'm so grateful you came over." Swift grinned and shook his head as he focused on chopping up ham for the cheese sauce. "I swear, any time you need a favor, I'm there for you."

Micha risked peeking up to catch his eye but quickly looked away before he did something dumb, like blush. Swift was a nice guy, and he was just being friendly. Micha needed to be grateful for that and not read anything more into it.

"Actually, it's just cool to get out of the house and do

something different," he admitted. "Not that I'm ungrateful to my folks!" he spluttered as an afterthought. "It's just kind of intense with everything that's gone on."

Swift looked thoughtfully at him as he began to stir the cheese sauce. "That must have been rough, what you went through. Did they treat you okay while you were being held in custody?"

Humiliation flared through Micha, and his gut instinct was to run out of there at the mention of his time spent in jail. But Swift's expression was sympathetic, as was his tone of voice. So Micha took a steadying breath, suddenly feeling like it might be nice to talk with someone about what had happened.

He glanced toward the living room where he could hear Imogen playing as she tidied. He'd rather she didn't hear any of this, but they were probably okay out here. Then he smiled as best he could at Swift, who was waiting patiently for a reply.

"It was okay, after the initial, awful shock. I was in custody – so just a jail, not actual prison – and I kept my head down. It's more…like after, the enormous relief of knowing I won't have to serve any more time, so long as I keep my nose clean." He laughed ruefully. "And I haven't been taking *anything* for granted. Having my own clothes back and eating what I want and sleeping in my own, quiet room." He shook his head, feeling a bit giddy. "I'm done hanging out with people like those guys who got me into trouble. I'm *not* doing any hard time. I'm so lucky my folks took me back in."

Swift frowned. "They love you," he said as if that was a given. "Besides, you didn't do anything wrong. Rhett said that guy set you up. I'm mad you were even held that long. But I'm glad that's behind you now." He looked as if he wanted to say something else, then changed his mind. But then he pointed at Micha's drink. "Hey, don't let it get warm," he joked. However, his expression changed as if he'd thought of something. "Oh, shit, are you worried about driving? You know, you're more than welcome to stay on my couch. It pulls out into a bed."

He beamed, looking hopeful. Micha's stomach swooped. Holy shit. Swift wanted him to stay for dinner so bad he was offering his couch?

Immediately, Micha was torn. He so desperately wanted to believe that the offer was genuine. That Swift wanted to get to know him better, maybe even become friends. But that nasty voice in the back of his head hissed, *'Why would anyone want to be friends with you?'*

He'd never been good at thinking with his brain, though. His cock was far more persuasive, telling Micha's brain to shut up. When else was he going to get the chance to spend time with Swift like this?

Doubt still held him back until Micha remembered what Swift had said about Imogen. "Well, if I stayed," he said slowly, "I could help you get Imogen off to school in the morning."

Swift's expression only got brighter, suggesting that hadn't occurred to him. "Oh, yeah! That would be awesome. Thanks, man. You're the best."

The rest of the night went mostly without incident. Imogen loved her pasta, had her bath without fuss, and even Butter spent most of his time lurking under Imogen's bed. Micha had some more thoughts about décor. Specifically, that Imogen's soulless room needed a makeover, immediately. But he felt rude telling Swift what to do again. If he asked, Micha could make suggestions, but other than that, he wasn't going to butt in uninvited.

Disappointingly, by the time they got Imogen off to bed, Swift looked utterly exhausted. Micha felt bad even allowing him to help put the sofa bed together, but he didn't know where any of the sheets were or anything. His hopes that they might stay up talking with another beer fell apart, but really, that was selfish. Swift was already being so kind and generous. Micha shouldn't be greedy and expect more.

So when he got into bed himself, he closed his eyes and took several soothing breaths, tallying up the good things from the day. He'd worked a whole shift without incident. He'd calmed down a distressed child and then been invited to socialize with a proper grown up. It didn't hurt that the grown up was fucking hot and sweet and pretty dorky, in a cute kind of way. He'd also escaped his family's well-meaning but pressure-inducing gaze for a while.

Yes. All in all, Micha had to say this had been his best day for a pretty long time.

He was almost asleep when his phone pinged. He frowned. He'd told Pops where he was, and Pops had already replied saying that was fine. (His exact word, in fact, was 'Wonderful!', which had made Micha chuckle. He was almost more excited about Micha making friends than Micha was.) Maybe it was a spam text?

Micha's stomach dropped, though, as he unlocked the phone screen and saw who the sender was.

It was an unrecognized number, so Micha didn't realize until he got to the end of the message. But then he gripped the phone case as nausea rushed through him.

Heard you were out. Your house misses you. When you coming back?

Dale.

He must have gotten a new number, as Micha had blocked the old one. Gritting his teeth, he locked the screen and dropped the phone back on the sofa arm, refusing to even think about replying.

Because the answer was *never*. He was never going back

to that house in Seattle.

But somehow, he didn't think that was what Dale wanted to hear.

7

SWIFT

They made the school bus by the skin of their teeth. Swift had been completely oblivious as to how long it could possibly take to get one little girl ready and out the door, but apparently the answer was three times longer than he'd expected. In the end, he'd picked her and her small backpack up, running out the door as Micha thrust a lunch box into his free hand, and he'd sprinted down the road just as the yellow bus appeared.

Mercifully, Swift got a whole thirty seconds before it pulled up to the stop, so he'd been able to place a startled-looking Imogen on the sidewalk, straighten up her sweater, and put her lunch in her bag.

"I hope you have a great first day, little bit," Swift said, beaming at his daughter as he held her hands. "You're going to make lots of friends and have a ton of fun in your new kindergarten class, okay?"

Imogen puffed out her cheeks and pushed her glasses up her nose. "Okay, Daddy. I'll do my best."

Swift squeezed her skinny arm gently and winked. "Your best is perfect. They're gonna love you."

When the bus door opened with a hiss to the chilly morning air, the middle-aged woman behind the wheel smiled down at Imogen. "Well, who do we have here?"

Imogen took a deep breath, then marched right up the steps. "Hello, I'm new. I'm Imogen Dillard, and I'm five and a quarter."

The driver grinned. "Hello, Imogen Dillard. I'm Lonnie Hall, I'm fifty-two and a half, and I'll be your driver. How about you take a seat for me, then we'll be on our way?"

"Okay, thank you." Imogen spun around and waved enthusiastically to Swift, even though he was only a few feet away. "Bye, Daddy!" she practically shouted.

"Bye, little bit," he said, waving back.

It was stupid, but he got a lump in his throat as the bus disappeared around the corner. He growled and blinked back tears, shaking himself as he walked back to the house. It was only then did he realize he was wearing his slippers.

He chuckled, doubting the neighbors would care. The only thing that mattered was getting Imogen on that bus with everything she needed, which he'd done.

Thanks to Micha.

Honestly, the man hadn't seemed fazed by anything this morning. Not by the missing shoe that had turned up in the microwave or what to pack for lunch or brushing Imogen's crazy long hair with that new tangle brush. Micha hadn't panicked once, whereas Swift had been convinced he was going to lose his mind numerous times before seven-thirty.

The real icing on the cake came, though, when Swift walked back into the house to find Micha completely absorbed in a YouTube video. When Swift peeked over his shoulder, he realized it was a tutorial on how to braid hair.

His heart flip-flopped as he took a moment to step away again before Micha realized he'd come back inside. Honestly, where had this man *come* from? Swift had kind of thought he was cool before he'd moved out to Seattle, but he would never have imagined that he would have grown up like this.

Swift felt a sudden flare of anger as he thought of those assholes who had so nearly ruined his life. How could someone take advantage of such a sweet person like that? Micha had almost taken the fall for something he'd had nothing to do with. Thank fuck he'd managed to avoid any serious repercussions.

Swift had almost asked Micha outright last night how long he was planning on staying in Pine Cove. He'd had every intention of dissuading him from going back to the city and being anywhere near those jerks who obviously didn't think enough of him. But that wasn't really Swift's place. As much as he wanted to, he'd learned through his twenties that he couldn't control everything. In fact, it was occasionally unhealthy the way he wanted to help other people. Sometimes they had to make their own mistakes, no matter how much anxiety it caused Swift.

So he kept his thoughts to himself, on that matter, anyway. No one said he couldn't give credit where it was due, and Micha had knocked it out of the park this morning.

"I'm serious," Swift said to let Micha know he was back as he walked into the living room again. "You're a wizard. It's got to be magic that got her out the door on time."

Micha blushed. Swift was mildly surprised how much he liked that. He was also startled that his cock twitched, too. It needed to behave itself, for fuck's sake. Micha was off limits as Rhett's baby brother. Besides, everything Swift knew about him told him he was straight.

The facts did, anyway. Micha had never come out or anything, but Swift had never known him to date anyone, either. But *Jesus*. The way he was peeking at Swift through those long dark eyelashes made Swift question himself, even just for a second. That wasn't a usual kind of way a straight guy looked at another guy, was it? Mind you, there was nothing 'usual' about Micha Perkins.

He was special.

"You'll get the hang of it in no time," Micha promised, then held out his phone. "I found a hair video that might help, as well. I get the feeling braids might be the only way to tame that plume."

"Plume," Swift repeated with a chuckle as he took the phone. "Cute."

He perched on the end of the sofa bed where Micha was sitting, watching the tutorial in silence for a few minutes. "Yeah," he said, nodding and handing the phone back. "That's awesome. Could you send me the link?"

He stood and stretched, making his back click. He hadn't been able to work out like usual over the past few days, and his body was already beginning to protest. But he was planning on heading to the Aspire gym where he worked and squeezing in a quick run at least before his first class.

"You want some coffee? Oh, how was sleeping on the sofa bed?"

Micha laughed and shook his head. "The bed was fine. Being woken up by menacing purring and being stared at… not so much."

Swift had to laugh. "Speaking of which, I'd better feed the beast. Honestly, he's so sweet with Imogen. I swear he's got a split personality, like that guy in those Hobbit films."

"Gollum, yeah," Micha said, ruffling his thick dark hair. "Um, sure. Coffee would be great. Then I'll get out of your way. You must need to head to work."

Swift shrugged. "I will, but I have some time yet. Listen, I don't think I can say this enough, but thank you. I don't know how people manage this by themselves. I think you're literally keeping me sane right now."

There it was again, that blush. Even if it meant nothing

more, Swift was pleased that he'd possibly made Micha feel good about himself.

"Most people work up to a morning routine," Micha said with a shrug. "Although I can't imagine feeding a screaming newborn and changing diapers is much easier. I wasn't so involved with that part of my nieces and nephews, but I saw how exhausted my siblings and their partners were in those days."

They'd wandered into the kitchen where Swift had thankfully already thought to get the coffee pot going amidst all the chaos. Guilt and worry swirled inside him, though, as he tipped some food out for Butter, then fetched a couple of mugs from the tree on the counter.

"Amy was all alone," he said ruefully. "Her mom was a waste of space, and her dad left a long time ago. I wish she'd *told* me. Did she think I wouldn't help?"

Micha came and stood beside him, gently taking one of the mugs from Swift's hand. Swift got that zing of electricity again as their fingers brushed against each other.

Micha looked small and young in the T-shirt he'd been wearing under his uniform. A lot of his tattoos were on display. Swift had lent him some sweatpants to sleep in. Despite Micha tying them up as much as he could, they were still slipping from his hips.

God, he was cute. He made Swift feel better just by being there, by smiling sweetly up at him.

"I think it's really tough being a parent," said Micha, "and people react differently to it. Some struggle and don't ask for help when they should."

He bit his lip and looked at the gurgling coffee. Swift thought of that little baby, wrapped in nothing but a sweater with a note begging for someone to take care of him. Maybe Micha's birth mom hadn't been able to ask for help until then? They'd probably never know.

Swift puffed out his cheeks and pulled the pot out of the machine, pouring Micha a cup. "You're right. The important thing is that Amy's getting help now and Imogen is here. She's safe."

"Agreed," Micha said.

They locked eyes for a moment. Then Micha cleared his throat and turned to get cream from the fridge. It gave Swift a strange burst of pride that he felt comfortable enough to do that and that he already knew his way around the kitchen.

"So, I was thinking…" Micha started. But then he broke off shaking his head. "Sorry, I need to stop interfering."

Swift frowned and scoffed. "Dude, you've been a lifesaver. If you have any more ideas, please, for the love of god, help a fella out. I'm all ears."

Micha laughed and sipped his coffee. Swift indicated they could sit down at the dining table, which they did. After another sip, Micha nodded.

"Seeing as Imogen's going to be a part of your life now, no matter what, I thought you could work on making your spare room actually into *her* room as soon as possible." He rubbed his thumb on the rim of the mug. "You could get new bedcovers and a toy chest, you know, things like that. Anything to make the room seem less…"

Swift was inappropriately distracted by the movement of Micha's thumb back and forth. Damn it, this was apparently turning into some kind of crush. Well, Swift needed to put a lid on it. There were far more important things to prioritize, like what Micha had just suggested.

"Cold? Sterile? Painfully sensible?" Swift offered after Micha was too polite to comment any further on his design choices. He knew he'd been uptight and fussy when working on his house. When faced with what seemed like an infinite amount of decorating options, sleek and monochrome had been the only scheme that Swift had felt comfortable with.

Until now. He was aware how out of place Imogen's toys felt in here, and he wanted her to feel as at home as possible.

"Sorry," Micha mumbled bashfully. "It's just, kids generally like colors."

"No, that's a great idea," Swift told him enthusiastically, shaking his head. "I could get pretty pink things and ballerinas and stuff. I bet Sweet Cherry Sue's in town would have things like that."

Micha opened his mouth, eyebrows raised, then grimaced as if he wasn't sure whether or not to speak. But Swift nodded as he took a mouthful of coffee. He needed to jump in the shower soon, but he didn't really want this one-on-one time with Micha to end.

"From what she's said," Micha said tentatively, encouraged by Swift's nod, "while we've been playing, I think she likes explorer stuff. Treasure maps and compasses and pirates and almost sciencey stuff. But," he added hastily, "if you think she'd like princesses and ballerinas, do that. So long as she feels like the room is hers."

Swift felt himself give a lopsided smile. "No, you're right. She does like pirates, doesn't she? And mermaids! If I got a mix of girl and boy things, then hopefully I'll get something right." He frowned. "Actually, my sister would smack me over the head for saying 'girl toys' and 'boy toys.'"

Micha laughed shyly from behind his mug. "I like the sound of your sister."

It was crazy the bolt of jealousy that sent through Swift. But that was so stupid. Micha was allowed to be interested in women. Except…

"I'm surprised you guys never met," Swift said as casually as he could. "Although Kestrel is a lot younger than me. Only fifteen."

Micha's reaction wasn't what he'd expected. He clicked his fingers and smiled. "You know what, I think she's friends with my niece, Pepper. Darcy said something. Damn, it's a small town, isn't it?"

Swift struggled to read the reaction, but he kind of felt like maybe Micha hadn't been interested in his sister in that way after all. It was ridiculous the spark of joy and relief that gave him, but he was having a heavy few days, so he cut himself some slack.

"It sure is a small town. It must be a bit of a shock after city life."

Fuck. Swift wished he hadn't said anything. Micha's expression dropped immediately. "It's nice," he said, looking at his coffee as he swirled it in his mug. "Seattle got pretty crazy. But I don't…" He glanced at Swift and sighed. "I'm not sure how much I fit in here."

He'd said something like that last night as well, which confused Swift. He might not have been fostered by Sunny and Tyee until he was ten, but he'd been adopted not long after, and Pine Cove had been his home for several years after that until he'd moved out. Did he really not think he belonged here?

"Your family is happy to have you back, though, right?" Swift asked quietly. He didn't want to pry, but he was kind of upset at the idea that Micha wouldn't feel welcome. "They're glad you're okay?"

Micha sighed deeply as he nodded. "Yes," he said firmly. "But that's kind of it. I'm the black sheep. I barely scraped through high school, didn't go to college, never fit in anywhere. I seem to just attract trouble." He shook his head. "They're so forgiving, but I'm the one that made myself into that black sheep, and I don't really feel like I deserve so much patience and understanding."

Swift didn't really follow that at all. What had Micha done that was so bad? The arrest wasn't his fault, everyone agreed on that. Sure, he'd fallen in with a bad crowd, but that was over now.

"They're so perfect and happy," Micha carried on, sounding sad. "It's hard to explain, but being around them makes me feel like more of a fuckup." He sipped some coffee and glanced at Swift with a little smile. "Some time away from them has taken the pressure off, though. So thanks a lot. I think if I can just reset a bit, get my head on straight, I'll stop taking their mere existence as a signal of my failure." He laughed bitterly and rolled his eyes. "I do love them very much."

Swift considered that a moment. "No, that kind of makes sense," he said genuinely. "My mom was more than happy to have me home after college, but I needed to spread my wings, you know? It wasn't that I didn't love my family. I just had to do my own thing."

Micha looked relieved but then huffed as a smile played on his lips. "In my case, this is sort of my second attempt at doing my own thing, but that makes it more important. I *can't* screw this up. I have to find a new path. A good one. Something that'll make my folks proud."

Swift didn't realize what he'd done until his hand had reached out and covered Micha's smaller one. "They *are* proud of you. You're their kid. But I totally respect wanting to forge your own way. And you will. I know it!" He grinned.

Micha was staring open mouthed at him before his gaze dropped to their hands. Swift hastily pulled his back to his coffee mug, laughing sheepishly.

"Sorry, I went into pep-talk mode there."

Micha chuckled nervously. "It's okay," he mumbled. "Thank you."

It was like a lightbulb went off in Swift's head. A million thoughts felt like they raced through his mind all at once as he stared back at Micha.

Micha squirmed in his chair. "What?"

Swift shook himself and excitedly waved his hands. "Sorry. I had an idea. Several. Uhh. Would you like some space while you're job hunting and all that?"

Micha shrugged. "It's okay," he said hesitantly. "Everyone has their own work, and my sibs live in their own places. I get time alone. I'm just being a baby."

Swift blew a raspberry. "I know Rhett, remember? Don't get me wrong. I love your family almost like they're my own, but they are chaos personified and always in everyone's business 'helping.'" He used air quotes, making Micha smile a little and bob his head in agreement. "So," Swift pushed ahead, hoping he wasn't about to put his foot in it. "Why don't you stay here?"

Micha almost spat his coffee over the table, only just getting most of it back in the mug. Swift sat back in shock as Micha hastily wiped his mouth. "W-what?"

Was this a terrible idea? Swift didn't think so. Even if he had a tiny, minuscule ulterior motive with his little crush, he would never act on it.

Not unless he thought Micha felt the same.

He mentally clicked his fingers in front of his face. That had *nothing* to do with this.

"Look, I promised I'd return the favor for all of your amazing help if I could, and, well, wouldn't this help give you some breathing room?" He waved his hands and awkwardly rubbed the back of his neck. "Oh, god, it sounds like I'm asking you to babysit or something, doesn't it? I didn't – that's not – fuck. Just forget I said anything. I was honestly just thinking of my sofa bed, but my life is way more complicated than that now-"

"I don't mind complicated," Micha said in a small voice, fidgeting on his chair again. He looked up at Swift with those big brown eyes, half a smile twitching at his lips. "I definitely don't mind kids. And breathing room sounds incredible, if only for a few days. I – just – are you sure I wouldn't be in your way?"

Swift blinked at him. "In the way? Dude, no, not at all. It would be great to hang out some more. I kind of feel like this is what we missed out on back in the day with Rhett. Seven years seems like a big gap at that age, but now we can be friends, right?"

There he went again, trying to collect everyone who stumbled into his life. But Micha smiled, not seeming to mind. "I'd like that," he said hesitantly.

Swift realized he was grinning, holding Micha's gaze. Then he snapped out of it and looked at the clock on the wall. "Fuck, I need to get going. I still haven't sorted out my reduced hours." He pinched the bridge of his nose and tried to quickly make a mental list of what needed doing. "I'll find you my spare key before I go. Imogen should be back from school at three-thirty, but I should be able to at least take a break then, if not wrangle leaving early. I don't have clients this afternoon."

No way he was missing the first time his little girl got off the school bus. He wanted her to feel secure here and in no doubt that she was safe and not going anywhere.

Micha nodded. "Okay. Well – I could head into town and maybe get some things for Imogen's room. Oh, no, unless you wanted-"

Swift waved his hands. "I've got no idea what things you have in mind, but it sounded good. Why don't you pick out a few items to get us started, then I can take her shopping over the weekend? It would be an awesome surprise if her room had a mini-makeover before she got home from school."

"That's what *I* thought," Micha cried, sitting up in his seat.

Swift spun around in his chair, reaching over to get his wallet from where he'd left it on the side. Micha started to protest, but Swift wouldn't have any of it. "Your family gave me a ton of secondhand stuff and wouldn't take a dime. No way I'm not paying for this."

He pulled out a couple of hundreds, aware that Micha's eyes widened, but he wasn't going to react to that. He didn't hesitate to give Micha his money or encourage him to pick out cute things to make his little girl happy.

"My taste is, well…" Swift held out a hand and indicated his house. He knew he was uptight and too neat and basically allergic to color. "You get kids. I bet you'll find Imogen some awesome things that make her feel so at home. I trust you."

Something passed over Micha's face that Swift couldn't quite read. But he gave him a small smile and accepted the money he was being offered. "I won't let you down."

Swift beamed.

He wasn't sure Micha could *ever* let him down.

8

MICHA

What the hell was Micha doing?

He didn't get to have this. That was the deal he'd made with himself a long time ago. There was no way he could indulge in anything like this while he was within the town limits of Pine Cove.

And yet here he was, staring at the ceiling in Swift Coal's living room for the second night in a row.

Of course his folks had been understanding about it. Hell, Pops had practically packed a bag for him and kicked him out the door when he'd gone home to get some things. "Swift is a good boy! A good friend! This is *just* what you need," he'd loudly declared as he'd pushed Micha into his truck, which Micha was apparently still borrowing. Pops had insisted Dad would take Pops wherever he needed to go for the next few days, while Dad had grumbled something incomprehensible at the TV.

Micha had tried to go to sleep a good couple of hours ago – after Swift had cooked the three of them dinner yet again and shared another beer with Micha. But his thoughts were so confusing.

He was racked with guilt for indulging in this little domestic fantasy for even a second. Because the truth was, he hadn't felt this valued or purposeful in years. *Years* and years. And while he was busy – shopping for bedsheets or groceries or cute little kids' portion plates – he felt dedicated and content. But afterward – like now – he was left feeling guilty and selfish. Was he taking advantage of Swift and Imogen?

He really hoped not. That wasn't his intention. But he liked this family stuff, and was it really that bad he thought he was good at it? Take Imogen's room. Micha had been so nervous suggesting that to Swift, only to have been left entirely in charge of the mini-makeover. Micha had been thrifty, but he'd been so lucky with the few stores he'd gone shopping at.

He'd managed to get her lots of beautiful mermaid things, as that was almost as popular as unicorns these days. He'd bought a poster in a cheap but really nice silver frame, a mermaid cookie tin, a bedside lamp. and a blanket that she could wrap around her legs that looked like a mermaid tail. He'd also gotten fairy lights, some colorful picture frames, and a toy chest. He couldn't find any treasure maps in Pine Cove, but he'd found one online and ordered it.

When Imogen had come home from school, she'd screamed and jumped around for a good five minutes. Swift didn't like to talk poorly of her mom, but Micha got the feeling Imogen hadn't had an awful lot before. He couldn't help feel a small sense of pride that he'd brought such joy to this girl's life with a few simple knickknacks. He needed to be careful, though, that he didn't slip into feeling like he belonged here. He was just crashing for a few days, that was all.

But then there was the other, glaring problem, which had made itself more than apparent when Micha had accidentally run into Swift just before they'd started dinner.

Right after Swift had stepped out of the shower, only wrapped in a bright white towel, still glistening with droplets of water on his perfect, sculpted, slightly fuzzy, tanned, and lickable chest.

Micha was going straight to hell.

Swift was his brother's best friend. Rhett was the closest thing Micha had to a best friend himself. There was probably no one in this world Micha was closer to, even though that wasn't really saying much. But Rhett had been a great friend and the best brother Micha had ever known. How could he be salivating over his closest bud like this?

Quite easily, it turned out. Christ alive, how many times had teenage Micha jerked one out, fantasizing about Swift wanting to experiment with a boy…just to see what it felt like…what it tasted like…

Micha squirmed on the sofa bed, angrily grabbing handfuls of the bedsheets and breathing deeply until his cock calmed down.

This! This was exactly what he was afraid of. That he would out himself after all these years. Or worse, embarrass Swift after he'd been so kind and generous. He didn't deserve some fuckup lusting after him, not when he had real, grown up problems to deal with.

Micha exhaled, his thoughts still warring. Because amidst all the guilt and shame and worry, there was also pride and hope. Swift kept telling him he was doing a good job assisting with Imogen, and Micha could *see* he was helping out. Imogen was doing so well with all the changes in her life, everything considered. He was just helping to steer her and her dad on the slightly easier path.

But what qualifications did he really have for that? Yes, he'd helped out a bunch with his nieces and nephews, not to mention a whole load of foster kids he'd probably never see again from the group homes. He thought about those little ones from time to time. He hoped they'd found homes, too. Like Imogen had.

Like he had.

He huffed and turned on his side on the bed. It was surprisingly comfy, considering it was a pullout. Better than the thin mattress he'd slept on while he'd been waiting to be processed.

No. He'd promised himself he wasn't going to dwell on those couple of months. All that mattered was that he never, *ever* got even close to breaking the law again. No jaywalking, no littering, and he wouldn't even *think* about driving if he'd had even a sip of beer. He'd had enough of living life on the edge. He'd done what he'd had to in Seattle. Sometimes it wasn't things he was proud of, but those days were over and he wasn't going back.

No matter what Dale said.

Micha bit his lip and looked at his phone, which was plugged in and charging next to the sofa. *Fuck Dale.* He hadn't even left it twenty-four hours before messaging again, asking Micha when he was coming home.

Brie misses you.

That was a low fucking blow, and Dale knew it. But what could Micha do? He'd tried telling Brie to get out before all this shit blew up. If she was still there after Dale had thrown him under the bus – and tried to throw her under the bus too by leaving her behind – what could he say to change her mind? He hated it, but he could help her better down the line by staying out of prison now.

There was something ingrained in Micha that made him feel like taking care of himself was nothing but selfish. But it was what everyone kept telling him to do, so he should try.

Wait, no. He didn't have to do it for himself. He could do it for his family, sure, but that wasn't as powerful as Micha telling himself to do it for Swift and Imogen. They *needed* him. At least for now, when they were still getting on their feet as father and daughter, something Micha was miraculously able to offer advice on. He couldn't let them down.

That was easier. Telling himself he was going to try a little self-care for the sake of them and his family eased the knot of tension in his chest. Micha had once read that you could try treating yourself like you would your best friend. He'd certainly never talk to anyone the way he spoke about himself. But somehow, it was just easier to make a promise to be a bit kinder to himself if he took his feelings out of the equation altogether.

With that decided, he exhaled in the dark, finally feeling he could sleep.

Then he heard it.

In the Perkins household, Dad and Pops had always been strict about leaving bedroom doors ajar at night until all the kids moved out. Micha had always felt it ridiculous that Pops was convinced if they didn't, someone would stop breathing. But it had come as second nature to Micha as soon as he was even vaguely responsible for a child that he'd left the living room door open a crack. It wasn't even a question that he had to keep an ear open for Imogen. Finally, all these years later, he felt a little bit closer to understanding his parents.

He was glad. That had definitely been a soft little sob from the direction of Imogen's room, like she'd been trying to hide it. But Micha had heard it plain and clear, and he was already out of bed and across the hall before she had time to let out another pitiful whine.

Carefully, Micha pushed the door that was also ajar, peering into the gloom.

He'd managed to get a nightlight that projected stars onto the ceiling – not cartoon-shaped stars, but real constellations that he and Swift had been able to name for Imogen, like the

Big Dipper. So he was just about able to see her huddled up in her bed with the nefarious Butter curled up by her feet, his eyes flashing like something possessed as he watched Micha step over the room's threshold. His ears moved like satellite dishes, swiveling for any hint of something to attack. Micha was eager not to give him an excuse.

"Hey, hon," he murmured. He sat tentatively on the end of her bed, not wanting to spook her or the cat. He'd half expected Swift to come out as well, but maybe he was already asleep. "You okay?"

"I had a bad dream," she said with a sniff. "Mommy was out in the back yard calling for me, but I couldn't run fast enough. Is she okay?"

Micha bit his lip and patted her leg through the comforter. "Your mommy is getting lots of help from very clever doctors and nurses. I'm sure she'll be feeling better in no time."

"No more crying?" Imogen asked.

That was a bit of a gut punch. Micha had never met Amy, but it sounded like she'd been struggling. He didn't want to misrepresent the situation, but he did want to comfort Imogen. "Sometimes it's good to cry," he said, sidestepping the question. "It helps us feel better. But yes, the doctors and nurses will help her feel less sad."

Imogen took a shaky breath and nodded as she petted Butter's stomach. It made Micha nervous even watching her do that. He was pretty sure the cat would have taken anyone else's hand off if they'd tried to touch him on his soft, fat tummy.

"Good." Imogen rubbed her face dry of tears. "I want her to be happy."

Micha nodded. "Everyone does, hon."

Imogen reached over and turned on her bedside lamp, making Micha blink as she slid her glasses on her face, presumably to see him properly. He smiled at her and tried not to feel nervous about whether or not he was handling these questions okay.

"When she gets better," Imogen continued as Butter writhed unnervingly under her clumsy petting, "will she and Daddy be friends?"

Oh, god. How was Micha supposed to answer that? "We'll have to wait and see," he said evasively, hoping it was enough.

Unfortunately, he'd forgotten that along with kids' innocence came their total lack of filter. 'Out of the mouths of babes…' as the saying went. Imogen smiled up at Micha. "Are your mommy and daddy friends?"

Micha felt like he'd been thrown into the Pine Cove lake in the middle of winter. Familiar feelings of shame and guilt and abandonment flooded his insides as his throat constricted. "Uh…"

Imogen's mouth dropped open. "Oh, no," she said. "Are you sad, Uncle Micha?"

He blinked back his tears and tried to clear his throat. "No, I'm okay-" he began.

But Imogen scooted over and opened her arms out. "Would you like a hug?"

Micha's heart could have cracked in two. He was the adult, and yet the small child was trying to be the one to comfort *him.* "How about we give each other a hug?" he suggested.

Imogen frowned as if she was really giving his words proper consideration. "Yes, that's a good idea." She patted next to her, pushing Butter off the bed. Micha gasped, but Imogen didn't even seem to notice. Butter rolled and hopped down to the floor with a resentful flick of his tail, but he didn't even hiss. "I give good hugs," Imogen continued as if nothing had happened. "Everybody says so."

Micha laughed nervously, watching as Butter stalked out of the room. Micha let out a breath of relief. "I bet you do." He moved carefully, then sat on top of the comforter with his back to the wall and his legs stretched in front of him. As soon as he was settled, Imogen launched herself against his side, attaching herself like a barnacle on a pirate ship. Micha laughed. "Wow, yeah, good hug," he said.

"I *told* you," Imogen said, sounding smug. Carefully, Micha draped his arm over her back, aware this was someone else's kid and he should tread very carefully. But she gave a happy sigh as she patted his arm. "Does that make you feel better, Uncle Micha?"

He chuckled and looked down at her. "A lot. Thank you for the excellent hug."

She nodded, then sat back up and clasped her hands in her lap. "Were you sad about your mommy, too?"

Micha did his best to hide the lump that threatened to rise in his throat. But maybe being honest would help Imogen feel better about the crazy situation she'd found herself in. After all, like Pops had said, the Perkins family was pretty far from normal in so many ways, but they were an amazing family.

Even with a black sheep like Micha.

"Uh," he said shakily as he searched for the right words. "I never met my mom. She, um, gave me up right after I was born."

Imogen gasped and covered her mouth, looking up at him with a horrified expression. "Oh, no!"

"It's okay, it's okay," Micha said hurriedly. Damn, he'd been trying to make her feel *better*. "Because I was adopted." Micha just wasn't going to elaborate on how long that had taken to happen.

"Oh, *phew*," said Imogen, letting out a big breath. "So you *do* have a mommy and daddy?"

"Actually," Micha said with a smile, "I have two daddies. Dad and Pops. Have you ever heard of anyone with two daddies before?"

"Oh, yes." Imogen flicked her hand and scoffed. "Of course. Mommy says some boys and girls have two mommies or two daddies and that's just the same as a mommy and a daddy. And anyone who says it isn't is a dumb-dumb," Imogen added with a scowl.

For a second, Micha was completely lost for words.

This kid was only five. Yet she knew that Dad and Pops were just as good at being parents as anyone else.

If only everyone could be so enlightened.

Micha swallowed down the wave of emotions that threatened to undo him. He didn't want to tell her he was proud of her – or especially her mom for teaching her that – because he didn't want to make her think what she was saying wasn't right.

In fact, it was how the world should be. Families came in all shapes and sizes, after all.

"They are dumb-dumbs," Micha agreed with a chuckle that masked him clearing his throat again. "Thank you."

"It's okay," Imogen said sagely. Then she let out a big yawn that seemed to resonate through her whole body.

Micha glanced at the clock. It was late by anyone's standards, let alone a little kid's. "Do you think you'll be able to go back to sleep now?" he asked her.

Imogen nodded but looked up at him expectantly. "Will you stay until I fall asleep?"

Micha's heart ached. It was always hard thinking about his adoption, but Imogen made him feel like he was slightly less unwanted.

Just like her dad, Swift, did.

He gave her a warm smile. "Of course," he promised.

"Why don't you turn off the lamp so we can look at the stars?"

"Okay," she mumbled sleepily. Then she slipped her sparkly glasses from her face and clicked the mermaid light off, leaving the soft glow of the constellations on the ceiling. "Nite-nite, Uncle Micha."

"Nite-nite, hon," he said back.

Despite all the emotions that had been whirling in his head before and the feelings he'd just stirred now, Micha couldn't help the small amount of contentment that washed over him as he felt Imogen get heavier with sleep.

He decided he quite liked being Uncle Micha.

9

SWIFT

Swift almost didn't dare to breathe.

Was Imogen finally back to sleep?

He rubbed his face where he was sitting up in bed, the light by the baby monitor illuminating his room.

Micha didn't seem to know that Swift had heard everything.

And now Swift was completely torn with several warring emotions. Initially, he'd been stirred from his deep sleep by the confusing sound of voices. His mom had always sworn he could sleep through a hurricane. But when he realized Imogen was awake and he heard her saying she'd had a bad dream through the new little device by his bed, he'd been fully conscious in an instant, ready to spring from his bed and run into the next room.

Until he heard Micha's voice.

It was as if hearing his soothing tone calming his daughter paralyzed Swift. He stopped breathing, listening to Micha assure Imogen that Amy was getting all the help she could. He was so kind when he mentioned her. There wasn't a hint of scorn or disrespect, which wouldn't be totally out of place, considering the situation.

But Swift felt very strongly about not painting Imogen's mom as some sort of failure or villain. She just needed some extra help and had perhaps waited a bit too long to ask for it. It sounded like Micha might feel the same way, which made Swift's insides swoop with warm appreciation.

Swift had finally felt like he'd come back to his senses and was about to go join Micha in talking with Imogen when he was stopped in his tracks again.

"Oh, no," Imogen cried through the baby monitor. "Are you sad, Uncle Micha?"

A red mist of possession and protection flashed through Swift so fast it made him dizzy. He knew that Micha was going through a lot right now, and he was dealing with it as best he could. But hearing Imogen ask if he was sad with such concern was like a knife through his heart.

Swift bit his lip and made himself sit back down, gripping onto the bedsheets. He wasn't Micha's keeper. It wasn't Swift's responsibility to look after him or fix his life. But Micha was doing so much to help him and Imogen it was difficult not to argue that Swift was perfectly entitled to sweep in and save Micha, consequences be damned.

He took a deep breath and shook his head. That was crossing a line. This stupid crush of his was growing at a ridiculous rate. It was probably one of those things where intense situations made you think feelings were stronger than they really were, right? Just because Micha was staying here for a few days while things were really crazy didn't mean they were anything more than friends. It was a stretch to hope they were even that. Sure, Swift was getting good vibes from him, but that didn't mean they were going to be best buds.

Swift needed to stop being so desperate. It wasn't like he

was short on friends, after all. He had dozens he hung out with regularly here in town, not to mention hundreds on his Facebook.

So why was he so hung up on Micha liking him?

He knew why, he thought with a grumble as he heard Micha talking about his adopted dads. He had to say his chest burst with pride as Imogen so casually defended the rights of same-sex parents. Amy had taught her well.

Then a thought snuck into Swift's mind. *How would Imogen feel if her daddy had a boyfriend?*

That was crazy. He physically shook himself. This was in no way the time to come out of the closet, no matter how much he might think he liked Micha at the moment. Both Swift's and Imogen's lives had been turned upside down this week, and Micha was recovering from a dramatic change in circumstances himself. He was getting back on his feet after a brush with the law, Imogen and her mom would soon be recovering after Amy left rehab, and Swift was dealing with sudden fatherhood being thrust upon him.

This would be a disastrous time to even *think* about starting a new relationship, let alone trying to navigate dating a man for the first time. Not that there was anything wrong with it, or that his family would disapprove. In fact, he was sure they would have a lot to say about having a full set of queer kids. But Swift needed to keep his priorities straight right now and not overcomplicate things.

Falling for his best friend's little brother would definitely count as complicated.

Sure, Micha was a grown adult who could make up his own mind. But Rhett had always been super protective of his younger brother. Micha hadn't had the best start in life and definitely didn't deserve to be dicked around now by Swift, who was probably just reaching out to the nearest kind soul in his time of need, looking for affection.

Still, his heart couldn't help but ache as he heard Micha and his little girl say goodnight to each other. Swift trusted Micha as though it were Imogen's mom in there with her. He wondered if that was sensible, recalling how Micha had told him off for also trusting him to push her on the swing. But it wasn't in Swift's nature to go around thinking the worst of people, not when they hadn't given him reason to.

Besides, if he had run into Imogen's room too, yelling, *'What's wrong?!',* he might have made her think a bad dream was a bigger deal than it really was. He didn't want to overcrowd her and make her anxious.

Swift's mom had been very clear on that when his younger sister, Kestrel, had been little. She'd told him it was important to make kids feel like they could cope. Like when Kestrel fell over and skinned her knees or came off her bike or banged her head. Their mom would always say, 'Oh, dear. Let me take a look. Well, you're all right. Up you get!' Within minutes, Kestrel would be up and playing again, forgetting she'd even been crying.

Swift allowed himself a moment of pride. There. He *did* already know some parenting stuff! Between what he'd gleaned from his folks and Micha's advice, maybe he wouldn't totally screw this whole thing up.

He realized the baby monitor had gone quiet. Hopefully, that meant Imogen had fallen back asleep and Micha had returned to the living room. Swift exhaled, puffing out his cheeks as guilt began to creep in.

As much as he'd wanted to give Imogen some room, he had listened to Micha talking with her when Micha most likely wasn't aware of that fact. He'd need to come clean and bring that up tomorrow. He didn't want secrets between them, and he certainly didn't want Micha to discover or remember the baby monitor down the line and put together that Swift had eavesdropped.

That made it sound distasteful. He didn't feel like it was, though. More like he'd been given a gift, getting a glimpse of Micha sharing a moment with his little girl. Just so long as Micha knew and was okay with it, Swift thought it was kind of precious.

He was overcome with the urge to go give Imogen a hug, even though she was sleeping now and wouldn't know. But Swift would know. He still wasn't used to having her jump up and clamber into his lap. She was so fragile it made his heart leap into his throat, imagining all the harm that could come to her. But that was his job as her daddy. To protect her as best he could.

There would be other nights, no doubt, where Swift would need to comfort her after a bad dream. He was kind of glad Micha had gotten a chance to take a turn tonight, as he probably wouldn't get many others.

Now, why did that make Swift feel sad? It was ridiculous to feel a pang that Micha was only going to be here for a few days. Swift couldn't go around kidnapping his friend's brother, for heaven's sake. He rolled his eyes at himself. Yes, it was nice to have Micha around for the moment. But there was no reason they couldn't continue being friends after this. *That* would make Swift disappointed. He felt like they were getting along very well, after all. Hopefully Micha would want to stay in touch once he moved on, even if he was terrible with things like Facebook.

Swift pushed himself out of bed, slipping on his robe and slippers. There was no sense in turning on the hallway light, as it would only disturb both Micha and Imogen if they had their doors open. Instead, Swift silently eased his own door open and crept out into the hall, using the light from his bedside lamp to navigate.

Not very well, apparently.

"Oof!"

He slapped his hand over his mouth as he bounced off something that shouldn't have been there. Or rather, someone.

Micha looked up at him in horror, his expression just about visible in the gloom. "I'm so sorry!" he hissed in a whisper. "She had a bad dream. I just-"

Before he could second guess himself, Swift reached up and held Micha's shoulders. "It's okay. I know," he whispered back, rubbing Micha through his T-shirt with his thumbs.

Micha froze, glancing down, then back up at Swift. "You do?"

Swift squeezed his shoulders, then let him go. "Uh, yeah," he admitted, unable to stop himself rubbing from the back of his neck, feeling sheepish. "The baby monitor was on."

Micha's eyes went wide. "Oh, right." He licked his lips, drawing Swift's attention before he could drag his gaze back up to his eyes as quickly as possible. "I'm sorry. I hope you didn't mind, but-"

"Oh, no, no!" Swift cried, then remembered to keep his voice low. "You did such an amazing job. I didn't want to interrupt. Thank you."

Micha's expression transformed into a slightly dazed look with a lopsided smile. "Right," he said, slowly but happily. "Uh, you're welcome. It was no trouble."

Swift's heart fluttered. For a crazy second, he wished he hadn't let go of Micha's shoulders. It would be so easy to gently pull him closer, to see if he angled his head slightly, would Micha do the same? What would happen if their mouths slowly came together-

"Ow!"

He was amazed he managed not to bellow louder as ten horribly sharp claws suddenly sank into his calf. Apparently, Butter had liked the look of Swift's bathrobe and had decided to pounce.

Immediately, Swift leaped backward, dislodging Butter and thoroughly destroying whatever magic moment had been passing between him and Micha. However, maybe it wasn't totally spoiled. Micha covered his mouth with both his hands as he tried not to laugh. It was such a sweet action that Swift forgot to be mad at the cat as he chuckled back at Micha.

"You think that's funny?" Swift teased.

Micha bit his lip as he grinned. "I think it's just relief he didn't target me," he whispered.

"You're wearing sweatpants!" Swift hissed indignantly back. But that just made Micha laugh more. He stuffed his knuckles into his mouth as he looked down to watch Butter slinking back into Imogen's room, swishing his tail victoriously, as if he hadn't just maimed Swift's leg.

Although Swift had to say, he wasn't really thinking about the little stings on his skin right then.

He was redoing his robe tie, trying to cover up a fraction more before certain parts of him got too excited. God, he was *obsessed* with the way Micha's mouth looked when he laughed and smiled. It was such an unusual sight Swift was taken by surprise from it. But he looked so gorgeous and damn kissable. All Swift's cock could tell his brain was how kissing would also be an effective way to stop him from laughing.

That was completely inappropriate. Swift needed to do or say something fast before any more blood rushed from his head down to his crotch.

"So!" he blurted out, still whispering, but not sure where his mouth was going because his brain apparently didn't seem to know. "Are you coming tomorrow?"

Oh god, that wasn't good!

"I mean, coming with me?"

That was even worse!

"To lunch," he finally managed to splutter. "I think I mentioned earlier how my family is all having a big get-together to welcome Imogen. They're really excited. It's like a cookout with pumpkin carving and probably stupid games. I'd love you to come – *I mean* – it would mean a lot to me and Imogen if you were to be there."

He clamped his mouth shut, afraid of the words that might keep tumbling out if he didn't. How many times could he say 'come,' for crying out loud? Micha looked slightly baffled at him. "Oh," he stammered eventually.

For fuck's sake. This was the other thing Swift did. He didn't just try and collect people all the time. He was always trying to help people become friends with other people. It probably put them in awkward positions, and Swift knew he needed to nip it in the bud. Micha wouldn't want to be subjected to a noisy, hectic-

"I – I'd love to." Micha offered him a hesitant smile, wringing his hands as he peeked up at Swift.

Swift gaped back at him for a second. "Oh – oh, you would? That's, well, that's wonderful."

Micha's smile dropped, replaced by worry. "Unless it's an inconvenience. I'd hate to put anyone out."

"No, no," Swift said quickly, waving his hands. "My mom always makes enough to feed a battalion. We'll all be living off leftovers until Thanksgiving, I promise." He beamed down at Micha. "So you'll be there?"

Micha bit his lip, a hint of a smile returning to his face. "Yes, please. Thank you."

Swift was a bit embarrassed by how ridiculously happy that made him. Somehow, in his mind, Micha was becoming linked with Imogen, and he wanted his family to meet and love them both.

"Great, cool, neat," he said, nodding and cringing internally while he tried to keep smiling. *Neat?* Had he accidentally woken up in the nineteen fifties? How much of a dork could he be, seriously? "Okay, then. Well, uh, goodnight, I guess?"

Micha shook his head, as if remembering where he was as he glanced back at the living room. "Oh, yeah, sure. Sleep well."

"You too," Swift replied sincerely.

For a second, neither of them moved. They just looked at each other in the near darkness. They were so *close...*

Then Swift laughed, shaking himself back to his senses. Micha hugged his chest and took a step back.

"Night," he said shyly.

Swift waved, apparently unable to stifle his inner dork, no matter how hard he tried. "Nite-nite, Micha."

Despite the thoroughly embarrassing display he'd just given, Swift closed his bedroom door with a huge grin on his face.

Micha was going to lunch with him.

And because it was with pretty much Swift's *entire* family, it was definitely not a date.

No way.

10

MICHA

WHAT HAD MICHA BEEN *THINKING?*

This had seemed like such a good idea last night, in the near dark, with Swift looking at him all sweetly and telling him he'd done a great job calming Imogen and getting her back to sleep.

Now he was going to walk into a house filled with people he barely knew or didn't know from Adam, but all of whom he was pretty sure had proper jobs and love lives and, most notably, had not *ever* been arrested by the police.

The Coal family was *nice.* Respectable. Surely they wouldn't want someone like Micha and his tattoos and his suspended sentence coming into their lovely home.

Unfortunately, it seemed Swift wasn't giving him any wiggle room to get out of it.

"Of course you're welcome," he said in confusion while he attempted to help Imogen get a new pair of sneakers on. She was being pretty good about it. However, Butter was dangerously fascinated with the laces. They should have gone for a pair with Velcro. *"More* than welcome," Swift continued. "When I told my mom you'd be there, she seemed so happy. I think she's missed feeding Rhett since he got married. And my siblings will love getting to know you!"

Micha highly doubted that. What would someone like him have to say to all those cool people? Rhett said that Swift's other sister, Ava, had almost qualified for the U.S. Olympic archery team. Micha had spent the past few years tending bar. It was going to be one long humiliation.

But Swift looked back up at him from where he was kneeling in front of Imogen, disappointment flashing across his face. "You don't have to come, though," he said hesitantly. "I'd – they'd – understand."

Bless him for giving Micha an out. But for some unfathomable reason, Swift really did seem to want him to come, and Micha would hate to let him down. Besides, Imogen pushed her glasses up her nose, then squinted accusingly at Micha. "Don't you want to come, Uncle Micha?"

"No!" he cried. "I mean, yes! Of course I do! I just wanted to double – *triple* – check your grandma wouldn't mind setting an extra plate. But Swift's said it's fine, so, um, of course I'm coming, hon."

She broke into a huge smile. "Yay! There aren't any other kids there, Daddy says, but you and me can play, can't we?"

"Uncle Micha might want a chance to talk to some of the other grown-ups, sweetie," Swift began, but Micha shook his head. That gave him the perfect escape if he got overwhelmed.

"No, it's okay. I'm sure we'll get time to play some space pirates, won't we, Imogen?"

She punched the air. "Yes! Daddy, can I bring my ship to Grandma and Grandpa's house?"

For a second, Swift looked down at the shoes he'd just put on his daughter's feet, then at his hardwood floors. But he seemed to realize the shoes were almost brand new and didn't have any mud or anything on them. "Sure," he said, smiling with what felt like effort. Micha was proud of him that he was trying to let go of his fussy ways, though. "Why don't you pack a few things into your bag to bring?"

"Okay, thank you very much, Daddy!" With that, she hopped down from the sofa and ran into her room, chatting away to herself as she picked out some of her favorites.

Swift stood, brushing his hands against the jeans that were clinging sinfully to his muscular thighs. Then he looked at Micha through his golden lashes. It was a gorgeous October day, and the sunlight streaming through the windows made his skin almost glow.

Micha dug his fingernails into his palms and used every ounce of his strength not to swoon.

"Please don't be nervous," Swift said quietly, probably not wanting Imogen to overhear. "I mean it. You don't have to come if it's too much for you. But my family really is lovely, if a little odd at times."

Micha scoffed to hide his nerves – and other things, like how Swift being so nice to him was making his stomach swoop – and raised his eyebrows. "Odd? You've met my brood. We're basically the Addams family. If any of us had a 'traditional' family unit, we'd probably hold a séance."

Swift laughed wholeheartedly. God, Micha loved making him do that. His heart ached.

"Yeah, screw 'normal,' right?" Swift licked his lips and sighed. "I just – I'd like you to have a nice time. It's cool that we're getting the chance to get to know each other like this. So I guess I'm just trying to reassure you that if you do come, you've really got nothing to worry about."

Micha exhaled shakily and glanced toward Imogen's room, where she was still engrossed in packing half her toys, from the sounds of it. Mentally, Micha steeled himself and nodded. "I made a promise," he said, turning back and looking Swift in his blue eyes with as much conviction as he could muster. "I'm coming. And – you're right. If I quit worrying, I might even have a fun time."

Swift seemed determined to put Micha's heart through the wringer. He broke into a goofy grin and did a sort of jig on the spot. "Awesome. I promise that you'll have a *great* time. And if at any point you feel overwhelmed or out of place – I'm sure you won't – but if you *do,* just come find me, okay? I'll always take care of you."

God, how Micha wished that were really true.

But he managed a sincere smile and relaxed approximately three percent. "Thanks," he murmured.

"I'm ready, Daddy!" Imogen came running out of her room with her backpack strapped around her shoulders… and Butter cradled upside down in her arms, exposing his soft belly. In the sunshine, his irises had reduced to snakelike slits that he turned on Micha and Swift, like Medusa trying to turn them to stone.

Micha took a step back.

"Oh, no, little bit," Swift said, his expression half grimace, half fear. "I don't think you can bring Butter. He'll, um, be happier here."

Imogen's face fell as she looked down. She and Butter shared a look. "But…doesn't everyone want to meet him?"

Micha glanced at Swift, who was practically sweating at trying to convince his daughter that she couldn't bring her devil cat with them. "Well…" Swift clicked his teeth and furrowed his brow. "He might get lost. It's a big house with grounds, and, um…"

"Aren't some of your brothers and sisters allergic?" Micha prompted, hoping he wasn't overstepping the mark. But Swift's face lit up.

"Yes, yes. Very allergic." He nodded with exaggerated

concern. "But not to dogs! Uncle Robin and his boyfriend, Uncle Dair, will be there with their puppy, Smudge."

Imogen frowned down at Butter, who swished his ginger tail and seemed to realize he'd been unceremoniously uninvited. He twisted in her arms and dropped down to the ground, stalking off toward the kitchen.

"No," said Imogen, nodding seriously. "Butter wouldn't like meeting a dog. He doesn't like dogs. But I do. Is he a *nice* dog?"

Swift's relief was palatable as he grinned down at her. "The *nicest*," he promised. "What do you say? Shall we get going?"

Imogen looked to the side, with what Micha was starting to think of her 'pensive' face. She thought about everything, did this one. "Yes. Let's go. Do they all know my name?"

Swift ushered her out of the front door with Micha by his side. "Yep," Swift said as he locked up. "But you can still introduce yourself, sweetheart. And it's okay if you forget people's names. There's going to be a lot of people there. If you need to come and find Daddy to have a break from everyone, that's fine."

"Or Uncle Micha," Imogen said factually as she marched to the car. "I can have a break with him, too."

Micha stopped in his tracks, but Swift touched his elbow and smiled. "Or Uncle Micha," he murmured with a smile. "That's right."

The car journey over was something of a blur. Micha wasn't sure if time went too slowly or if the whole thing was over in the blink of an eye. But *damn it,* Swift was confusing him. The little touches, the fond glances, the confidence he had in him. How was Micha supposed to react to that? Was it just Swift being overly friendly? He always was a lost puppy sort of person, never letting anyone feel left out or abandoned. But if Micha didn't know he was straight, he'd be tempted to read something else into all these little exchanges.

If he was crazy, he might think Swift was into him. That he *liked* him. But that was insane. It could never happen.

Swift hadn't been kidding. From the number of vehicles parked up outside the Coal family home, Micha was tempted to think they'd invited half the damn town. Jesus, it was as bad as Dad and Pops' place around the holidays. Cars and trucks, a van, and even a motorbike. So many people.

Micha clenched and unclenched his hands, trying to dispel the nerves. Swift had promised it was going to be okay, so he needed to trust him. But his hands were still trembling slightly as he unbuckled, then exited the car to walk beside Swift up the drive toward the porch. The afternoon air was cool, and there was a fair wind, but the sun was shining brightly.

Imogen was quiet. She held her daddy's hand as they approached the steps. The three-story house was made of pale wood and surrounded by rich-scented pine trees. Micha thought he saw some of the curtains twitch through one of the large, square windows. Were people watching, waiting for them to approach? Nerves twisted in his guts.

He glanced at both Swift and Imogen, offering a tight smile. This was supposed to be a fun, relaxing afternoon. He just needed to keep breathing and make sure his anxiety didn't get the better of him.

However, it was difficult not to jump as he went to place his foot on the first of the wooden steps, because Swift rested his hand on the small of Micha's back, guiding him gently up toward the porch.

Micha wasn't sure if anyone had ever touched him like that before. Yes, he was wearing a jacket, a shirt, and a T-shirt. But it felt like Swift's palm burned a hole through all his clothes, it was so hot against Micha's skin. It wasn't unpleasant, Micha realized as he got over the initial shock. It was actually sort of wonderful.

As they reached the door, Swift beamed at him, then let his hand drop. Micha felt the loss immediately but hoped he didn't show any kind of disappointment on his face. Luckily, Swift chose that moment to glance down at Imogen.

"Do you want to ring the bell, little bit?"

Imogen looked up at the old-fashioned pull-bell Swift was pointing at. The gentle clacking of a wooden wind charm drifted through the air. It was hanging on the other side of the door to the bell and appeared to have little photos in ovals of wood that were tapping against the central cylinder. They kind of looked like school photos.

Dad and Pops were kind of obsessed with photographs. Well, it was mostly Pops. Micha figured it was probably because they missed out on seeing their kids growing up before they were adopted, but for as long as Micha could remember, Pops would always have a crappy old camera in his hand at every event. Dad wouldn't let him have a fancy one, because he always found a way to break it. Now, his phone case was like a fish tank it was so thick. But there Pops would be, filming and snapping away at every birthday or holiday. Micha was pretty sure he'd caught all the grandkids' first words and steps on celluloid, forever immortalized.

Micha was never keen on having his picture taken. In fact, he tried to avoid it most of the time, much to Pops' dismay. Photos always made Micha feel uncomfortable, like he was taking up space. Now, looking at the faded images on the wind chime, he wondered for the first time if he'd been wrong. If no one ever captured his image, would it be like he'd never even been there at all?

He was drawn from his reverie as Swift lifted Imogen up so she could tug on the heavy bell. "That's it! Great job, kiddo." She beamed as her dad put her back down, but then it felt like all three of them looked anxiously at the wooden door, waiting for it to swing inwards. Yet when it did, they all still flinched in surprise.

A teenage girl threw her hands up like a mime artist as she gasped. She had a boyish figure and a pixie cut of jade-streaked blonde hair. Her scruffy T-shirt read 'Here to break the gender binary system' in big, bold letters, and her spindly legs poked out of her shorts like tree saplings. By her feet, an excitable fluffy puppy was dancing around, trying to make new friends. But he was well trained. He didn't rush out the door, instead dropping his butt down and contenting himself by wagging his tail frantically.

"Holy cow! You must be Imogen!" The teen bumped her chest with her fist. "I'm your auntie Kestrel. It's so awesome to meet you."

Imogen blinked behind her glasses, her mouth hanging open as she gaped up at Kestrel Coal. "Hi," she said eventually, then thrust her hand forward. "It's a pleasure to meet you, Auntie Kay…Kes…"

"Kestrel," Kestrel supplied, reaching down to give Imogen's hand a good shake. "Don't you have perfect manners? Just like your daddy!" She wasn't wrong there, Micha thought longingly. "Hey! Do you like reading? I got you a present."

It was as if Imogen awoke from a spell and snapped back to life. She jumped forward and clasped her little hands in front of her chest. "Yes, yes! I love reading!"

Kestrel reached over to a table in the entrance hall and picked up a large but slim hardback book to present to Imogen. Micha caught the word 'rebel' on the cover. "Each page tells a story about a real-live woman who's done really awesome things in history," Kestrel said. "I can read a few of them with you later, if you like?"

Awestruck, Imogen accepted the book carefully into her

hands. "Thank you very much," she said quietly, turning it over to look at the back as well as the front. "I like your dog. May I pet him?"

"Of course!" Kestrel beamed, then seemed to notice Swift and Micha as Imogen patted the dog's head. "Hey, you!" she cried, flinging her arms around her brother's neck, which required her to stand on her tiptoes. "Oh my god, isn't this insane? How's being a dad? Everyone's here. They can't wait to meet Imogen. Oh, hey!" She looked at Micha and let Swift go, placing her hands on her hips as she gave Micha a bright smile. "You must be Micha. I'm glad you didn't go to prison."

"Kes!" Swift exploded indignantly, and icy cold shame rushed through Micha. He opened his mouth to say something, but words abandoned him.

Kestrel frowned at Swift. "What? I am supposed to be all white middle class about it and not say anything?" She blew a raspberry and turned back to Micha. "Pepper told me all about it. You're her uncle, right? I'm glad you were one of the lucky ones and didn't go down for some bullshit reason. And Mom said that *Swift* said that you've been, like, a total miracle worker this week. She's so happy you came today. Oh, come in! Why are we loitering on the porch?"

She laughed and shook her head as she stepped to the side, inviting them in. The dog jumped to his feet, making Imogen giggle in delight. Swift sighed wearily. "You couldn't have waited until we even crossed the threshold, huh?"

Kestrel looked genuinely confused. "Waited for what? I hope you're hungry! We've been cooking since yesterday."

"Of course you have," Swift said, shaking his head, but there was affection there.

Micha, on the other hand, was paralyzed by fear. Had they all been gossiping about him? Oh, *fuck.* He should never have come! He should leave before he embarrassed Swift…

…who once again placed a large, warm, reassuring hand

on him, this time by wrapping his arm around his shoulders. Micha's heart threatened to stop.

But then he looked up at Swift's kind smile which told him it was going to be okay without using words, and he tried to relax. Kestrel was right. It actually did kind of feel better to have her address the elephant in the room right away rather than skirting around the issue all afternoon. If the Coals knew it wasn't really his fault he'd been in trouble with the law, but were still okay with him being around Imogen and Swift, then what was the worst that could happen?

"You have a lovely home," Micha said automatically as they closed the front door. He wiped his feet on the mat and took a quick look around at the hundred more photos on the walls that Pops would certainly approve of. The worn tapestry rugs on the floor and handmade terracotta pottery on display immediately gave it a very homely feel.

"Where on Earth did you get your interior design taste from?" Micha murmured playfully.

Swift bumped hips with him and pretended to scowl. "Shush, you."

Kestrel glanced over her shoulder at them as she led them down a corridor toward a hum of happy voices. The dog was hopping around her feet, clearly very pleased he'd found three new people. Kestrel's expression was curious. Swift arched an eyebrow at her, so she smirked and looked forward again. Imogen was trotting dutifully in front of them, behind Kestrel, her book clutched in her hands and her backpack bouncing with each step.

Maybe Micha should have felt stranger about how much Swift was touching him, but honestly it was so comforting he couldn't bring himself to overanalyze it or move away. Was it really doing any harm?

He didn't think so until they stepped into a large kitchen

where half a dozen people were loitering with drinks. The conversation stuttered as everyone's gaze dropped to where Swift's arm was draped around Micha's shoulders.

Ah. Yes. That did look awfully boyfriend-like.

Several pairs of eyebrows rose, but before Micha could properly get a good look at any of their owners, Deb Coal flapped her hands and skipped over to where Kestrel had left Swift, Micha, and Imogen standing.

"Oh, hello! Hello! Look at you guys!" First, she swept Imogen up in her arms, making her giggle. Then Deb directed her affections toward Swift.

He chuckled in embarrassment as his mom managed to hug and rock him back and forth with her granddaughter still on her hip. Deb was about half Swift's size, but she didn't seem to realize or care. "You saw us like a week ago, Mom," he complained.

"Let me fuss," she chided as she lightly slapped his arm. At least her hug had separated him and Micha, but then she turned to face Micha and seemed to beam even more. "I'm so happy you came, dear! How is your family? Can I get you a drink? You must say hi to everyone. How's the job hunting going?"

"Mom," Swift almost growled as Deb steered Micha away from him. It was easy to see where Kestrel got her motormouth from.

"I-I'm good," Micha managed to stammer as they reached the fridge. "Been working a few shifts at the diner."

Of course they all knew he meant his folks' diner. He hadn't been gone so long he'd think they'd assume anywhere other than Sunny Side Up here in Pine Cove. So it was no surprise when several people nodded and beamed with little 'oh's.

"How's Sunny doing?" a slim guy with dark hair and glasses asked with genuine concern. When Micha didn't respond, because he wasn't sure how, the guy gave him a sympathetic look. "He burned his arm on the grill the last time I was there with some of the other teachers. He swore like a *sailor,*" he added scandalously, but there was real affection there too, so Micha didn't mind when the room chuckled lightly.

"Oh, of course, yeah." Micha went to fold his arms, then slipped his hands into his jeans pockets instead, still feeling too exposed. "Sorry. Growing up, he just always had some burn or cut or something. He never thinks to mention it. One time, Pops only realized he had glass in his hand when he, um-"

Oh god. He'd just been about to say when Pops had pulled Dad up for a kiss. Automatically, Micha slammed the brakes on the end of that sentence. But then he looked around the room at the expectant faces. He saw a muscular blond guy with dog tags who had his arms around a bespectacled redheaded man who looked a lot like the dark-haired guy who'd spoken. The dog was now curled up at their feet. Then he noticed a pretty Asian guy engrossed in his phone, but he was leaning against another stocky man who smiled encouragingly at Micha as he played with the hem of the twink's tank that read 'As if?' Kestrel was there with her gender T-shirt and the dark-haired guy had a subtle rainbow design on his bracelet.

This whole family was LGBT. What the hell was wrong with Micha? He didn't need to censor himself. But it was like shame had crawled up his throat, and his cheeks were burning. He didn't know how to recover the story.

The dark-haired guy grinned, though, and shared a glance with the redhead. "Sunny always was a stubborn son-of-a-" He widened his eyes and cleared his throat, glancing at Imogen, who was still perched on her grandma's hip, hugging her new book. *"Gun.* Son-of-a-gun.

You remember that time we snuck into the kitchen, Robin?"

Deb huffed and shook her head at Micha. "Those boys knocked over a whole stack of plates! But your father wouldn't let us pay for them!"

The redhead, Robin, smiled sheepishly, glancing at the blond attached to him. "Sunny made us wash dishes all summer, with no pay!"

"Yeah, you learned a thing or two, though, right?" Swift teased them fondly.

Ah. Of course, those were the Coal twins. Micha vaguely remembered about the plate incident, but it was years ago.

Swift bit his lip and looked at Imogen. Micha could feel his anxiety rolling off him at how to handle her with all these people. Without thinking, he reached up and touched Swift's arm. The second they connected, he realized what a dumb thing that was to do. He was hardly hiding his feelings in front of all these people. But in that moment, assuring Swift seemed more important than concealing his dumb crush.

It was worth it for the quick but heartfelt smile Swift flashed him. His confidence renewed, he reached out to take Imogen in his arms. "So, hey, everyone? I think you've heard a lot about my daughter. Imogen, I'd like you to meet my family."

Micha was pretty sure some of the guys weren't actually related to the Coals, but he loved that Swift was possibly including friends when he said 'family.' That word didn't just mean blood, after all.

Imogen clutched her book like a shield. Then she flung her hand out. "Hi!" she said a little too loudly, spreading out all her fingers. "I'm Imogen, and I'm five and a quarter!"

The dark-haired twin gasped. "Five?" he repeated.

Imogen nodded. "And a quarter."

"Wow, you're so big." He grinned, pushing his glasses up his nose with a single finger. "I like your glasses."

"Thanks," Imogen cried. "I like yours, too!"

Seeing as he was the only man in the room without another man draped over him (aside from Swift, of course) Micha might have been interested. But he was so put together and confident Micha knew he'd never really be brave enough to make a move.

The twin offered out a hand, which Imogen didn't hesitate to shake. Wow, these Coals just *bred* manners. "Hi, Imogen, I'm your uncle Jay. Did your auntie Kestrel get you that book?" Imogen nodded. "Yeah," Jay drawled. "For a second, there was a chance that not everyone in the room owned it."

Kestrel rolled her eyes. "Well, they should because it's *amazing.* Duh."

God, they were all so easy with each other, just like the rest of Micha's family. They bounced and rolled off what people said and teased naturally and knew when to give a wink or an eyeroll to keep the conversation going.

Micha could feel his breath getting short. He didn't want them to ask all the usual bullshit small talk questions people asked. They would only be being polite, but those kinds of questions always revolved around your job, your relationship status, where you lived, when you were going on vacation, what car you drove. Normal, common stuff most people could relate to.

Not Micha. He wasn't normal. And he desperately didn't want to let Swift down by stuttering over what the hell to say to his fun, accomplished family.

Except…Swift moved with Imogen in his arms and came to stand next to Micha. Just him being that close made Micha's heart rate slow down. He was okay with Swift by his side.

"Rather than everyone introducing themselves at once," Swift said warmly to the room, "how about we head outside to make some s'mores on the fire I know Dad has going?" There were several grumbles and titters of agreement. "That way you can maybe come out in ones and twos to say hi? Imogen told me she's never made s'mores before."

"That's right!" Imogen proclaimed to the room proudly. Micha's heart ached a little. She was such a loud, slightly strange but completely brilliant child. He knew he shouldn't get too attached when her situation was up in the air and Micha had a tenuous link to her at best, but he couldn't help it. He thought she was great.

Almost as great as her dad, who beamed at Micha unexpectedly. "What do you say, Uncle Micha? Shall we teach the little bit how to make s'mores?"

Embarrassment almost threatened to creep over Micha again. But if he just looked at Swift, it was as if there was no one else in the room, and that made it okay. He was pretty sure he could tell Swift anything.

"I, uh…I've never made s'mores either." He'd always insisted he was too cool as a teenager to do dumb kids' stuff like that, when the truth was, he'd always just been terrified of getting it wrong. But Swift wouldn't let him get it wrong.

Sure enough, Swift didn't look at him like he was an alien from Mars. He just jostled Imogen on his hip. "Shall us three go make pre-dinner s'mores, then?"

"Yes!" Imogen cried.

Deb grumbled something about not ruining dinner, and Swift mumbled something about not dreaming to. But all Micha heard was 'us three.'

He was scared how much he liked the sound of 'us three.'

11

SWIFT

Swift was fully aware of how many varieties of burgers his folks were likely to have lined up for the grill outside. The bowls of bean salad and corn salad and sweet potato salad. The apple and pork kebabs, and of course a vat of mac'n'cheese that had to be lurking somewhere.

There was no need for s'mores. But he was freaking out.

He knew he had no reason to. This was his family. They all just wanted to help. No one was judging him. But all he could think was as great as it was to see everyone – and he was fully aware there were still more of them to come – he suddenly wanted it to be just him, Micha, and Imogen again, like it had been all week.

How crazy was it that Micha had never made s'mores? Swift was oddly proud he was going to get to share his first time with him. That was much easier to think about than worrying about Imogen being overwhelmed and how best to cope with parenting her in a big group like this and the hundred ways he was probably already doing things wrong.

Swift had always been a pretty confident guy, but now he was responsible for a human being. Each new situation was leaving him reeling. Every decision had him clamming up, panicking that if he made a mistake, it was going to be added to the now growing list of things she'd one day have to speak to a therapist about.

Micha made things better, but Swift was fully aware he was being too clingy with all the touching and putting Micha in an awkward position.

So, s'mores. It was his go-to comfort food, bringing him back to his days of camping as a kid and that sense of freedom, toasting marshmallows under the stars over an open flame.

That was, if they ever managed to escape the kitchen.

His mom had apparently decided the best way to dissuade him from spoiling his appetite was to enlist Kestrel in ferrying out some dishes to the tables outside. Swift was pretty sure he could see his dad and other sister, Ava, tending to the grill. They were two peas in a pod, neither of them the best at small talk or big groups.

Robin was saying something to his boyfriend, Dair, about getting a text. It sounded like their friend, Peyton, was on her way. It was lovely that family time often included adopted friends and partners these days, not just their core seven. That was why Swift had felt so comfortable bringing Micha. They'd suddenly created quite the bond over Imogen and living together for a few days. It felt right that he was here.

Speaking of family friends, until that point, Ava's best friend and the twins' former classmate had been silent. With a dramatic flourish, Emery Klein suddenly locked his phone and looked up with a full-body shiver and a sigh of relief.

"Oh em gee, I'm *so* sorry about that. She's all *work, work, work.* But I'm done now, I *swear.*" He slipped his phone into his back pocket…where his boyfriend, Scout Duffy, promptly plucked it back out again without Emery even noticing. "So, what's happening? How's everyone feeling? Do we all have drinks? Snacks?"

Scout winked at Swift as he put the phone in his own jeans' pocket, presumably to stop Emery from falling back into work again. Swift had been seeing a fair bit of the pair of them at the gym lately as they took more classes. He'd also been assisting Scout with ideas about setting up his own specialist gym. He was glad they were there with his family.

Or…he had been.

Emery pushed himself off the kitchen counter where he and Scout had been leaning, slinking over to Micha in a manner that made Swift think of Butter when he was on a mission to fuck something up. Swift really liked Emery. He did. But he bristled and hugged Imogen to him as Emery zoned in on Micha's exposed arms.

"Oh, baby. That ink is *gorgeous*." Emery lightly trailed a finger up one of Micha's forearms. "My boyfriend has tattoos as well. Did everyone hear I have a *boyfriend* now?" He batted his eyelashes around the room.

Jay rolled his eyes behind his glasses. "Honey, they got a memo on the *moon*."

Emery snorted inelegantly. "Don't be jealous, sweetie. It doesn't suit you. Anyway. Micha, was it? You and Scout should compare. Make notes." He winked. "Maybe take your tops off?"

"Okay!" Swift said a little too loudly, feeling irrationally angry at Emery. Well, it wasn't irrational. Micha wasn't like that, Swift was pretty sure. It was okay to flirt with guys who easily dealt shit back or other gay guys, but Emery was overstepping a mark. Swift would lie in hell with a bad back before allowing Micha to feel uncomfortable if he could help it. "Let's keep it PG-13, okay?"

Emery smiled his charming-as-fuck smile, though, and

popped a hip to address Swift. Or rather, Imogen. "Of course! Hey, cutie pie, do you like glitter?"

Oh, fuck. *Glitter?* Swift almost broke out into a cold sweat just thinking about what that would do to his house. *But* – he firmly reminded himself – his house included Imogen now. So if that meant glitter sneaking its way into every damned crevasse, so be it.

Maybe.

However, Imogen didn't seem so sure. "I guess?"

Micha looked up at her in Swift's grasp. He was always so much more confident talking to her than he was with adults. He'd looked close to passing out when Emery had touched his arm. But to Imogen, he just smiled. "Stars glitter," he said simply.

"Oh, I love stars!" she said far more enthusiastically back at Emery. "I learned the Big Dipper and Cassy Cassy and Omlin's Belt."

Micha smiled shyly at Emery. "Cassiopeia and Orion's Belt," he corrected softly, but Imogen didn't seem to care.

Swift did, though. Emery had a boyfriend. What was he doing looking Micha up and down like that?

"Oh, pumpkin," Emery said playfully. "It sounded like she got them right to me." He winked and bit his lip before gasping at Imogen in delight. "Well, your uncle Emery brought some special, biodegradable glitter *just* for you. So you can make as many stars as you want! Do you want to come and get it while Uncle Emery remembers?"

"Yes, please!" Imogen cried, already reaching out for Emery.

Emery looked surprised and took a step back, almost scared. "Oh, fabulous. Uh, Uncle Scout will handle transportation. Shall we, Uncle Scout?"

Scout rolled his eyes. "She won't break, Emery."

Emery clutched at his chest. "A human child is different

from a hedgehog, Scout," he ground out through gritted teeth and a smile. "I'm not strong enough."

Swift laughed, grateful that as much as Emery had irritated him, he was thinking about Imogen's safety. Swift trusted someone of Scout's physique, not to mention a former bodyguard, to hold his little girl, and she was excited about the glitter now.

Plus, it got Emery out of the room and away from Micha. Everyone knew that even with a boyfriend, Emery Klein flirted when he breathed, but he had no right making Micha uncomfortable like that.

Except, Micha didn't look uncomfortable. In fact, he beamed over at Swift as if nothing was amiss.

Maybe nothing was. So long as Micha was looking at Swift like that, things couldn't be too bad, could they? So long as Micha was happy and not worrying, what was really that awful? And honestly, what had been Swift's problem anyway? He knew Emery and Scout were *madly* in love. Swift had nothing to concern him there.

And – *what?* Why the hell was he even worrying? Micha wasn't 'his' in any way, shape, or form. He had no reason to be jealous or protective or any other crap like that. Micha wasn't gay – because surely Swift would know if he was – but *if* he was – he could make eyes at whoever he liked, right?

Right?

The thing was, right then, Micha was only making eyes at Swift.

"How about those s'mores?" Swift blurted out, feeling heat rise at the back of his neck. God, this was confusing.

He'd always kind of suspected he might be bi. Sometimes, being around certain guys made him all fuzzy just like he would around a nice lady. But he'd never acted on it, feeling like that would somehow be encroaching on his siblings' territory. They were the queer ones. Who was Swift to jump so late on the bandwagon when he wasn't even sure how he felt?

But when it was just him and Micha, he felt like it was pretty simple. Swift just *liked* him, that was all. They didn't have to act on it – in fact, they shouldn't – and until Micha gave him a hint about his sexuality, Swift was determined to be nothing but friendly.

But his protective streak was hard to control. He just wanted to take Micha someplace quiet again, like a reward for meeting so many people at once.

"S'mores sounds great, don't they, Imogen?" Micha said sweetly as Emery and Scout brought her back in. Swift was pretty certain his daughter wasn't even that sure what s'mores were, but she still nodded enthusiastically. So once they'd carefully placed the containers of glitter by the front door, Swift carried her out into the back yard with Micha by their side.

Sure enough, his mom had gotten out the two picnic tables and covered them with red-and-white-checkered tablecloths. There was a nip in the fall air, but with the bright sunshine beaming down, it was bearable at present with shirts and light jackets on.

The tables were already groaning under the weight of so much food, and that was before Dad and Ava started plating up anything from the grill. There was meat, fish, veggies, and cheese, all waiting to go over the flame. Swift's dad and sister both saluted from where they were tending the flames, each with a beer in hand. The mouthwatering smell of sausages drifted through the air.

Swift was driving, but Micha wasn't. "Hey, did you want a beer, too?" he asked, thinking it might help Micha relax. But he smiled and shook his head.

"I'm good, thanks. Do you want a cherry cola?"

It was dumb, but Swift was still touched that Micha had noticed that was his favorite soda. "Sure, thanks." Swift watched as Micha fished around a cooler for a couple of cans, while Swift placed Imogen down to walk with him. She was a little too big to be carried everywhere, after all. But Swift couldn't help himself at the moment when he was feeling protective. "Hey, kiddo. We can still do s'mores, but look what Grandma and Grandpa have set up. You wanna have a go?"

He pointed at another table on the vast lawn that was surrounded by pine trees. This one was a simple folding table with a plastic sheet on it, as well as half a dozen pumpkins and some plastic carving tools. With everything that had been going on, he'd almost forgotten Halloween would be coming up in a couple of weeks. Obviously his mom hadn't, though. They'd carved pumpkins as a family every year, and now Swift could pass on that tradition with his own child.

And Micha.

He held two soda cans and looked between the grill, where Swift's dad and sister were standing, and the pumpkins. It wasn't that Swift's sister, Ava, was scary per se, but she didn't exactly have a warm or inviting demeanor. That was before you considered the black leather pants and jacket and the suspicious glare she wore under a mountain of black curls. Swift knew she was awesome, really, but he didn't blame Micha when he turned back to the pumpkin table instead.

"Are we carving?" he asked hopefully.

There was a sparkle in his eye. Unlike when he'd asked about s'mores, he seemed interested rather than apprehensive. That made Swift even more sure of their slight change of plan.

"Yeah, we can save the marshmallows for later and not spoil our appetites." Swift caught his mom's eye as she came out with a plate of rolls and gave her a wink. She smiled gratefully at the pumpkins and then looked purposely at all the food that was on display. He rolled his eyes and nodded. Yeah, she had a point. They could wait for sweets.

Pumpkin carving was an activity they could do just the three of them, not even having to deal with people around the grill, and the rest of the friends and family could come and visit them in smaller groups, much easier to manage. Swift told himself he was thinking purely of Imogen, but it didn't hurt that it would probably make Micha feel more at ease too.

Swift wasn't very artistic, so he usually made use of the stencils his mom always printed out when they'd been kids. He could draw around basic patterns and then cut a goofy face out of the hollowed pumpkin. But as he and Micha helped Imogen scoop out the wet flesh into a bucket, Swift was surprised when Micha picked up a marker and drew a damn good scary, toothy face for Imogen to hack at with her little plastic knife.

"That's really good," Swift said as he tilted his head and marveled at Micha's skill. "Where did you learn to do that?"

Micha blinked and looked between Swift and the pumpkin. "Uh…it's just a standard design. I don't know. I must have seen something similar a thousand times."

Swift smiled and gently touched his arm. "So have I, but I couldn't bring it to life."

Micha's mouth popped open in a pretty 'O' shape. "Thanks," he said weakly. *Fuck*, his lips looked kissable.

For a second, they just stared at each other. No matter how much the voice in Swift's head screamed at him to back off, the rest of his brain really couldn't remember why he should. Because Micha was looking at him all warm and dazed. It would be so easy to just lean down and plant a kiss at the corner of those sweet lips…

"Daddy, look – *look!*" Imogen's impatience pulled him sharply from his reverie. He shook himself and turned his attention to the partially mutilated pumpkin. Although to be fair, Imogen had mostly stayed inside Micha's lines.

"Wow," Swift said enthusiastically. "You did a great job, honey. Are you done?"

Imogen frowned and scoffed. "No, Daddy. I have to make the lines straight."

Swift felt his mouth twitch, and Micha grinned affectionately too. "Quite right," Swift agreed. "Of course you do, silly Daddy." Imogen huffed in agreement, then went back to work.

At that moment they were distracted by Swift's brother Robin coming out through the back door. He wasn't alone, but it wasn't his boyfriend by his side. It was an androgynous-looking woman with her short hair styled with a skin fade on the back and sides and the rest brushed forward. Slim with tattoos and a few piercings, she wore biker boots and overalls on top of a flannel shirt. Her smile was so bright, however, she turned what could have been a harsh look into something fun and edgy.

"Hey, everyone," said Robin cheerfully. "You remember my best friend, Peyton? She's also moving into town."

Swift raised his hand to say hello but was distracted by the almighty clattering of a tin platter of uncooked burgers and a pair of tongs being upended by Ava and hitting the stone patio. He wasn't the only one. Everyone swung around to see the usually cool Ava standing like a deer in headlights. Peyton covered her mouth in dismay.

"Oh, no, Ava!" she said earnestly. "Never mind, accidents happen. There's lots more food, after all. Let me help you clean that up."

She skipped forward while Ava watched her in apparent terror. Why was she acting so weird? Dair slammed the kitchen door shut, just stopping an eager Smudge from running out to also 'help.'

Swift's dad nudged Ava. "That's nice of you, hon," he said to Peyton. "Isn't that nice of her, Ava?"

Ava's eyes widened as Peyton reached her, smiled, then dropped to her knees to start putting the ruined meat back onto the platter. Robin rolled his eyes as Jay came to stand next to him with a snicker. Swift wondered if they knew something he didn't?

"I have to…go check…my umbrella," Ava stuttered. She skirted around Peyton and the burgers like she was playing the floor is lava, then dashed into the house. The twins laughed, and Peyton looked confused at them, while Swift glanced at Micha, who shrugged.

"Maybe her umbrella is lonely?"

It was a silly joke, but it broke the mood and made other people laugh, too, which made Swift proud. It was kind of dumb how much he wanted everyone to like Micha as much as he did.

A fact that might not have gone unnoticed.

Swift had just convinced Micha he could also carve his own pumpkin as there were loads and he wasn't sure who else was going to bother when the twins came over. Peyton had taken Ava's place by their dad at the grill, and Imogen was still engrossed with stabbing away at her own jack-o'-lantern.

"This looks cool," Robin said to her. "Can Uncle Robin join you?"

Imogen looked up. "Uncle Bobin?"

Robin chuckled ruefully. "That's what Grandma calls me," he said fondly as he sat on the other side of the folding table. "Hey, man. I'm Robin."

Micha seemed slightly wrong-footed when Robin reached out his hand to shake. But then Micha appeared to collect himself and pumped Robin's hand a couple of times.

"Nice to meet you," he said almost confidently.

"Can I have a word?"

Swift looked around as Jay murmured in his ear, quiet enough Micha probably hadn't heard him. Swift cocked an eyebrow, but Jay simply jerked his head, indicating they step away for a minute.

Swift followed him. "Is everything okay?"

Jay smiled and took a swig of beer from his bottle. "Sure, I'm fine. How about you? It's been a hell of a week."

They wandered down the lawn before loitering by one of Mom's rose bushes. Swift sighed heavily and ran his palm down his face, flicking the stay tab on his cherry cola with his index finger on the other hand. "You're telling me. It's like I don't even know who I am right now. If I stop and think, I kind of just want to get under my bedcovers and never emerge." They laughed, and Jay gave him a sympathetic look. "But it will be fine. Thank god for Micha, I swear."

"Yeah." Jay frowned and nodded. "That's, uh, yeah. Since when have you been best buds with your actual best bud's little brother?"

Swift gave Jay a considered look. "We kind of hung around before. But he's great with kids and needed a place to crash for a few days. That's all."

Jay scoffed around the lip of his bottle and sipped some more beer. "That's not all, dude. Come on, is there something you want to tell me?"

Swift felt his palms get sweaty, and he flicked the stay tab a few more times. "Like what? Being around someone twenty-four seven can make you become good friends pretty fast." He was aware he sounded a little defensive, but he didn't like his brother questioning Micha. "Have you got a problem with him?"

"What? No," said Jay.

"Because that thing in Seattle wasn't his fault," Swift said a little more heatedly.

Jay raised his hands and his eyebrows. "I know, I know," he said gently, then he laughed. "That wasn't what I was asking. Chill. It's just, I've never seen the two of you together, and it's like I'm seeing a whole new you for the first time."

Swift licked his lips, tasting the cherry tang. "Well, finding out you're a dad and gaining full-time custody of a five-year-old will change you, trust me."

"Okay," Jay said, shaking his head. For a second, Swift was hopeful he'd drop it. But then he wagged his finger. "Swift, I'm your brother. Your *gay* brother. Are you seriously telling me that there's nothing at all going on between you guys? All those looks and touches between you?"

Swift laughed, probably a bit too loudly. "What? No! Jay, I'm *straight!*"

Jay tutted. "No need to sound so offended."

Ice raced through Swift. God, he wasn't sure what he wanted to say or how much he wanted to admit. He wasn't even sure what was really true at this point. But the very last thing he wanted to do was make his brother, or any of his siblings, for that matter, think he had *any* kind of problem with them being queer.

"I'm not," Swift said lightly, trying to dispel the awkwardness as fast as it had appeared. "That's not what I meant. Look, I'm pretty sure Micha's straight, and he's shy. I don't want him feeling like he's being examined in a petri dish. He's been through a lot."

"Are you sure?" Jay asked, narrowing his eyes over at the pumpkin table, where everyone was still working hard.

Swift felt his irritation rising. "Yes, I'm sure. That thing in Seattle was awful, and-"

"Are you sure he's *straight*," Jay cut across him bluntly, turning his firm gaze on Swift. "Have you asked him?"

Swift was feeling horribly put upon. "That's kind of personal, don't you think?" he mumbled.

But Jay's expression softened. "I'm only asking because he looks at you. A lot. Like you hung the moon." Swift opened his mouth to protest, and Jay raised his hands again. "I'm just saying what I've noticed in the whole twenty minutes since you walked through the front door. Don't shoot the messenger. If you're not interested, you might want to think up some words to let the poor boy down easily."

No. That was crazy. Jay couldn't be right, could he? Despite his best efforts, a spark of hope flickered inside Swift, and he couldn't help but glance over to see where Micha was absorbed in whatever sweet thing Imogen was babbling about, a smile on his cute face.

"Or…" Jay said pointedly, dragging the word out. "Do you want to have a think about how *you* feel instead? I know we've always teased you about being the only straight one, but it's not too late to come out, you know?" He laughed and shook his head. "If you need help settling on a label, you can always ask Kestrel. I think she's up to four or five now."

"What?" Swift asked, not quite following.

"Labels," said Jay with a wink. "I thought I was exotic being gay, but she's got a string of words as long as your arm. Pansexual, nonbinary, demisexual, genderfluid, polyamorous – I think those are all the current ones." He grinned, but Swift felt a bit sick. Rather than think about himself, he considered what Jay was saying about Kestrel.

"She's fifteen. How does she know all that stuff? Is she dating?"

Jay looked thoughtful, then shook his head. "Not that I'm aware. I think she's just grown up with the internet. Gen Z, you know? They have an opinion about everything." He shrugged, then lightly clapped Swift's arm. "Look, dude. I didn't mean to freak you out. I just thought you might like someone to talk to. And the offer's still there. It *really* wouldn't be a big deal if you were bi or something, you know. Ava's bi, even though she seems allergic to people most days."

But that was where Jay was wrong. It *would* be a big deal if Swift gave into this. Forget coming out. If he wanted, yeah, he could probably do that any day of the week, and his family would hardly bat an eyelid. But to have feelings for Micha, the youngest and most vulnerable of the Perkins siblings, the brother Swift's best friend had always been extremely protective over?

Yeah, that qualified for a problem in Swift's eyes.

But he didn't want to get into all of that with Jay, who really was just trying to be nice.

Swift gave him a lopsided smile and tapped his bottle with his can. "Speaking of dating, what's up with you? I feel like you haven't brought anyone home in forever."

Jay was one of those people who seemed to easily get over heartbreak and walked from one relationship into another. But lately – maybe the last year or two – he hadn't seemed interested in anyone.

Sure enough, Jay gave him a smile that didn't reach his eyes. "I'm just focusing on me right now," he said evasively. But then he steered the conversation right back to Swift. "Look, it's cool if you don't want to talk about this. I didn't mean to pry. But if you have any questions or need any advice, I'm here for you. Cool?"

Swift sighed. That was the best exit from this conversation he was going to get. So he didn't outright deny any of Jay's assumptions. He just let them lie. "Cool," he agreed. "Shall we go carve a pumpkin?"

Jay pulled a face. "Oh, hell no. I've been doing that all

week for the kids at school. It's taken me all weekend to shower off that smell. What I need is another beer and something smothered in ketchup."

Swift laughed as they made their way back down the lawn toward the rest of the group. It seemed everyone was congregated outside now as sausages started migrating from the grill into buns. Imogen's glasses were smeared with the insides of her jack-o-lantern as she grinned toothily up at him.

"Look, Daddy! I did it all by myself!"

The neat lines on the finished design and Micha's fond smile suggested otherwise, but Swift didn't care. "Wow!" he cried. "I can't wait until it gets dark and we can put a light in it!" He tried not to gush with praise as he glanced over and saw Micha had carved an honest-to-god spider's web, complete with spider, in the few minutes Swift had been talking to Jay.

It was criminal how little that man thought of himself when he clearly had so many hidden talents.

Swift tried not to worry, but he felt like he was standing on the edge of a precipice. Was there a shred of truth to what Jay had said? *Did* Micha like him in that way? Was there a chance he might not be straight and was feeling something of what Swift was feeling?

But even if he was, then what? If they made a move, it could ruin everything. The situation with Imogen was so delicate, and Rhett might never forgive Swift for messing his little brother around.

Although…as Swift came and stood by Micha and he smiled sweetly up at him, Swift had to admit he had absolutely *zero* intention of messing Micha Perkins around.

In fact, if anything were to ever happen at all, Swift was pretty damn certain he'd treat cute and lovely Micha like a damn prince.

12

MICHA

Who knew a five-year-old had such lungs?

Imogen's new favorite trick was to wrestle Micha before the school bus arrived while he was trying to braid her ridiculously long hair. Only on the mornings Swift had already left for work, of course.

"I want *Daddy* to do it!" she was currently screaming with tears running down her cheeks behind her glasses. "When Daddy brushes it, it doesn't hurt! I want *DADDY!*"

Her words cut like a knife through Micha's heart, although she couldn't possibly know that. But the only reason he was really there was because Swift said he was doing a good job and helping. So if Imogen didn't want him there...

Imogen was a kid who had temporarily been separated from her mom and dumped into a town she'd never been to before. Micha was a grown adult and needed to get a thicker skin. He was used to his nieces and nephews throwing tantrums. He wasn't going to be cowed by this. Besides, he knew he was damn good at doing her hair when she stayed still.

"Imogen. If you don't sit still, it's going to hurt when I brush. If I don't get your hair done, you'll miss the bus, and you won't get to school in time, and Daddy will be upset. We don't want Daddy to be upset, do we?"

Micha's heart ached far more than it should have at that silly little threat. He tried telling himself that Swift *wasn't* mad at him. But things hadn't quite been the same since the cookout.

How could they be? Not with what Micha had heard.

Imogen's lip wobbled. "Sorry, Uncle Micha," she mumbled. "I'll be good."

Micha's heart melted. "You *are* good," he told her gently. "But if you wriggle, Uncle Micha's magic brush will pull on the nasty tangles. We'll be done in no time, though, if you sit on your hands. Why don't you tell me a story?"

That always did the trick. Imogen meandered excitedly between telling Micha about one of the scientist women from the book Kestrel had bought her and a car ad she'd seen on TV that morning. Micha said 'uh-huh' about a dozen times, and 'oh really?' even more as he focused on brushing the hair that was by her butt, working all the way up to her shoulders. Once it was detangled, he hastily braided it down her back, grabbed her lunch box, then ran down the road with her to the bus stop.

Lonnie the bus driver chuckled as they just made it in time. "Are your daddies ever going to get you here in time, sweet pea?" she asked Imogen, much to Micha's horror.

"No, we're not-" he spluttered.

"Bye, Uncle Micha!" Imogen called over her shoulder as she hopped up the bus steps. Then she waved down the whole bus. "I'm here!"

Micha's mouth was still hanging open as Lonnie closed the doors and drove out of sight. He stood there for a full two minutes before he trudged back to Swift's house.

It was always so quiet when it was just Micha in the house. Well, him and Butter. But Micha's hands were itchy all over from healing scratches, and they were on their second box of Band-Aids in so many days, so he wasn't exactly feeling warm and fuzzy toward the little ginger nut.

The cat was thankfully nowhere to be seen as Micha poured himself some coffee and sat at the kitchen table for a moment. He really had no right to be complaining. For two months he'd worn state-issued clothes right down to his underwear. He'd been lucky to hold on to a bar of soap for that time and escape those showers without anything growing between his toes. He'd been told what to eat and when to sleep and spent every day in a state of downright terror that this was going to be his life now.

He was *lucky.* He was free, and his family loved him. They were even understanding about him needing space and staying at Swift's for a while. He could forge his own destiny.

If only he had any clue what he was doing.

If only staying with Swift still felt like an escape and not an endurance test.

Micha sighed and pulled his phone out from his jeans so he could slouch more comfortably on the kitchen chair. He put it on the table and toyed with the edge of the case, then the handle of his coffee mug. But there was no getting away from what he'd heard.

"I'm *straight!*"

It had been the spluttering indignation that had been the hardest to swallow. Micha hadn't heard another word that Swift and his brother had said between them. But Swift's heightened voice and the particular direction of the wind in that moment had meant he'd heard enough.

Really, though. What had he been expecting? For Swift to suddenly declare he liked men after all? That he was madly in love with Micha and couldn't bear another minute apart?

What they had here was just a business arrangement. Micha got a space to crash with a little privacy in return for some babysitting duties. It had been ridiculous to think he and Swift would really become friends. They had nothing in common. Sure, the beers were nice, and Micha hadn't felt this comfortable talking with anyone in a long time. But it was temporary.

At some point, it was all going to end.

Alone in the house, Micha indulged in allowing a dry sob to escape. Then he covered his mouth and tried to calm himself. He was just so desperate to fit in somewhere that he was fooling himself into believing that place was here, with this family. But Imogen had a mom. Swift had his parents and siblings and friends. Micha didn't really belong with them, and he knew it.

He busied himself for a while, loading the dishwasher, tidying toys, and putting laundry away. Domestic things that kept his hands busy and his mind a little less frantic. Butter was most likely off murdering things, so Micha quickly changed his litter box and washed up his food bowl, putting out fresh wet food for whenever he deigned to return.

Micha had a shift at Sunny Side Up in an hour and a half, and after puttering about the house for a while, he felt less fractious with his situation. Even if he was going to leave in a few days, he couldn't help but feel he'd still left a mark on the place. It was mostly through helping Swift adjust to Imogen's presence, but it still felt good to see how well he had adapted. There were already a couple of her drawings stuck on the fridge (treasure maps, of course), and her room was almost unrecognizable now from the cold, sparse space it had been before.

Where the now shattered vase had stood, there was the first photo of Imogen to be displayed in the house. She was proudly holding up the pumpkin she'd carved. The one

Micha had helped her with. It wasn't like he was in the photo – that would be weird. But it was nice to feel he was sort of in it in spirit.

He had a little time to job hunt before he had to leave. He wasn't feeling passionate about anything, but he couldn't keep relying on his folks for shifts at the diner. When he picked up his phone and realized he had four missed calls from an unknown number, he guessed it could have been one of the jobs contacting him. That gave him a tiny bit of joy not necessarily for the job itself but for the sense of achieving something.

Except it wasn't a prospective employer who answered.

"Micha?" Brie's panicked voice squeaked down the end of the line.

It was good Micha hadn't been carrying anything. Otherwise he would have certainly dropped it at the sound of hearing his friend. Brie was like the younger sister he'd never had or an adopted niece. Her distress immediately sent adrenaline shooting through Micha's system.

"Brie! What's wrong? Is everything okay?"

She exhaled on the other end of the line. "No, I'm fine," she mumbled, her voice more subdued. "I just haven't heard from you, that's all."

Micha bit his lip and looked around the spotless kitchen. Something wasn't right. "I sent a few texts," he said apologetically. "How come you've got a new number?"

"Dropped my old phone," Brie said distractedly. There were noises in the background, like there were other people around, but Micha couldn't work out if she was in a café or what. It didn't sound like she was outside as there was no wind or traffic sounds. "Dale got me a new one."

The mention of Dale's name sent goose bumps rippling over Micha's skin. *Asshole.* "Is he treating you okay?" he asked.

Brie spluttered. "Yes, yes, of course," she said hurriedly, followed by a shrill laugh. "I told you he got me a new phone, didn't I?"

Micha wasn't sure why, but the prickle on the back of his neck told him that Brie hadn't 'dropped' her last phone. He'd bet any money that Dale's temper had flared and her phone had been the casualty. He loved doing that, breaking something of yours, then making you feel so cherished when he apologized and replaced it. But Micha could see what a manipulative tactic that was now. It made you feel like you owed Dale, even though he was the one who had trashed your things in the first place.

"Brie," he said as he sunk into one of the kitchen chairs, "I'm so sorry I left. I just couldn't be around Dale anymore. You know what he did was awful and shitty, right? He could have ruined both our lives."

The was a slight pause. "We miss you, though," Brie said, an anxious clip to her words. "When are you coming home?"

Micha sighed. It felt like shit that he wasn't there to be a shield between her and Dale. Even though she was seventeen and almost an adult, hell bent on making her own decisions, she was still so young. Micha was pretty sure she had a hero worship thing going on with Dale because he'd given her a bed to sleep in. However, Micha worried she still didn't fully understand that anything from Dale came with strings attached.

How long before Dale insisted that the bed she slept in would be his? He didn't usually bother with women, but Micha had a bad feeling about this. It wouldn't matter to Dale that Brie was a lesbian. He'd make her feel so special, of course. Almost like it was her idea. But there would be that implication that she couldn't really say no if she wanted to stay in the house. Then he'd get bored, move on to his next fancy, and laugh at her while she cried.

Micha was ashamed to admit he knew exactly what that would feel like.

Brie wouldn't be told what to do, though, not by him. Dale had her enthralled with his motherfucking charm, but Brie had been let down by too many adults to simply follow orders unless she wanted to. Or thought she wanted to. If Micha was going to help her, he'd have to try and nudge her in the right direction rather than be direct.

"I don't think I'll be back in Seattle anytime soon, hon," he said gently. "I miss you too, though, so much. Hey, you been to that ice cream place again since I've been gone?"

That cheered her up immensely. She got all giggly as she told Micha about a girl she'd made friends with, and they'd been back there a couple of times to share a banana split.

"That's great," Micha gushed. "She sounds sweet. Do you think you'll spend more time with her?"

"Maybe," Brie said.

Micha could practically hear her shrug down the phone line. She always got defensive of anyone she had a crush on, pushing them away before they really got a chance to hurt her. Or even try and love her. He hoped maybe things might be different with this girl until he realized that they hadn't gotten until the true point of the phone call.

Until now.

"Maybe I could come visit you?" Brie said in her best casual voice. "Where are you living now, anyway?"

Micha paused, straining his ears extra hard. As if he did that, he might hear Dale listening in on the conversation. Was that why he could hear so much background noise?

Was she on speakerphone in the house sitting next to him?

"With my folks," Micha said, doing his own best casual voice. "It's a tiny little town that no one's ever heard of it. I'm working at a diner, though, and I get free food on my breaks."

"That's awesome," Brie said, but there wasn't much enthusiasm in her voice. "Well, what's the town called? I can Google images of it. I bet there's lots of trees and shit, right?"

Micha bit his lip, feeling the tears burning behind his eyes. He wasn't telling Brie where he was living, because Dale would get it out of her, even if he wasn't already listening in. Micha wasn't going back to that life. He *refused.* Even if things weren't perfect in Pine Cove, he could cope with a little heartache far better than trying to stay out of the trouble that followed Dale around like a storm cloud.

"I-I'm sorry, hon, I've got another call coming in," Micha babbled, trying not to let his voice break. "I think it's work. I have to go. I'll text you, okay? Stay safe. Love you."

"Micha-"

He could hear the defiance in her voice. If she asked him again for his town name, or worse, his address, he'd have to tell her 'no.' That might get her into trouble with Dale. Micha couldn't save her like he wanted to right now, but he could try and protect her by not allowing her to do Dale's dirty work.

"Bye, hon!"

He hung up. And because he was a coward, he turned the phone off. He'd have to do that for his shift in an hour anyway, but he couldn't take it if she called back again.

He *hated* Dale for using her to get to him. What a piece of shit. *He* was the coward, not Micha. Micha would still try and do everything he could to encourage Brie to get out of his clutches, and if she left him, he'd be there for her, one hundred percent. Hell – maybe he could take half of his next paycheck and mail it to her?

The thought cheered him up for a second as he resolved

to do exactly that. But she was so far away, and a lot could happen in no time at all.

Micha buried his head in his hands as the tears finally came flooding out while he wished that so many things were different. "Please, Brie," he whispered to himself. "Listen to me – save yourself."

But Micha hadn't even saved himself, had he? He'd gotten lucky in his day in court and was now relying on his parents to keep him afloat.

And Swift.

Shame burned through Micha as he rubbed his face and stood angrily up. It was humiliating imagining what Swift must really think of him, leeching off his hospitality.

No, Micha needed to step up. If he got his own place, he could go and *get* Brie, and they could start over again together, here in Pine Cove, where it was safe. She could get a job somewhere and record songs in her bedroom. They could help each other with the rent, and more importantly, stay far away from Dale's grasp.

And if Micha didn't see Swift every day, that would probably be best for everyone. At least, that was what he kept telling himself until he stopped crying and finally left for work.

13

SWIFT

"All right, everyone! Great job! Make sure you stretch out with your partners, and hopefully we'll see you again next week."

Swift was thrilled he was finally able to teach a weekly defense class that had been growing steadily in popularity over the past several weeks. Ava's best friend, Emery, had been the victim of a violent crime a couple of months ago. As a result, he'd championed Swift's long-held desire to start the class and had also made a personal recruitment effort to make sure the class got traction.

Swift was glad that word-of-mouth was spreading naturally, but also that he and Emery were becoming friends themselves now. It was like Emery was collecting all the Coal siblings. Swift was sure as soon as Kestrel was old enough to drink, Emery would be taking her off to big city prides and championing her LGBT activism, too.

So it wasn't unusual that Emery came over to say hello once class was done. He'd only missed one session when he'd been out of town, and all the others he had made a point of chatting with Swift afterward, even if only for a few minutes.

Which was why Swift didn't see the ambush coming until it was too late.

"Hey, cutie pie," Emery said with a wink as he screwed the cap back on his metal water bottle. "That was a great class, thank you."

Swift wiped the back of his neck with a towel. "No problem. You were really nailing that last move. I can see you've been practicing."

Emery fluttered his eyelashes and ran a hand through his dark hair. "She's got a *great* workout partner at home, if you catch my drift."

He waggled his eyebrows, and Swift had to laugh. Now that Emery had a boyfriend and was crazy in love, he was almost insufferable. If Swift wasn't so happy for him and Scout, he'd have told him to get over it by now. But it was sweet seeing how much good their relationship was doing. Emery was a lot less prickly these days and better at communicating what he really meant.

Usually, that was a good thing.

"Sooo," Emery said devilishly as one of Swift's PT clients also approached. He probably had a training question, which made it all the mortifying when Emery's words left his lips, loud and clear. "How's that hot little boyfriend of *yours* treating you?"

"What? No!" Swift spluttered with a laugh. "Micha? No. He's – we're just friends. New friends. Well, not new, he hung out with Rhett and me all the time years ago. But, uh, he's just – we're helping each other out."

Emery narrowed his eyes at Swift as the PT client frowned. Swift was pretty sure his name was Elias. "Is this a bad time?" he asked.

"I-" Swift began.

"No, it's a good time, baby," Emery said slyly. "Let's outnumber Mr. Coal and get him to tell us the truth."

Swift hated being put on the spot for the second time in so many days. The *truth* was he really wasn't sure how he felt about Micha. Sure, he liked him a hell of a lot, and whenever he walked into a room, Swift could feel himself lighting up with happiness. But he still wasn't sure where they stood in terms of their sexualities or if dating a man was something either of them wanted.

No, not dating any man. Dating *each other*. Swift could probably answer that question, if he was being honest. He was dangerously close to admitting he might want to give it a try, even though he was scared what Rhett might say. Swift was pretty certain his feelings for Micha were real, and his last intention would be to mess anyone around. Sure, it would be his first relationship with a man, but everyone had to start somewhere, didn't they?

But he had no clue what Micha might say. If anything, he'd been more distant since the cookout, even though Swift had thought the whole thing had gone really well. Micha had seemed to cope well talking with everyone, and most of his family had called to praise the way Micha was with Imogen as well as saying how nice he was himself.

But for Emery to assume they were dating already was too much. Despite what Jay had said, Swift really couldn't say if Micha was interested in men or not. Just because they got along well didn't mean that Micha was interested in anything more.

"Emery," Swift said firmly. "I'm telling you that we're just friends."

Emery rolled his eyes and shook his head. "Jay filled me in on the whole so-called 'straight' thing. Honey, a lot of people aren't as straight as they seem. You should worry less about putting a label on it and have some fun."

"I'm not-" Swift began, frustrated. He was aware Elias was still there, involved in the personal conversation now thanks to Emery's invitation, whether he or Swift liked it or not. "Okay, I can only speak for myself. And – sure – if it came down to it, I'd be less worried about labels than I would being happy. But Micha is my friend and my guest. He's helping look after my child. I wouldn't dare to presume anything that goes beyond that."

"Micha?" Elias said, raising his eyebrows. "Not Micha Perkins?" Swift nodded. "I'm friends with his sister, Darcy. He seemed like a good kid. Well, not a kid anymore. But he was always great with her children."

"He was," Swift agreed with a smile, but inwardly he was freaking out. Of all the people who had to overhear this, it had to be one of Darcy Perkins' friends? What were the chances? Could Swift trust Elias not to mention anything about this to her?

Unfortunately, it looked like there was no stopping the conversation now. Emery was all puffed up.

He arched an eyebrow at Swift. "Are you serious? Are you implying that sweet thing isn't mad for you? Have you seriously not seen the way he looks at you?"

"No." Swift was trying not to get irritable. "I haven't. And I don't know what Jay has said, but neither of us has come out, and I'm kind of annoyed that everyone is making assumptions and pushing things. He's been through a lot. He doesn't need anyone making him feel awkward."

Emery slowly raised his eyebrows and glanced at Elias. They were the only three left in the glass-fronted studio now. Luckily, there wasn't a class scheduled for another half an hour, so they had some semblance of privacy for the time being. As much as you could get in a glass bowl with all the people on the exercise machines facing toward you.

"No one should be forced to come out," said Elias comfortingly. "And no one should out you, either. If that's something you want to do, think about it on your terms." He smiled warmly.

He was a gentle sort of guy. Soft brown hair, medium height and build, although he'd really toned up and bulked out a little over the past few months. He'd started working out this year as he was approaching his fortieth birthday, and Swift got the impression he was heading off some sort of midlife crisis by getting in shape. To his credit, he'd been busting his ass and was looking great. Swift had always suspected Elias was gay, but his interest in the conversation and that comment felt like confirmation. Although as Elias had just said, he wasn't going to make any assumptions.

"But…" Elias glanced at Emery, who wasn't looking convinced with Swift. "Trust me when I say life is short. Too short. If you like this guy, tell him. Don't tiptoe around until it's too late." Elias offered Swift a sad smile that suggested he had a story to tell there.

"Exactly!" Emery clapped his hands together and winked, a sassy spring in him as he popped his hip. "All I'm saying is you guys make such a super adorable picture of domestic bliss. If I assumed you were dating, that's because you have all this gorgeous chemistry! And while Jay and I might have discussed you guys an itty-bitty bit, we both noticed all the cuteness all by ourselves. It would be a waste not to make a move while he's literally living under your roof!"

Swift sighed. "That's the thing. What if I'm wrong? He'd feel like he'd have to leave. That'd be the last thing I'd want. If I was staying with someone I just saw as a friend and they tried it on, I wouldn't feel comfortable hanging around at all."

Swift knew what he was admitting. He'd rather keep his feelings secret and protect the delicate, blossoming friendship they had than risk it all for some dumb crush.

Emery rolled his eyes. "No one is suggesting you start by

sticking your tongue down his throat, cherub. Use your words."

Elias nodded. "Maybe suggest going for a walk, so it's not in your place. Then if he's not comfortable, he doesn't feel trapped."

"But you know," Emery said as he shimmied his shoulders and poked Swift's arm, "I'd bet good money he doesn't want to walk away. I've had my gay card for a long time, sweet cheeks, but almost anyone could see a candle being held when it's burning that brightly."

Elias took the sweeter approach. "I've also had my gay card for a very long time, now," he said, making Swift feel relieved he didn't have to assume anything anymore. "If you're struggling with how you're feeling, you can talk to me anytime. I mean that."

Swift bit his lip. "I'm pretty sure I'm not gay," he said as carefully as possible. He didn't want to leave any room to imply he thought there was a problem with being gay. "I definitely like women still."

Elias nodded, his expression still warm and welcoming. "That's great."

"Yeah," Emery agreed. "You're probably one of the other letters. Or maybe you're just 'Micha-sexual'?"

Swift laughed with both of them. "Oh, god," he said ruefully, shaking his head and running his hand through his damp hair. "Did I just come out at work?"

"Yep," Emery said proudly. "The sweat makes it even more special. We're bonded now, like a blood pact."

Elias looked mildly alarmed, probably because he didn't know Emery's sense of humor. But Swift appreciated him making a joke out of it. After all, this wasn't really that big a deal in this day and age. He took a deep breath. "I'm bisexual," he said aloud for the first time in his life. He smiled bashfully while Emery squealed and spun on the spot. Elias clapped him on the arm.

"Good for you," he said affectionately.

Swift puffed out his cheeks. As good as that felt, it didn't rule out his other concerns. Emery stopped spinning and huffed.

"I can already see you coming up with new problems, Swift Coal. If you like this guy, just tell him. It's that simple."

"Well," said Swift, grimacing as he drew out the word. "He's my best friend's younger brother. Rhett's very protective of him."

"So's Darcy," Elias said with a head tilt. "But I'm pretty sure she'd love nothing more than to see him happy. He hasn't had the best luck in life."

Emery scoffed. "Just don't be an asshole, and no one will get a stern talking to. Seriously. None of us can guarantee a relationship is going to work out. You just have to give it your all and hope for the best."

"One boyfriend and suddenly you're Dear Abby," Swift grumbled, but his mouth still twitched with a smile. Emery did have a point. Swift had already thought so himself. If he went for it with Micha, he'd be in with both feet and treat him with the utmost respect. Rhett couldn't really have a problem with that, could he?

"You know it, honey," said Emery with a wink. Elias chuckled.

But there was an even bigger consideration Swift couldn't ignore, even if he wanted to. "Okay, maybe I'll think about it. Thanks, guys. But this whole situation with Imogen is my priority right now. I'm not going to do anything to jeopardize that."

"Babe," said Emery sternly. "I saw that boy with your kid. He's a damn natural. He adores her and knows just how to handle her."

Elias nodded. "Pepper and Charles love their uncle Micha. It's like he speaks 'kid' fluently."

Emery wagged his finger and gave Swift a devilish look. "I think you're creating excuses, Mr. Coal. I'm going to make you promise me you won't let this pass you by."

"If you think you could have something special with this young man," Elias said sagely, "don't let it slip through your fingers. Otherwise you'll turn around and wonder what you've done with your life."

Swift wanted to ask Elias if there was anything he wanted to talk about, but after he spoke, he put on a bright but tight smile and took a slight step back, clearly saying this conversation wasn't about him. Maybe Swift could ask if he was all right another time.

For now, he sighed and smiled at both men. "Thank you," he said sheepishly. "I guess…I guess you're right. I should at least *try?*"

"Hell, yeah!" Emery cried. "That's the spirit. You go get your man, sugar!"

Swift wasn't quite sure about that. But…maybe Emery had a point. Had Swift been creating excuses because he was afraid?

Well, Micha had been through far more hardship than that and had come out the other side even lovelier and sweeter than before. Swift owed it to him to be honest. Be brave.

He began working on a plan.

14

MICHA

Micha had convinced himself over the past few years that he was a city boy. There was no doubt he loved the hustle and bustle of Seattle, that feeling of always being connected to everything. But as he strolled along Main Street toward the lake, he felt like he could breathe again.

He'd been into the center of town many times since he'd been back, but that had been for work. He hadn't come to just enjoy his surroundings until now.

Until Swift had asked him to.

It had been a tense few days where both of them had been busy with their jobs and running around after Imogen. It hadn't felt like there had been much breathing room, but Micha had still managed to busy himself with plenty of worrying. Surprisingly, Brie hadn't called back or even texted after their conversation, which actually troubled Micha even more. What was happening back at the house? Was she okay?

And this Swift situation was shredding his heart in two. He loved being around him, but he knew it was wrong and couldn't shake the feeling that Swift was just putting up with him. Secretly, he must want Micha out from under his feet by now, surely?

But then they had both worked an early shift, so Swift had suggested they go together to pick Imogen up from the bus stop, after which they could all take a stroll along the boardwalk. First, though, was a trip to Rise and Shine, Pine Cove's premier bakery. God, Micha had forgotten how good it smelled in there.

It was so cute Brie would definitely refer to it as being 'Instagramable,' which definitely wasn't a word, but Micha couldn't help but think of it as they approached the shop with a very excitable Imogen. A vintage bike with flowers in the handle basket was parked outside as a permanent feature, and the sign was painted in flowy gold lettering. Inside were more flowers and burlap bags on shelves printed with fading stamps of different grain names. The counter at the end gleamed as they approached.

"Hi, there," the server behind the glass display case said cheerfully. He was a petit guy with honey-blond hair, hazel eyes, and a bright smile. His name badge read 'Ben.' Micha didn't remember him from before, but he was probably younger than him. It reminded Micha just how long he'd been gone from this town. "What can I do for you today?" Ben asked.

Swift grinned and picked Imogen up to sit on his hip. "This is my little girl's first visit here," he said proudly, "and she's heard *all* about your famous cupcakes."

"Is that right?" Ben said, beaming even more and raising his eyebrows. "Well then, would you like to try one? You know, I made these myself." Ben winked and made Imogen giggle.

He indicated the selection of colorful, mouthwatering iced cakes in the display case. They were all the shades of the rainbow and then some, garnished with stars and butterflies and sprinkles and a dozen other cute things that couldn't help but make Micha smile.

He'd always thought of baking as kind of pointless. Why labor over something so much that you were just going to eat or that was going to go bad? But as Imogen spied a sparkly blue-and-green creation with a mermaid tail sticking out of the icing, he kind of understood the appeal for the first time.

They were joyful, pure and simple. Who knew how long Ben had spent decorating that cupcake? But it felt worth it for the way Imogen gasped and pointed.

"That one! Daddy, can I have the mermaid one?"

"Of course, little bit," Swift said happily. He turned to Micha, but Imogen pushed her glasses up her nose and pointed again, looking at Ben. "Is it vegan?"

Both Micha and Swift stared at each other, then couldn't help but laugh. "Honey?" Swift said, slightly confused. "I didn't know you were vegan."

She rubbed her nose and scrunched up her face. "Cathy at school is vegan, and she said I should be too."

Swift opened and closed his mouth, looked at Micha, then back at Imogen. "Of course you can be vegan, hon. But…do you know what that means?"

She pressed her hand to the side of her cheek. "It means good?" she said, definitely guessing.

Swift chuckled and caught Micha's eye, making him feel all warm and fuzzy inside. It was so difficult not to feel like they weren't sharing a special parental moment. But Micha was just the babysitter, and he needed to remember that.

"It means you don't eat any meat or fish or milk or eggs," Swift explained. "Is that something you'd like to try?"

"Uhh…" Imogen looked confused. "But I like sausages. And chicken nuggets."

"You don't have to make any decisions now," Swift assured her despite the fact that there were a couple of people waiting behind them. Another server appeared, so Ben could take his time looking after them.

But Ben had been listening. "We actually *do* have some vegan cakes made up," he said with his eyebrows raised. "If you don't mind waiting a minute, I can fix up a new mermaid one?"

"Oh, yes, please!" Imogen cried.

Swift grinned and shook his head. He was probably thinking the same as Micha. That she still probably didn't quite understand what she was asking for, but it was super nice of Ben to put himself out like that, and if it made her happy, so be it.

"Is there any chance you could do three?" Swift asked with a wince. "One for each of us?"

"Oh, no, you don't have to-" Micha began.

"Of course!" said Ben, disappearing into the back room of the store.

Swift fixed Micha with a firm stare. "You've been a *saint* the past couple of weeks. Please let me buy you a vegan cupcake."

Micha worried that he blushed, but he couldn't help it. "Okay, thank you," he mumbled with a shy grin. That was really nice of Swift.

It was behavior like this that noodled Micha's brain. He'd never had a guy buy him sweet treats before. His parents had, and Rhett had always made sure to grab him whatever he and Swift bought with their allowance. But Swift made it feel special.

Like a romantic gesture.

Urgh, Micha needed to nip that in the bud. It was inappropriate! But the way Swift smiled when he presented Micha with his cupcake – after giving Imogen hers but before claiming his own – made Micha's weak heart flip. He held his gaze for just a second longer than expected, their fingers grazing against each other.

"That'll be $11.35," Ben cried cheerfully, ringing up the cash register, which was such an antique it actually dinged. It certainly got Micha and Swift's attention enough to make them spring apart.

Micha felt vaguely guilty as Swift batted away Micha's feeble attempt to pay for his own as he reached for his wallet. Micha had to admit, it felt really nice for someone to buy him something without expecting anything in return.

Unlike Dale.

Micha pushed that dark thought away. This was a pure moment, and that asshole didn't belong in it.

That was just the thing. Swift probably had *no* idea how adorable he was being right then. How much Micha's heart was aching for him. It was pure and innocent, and Micha needed to stop imagining something that just couldn't be there.

Or so he thought.

Swift led them down to a bench that overlooked the lake where they happily ate their cupcakes. Personally, Micha couldn't tell that they weren't 'normal.' They tasted just like regular cupcakes. He realized he'd probably been harboring an unfortunate prejudice against vegan alternatives until that very moment.

"Hey, I think Farm Fresh sells some meat-free things," Micha said as the thought popped into his head. "We could buy them and give them a go, if you like, Imogen?"

She had icing on her nose as she considered Micha's words. "Does that mean they're vegan?"

"I think so," said Micha. "We can double-check the labels."

She nodded. "Then yes, please, Uncle Micha. Thank you." She mashed the rest of the cupcake into her face. "'Addy?" she asked with her mouth still full. "Cam I go brow pebbles inbo da lake?"

Micha looked up to see Swift's response…but Swift was staring sort of funny at Micha. *Shit!* He should have checked about those veggie sausages before offering them to Imogen. *Stupid!*

Swift blinked, then grinned down at his daughter. "Chew and swallow first," he said firmly, cleaning her face with a wet wipe that he'd produced from nowhere. "Then yes, you can go throw some pebbles. But don't go into the water, okay? You're *very* precious, and Daddy would cry and cry and cry if a sea monster snatched you up!"

She squealed and squirmed off the bench. "It's not the *sea*, Daddy. There are no monsters!"

"What about the Loch Ness Monster?" Swift asked in all seriousness. "He lives in a lake."

Imogen paused. Then she laughed. "He's in a – a – a place the other side of the *world*, Daddy. You're *silly!*"

Swift winked. "Yes, I am. But still be careful, please?"

"I will!" she cried as she ran off, her neatly braided hair streaming behind her.

Micha tried to hold Swift's gaze as he looked back at him, but he was grinning too much, so he looked away. "You're doing so well with her," he mumbled. "That whole vegan thing and the lake. You even came prepared with wet wipes!"

Swift scoffed and flipped open his satchel. "I've got Band-Aids, juice, raisins, my iPad, tissues – you name it!"

Micha toyed with his cupcake wrapper. "You're nailing it." He meant that. Swift was doing so well parenting after just a couple of weeks.

What did Swift really need Micha around for any more?

He startled as Swift touched his knee. "What about you, offering to try veggie sausages? That's a really good idea. We can teach her what veganism means, then she can make her own mind up – but informed. Not just do it because her new best friend told her to."

Swift laughed, but Micha licked his lips. We?

"Sorry, I should have asked first. It's your choice what you guys eat."

Swift frowned. "Well, no," he said with another laugh. "You're eating it, too. I love it when you suggest things for us all. I've been so used to focusing on protein levels and low-carb everything, I need a lot of real-world input."

Micha folded his cupcake wrapper until it wouldn't bend anymore. This was the perfect moment. He should tell Swift it had been lovely – wonderful – but it was time for him to move back in with his folks. Swift and Imogen didn't need him anymore. He was just encroaching. So no, Swift shouldn't make dinner choices based on Micha.

Except the words wouldn't come. His head knew he needed to leave the little family to get on with their life. But his heart couldn't bear to rip himself from the first place to feel so much like home in, well…forever.

Nowhere had felt as comforting as Swift's house. But Micha couldn't stay there. He didn't belong.

Unfortunately, because Micha didn't talk, Swift carried on.

"You know…" He pulled the crumbs off the edge of his wrapper, letting them fall to the ground, no doubt where some birds would enjoy them later. Then he screwed up the wrapper and put it in the bakery bag. Micha did the same. His fingers were getting sticky. "I'm so glad you've been here these past few weeks, Micha. I don't know what the *hell* I would have done without you. I – is it stupid to feel like it was fate that brought us together?"

A lump formed in Micha's throat that he tried to swallow around. Swift was just trying to be nice. "You'd have been fine," he said, attempting to act blasé. "You're a quick learner.

Like I said at the start. You love her. You took her in. The rest would have fallen into place eventually."

His gaze had drifted down to his sneakers as he spoke. There was a pause in which Micha's gut twisted, trying to work out what else he could say to steer this conversation to its natural conclusion. Micha needed to leave.

Except, Swift's toe nudged his own. "Micha?"

Micha frowned and looked up. Was Swift slightly closer to him? "Uh, yeah?"

Swift bit his lip. God, his mouth looked strong, kissable. Micha had dreamed of what it might taste like for so long. It was painful to be this close and yet so far. Swift nibbled that damn lip.

"You've been amazing with Imogen, but-"

Micha smiled, trying to keep the tears that stung behind his eyes at bay. "But it's time to go."

"W-what?" Swift spluttered. "No – that's not – why would you say that? Do you want to move out?"

Micha studied him. He seemed genuinely upset. "No – not yet. I wouldn't leave you in the lurch with babysitting. But you must be sick of me by now?"

Swift exhaled with a nervous laugh.

Then he took Micha's hand in his.

Micha was pretty sure his heart stopped.

"Why would you think that, hon?" Swift asked, playing with his fingers.

Micha licked his lips, his gaze transfixed on his hand being cradled between both of Swift's. What the hell was going on?

"I – I've been crashing on your couch for days?"

Swift chuckled. "And I've *loved* it," he said softly. "Micha, please stop me if I've got this all wrong. But…are you interested in me?"

"What?" Micha's skin felt like it was burning, and he couldn't breathe properly. He'd been so *careful.*

Swift licked his damn lips again. "Are you gay?"

Micha snatched his hand away like he'd been burned. *No, no, no.* This couldn't be happening! He'd sworn to himself no one in this town would ever know his secret. His eyes and throat burned, and sickness rolled through him.

Swift looked horrified. "Whoa! Micha, I'm so sorry! I-"

"Swift," Micha choked out, hugging himself and squinting over the fall sunlight as it played on the rippling surface of the lake. "You're a...*wonderful* guy. I'm sorry I can't – I don't..." Micha sniffed and scrubbed his face, hoping to hide the tears that were leaking free. "I think it's best if I go. You don't want me around, trust me." He stood up.

Swift sputtered indignantly. "Wait a minute. I was just trying to tell you the opposite! I like having you around, Micha. I *really* like it. In fact, I sort of love it. I'm so sorry if I've offended you. That wasn't my intention."

Micha squeezed his eyes shut. Swift was such a sweetheart he couldn't bear it. "You haven't offended me," he whispered.

This was worse than he could imagine. The only thing that could hurt more than Swift not being interested in Micha was suddenly discovering he might actually be and Micha knowing he couldn't do *anything* about it. *Fuck!* How could this be happening? Swift was supposed to be straight and therefore safe!

"I promise, it's me," Micha said, biting back tears. "I'm just a fuckup. I need to get out of your perfect life before I spoil it."

Swift stood as well, but Micha turned and walked away before he could say anything else. Jesus *fucking* Christ! What had he done in this life to deserve this? Had Swift really just told him he *liked* him? That he was interested? He'd held his hand – in public!

He knew exactly what he'd done to deserve this, however.

But none of that mattered. It didn't matter when Swift called his name out after him. It didn't even matter when Imogen cried for Uncle Micha. He had to go.

It still hurt like fucking hell, though.

15

SWIFT

What the hell had just happened? This was a nightmare.

"Is Uncle Micha okay, Daddy?" Imogen asked from the back seat.

Swift swallowed and smiled at her in the rearview mirror. He wasn't going to lie to her. "I think Uncle Micha is a bit sad. Hey, would you like to stay at Grandma and Grandpa's tonight, hon? Then Daddy can look after Uncle Micha and make sure he's okay."

Imogen's lip wobbled. "I could look after him, too," she said in a small voice. "So he doesn't leave."

Poor little bit. She was probably thinking of her mom. But that was exactly why Swift wanted to protect her. Something must be badly wrong for Micha to get this upset, and Imogen had seen too much upset lately.

"Uncle Micha knows that you love him very much, hon," he said gently, already taking the route to his folks' place. "And Daddy's going to do everything he can to convince him to stay in our house. But even if he moves back in with his own family, we'll still be able to see him, I'm sure." *If he doesn't disappear back to Seattle,* the voice in the back of his head warned him.

Please, god, that wouldn't happen.

This was *exactly* what he'd been worried about, what he'd tried to explain to Emery and Elias at the gym the other day. Deep down, Swift wondered if he'd known Micha would bolt if he tried to bring up his feelings. But seeing it happen was more painful than he could have imagined.

He really couldn't work it out. Micha had reacted very badly to the suggestion that he could be gay. But he hadn't corrected Swift. So had Swift been wrong or not?

"Does Uncle Micha love Imogen, too?" she asked. She very rarely spoke about herself in the third person, only when she was overtired or stressed. Damn.

"He does, sweetie. But sometimes grown-ups get sad, and they need other grown-ups to help them. Hey – maybe you could draw him a present for when he's feeling better?"

Imogen's little face lit up behind her sparkly pink glasses. "Would he like a treasure map, Daddy? A Halloween one? With ghosts and pirates and Captain Marvel?"

Even though his gut was in worried knots, he had to smile at that. "I'm sure that would make Uncle Micha feel a hundred times better. Aren't you thoughtful, sweetheart?"

Imogen bounced her legs and sucked her thumb as she looked out the car window. Swift quickly called his mom on speakerphone with the cell mounted on the dash. He was beyond grateful that she didn't ask him any questions. She just said they would be utterly delighted to have a sleepover. Naturally, she'd already set Swift's old room up as a room for Imogen, stocking up on spare sets of jammies and a kid's toothbrush. She even had stuffed animals there and storybooks for bedtime.

It wasn't until Swift dropped her off and pulled into his

own driveway that he realized how nervous he was. Would Micha even be here? How had he gotten home if he was?

His first question was answered immediately as Swift opened the front door and found it wasn't double-locked. He only just caught some shuffling noises as the door swung inward before everything went still. "Micha?" he called out, his heart in his mouth.

There was a pause that stretched out forever until Micha finally replied, "In here."

Swift made sure the door was shut and secure, then followed Micha's voice into the living room, where he was packing. But he had more stuff than when he'd arrived, and it looked like it wasn't all fitting into his backpack. Swift was eternally grateful, as it meant he was still there.

"You're leaving?" he asked, aware how pitiful his voice sounded. How had this backfired so spectacularly?

Micha bit his lip and looked at his too small bag. He'd folded up the sofa bed, like he did each morning, except this time he'd stripped the sheets and folded them neatly on top of the cushions. "I can't stay," he practically whimpered.

"Oh, god!" Swift moaned. He ran his fingers through his hair as he sunk into the regular sofa against the other wall. "I'm *so* sorry. I didn't mean to make you uncomfortable. I – yes, I like you. But it's just a dumb crush. You're more than welcome to stay, hon. I don't want to spoil our friendship, and I don't want to make you feel so miserable!"

Micha sniffed and took in a shaky breath. "A crush?"

Swift sighed, feeling like the worst person in the world. He dropped his hands between his knees. "It's nothing. It's stupid. If I made you uncomfortable or crossed a line, I can't apologize enough."

Micha blinked several times, still staring down at his bag. "Are you gay?"

This was it, the moment of truth. Swift had sworn to

himself that he'd never do this unless he truly meant it. And although it was all going horribly wrong, he couldn't help but feel that moment was now. This was his truth.

"I'm bi," he said as firmly as he could. The more he said it out loud, the more natural it might become.

Micha let out a high-pitched whine and covered his face. The sound just about broke Swift's heart. Before he knew it, he was up in a second and by Micha's side, slipping his arm around his back. But then he froze.

"Should I stop?" he rasped.

To his surprise, Micha turned and slammed into Swift's chest, his face still covered as he howled, leaning into Swift for support. Swift immediately wrapped his arms around him, making soothing noises as to his horror, Micha began to sob.

"Shh, sweetheart, it's okay," Swift murmured, resting his cheek on Micha's hair and rubbing his back. "I've got you. It's okay."

"You weren't supposed to like me!" Micha cried between hiccups. "I can't – I *can't.*"

"Can't what, hon?" Swift *hated* seeing him so distressed like this. He hated even more that he'd caused it, but he didn't understand how. "If you're not into men, that's totally fine. I never meant to overstep any lines. Your friendship is important to me. If I freaked you out, I'm so-"

"I'm *gay!*" Micha all but screamed.

He was crying hysterically now into Swift's hoodie. As his knees buckled, Swift took most of his weight, sinking them both down into the sofa. Micha curled into the fetal position against his side, clinging on for dear life while Swift held him tightly, rubbing his back. He kissed his hair, wishing he understood why Micha was so broken by this.

"That doesn't mean you have to like me back, hon," Swift

said gently when his sobs seemed to ease a little. "I'm mortified if I made you feel obliged or-"

"I like you."

Micha's voice was so small Swift almost missed it. But he just caught the words, and his heart skipped a beat. "You do?"

Micha scowled into Swift's shoulder as a fresh wave of tears cascaded down his face, absorbing into the material of Swift's sweater. "But I can't – I *can't!* I promised myself. Not here. Not in this town."

Swift chewed his lip as he stroked Micha's hair. "Why not, sweetheart?" he asked gently. "Did Rhett say something?"

That finally seemed to get Micha's attention. He leaned back, blinking his beautiful brown eyes, which were all red and puffy. They looked sore. Swift reached up and brushed a stray tear away from his cheek. Micha closed his eyes, but he didn't screw them up, at least.

"Rhett?"

"Yeah." Swift shifted uncomfortably. "I know he's protective. Is that why you don't want to date, um, anyone here?" Best to keep it generic and not specific. He'd almost said 'date me.'

But Micha looked even more confused. "No, he doesn't know. No one does. Hey – where's Imogen?"

"With my folks," Swift said warmly. Trust Micha to be more concerned about her than himself. "How did you get home?"

"I called that Uber guy you said to use." Micha frowned. "He talked a lot."

Swift couldn't help but smile. "What, Kamran? Yeah, he'll chew your ear off."

Swift wasn't sure of the details, but Kamran had somehow helped with that nasty business that Emery and Scout had gotten wrapped up in back in August. Since then, Scout and

Kamran were best buds, and Emery had insisted that everyone he knew – and everyone *they* knew – made Kamran their first call if they needed a cab. Emery wanted his business to be overflowing. Swift was glad he'd given Micha that number last week in case of emergency. He would have hated to think of a stranger taking a distraught Micha home.

Because this *was* home. It had only been a few weeks, but Swift already knew it would feel wrong without Imogen and Micha there, too. He wasn't ready to give up on this without a fight, even if he and Micha just stayed as friends. That would be preferable to this deeply upsetting scenario unfolding before him.

"Micha," Swift said firmly, sensing he needed to take charge. "Why are you so upset? If you're saying I didn't do anything wrong and you like me too, then what's wrong?"

Micha's face crumbled, but he stayed sitting up in Swift's arms so he could see his face. "I can't be gay. Not here. I made a promise. It's not allowed."

"Who says it's not allowed?" Swift could feel his temper rising. If anyone had told Micha that, Swift was going to have stern words with them, that was for sure.

But Micha's answer was more upsetting and more confusing than that. *"I say."*

What? "Micha-" Swift began. But Micha stopped him.

"I had a lot of foster families," he began explaining, his eyes staring listlessly at one of Imogen's toys left lying on the floor. A stuffed rabbit. "But I was with the Brays for a few years when I was young. I don't remember much before living with them. They took a lot of us in. The guy, Craig, he…he didn't like sissies."

Swift's blood ran cold. When Micha paused, Swift had to ask, "What happened?"

Micha bit his lip. Two fat tears slid down his cheeks. Swift didn't hesitate to brush them away with the knuckle of his index finger. *Jesus,* he'd give anything to make this pain stop for Micha.

"Boys should be boys, not sissies," he whispered like he was repeating a mantra. "If he caught me playing dolls with the girls…looking at pony books…waving a stick like it was a fairy wand…" He screwed up his eyes and gritted his teeth. "He had a slipper."

Swift thought he was going to be sick. Someone *hit* Micha with a slipper? When he was only Imogen's age?

Fury like he'd never known raged through him. He didn't know what to do. He wanted to scream or punch the wall. How *dare* anyone do anything so cruel?

"I'm so sorry that ever happened to you," he managed to bite out. "That sick fuck belongs in jail."

Micha shrugged, his eyes still on the stuffed rabbit. At least he wasn't pulling away from Swift's touch.

"I don't think he is. No one checks these things. Eventually, he realized he couldn't beat it out of me, so they sent me packing. I bounced around homes with all my stuff in a trash bag." His face dissolved again, and a sob wracked his body. "Then Dad and Pops took me in."

Swift would have thought that was where this story got happy, but the anguish on Micha's face told him to shut up and listen some more. These demons were clearly still haunting him, all these years later.

"I didn't *want* them," Micha snarled, his face blotchy and wet. "They were everything I'd been told was wrong. They were the reason I got hit again and again and *again*. I *hated* them. I was awful, so bad. I got into fights at school and told them to send me back away…*away from the perverts.*" He was crying in earnest now and collapsed back into Swift's arms. "But they just kept *loving* me. Telling me it would be okay, that they weren't sending me back. That I was family now and family didn't quit."

For a few minutes, he cried some more until his sobs became shudders and sniffles. Swift reached out to grab the box of tissues from the coffee table, letting Micha blow his nose a few times and mop up his eyes.

Swift felt like his horror was a living thing in his throat. Micha had been bottling all this up, for all this time?

"When I got older," Micha continued, his voice so subdued it was barely more than a mumble, "I realized everything Craig had said about me was true. I was gay, just like my dads. But…but how could I be? I'd been so cruel to them. I broke things and hurt my siblings and tried to run away. I called them every filthy slur I knew. I couldn't be allowed to turn around and get to be the same as them. I'm not…I'm not worthy of that. So I made a promise. I could leave and make my own way, but I'd never tell them what a horrible, selfish hypocrite I was."

He sounded so disgusted with himself that it broke Swift's heart. "You were a *child*," he said through gritted teeth. "You'd been *abused*. You're right. Sunny and Tyee love you. They love all of you. They'll understand."

Micha blew his nose again, then stared lifelessly at the bunny rabbit on the floor. "You know no one wanted all my siblings? They said four was too much or that Darcy's chair was a problem – like that's all she was?" He screwed up his face. But then he closed his eyes and smiled. "Gay couples didn't adopt back in the eighties. But Dad and Pops…." He shook his head, and Swift knew what he meant. Those men had never cared much for the rules. "They fought to get all four kids. Keep the siblings together. Gave them a home when no one else would. That's why the same agency reached out to see" -he gulped- "to see if they'd take a troubled kid like me."

Swift stroked and kissed his hair. "Thank god above they

did. You deserved a loving family, Micha. No one should ever go through what you did."

Micha shook his head against Swift's damp chest. "I don't know that I do. But it seems grotesque for me to...I can't come out to them. I just can't."

Swift bit his lip. "Do you want to hear something totally ridiculous? I've suspected I might be bi for years. But I never knew for sure. Whereas all my brothers and sisters always knew so strongly what they were. So I convinced myself it probably wasn't a thing. Then..." He sighed. "Then it felt like I couldn't come out, because that was *their* thing. If I didn't know for sure, I shouldn't. It was like it was trivializing what they'd been through. I didn't want to jump on their bandwagon so late. So I told myself I wouldn't come out unless I was *really* sure. Unless I met someone."

Micha went still in his arms. "Swift," he said cautiously, looking at his sweatshirt as he clutched a handful of the material tightly. "You're not – don't come out for me."

Swift felt like his heart cracked. But he tried to keep his voice light. "No, it's okay, hon. If you're not interested-"

"I'm crazy for you." The statement hung there, and Micha stared at his fist on Swift's hoodie, and Swift stared at the top of Micha's hair.

"You – what?"

Micha closed his eyes, his dark lashes gracing his cheekbones. "I'm not worth it, Swift. Hold on for someone else."

Well, that got Swift all fired up in a flash. "Now just one second," he said, taking Micha by the shoulders and moving them both so they were looking at each other. Micha's expression was startled, but Swift needed to make him understand this. "I *hate* hearing you talk about yourself like that! You're smart and cute and fun and hardworking and have so many talents and...and did I mention cute?"

A hint of a smile twitched at the corner of Micha's lips. He looked down at his hands as he very carefully laid them on top of Swift's chest. The contact sent an electric current all through Swift's body, making him feel like he'd lit up like a Christmas tree. But he did his best not to move in case he spooked Micha.

"You said cute, yeah," Micha whispered.

Swift licked his lips. "I can't stop thinking about what it might be like – only if you wanted to – but, uh, I've been picturing-"

Before he knew what hit him, Micha's lips crashed against his.

They were perfect, just like he'd imagined.

16

MICHA

Micha's first thought was, *FINALLY!*

But it was closely followed by a second thought of, *what the hell?*

He pulled away from Swift in horror. "Sorry, sorry!" he squeaked.

Swift blinked, smiled, and hugged Micha to him. "Now why on Earth would you be sorry?" he gently murmured, stroking Micha's back again. *God,* that felt good.

"Uh, I kissed you. I sort of launched myself at you."

Swift chuckled. "It might have been the only thing to stop me babbling by that point."

Micha frowned and took a couple of deep breaths. "You didn't mind?"

"No."

Swift kissed the top of his hair. He'd done that a few times since Micha had lost his shit. He was ashamed to say it was one of the nicest things he'd ever felt from anyone else, even when he'd been spilling all his terrible secrets. When Swift pressed his lips to the top of his head, Micha felt like maybe things weren't so bad after all.

Swift had called him cute. Twice.

But Micha had also told him his deepest darkest secret, his most shameful truth. Couldn't he see what a terrible person Micha was? He didn't deserve to be held like this, how he'd dreamed of it for so many years.

"Swift, I shouldn't-"

Swift puffed out his cheeks. It was an adorable little habit he did quite often. It made Micha's heart ache. "Shouldn't what? Be happy? Live an authentic life? Because you acted out after you were traumatized by a monster as a child?"

Micha opened his mouth to protest, but he didn't know what to say. It all sounded very logical when Swift explained it like that.

"I don't know," he whispered.

Swift brushed his fingers across his cheek, sending shivers down his spine. "I do," he murmured. "I like you, Micha. You make my day better. You brighten up any room you walk into. And if it's quite all right, I'd really like to try that kiss again. This time less rushed."

Micha bit his lip and hummed. The nasty voice in the back of his head was telling him Swift couldn't mean that. He was far too good for Micha. But the evidence was there in the way he was cradling Micha's body to him, the way he cupped his hand to his cheek, waiting for permission to kiss him again.

Fuck, that was romantic.

Micha hadn't put much stock in kissing before. It was something you did to basically let the other guy know you wanted to fuck. Then there might be a bit more once they started getting naked, but usually Micha felt his mouth was better used in other places.

But Swift…Micha just sort of wanted to lie there and bring their mouths together again. Softly, sweetly.

So that was what he asked for. "Please," he whispered,

touching his fingertips to the side of Swift's square jaw. It was slightly prickly with a day's worth of stubble, just the way Micha liked it.

Swift studied him with his sky-blue eyes. Not just any sky. A crisp fall sky when the temperature had just dipped but the sun was still shining and there wasn't a cloud to be seen. The kind of day that made you want to take in a lungful of air and hold it until you burst.

It was the kind of sky that looked like freedom.

Carefully, Swift moved them a little so Micha was more snuggled into the corner of the couch with Swift's strong hands splayed across his back and caressing the side of his cheek. His warm breath ghosted over Micha's mouth, tasting faintly sweet from the earlier cupcake. Swift's tongue darted out, wetting his lips, making them glisten.

Then he leaned in, touching them to Micha's, almost reverently.

Micha moaned. He couldn't help it. His hands tightened around the back of Swift's hoodie, feeling the soft material and hard muscles under his fingers. Swift nuzzled his nose against the side of Micha's, moving his lips a little, deepening the kiss. He was warm and smelled of the fresh air from the lake and a masculine musk that Micha had picked up on from when he came back after the gym. A manly man scent that drove Micha wild.

His body was heavy on top of Micha's in the most perfect way. Tentatively, Micha slipped his tongue out as his lips moved, delighted that Swift copied him, the kiss becoming open-mouthed.

Micha wasn't sure how long they lay like that, hands exploring torsos and mouths traveling over lips, jaws, earlobes. It just suddenly occurred to Micha that he was so relaxed he felt boneless.

Swift made him feel safe. Cared for.

He dared run his hands between Swift's jeans and hoodie, feeling the strip of warm skin along his back. Just once – when his sweatpants had ridden down to his hips – Micha had spotted a matching pair of dimples on either side of his spine, where his back met his butt. He'd felt at the time it was the most mouthwatering thing he'd ever seen, and now his fingers were skimming over those delicious little dents.

Swift was a gift from above.

Micha knew he was being greedy, selfish. He shouldn't get too close to Swift, because he ruined everything he got too close to. It was just inevitable. But Micha was weak, and he couldn't seem to help himself. He'd wanted this for years and years – over a decade. It would be impossible to even try and estimate how many fantasies he'd had about Swift Coal in all that time, and now here they were, and it was better than Micha could have ever imagined.

But was that wrong? Swift didn't know that. Micha pulled back, starting to feel breathless again but not in a good way. Swift frowned, touching his jaw delicately with his fingers.

"You okay?"

If Micha had told him the worst secrets about himself, if he was admitting to being gay when he'd sworn to himself he'd never do that back home, maybe he should go all the way and spill his last truth?

"I…" He inhaled slowly, trying not to panic. He felt like any wrong word could make this all go away in a puff of smoke. But he didn't want to lie anymore to Swift. Not when he made him feel so protected. "I've always liked you," he mumbled, playing with his hoodie strings.

Swift touched his chin, encouraging him to look into his eyes. "Always?"

Micha chewed his lip and glanced away. "When I was a teenager," he said, feeling himself blush, "you helped me realize…you were one of my first…" He closed his eyes and took another breath. "It was just a dumb crush. But then you showed up in our kitchen after all those years, and it wasn't so dumb anymore."

Swift's laugh was a deep rumble, and he placed a gentle kiss to the corner of Micha's mouth. Then he brushed his lips against the shell of Micha's ear. "Holy fuck, that's hot," he murmured.

Micha screwed his eyes shut tighter and bit his lip so hard he almost tasted blood. His dick was starting to throb in his pants, getting harder and thicker. "You don't think it's kind of pathetic? A silly kid mooning after you?"

"No," Swift replied as he nipped at Micha's earlobe, making him gasp. "Because that kid was adorable and I always liked him. But then he went and grew up into a real hottie that finally yanked my dumb ass out of the closet." He was trailing kisses down his jaw now. "Micha, I don't want to put any pressure on you to do anything you don't want. It's been an emotional day. But now I've finally got my hands on you, I'm sort of losing my mind here."

He brushed their noses together and skimmed his lips across Micha's, dotting little teasing kisses. Then he glanced down, encouraging Micha to do likewise. It was easy to see the bulge that had grown at the top of his leg.

Micha was doing that. Micha had made Swift Coal so turned on he was straining against his pants.

He took a steadying breath and tried to organize his many frantic thoughts. His sex-brain was taking over, and all he really wanted to do was lose himself in Swift's naked body. But his hadn't been the only confession of the evening, and Micha shouldn't be selfish.

"You, um..." He swallowed but then mustered enough courage to look Swift in the eyes. "You've really never been with a man before?" Swift shook his head. "And you're not, uh, freaking out about it now?"

Swift smiled. "Nope. It feels nice. Better than nice. Just because something's new doesn't mean it should be scary."

Fucking hell, he was such an adorable Hufflepuff. Always seeing the glass half-full.

Micha couldn't help the rueful laugh that escaped his lips. "I've been with a couple of guys who wanted to experiment. I don't know if they were gay or bi or what, but they were definitely in denial, calling themselves straight, even after we…well, you know." He sniffed. Those guys weren't worth thinking about now. In truth, Micha felt kind of sorry for them, drowning in their own toxic masculinity.

But had he been any better, denying who he was at home for so long?

Swift kissed his cheek. "I'm not like them. It might have taken me a while, but I know who I am. I'm here, with you, and it's amazing."

Micha breathed out, a real smile tugging at his mouth as he ran a hand up Swift's muscular arm. "It is," he whispered.

"But it's also a lot," Swift said seriously, caressing the side of Micha's neck and giving him full-body shivers. "We've talked about some deep things and both come out. We don't have to do anything more now or make any decisions. Except…I'm going to beg to you unpack that bag. Please. We can take this as slow as you want, but please don't leave."

Micha sniffed and rubbed his damp eyes. Swift knew how to make his heart twist and ache in a way that somehow felt good. When he'd been a kid, Micha's family had begged him to stay, and luckily, they'd had the power to make that happen until he was old enough to see what a blessing they truly were.

But no man had ever pled to keep him in his arms. Dale had always made it feel like a threat, no matter how subtle. Swift was making Micha feel like the most important person in the world.

Well, second most important.

"What about Imogen?" Micha asked, feeling a frown crease his brow. "She's the priority. I don't want to confuse her."

Swift huffed and smiled, his eyes glassy. "On that, we're both a hundred percent on the same page. But she loves you. She was very worried after you left. I promised her I'd ask you to stay with us. I think…I really do think if she knew you were Daddy's special friend, she would be very happy."

Micha's heart skipped a beat. 'Special friend' sounded an awful lot like 'boyfriend.' But that was leaping ahead. Swift's talk of taking things nice and slowly calmed all his frantic thoughts, helping him focus on the here and now. And what he was saying was that it maybe wouldn't rock Imogen's world again if his and Micha's relationship altered slightly.

"Okay," Micha whispered with a twitch of a smile.

Swift leaned down and captured his lips again in a slow and easy kiss. "I…can we…uh…"

Micha giggled. "What?"

Swift rolled his eyes. "Don't get me wrong. I'm loving making out on the sofa like horny teenagers. But I feel wrecked and you must, too. Do you want to, uh, maybe go snuggle in bed?"

Micha didn't know whether to laugh or cry as he grinned and cupped the side of Swift's face. "No one has *ever* asked me to snuggle before."

Swift grimaced and laughed. "It that totally lame?"

"I love it almost as much as the hair kisses," Micha blurted out before he could change his mind.

Swift's expression softened as he caressed the back of Micha's neck. "Hair kisses?"

Micha only felt a little shy as he tapped the top of his head. "Nice little kisses, here. Sweet kisses." He couldn't bring himself to say it, but they were so wonderful because they were given with nothing expected in return. They made Micha feel free and safe.

"Come to bed with me, Micha," Swift murmured, trailing his hands along Micha's back and sides. "You can have all my sweet little kisses, darling."

Pet names. That was another thing Micha wasn't used to. Most guys didn't bother, or when they called Micha pretty or whatever, it kind of felt derogatory. Micha had told himself he didn't mind that during sex, especially good, rough sex he could totally lose himself in. But he'd never really experienced this light, heady feeling coursing through him as Swift led him by the hand to the bedroom. He believed Swift when he said he was cute. He almost believed him when he said other things too, like how he was talented.

Micha wanted to stay in this bubble, where Swift's version of Micha wasn't a failure, where he hadn't made all the wrong choices.

Micha had been born unwanted. But Swift made him feel like he was cherished.

That little voice tried to rear its ugly head as they kicked off their shoes and slid between Swift's bedsheets. It tried to tell Micha that Swift only wanted sex. That he didn't really like or respect Micha. But Micha wasn't stupid. He could see what was in front of his own eyes, and in that moment, he was very much wanted.

Micha wasn't going to waste time worrying where it was going to head. Life was short and full of disappointments. Right now, Swift's lips were seeking his out again, his hands were skimming over his hips, and it felt *so* good.

"I've been wondering," Swift said as they lay side-by-side on his sumptuous memory foam pillows under sheets that felt like they had a thousand thread count, "if you have any more tattoos?"

Micha snorted, not even caring if he sounded terrible. "Have you now?"

Swift nodded, playing with the hem of Micha's sweater, tugging it ever so slightly upward. "Can I look?"

"I see exploring runs in the family," Micha teased, and Swift laughed. Micha's heart was racing, but as scared as he was, he was also desperate for this. "Um, okay."

Swift grinned as he slid his hands under Micha's sweater, touching his soft belly. Micha felt a little embarrassed when comparing himself to Swift's hard abs, but Swift hummed and stroked his skin.

"Lovely," he murmured against Micha's neck. Then he bunched up the sweater and pulled it up Micha's chest, encouraging him to lift his arms above his head so he could slide it off all the way. He discarded it by the side of the bed while Micha tried not to shiver in anticipation. His nipples were already budded as Swift ran his hands over his torso, drinking him in. "I like this." He stroked the thorny rose above Micha's heart. Micha had to admit it was one of his favorites.

"Thank you." He didn't really have a story behind it. It had just felt right to put it there. Micha had designed a lot of his ink himself, such as that rose, as well as the pirate ship and the mermaids on his arms. Silly doodles, really, but they made him happy.

When Swift kissed the rose, though, he moaned and slid his hands through his blond hair. His cock was throbbing, pressed against his clothes. He thrust upward, chasing some friction to give him relief.

Swift chuckled. "Do you need some help there?"

Micha froze and bit his lip. He felt how wide his eyes were as he looked up at Swift. "No, it's fine," he uttered. "We said we'd go slow."

Swift arched a golden eyebrow at him, making his insides

squirm. "Part of me testing my 'am I bi?' theory was watching a fair amount of porn. It was hot, leading me to think cocks might turn me on a bit. I'm not scared of yours. I'm quite excited, actually."

Micha's breaths were shallow and ragged. How could Swift make something so matter-of-fact sound so fucking scorching? "Do – do you want to touch it?" Micha squeaked. Swift nodded, adorably flushed, then slid his hand down Micha's ticklish ribs and over his hip, skimming the inside of his thigh. Micha groaned with want, rutting upward, seeking attention.

Then he got it.

Swift firmly cupped his crotch, rubbing Micha through his jeans as he kissed him deeply, his tongue probing Micha's mouth, claiming him. Micha clung to his strong shoulders, like an anchor in troubled waters, allowing himself to be conquered.

It appeared Swift was correct. He had no problem touching another man's junk. He even started undoing Micha's fly.

"Oh, fuck," Micha whispered. To his dismay, Swift paused.

"Too fast?"

Micha ground his teeth together and shook his head. "Not if it's okay with you. I just…I can't believe this is happening."

Swift's smile was sinful as he hummed and kissed Micha's lips again. "Believe it, gorgeous. I've finally got my hands on you, and I want it all. Can I make you come?"

Micha spluttered and whimpered, pressing his forehead against Swift's. "Y-yes, please."

He felt like he might tremble apart as Swift finished unzipping his flies, then slid his fingers through his briefs to wrap them around Micha's hard and leaking cock. He bucked, clinging on to Swift's hoodie. They were still mostly clothed, but it still felt so intimate, and Swift began to stroke him. Christ. This wasn't going to take long.

Micha's fingers fumbled downward, trying to find Swift's pants button without breaking the momentum, but Swift halted him with a touch of his hand. "Let me look after you first," he insisted.

No one had ever done that before. Micha had always been expected to pull his weight. Making the other guy come first was his priority. But Swift rolled them, letting Micha lie on his back while Swift kissed and jerked him off. All Micha had to do was run his hands over Swift, and even that didn't seem to be expected. Swift just wanted to take care of him.

Micha's heart clenched as he came suddenly, shooting his load over them both. "Sorry," he gasped as his vision swam.

Swift chuckled and – *holy fuck* – brought his hand up to tentatively lick one of his messy fingers. "Why would you be sorry, sweetheart?" he asked with a devilish grin on his face.

Micha panted, still high from his climax and disbelieving what he was seeing. "You're kind of a little bit kinky," he said breathlessly. "You know that?"

Swift grinned. "Only with people I really like. Was that okay?"

"I came too fast," Micha lamented, but Swift shook his head.

"No such thing if it was good. Next time we can try something else."

Next time? God, Micha could only dare to hope.

As he gradually floated back down, he and Swift kissed leisurely, not caring about the mess that Micha had made. As soon as he had his wits back, Micha made a second attempt to reach for Swift's crotch. This time Swift let him.

In fact, he moaned wantonly into Micha's mouth as Micha rubbed his hard length through the denim. "Can I?"

Micha whispered. Swift nodded, brushing their noses together, their breath hot against each other's mouths.

Micha did his best to steady his hand as he freed Swift's length. It was fat and long, sturdy looking, just like he was. Micha held his breath as he encircled the girth, loving how much Swift gasped at his touch.

"Okay?" Micha asked, checking in like Swift had done because that had felt so good. Swift nodded as Micha stroked him, burying his face against Micha's neck and moaning.

Micha was the first man to do this. Swift had never experienced this from a guy before. Micha concentrated on giving the very best hand job he could, but he also couldn't help but feel a little bit of pride. He was the lucky one that Swift had trusted into his bed.

They rubbed stubbled cheeks and panted as Micha stroked him, coaxing his climax to build. Never in all his teenage years would Micha have thought he'd be here now with gorgeous, kind, cool Swift Coal. Even if it was just for tonight, he was going to enjoy this moment.

As Swift came, he held Micha tightly while he gasped, their bodies trembling together. Swift shook while he caught his breath, then blinked his eyes back open, his eyes finding Micha's.

Then he smiled like warm sunshine, hugging Micha against him in spite of the mess. Their clothes had taken the brunt of it, so Micha didn't feel so uncomfortable, even though he was bare-chested.

Swift kissed the top of his hair. Despite the doubts already kicking in, Micha melted into the embrace, letting Swift cradle him. "That was amazing," he said reverently.

Micha smiled against his neck. "Yeah? I didn't do much. Sorry, I-"

Swift halted him with a long and tender kiss. "Please stop saying sorry. Making love doesn't have to be complicated and last for hours when you care about the person. At least, that's what I think." He shrugged while Micha stared at him. "What matters is that we're sharing something special together."

Micha guessed that was a good point, actually. He'd had some spectacular fuckings in his time, but how many of those guys had cuddled him afterward? "Yeah," he said shakily, but he was smiling.

Swift kissed his temple, then his hair, stroking the top of his bare arm. "I'm sorry it took such an emotional push to get us here," he said somberly. "But I'm glad we talked, and I hope we'll talk some more. Because I care about you, Micha. And…well, if you're interested, I'd like to see where this relationship takes us."

Within less than thirty seconds, worry rinsed away all of Micha's joy and contentment. Oh *god*. He'd told Swift everything. Of course he wanted to talk more. Shame washed over Micha. He didn't deserve to feel this happy. He didn't deserve to get the thing he'd always wanted when he'd thrown Dad and Pops' kindness back in their faces for years. Especially not when they'd taken him back in after he'd narrowly escaped going to prison.

It was only early evening, but it was getting dark outside, so it wasn't that surprising when Micha felt Swift doze off against him. Once he was sure he was properly asleep, Micha very carefully extracted himself from Swift's arms, intending to get cleaned up. When he looked down for his sweater, he realized Butter had claimed it as a bed and was looking back at Micha with half an enormous dead spider hanging from his mouth. At least, Micha hoped it was dead. Either way, he decided to leave the sweater where it was, resolving that he'd probably get it back covered in holes. But he couldn't really muster the energy to care.

In the moment, what he'd just shared with Swift had been

incredible. Micha had fucked a lot. However, he wasn't sure how many times he'd made love. But what was going to happen now? Swift couldn't really mean what he'd said about wanting to be together. If Swift came out, it should be to date some lawyer or environmentalist or someone else cool and smart and respectable.

Not some punk kid who'd managed to screw up the few good things he'd been handed in this life.

As much as Micha wanted to crawl back into Swift's bed and stay in Swift's imaginary bubble, the reality was that this was never anything more than a silly teenage dream. So Micha trudged back into the living room, pulled his pajamas from his backpack, then curled up on the sofa under one of the sheets he'd stripped from his foldout bed. Eventually, he dozed off, trying to figure out what the hell he was supposed to do now.

17

SWIFT

SWIFT WAS DISORIENTATED WHEN HE SURFACED. HE WASN'T usually one for napping and felt discombobulated as he ran his tongue over his teeth and rubbed his gritty eyes in the dark. It was past nine in the evening, and he was fully dressed under the covers.

Almost fully dressed.

His memories came flooding back to him as he rearranged his underwear and did up his jeans. Everything that had happened replayed in his mind at high speed in full-color definition. Wow, that was an awful lot to take on board. Amazing in the end, although intense. But where was Micha now? He'd been in Swift's arms as they'd cuddled after sex. Had he woken earlier and gone for a shower? To get something to eat?

But the house was dark as Swift made his way from his bedroom. He flicked on a couple of lamps rather than any of the overhead lights, treading quietly across the floorboards. Micha's sweater was discarded on the bedroom floor, a suspicious amount of ginger hair all over it.

He wasn't in the bathroom or the kitchen. Just when

Swift was starting to panic that he'd left after all, he discovered a curled-up lump on the sofa, breathing softly. Swift sighed, partly relieved, but confused as to why Micha had moved. Swift sat on the edge of the cushion, then rubbed Micha's arm.

"Hey, hon," he said gently.

After a couple of seconds, Micha stirred, taking in a deep breath and blinking his eyes. "Swift?"

"Hi, sweetie." Swift rubbed his arm some more. "What are you doing out here?"

Micha looked confused for a second. Then he rubbed his eyes and sat up a little. "Oh," he said, sounding sad and maybe guilty.

Swift didn't really want to talk in the dark, so he leaned over and turned on another lamp, basking them in a soft glow. Micha hugged the sheet over his chest. He'd changed into his pajamas.

Swift tried not to let sadness overwhelm him, but he figured it was better to ask the question right away. Like ripping off a Band-Aid. "Do you regret what happened?"

Micha licked his lips, his dark hair disheveled. "No," he said slowly, looking down at that stuffed rabbit again. "It was amazing. I just…I thought maybe you'd need space. I don't know what we're supposed to do now."

Swift exhaled and rubbed Micha's propped-up knee. Mercifully, he didn't pull away. "I don't need space," Swift said with a smile. "Slow is good, but when I have sex with someone, I think it's nice to cuddle with them when we wake up."

"Oh." Micha's Adam's apple bobbed as he swallowed. "Sorry."

Swift didn't want to push Micha, but he also wanted to make sure he made him aware of how he was feeling.

"It is a lot," Swift said. "What you told me about your

past…" He balled his fist, then flexed it back out again as his anger dispelled. "I'm really, really glad you told me all that. I'm so sorry you've been holding on to it all for so long. We can talk about it whenever you like. Because well, I'm here for you. I'm all in for you, Micha Perkins. If you want me."

It took him by surprise as Micha's hand suddenly flew out and covered Swift's on his knee. A fluttering of hope blossomed in Swift's heart.

"I-I do. Want you." Micha fiddled with his fingers, his gaze on them rather than Swift's eyes. "I just don't really see why you'd like me. But you said you do. So I should stop asking why, or you'll stop."

Swift chuckled, flipping his hand so they could entwine their fingers. "Not likely. But I'll do what I can to stop you from second-guessing stuff. Slow doesn't mean I want you doubting everything I say or do, or worrying that you've upset me. I promise I'll *tell* you if there's something that makes me sad or pissed off or even just confused. Someone told me recently that we all go into relationships just trying our best."

Micha peeked from underneath his dark eyelashes. "Relationship?"

Swift grinned. "This is me not rushing into anything, can you tell?" He rolled his eyes. Luckily, Micha laughed softly, and Swift rubbed the back of his hand with his thumb. "But, um, I'm not planning on seeing anyone else for the foreseeable future, if you get what I mean?"

With a shaky breath out, Micha nodded. "Me neither. And I want to try to freak out less. But I've never been in a relationship before, and I'm used to things falling apart around me for one reason or another. I might need some help."

Swift lifted his hand to kiss his knuckles. "Asking for help is a really good start. We'll just try our best together, like the whole parenting thing, okay?"

Micha laughed and rested his head on the side of the sofa. "Okay."

"So," Swift said, hoping he wasn't going to drop too much of a bombshell. "If you want, rather than pull this thing out every night, you can come share with me."

Micha lifted his head again, his eyebrows raised. "The bed? That seems…a little fast."

"You don't have to," Swift assured him. "But if you did, I'm not talking about getting wild. I just…" Oh god, he was going to sound so lame. "It sort of upsets me thinking of you out here when we could cuddle in there."

Micha bit his lip as his expression softened. "Cuddle?"

"And snuggle," Swift said, grinning. Micha laughed and even blushed a little. "Seriously, though. I'm not pushing for anything more than maybe a little kissing. You can call the shots. Only, someone *else* told me that life is too short, and it seems an awful shame not to have you in my arms when I quite like you there."

Micha rubbed the back of his head with his free hand and laughed bashfully. "I quite like being there too. I *really* like it. Okay, I guess we could try?"

"Amazing," Swift gushed, feeling giddy. "Excellent. Yes." He kissed the back of Micha's hand again.

"You're such a dork," he said, sounding fond at least.

Swift nodded proudly. "Darn tootin'. Now, Mr. Perkins, I would very much like to cook you some dinner. Would that be acceptable?"

Micha blushed even harder and buried his head on his knees. "Very acceptable," he squeaked. Swift laughed and kissed the top of his hair.

"It's a date, then. Oh, don't act all surprised," he scoffed fondly when Micha looked up at him with wide eyes. "I'm trying really hard to go slow here, but you're too adorable. Let me make you dinner, and you can pretend it's not a date if you don't want that."

Micha bit his lip as he grinned. "No…it can be a date. If you want that?"

Swift did want that. Very much.

"So come on," Rhett said a few days later. "Spill."

Swift fiddled with his soda can as they sat on the back porch, watching Imogen run around the yard with a very enthusiastic but rather unstable Mateo and Luis tottering after her. The twins were mostly babbling in Spanish, but their mom – who was also Puerto Rican – was chasing after them, translating for Imogen and teaching her boys new English words.

"God, man," Swift said, not deliberately avoiding Rhett's question on purpose. He was just suddenly overwhelmed in the moment. "Look at us. We've gone from nothing to three babies between us in less than four months. Isn't that insane in the best kind of way?"

Rhett chuckled and sipped his beer. "Completely. But I'm going to have to get my ass off the bench and into the game in a minute, so out with it. What's been eating you?"

Swift almost blushed. He and Micha hadn't gotten any further than heavy petting yet, but Swift was far from innocent. He had a feeling they might progress to third base sooner rather than later. Not that he was telling Micha's big brother any 'eating' plans he had. *Fuck* no.

Suddenly this seemed like a terrible idea. It had been a couple of days since their relationship had shifted, and Micha was doing okay not letting his fears and doubts get the better of him. Why had Swift even arranged this get-together?

Because Rhett was his best buddy and the person Swift turned to when he needed to hash something out. He was just going to have to be careful how he did it. But he wasn't sure how much longer he and Micha were going to be able to keep what was happening between them on the down low. So far, they hadn't changed anything in front of Imogen. But soon enough, Swift was going to want to give her a sanitized version of events. Micha made him happy, and he wanted them to be able to hold hands or share a kiss like any other couple.

Coming out to Imogen meant coming out to everyone, though. Otherwise she'd blurt it out in her natural, excitable way, and Swift didn't want Micha being wrong-footed.

And Swift didn't want Rhett hearing about it from anyone other than him. He was serious about his little brother and would want to head off any concerns right off the bat.

Swift watched the plastic skeletons swinging from the tree in Rhett and Louella's back yard. Halloween was getting close, but Imogen kept changing her mind on what she wanted to dress as. *Welcome to parenthood,* he thought with a little smile. Whatever she decided, Swift knew Micha would be there to help him navigate his first attempt at fancy dress with his kid.

"I think I've met someone," Swift said as the kids all piled on top of Louella, shrieking and laughing.

"Really?" Rhett said, intrigued. It was enough to get Swift's attention. His expression was amused. "Dude, that's fantastic. Congratulations."

Swift frowned. "You don't seem all that surprised."

Rhett shrugged. "I knew *something* was up. I'm glad it's a good thing, not a worrying thing."

"Well," said Swift, "it is a little tricky, what with Imogen in the picture now."

Rhett scoffed. "Dude, you're a parent, not dead. If anyone can date and look after that little munchkin, it's you. So come on. You're killing me here. What's her name?"

He studied Swift as if he was waiting for a particular answer. Swift wasn't sure what that might be exactly, but he shifted on his seat. "That's the thing. It's not exactly a conventional relationship."

Rhett reached out and gave him a friendly punch. "My family specializes in unconventional. You can't scare me. So long as this person knows about Imogen and is nice to her, I'd say you're good."

"Oh, no, yeah," Swift spluttered, pulling a face. "There's *nothing* to worry about there, trust me."

Rhett shook his head and smiled. "Great, then. So, what's the deal?"

Swift sighed and toyed with the stay tab on his soda can. He decided not to dive into why it had taken him so long to come out and just get on with it. But this was a big deal, telling Rhett. It took him a second to pluck up the courage. "I'm bi," he blurted out. "And this person is, well, a guy."

Rhett's lack of reaction could have been surprising, except as he'd just said, his family had a lot of members who you could argue were outside the mainstream. "That's wonderful, Swift," he said. "I mean it. I had thought maybe you might be before, once or twice. But I'm happy you got there on your own and you've met someone special."

'Met' wasn't quite the right word, but Swift was so relieved that Rhett was on board he wasn't going to worry about that detail just yet. "Thanks, man. Thanks." He beamed and clapped Rhett on the leg, then looked over at Imogen again.

Not everyone was going to feel the same way.

Swift swirled his cherry cola and sighed. "But I don't know where I stand with my custody rights. If some asshole didn't like me dating a guy, could they take her away?"

At that, Rhett did become quite serious. He inhaled deeply and sat forward, leaning his elbows on his knees. "Yeah," he said, nodding. "Someone might come along and be an asshole. Then, my friend, unfortunately all you can do is fight. Because *you're* right, and *they're* wrong. But you're also Imogen's biological dad, so it should be easier for you to keep custody. Hell, any moron can see what a wonderful life you're giving her. I'm sure you'll be fine if anything even ever happens like that."

Swift watched as Rhett rubbed his mouth. He looked over at his wife doting on all three children, all smiles as Imogen attempted to braid Louella's long dark hair (badly) and the boys played with plastic dinosaurs, using Mama's knees as volcanos.

Rhett and Louella had gone through hell and back to adopt those boys.

"Argh," Rhett said, smiling, even though his eyes were glassy. He shook his head and fixed Swift with a firm stare. "I'm aware I've said it before, but I'll just say it once more to make a point. I didn't know Lou was trans when we met. Not that she should have to wear a fucking sign or anything," he added with a scowl. Swift nodded. He did know that, and he agreed. Other people needed to mind their own damn business. "But trans people weren't something I was all that aware of. I hadn't thought about people like her much or thought that's who I'd fall in love with. But I did." He beamed and waved to his family across the lawn, and they waved back. "I feel very strongly about that, man. You fall in love, and that's it. Doesn't matter with who if you both feel the same. And if you and that person love your kids, what the hell else is there to say? Lou was determined to adopt from back home, so we jumped through every hoop to make that happen. And yeah, some assholes tried to stop us. Just like they tried to stop Dad and Pops." He grinned defiantly. "I feel sorry for those sad bastards. I really do. Because this is what family looks like. I'll die on this hill."

"Amen," said Swift thickly. He was proud of them both for fighting so hard, just like he was proud of the five children Sunny and Tyee had worked so hard to save. Not to mention the other kids they'd fostered along the way, giving them a few months to get back on their feet.

Some people – like Micha's fucker of a foster dad – would call them all abominations. Swift would call them saints.

"So, no," Rhett said firmly as he stood, brushing his hands on his jeans. "If you've met someone you like, don't let anyone tell you it's wrong when it damn sure ain't." Then he fixed Swift with a mildly terrifying glare. "Just so long as you treat this guy with *respect* and know that if you fuck him around, he might have older siblings who won't be happy about that."

Then he winked, took a last sip of beer before jogging down the porch steps to roar like a T-Rex, and started chasing his squealing boys around.

After the initial shock passed that Rhett had likely guessed *exactly* who the object of Swift's affection was, Swift took a moment to process what his best friend had said.

If he was going to go down this road, it might not be easy, but it could be worth it…for love.

Swift wasn't quite sure he and Micha were there yet or if they ever would be…but he still sat on that porch with a goofy smile on his face for a little while longer.

18

MICHA

Micha didn't want to jinx anything, but he was pretty sure this was going okay. It was, wasn't it? Thinking that wasn't going to ruin it, right?

"Uncle Micha, the water!" Imogen cried.

They were both in the kitchen, her sitting at the table, coloring, Micha washing up a pan for dinner. They'd had leftovers from Sunny Side Up the past couple of days, but tonight he'd been determined to cook up some of the vegan burgers from Farm Fresh with some potatoes and roasted veggies. But he'd let the water in the sink get so high it was almost going to spill out onto the floor.

Micha shrieked and slammed the faucet off. "Nice save, Captain."

"Aye, aye!" Imogen cried with a salute.

Micha shook his head and looked for the dish sponge, but it was nowhere to be seen. That was odd. He could have sworn...

He turned and froze. Butter was on the other counter, crouched and ready to pounce. The sponge was in his mouth, his ginger tail swishing, his ears flattened back, and his green eyes narrow slits. Micha could have sworn his expression said 'This is mine now. Fight me.'

"Or I could just get a new sponge, you monster," Micha mumbled under his breath as he dived below the sink to get a new sponge from the cupboard. That was *not* a battle he was prepared to have today.

"Sorry, Uncle Micha?"

Micha cleared his throat. "Nothing, hon. Say, what are you drawing there?"

Imogen pushed up her glasses. She had chalk smudges all over her face. There was practically a rainbow rubbed along her nose. Micha laughed, making a note to get a photo for Swift before he washed Imogen's face. He was working a late shift today, so would probably be home after her bedtime. She was surprisingly good about Swift not always being there.

She trusted he would come home.

Once her glasses were back in place, she proudly brandished a sheet of paper so covered in color it looked to be losing its structural integrity in places. Typical Imogen, always going full out on everything.

"It's for school!" she announced. "We have to draw our family! Look! That's me. That's Mommy. That's you and Daddy. And that's Butter."

If Micha was honest, he was looking at a lot of round blobs and fierce straight scribbles that could have been limbs or hair, it was hard to say. But to Micha, it was one of the most beautiful things he'd ever seen.

"Y-you put Uncle Micha on your picture?" he asked, crouching down so he was her level. She thrust the paper at him, so he took it by the corners so as not to smudge any more of the chalk.

Imogen looked perplexed. "Yes. Do you like it? Look! There are the frogs! And the toast!"

Micha had no idea why there would be frogs or toast or why the sky would be green, but honestly, that all made it all the more awesome. "I love it, hon," he said, hugging her side as he carefully gave her back her masterpiece. "Once your teacher has graded it, can we put it on the fridge?"

They already had a treasure map pinned there with a magnet. It was the drawing Imogen had done for Micha when she'd stayed with her grandparents after they'd bought cupcakes and Micha had freaked out and almost left. He'd been delighted with that picture, but this one was something else.

She considered the drawing with a little frown. "My teacher might put it on the wall at school. If it goes on the wall, I can make *another* one. Is that okay?"

Micha grinned. "Of course."

Absorbed in her work again, Micha turned back to the pan he'd been planning to scrub and also to the thought he'd been chewing on before he'd almost let the water overflow.

Things seemed to be going well with Swift. It was *nice*. It scared the shit out of Micha if he was honest, but at the same time, it was kind of amazing.

In some ways, nothing had changed. He was covering even more shifts at the diner now, so he and Swift were juggling their schedules with that and the gym and Imogen's school hours. So far, though, there had always been someone home with her, even if they'd had to subcontract in Grandma and Grandpa. Micha and Swift cooked dinners and did chores and played board games, and before bedtime, they gave Imogen her bath and read her stories.

It was after she fell asleep that things had gotten a little different.

Sometimes Swift and Micha would have a beer while they snuggled on the sofa with the TV. Sometimes they listened to music and talked, mostly reminiscing about the old days or what Swift had gotten up to during college. He never asked about Seattle, for which Micha was very grateful. That life was feeling more and more distant.

And most nights ended with brushing their teeth, some stretching for Swift, and then cuddles as they fell asleep.

The first night, Micha had hardly dared breathe, expecting Swift's hands to wander. But they'd just spooned until to Micha's surprise, Swift had fallen asleep. It was oddly charming that Swift had kept his word. He truly just wanted to cuddle.

And so it had been most other nights. Sometimes Micha was even the big spoon. He got a real kick from that. But there had only been one night so far that they'd made out properly again, and that had been when Micha had felt horny as hell, so he'd made the first move.

Swift was considerate and thoughtful and tender and, most surprisingly, fun in bed. The second time had taken a lot longer, and Swift had even let Micha go down on him. There was no pressure. Micha called the shots, and he was finally starting to feel relaxed. Like he was close to telling Swift he could make a move too, whenever he felt like it. Because if Micha was hesitant or didn't feel quite right, he was sure now he'd have the confidence to tell Swift that.

Things were feeling more balanced between them. In fact, Micha had started considering a crazy plan. He was thinking – maybe – he might stop looking for full-time jobs. If he could keep picking up shifts at the diner, then he was building up to admitting to himself and to Swift and his family that he was *possibly* considering community college.

He might not. But he also just might.

Pine Cove didn't have a college, but Penny Falls, the town over, did. Pops had dropped several hints now that he might sell his car to Micha for fifty bucks, since he was driving it all the time anyway. Pops made it sound like he was tricking

Dad into buying a new car with him, but secretly Micha suspected they knew he wouldn't just take the car. But he might 'buy' it for fifty dollars.

Micha caught his reflection in the window. It was getting dark outside, so it was more like a mirror. For a moment, he stopped to appreciate everything that was going for him right now. Yes, it was a simple life with simple goals for the time being. But he was daring to think he might be *happy*. And sure, he was starting small, but for the first time in his life, he felt like his ambition could grow. He might actually make something of his life if he wasn't careful.

The thought made him giddy.

Of course, he'd temporarily forgotten that karma was a bitch.

A knock came at the door just as Micha was done drying the pot. So he wiped his hands, winked at Imogen, then went to see who was calling. They weren't expecting anyone.

Definitely not who Micha saw when he pulled open the door. In fact, Dale and Brie were pretty much the *last* people he expected to see illuminated by the light on Swift's front porch.

"What the-?" he cried, almost taking a step back in shock. But then he gripped the side of the door, straightening his arm like a barricade. He felt his lip curl at Dale as his heart began to pound. "How did you find me?"

Dale laughed like Micha had just said something hilarious. "Perkins? Is that anyway to greet your friends? We've been worried sick about you."

Micha tried to control his breathing as his eyes flicked to Brie. To be fair, she beamed at him in relief, and he had to admit he *was* glad to see her. Her freckles had faded on her pale skin, but her red hair was just as messy up in its usual bun. He leaned forward and gave her a one-armed hug. But he wasn't letting go of that door.

"Dale," he said firmly once he let her go. "There's a reason I didn't contact you, and you know it."

Dale scoffed, sniffing and rubbing his nose. "Oh, please. You're not still upset about that, are you? I needed the cash – for the house. *We* needed it. It's not my fault you got picked up by the cops. I told you to run."

"Yes, it *was* your fault," Micha growled, feeling an anger he'd never dared direct toward Dale before. "You tricked me into going with you to commit a crime and be your getaway driver! Was that what happened to Rick, huh? Did he move away, or did he actually go to prison?" Micha had been thinking about their former housemate for a while, and he was pretty sure he knew the truth.

Dale rolled his eyes. "You're overreacting. You're here, aren't you?"

"I did two months' time served! I'm on a suspended sentence!" Micha barked. He was aware Imogen was still coloring in the kitchen, so he swore to keep his voice down after that.

"Oh, a whole two months," Dale said in a mocking tone, sniffing again.

Jesus, was he on coke again? There had been a time when his using had gotten pretty out of hand. The only thing worse than Dale arriving on his doorstep was a coked-up Dale being anywhere near Micha.

Or Imogen.

"Dude," Dale continued, "we've been *worried*. We're your family, and we didn't know where you were!"

Micha shook his head and closed the door by a few inches, hoping he could slam it in time if he needed to. "You're not my family. You abandoned me. My *real* family have supported me."

Dale tapped his chin. "Oh, you mean your *adopted* family?

You don't know who your real family is, do you? The records were sealed."

Micha didn't blame Brie for telling Dale that. Sure, he'd confessed those details about his past to her in confidence, but he should have realized by then what a manipulative and forceful shit Dale could be.

"Yeah," Dale continued, nodding as he looked between Brie and Micha. "Lucky the little missy here knew that. It meant we could find you, didn't it? A simple internet search brought up your adoption fifteen years ago. Apparently, it was *quite* the talk of the town."

He put his hand on the back of Brie's neck and rubbed the side with his thumb. It could have been seen as a comforting gesture, but Micha recognized it immediately as the threat it was. In a flash, Dale could dig his fingers in and shake her by the scruff like a puppy.

Dale sighed. "It was easy then to work out your parents own that tacky diner in what passes for a town center here. Honestly, how have you not blown your brains out from boredom yet?"

"So you followed me home from work," Micha snarled. "Well, I'm sorry you wasted the gas money. I'm not going anywhere."

Dale laughed and shook his head, his hand still on the back of Brie's neck. She flinched, ever so slightly. "Oh, I'm sure you'll come around. You don't belong in a nice place like this, Perkins. It's okay, though. You'll always have a *real* home back at the house. No hard feelings and all that."

Micha ground his teeth and scowled. "I think it's best you leave. Now."

That could have been it. It wouldn't have been good, but the situation would have been reasonably handled. Except of course it wasn't the end.

"Uncle Micha! I finished it! Who are you talking to?"

To Micha's absolute horror, Imogen pushed her way through his legs and gaped up at Brie and Dale. Brie appeared perplexed by the appearance of a small child. But Dale's face split into a dangerous grin. "Well, hello, there! Who are you?"

"Imogen," she said warily, looking him up and down. "I'm five and a quarter. Who are you?"

"He's leaving-" Micha tried to say as he scooped Imogen protectively into his arms. Luckily, she must have left her drawing on the table, so he didn't crush it.

Dale smiled like a shark. "I'm Dale, Imogen. It's *very* nice to meet you. I'm Uncle Micha's friend."

"No, you're not," Micha said, trembling. He'd never stood up to Dale before. He'd been duped into believing he owed him for so many things when the truth was, he didn't owe Dale jack shit. "Get out of here. Leave town, or I'm calling the police."

"Ooh," Dale said, sounding like a ghost as he waved his hands. At least he'd let go of Brie. "On what grounds?"

"Trespassing," Micha spat. "Harassment. Intimidation. I don't ever want to see or hear from you again." Then he looked away from Dale. He was dead to Micha, as far as he was concerned. But Brie? "Hon, you could stay," he said urgently. "You don't owe this creep anything. You don't have to listen to him."

"Oh, and what?" Dale snapped, grabbing the back of her neck again. Both Micha and Brie winced. "She's going to listen to you? *I* have her back! *You* left us when we needed you! Why the hell would she trust you?"

Brie looked scared as she opened her mouth. But then she probably knew anything she said would only make things worse, so she shut it again. Imogen whimpered into Micha's neck, hugging him as tightly as he was holding her.

"Dale-" Micha began.

But a ginger streak shot from inside the house, launching itself at Dale's pants, ten sharp claws lashing out. "What the *fuck?*" Dale bellowed as he kicked his foot.

However, Butter was too fast for him, leaping to safety behind Micha's legs with a vicious hiss that showed off all his fangs. He swiped with his paw, wrinkling his nose and growling all the way from his belly.

Dale rubbed his face and straightened up the lapels of his leather jacket. "Right, fine. Fuck you, Perkins. I'm sure we'll see you around. *Bye, Imogen.*" He gave them a nasty smirk as he waved. Then he grabbed Brie's hand to drag her back down the yard, deliberately stomping on the wood chips instead of the flagstones.

Brie glanced over her shoulder. "Wait!" Micha called to her. But then they were in a banged-up car Micha didn't recognize, spinning the wheels, kicking up stones from the street, then driving down the road.

Taking a sudden breath, he stepped back inside and slammed the door, shaking, dizzy, with his mouth salivating as he considered throwing up. He looked down at Butter in shock. But he was cleaning his paw like nothing had happened. Then he meowed, swished his tail, and stalked off back toward Imogen's room.

"That man said a bad word," Imogen said. Micha's attention was immediately back on her, brushing her hair back from her forehead as her lip wobbled.

"I know, baby," he said. His voice trembled as he picked her up and walked her down the hallway, rubbing her back. "He was a bad man, and Uncle Micha is so sorry you had to see that. He won't come back, I promise."

Micha was light-headed. That fucker had been *so close* to Imogen it made him want to scream. He'd tracked Micha down – why? To intimidate him? To force him back to Seattle? How deep were that asshole's control issues?

It wouldn't have been so bad if they'd cornered Micha on the street or a parking lot. Hell, even in or outside Sunny Side Up would have been manageable. But the fact that Micha had brought this shit to Swift's front door, literally, was deeply troubling. And he was pretty sure Dale had been high.

He dropped into one of the kitchen chairs, clutching Imogen to his chest and rocking them both back and forth as a sob escaped his throat. "It's okay," Imogen said quietly, patting Micha's arm. "Don't cry, Uncle Micha. I'm sorry."

"No, no," Micha said, pulling himself together and managing to fake a weak smile. "You don't need to say sorry. You're a good girl. Look at the amazing drawing you did. Is it finished? Can you show it to me?"

They twisted around to look at the chalk family portrait. Then Micha suggested they draw something else together. Gradually, both of them calmed down enough to stop trembling and start smiling again.

Micha abandoned the fancy veggies and microwaved them some macaroni and cheese for dinner instead. At least Imogen ate most of hers. He barely managed a couple of bites. His stomach was still rolling with fright. It was going to be okay, he told himself. He'd save the special dinner for when Swift was home. That would be better, anyway, to share with all three of them.

Micha attached Imogen's new drawing to the fridge with one of the new novelty magnets Swift had collected over the past few weeks. The drawing was a pirate ship that Micha had helped a little to draw and then let Imogen color it in all its crazy glory. It and all the other art made the room so vastly different to the sterile, monochrome kitchen it had been only a few weeks ago.

Micha was proud of himself. He made it all the way through bath time and through reading one of Imogen's favorite stories from Kestrel's rebel girl book. Then he kissed Imogen on the head and turned her nightlight on. As he did, Butter leaped onto the bed, curling against Imogen's chest and neck, purring loudly as soon as she hugged him close.

"Good kitty," Micha whispered, meaning it for the first time ever.

Then he pulled Imogen's door almost all the way closed, made sure the baby monitor was working on Swift's nightstand, crawled under Swift's covers, and cried himself to sleep.

19

SWIFT

NORMALLY WHEN SWIFT CLOSED UP THE GYM AND CAME HOME late, Micha was still awake, waiting for him. But when he arrived back that evening, all the lights were off, aside from the glow coming from the crack between the door and doorframe into Imogen's room. Her night light and glow-in-the-dark stars led Swift's way as he tiptoed through the house.

Even though she was sound asleep, Swift sat on her bed and leaned down to give her a kiss on the forehead. Butter gave him a fright as he silently jumped onto the mattress, stalking toward Imogen's pillows, purring. But as Swift froze, expecting to get a scratching, Butter just threw himself down against Imogen's form under the comforter. She reached out in her sleep, placing her hand on his back.

Swift stared down at the cat, but for once, the ginger creature simply stared back.

Using the flashlight on his phone to navigate, Swift pottered around the house. He dumped his dirty laundry into the hamper in the utility room just off the kitchen to do tomorrow, stretched, then raided the fridge for a snack to eat before brushing his teeth. His heart melted as his eyes landed on a Post-it note attached to a wrapped-up sandwich. Micha might have gone to bed already, but the simple heart on the sticky label was almost as sweet as a kiss from the man himself.

Swift took his time munching through the bread and tasty fillings, scrolling idly through his social media to help his brain wind down from work. Then he placed his plate in the dishwasher before dutifully using his electric toothbrush for a timed two minutes. Yawning, he made his way into his bedroom as quietly as possible, hoping Micha wouldn't mind if he slipped his arms around him for a cuddle.

Swift couldn't believe how lucky he was that this was his life now. It was a dream.

Or so he thought.

"Swift?" Micha mumbled as soon as Swift wrapped his arm around him to spoon a little.

"Yeah, it's me. It's okay. Go back to sleep, hon."

But Micha let out an anguished cry and turned in his arms, grabbing Swift's T-shirt and burying his face in his chest. "Oh, Swift! I'm so sorry! It's all my fault! I never meant to cause any trouble! If you want me to leave, I understand."

"Hey, no, shush," Swift said soothingly despite his complete confusion. "It's fine, Micha. What's wrong? What happened?" Fear lanced through his chest, even though he'd just been in his daughter's room. "Is Imogen okay?"

"Yes, yes, she's fine." Micha scrubbed his face and gave Swift a wretched look in the near dark. "But the douchebag I used to live with showed up *at your front door.*"

Swift felt his eyebrows rise, unable to stop the slight alarm that filled him. "Are you okay? What did he want?"

Micha took a shaky breath. "He's trying to get me to come back to the house in Seattle. I think he hates the fact that I 'got away' from him or some shit. I told him 'no' and slammed the door."

Swift exhaled. "Good, that's good!" He rubbed Micha's arm and kissed his cheek. "That was the best way to handle it. If there are any other issues, we can contact the police."

Micha gave him a weak smiled and sighed. "I also told him that."

"Excellent. In fact," Swift said, "let's call the police tomorrow anyway and just let them know we've had an incident. That way it's on file. Okay?"

"That's a great idea." But Micha didn't look entirely convinced. "I just feel awful. If I wasn't staying here, he would never have shown up. He's bad news, Swift."

Swift hugged him close and rubbed his back. "It's just one of those things," he assured him, meaning it. "Sometimes bad things happen. It's not your fault. I don't blame you."

Even though Swift really didn't like the idea of anyone problematic hanging around his house or getting anywhere near Imogen, he absolutely didn't blame Micha. He'd been tricked into almost breaking the law, and this guy had shown up unannounced and uninvited.

"I'm just going to deadbolt the door," Swift said.

Micha nodded as he kissed his cheek and gave his shoulders a squeeze, then slipped from the bed. He didn't just double-lock the front door, but he also made sure the back was secure and all the windows, which he knew had security glass. Happier they were definitely safe, he hurried back to Micha, wrapping him up in his arms again.

"I swear," Micha said as he clung tightly to Swift's back and rested his temple on his shoulder, "I never told him the town name or anything. He tracked me down."

"Asshole," Swift growled. "Well, hopefully now you've told him 'no' in person, that's the end of it. You're safe with me, baby."

Micha released a shuddery breath and nuzzled their cheeks together. The feel of stubble was novel to Swift, but he really liked it. He wasn't sure if it was a general man thing or he just liked it because it was part of Micha, but he figured it didn't really matter.

"I know I'm safe with you," Micha murmured as he carded his fingers through the back of Swift's hair. "Even as a teenager, you made me feel like I was wanted. I'm glad you came back after college."

"I'm glad you came back after Seattle," Swift said, trailing little kisses along Micha's jaw.

They hugged tighter, Swift's thigh nudging between Micha's legs as they started to kiss. This wasn't a sweet goodnight or even a way to calm down after a fright. There was passion beginning to simmer. It tingled in Swift's belly… and below. His heartbeat was picking up, and his breaths became more ragged.

"Micha," he murmured against his lips.

Micha whimpered. They both knew they had to be quiet, but that kind of made the desperation more intense. "Want you," he mumbled as he dug his fingers into Swift's back.

"You've got me," he assured between kisses. They were slightly sloppy as tongues and lips clashed, hungry for more.

But Micha shook his head, tugging at Swift's T-shirt. They were both clearly starting to harden in their briefs. Swift's heart skipped a beat.

"Hang on a second, baby," he said softly, stilling Micha's hands. "You're upset."

Micha nodded. "I was, but you're here, and everything's okay again, and I just *want* you." Then he froze, looking up at Swift with concern. "Sorry, sorry," he said breathlessly, letting go of his pajama top. "This is – you haven't – I'll calm down."

Swift cupped Micha's face with his hand. "If you're

worried I haven't been completely naked with a man before, that's not the issue. Or that I haven't done anything more than our fumbling, that's fine. But you were just crying. I want you – badly – but only if it's not too fast."

Micha spluttered a little giggle, then covered his mouth, his eyebrows raised. "Too fast?" he said, dropping his hand. "Swift, I wanted you when I was fifteen. This is ten years in the making. I-" He closed his eyes and exhaled. When he looked at Swift again, his expression was serious. "I want to take comfort in you. A lot. But this is *your* first time, so it should be special and not just any old sex."

Swift smiled and stroked Micha's hair back from his face. "I've had a lot of sex, sweetheart. But if I'm going to pop my man cherry, I'd be honored to share that with you. Kestrel's always telling us how virginity is a social construct, but I think it's kind of nice to share your firsts with special people if you can."

Micha smiled shyly, biting his lip. "You think I'm special?"

"Very," Swift assured him.

The truth was, Swift was extremely excited at the idea that he and Micha might move things forward, but he wanted to make sure it was under the right circumstances. He'd had his doubts that now was the right time. However, Micha was kissing him like it was the breath of life, his lips strong and needy against Swift's as he rolled his hips and thickening length against Swift's thigh. If he wanted comfort from Swift as desperately as he said he did, Swift was happy to give that to him.

More than happy.

He'd been getting familiar with Micha's lovely body over the past several nights. He'd been mapping his tattoos and gently touching all the secret places, like along his clavicle or the inside of his elbow. He wasn't sure Micha thought they were making out when he did that, but to Swift, that stuff was fucking crack. He *loved* the way Micha's eyelids fluttered closed and all the little breathy moans he let escape.

And now Swift was going to share everything with him.

He adored the dips between Micha's waist and hips. It was a subtle curve, but Swift's hands fit perfectly, just like his lips fit perfectly behind his jaw and under his earlobe. He'd been daydreaming of all the things he and Micha could do together in the dark, safe under the covers. Swift liked it here, where he could protect Micha from all the crap the world tried to throw at him. Now he wanted to please him, to make him wild with desire.

Micha Perkins didn't seem to appreciate how precious he was. So Swift was going to show him.

"Can I suck you?" Swift asked, nibbling at Micha's ear and playing with his nipples. They were always so quick to harden, eager for Swift's fingers to pinch and twist them. They'd only made out to completion once since that first night, but Swift was starting to feel like an expert in Micha's body. He hummed against Micha's throat, feeling him whine through his lips. If Micha wanted to lose himself in Swift, Swift was happy to take charge and make him as deliriously happy as he could. "Been fantasizing about your cock."

"You're killing me," Micha squeaked, grabbing Swift's face for another messy kiss. "Of course you can suck my dick. But if you want to fuck me, you probably can't do it for long. I feel like I might explode any second."

Swift rubbed his fingers along Micha's chest and throat, brushing his knuckles across his cheek. "You want to bottom?" He might not have had sex with a man before, but he'd tried anal with women and had been reading up on gay sex practices. He felt pretty confident topping so long as Micha didn't just expect it to be that way just because Swift was physically larger. He'd be happy trying it the other way around, he was sure.

But Micha was panting, his cock leaking against his briefs as his hands moved frantically over Swift's chest and shoulders, like he wasn't sure where he wanted to grab most. "Love it. I *love* bottoming. Usually it's with strangers. Want you inside me, Swift. *Need* it."

Swift kissed him hungrily, slipping his hand into his underwear and giving Micha's cock a tight squeeze that made him moan as loudly as he dared into Swift's mouth. He knew from experience wrapping his fingers around the base of his own cock stalled his orgasm while he was getting head, and if Micha wanted him inside him, Swift wanted them to come together.

"I'm going to swallow your pretty cock, baby," he whispered as Micha whimpered and bit his lip. "Then you're going to be the first man I ever fuck. Because you're amazing."

"Swift," Micha begged. Single tears leaked from his eyes, but Swift knew they weren't from sadness. They were from overstimulation, and he loved that. He brushed them away with his thumb and kissed Micha's closed eyelids.

"I'm right here, darling."

"Want that. Want you. Please."

Swift kissed his gorgeous lips a little longer while he stroked the wet, satiny skin of his hardening dick. He was like hot steel under his fingers. Swift was eager to taste it.

So he began kissing his way down his neck, finding that thorny rose tattoo he liked so much above his heart, then sucking on his hard nipple for a moment. *God,* he loved the way Micha was squirming under him, panting lightly, his skin damp, and his hands fluttering over Swift's back and through his hair. He was so vibrant and responsive to Swift's every touch, like he'd been starved of it.

In a way, Swift understood. It wasn't like he'd known this

was how his feelings would develop, but being close to Micha felt natural. Like it was meant to be.

There was a thatch of dark curls at Micha's crotch that Swift nuzzled his nose through, inhaling his unique musk. Swift's dick was so hard now, throbbing in his briefs, begging for attention. But part of the fun was ignoring it, letting it get harder from the inadequate friction of his underwear. By the time he sunk into Micha, he wanted to be desperate for him.

He licked a stripe up the underside of Micha's erection, looking up as Micha clamped his hand over his mouth to make sure he didn't get too loud. Swift adored knowing he was driving his lover crazy.

To start with, Swift just slipped his mouth over Micha's tip, running his tongue over the leaking slit and pressing tightly with his lips, which he'd wrapped around his teeth. He jerked off Micha gently with his hand at the base, getting used to his feel and flavor. It was slightly bitter, but Swift didn't really care either way about that. He cared that Micha's hips were jumping off the bed, chasing Swift's mouth and throat with his desperate cock. He cared that Micha was whispering *"Swift, Swift, Swift,"* like a prayer. He cared that this might have been brand new to him, but he didn't feel out of his depth in the slightest, because he was here with Micha, and that was what they did.

They worked things out together, as a team.

Swift could have kept going like that for much longer. He was eager to try deep throating after Micha had done it to him. But they'd agreed on going all the way. Swift wanted to feel as connected to Micha as he possibly could. So with one last suck, he popped off the top of his cock, kissing the top and in the dip where Micha's leg met his groin.

"Do you want to stretch out?" he asked as he came back up to kiss along Micha's jaw. He looked blissed out already, and his breaths were light and shallow. It was so beautiful how he didn't have a care in the world other than the pleasure Swift was giving him.

He nodded, meeting Swift's gaze. "Just a bit would help. Oh, shit. Do you have protection?"

"I bought condoms, yeah," Swift said. They couldn't get pregnant, but there were other things to consider, and Swift had meant it in every way when he'd promised to keep Micha safe. "And lube. Do you want to stretch while I suit up?"

Micha nodded, but he also leaned up, capturing Swift's mouth with needy little kisses. "Fuck, you're amazing," he gasped as their lips parted for a second. "Everything's so easy with you."

Swift kissed him some more, grinding down on top of him. "That's the way it should be," he whispered.

Micha's briefs were around his thighs still, so he kicked them off as Swift discarded his own pair on the floor. Eagerly, he reached for a condom from the box, then passed Micha the fresh bottle of lube he'd picked up. It wouldn't take him as long to get the condom on as it would for Micha to squeeze his fingers inside him, so as soon as he'd squirted out some of the gel, Swift started kissing his neck, looking down his body as he played with his hole, forcing that first finger beyond the tight ring of muscle.

"You're so hot, Micha," he moaned, watching him fuck his fingers with a growing need in his belly. A possessive claim washed over him to make Micha his right the hell now. "You look so pretty like that."

Micha whimpered, adding a second finger and kissing Swift's mouth urgently. "Fuck it," he mumbled. "That'll do. Just use lots of lube. I can't wait anymore."

Swift laughed, obediently ripping the condom wrapper open to roll it down his cock. He knew he would take his part in this slowly, so he didn't mind if Micha got impatient now.

"Are you okay lying like this?" Swift asked.

He'd seen all kinds of positions in porn, but he honestly had no idea what they felt like. He was glad when Micha nodded, though. He wanted to stay facing so they could keep kissing.

"Wait a sec," Micha said.

He reached for a pillow and wriggled to slide it under his hips. Then he held on to his knees. Seeing him display himself like that was honestly mouthwatering. After diligently smothering his cock with more lube, Swift maneuvered himself between Micha's legs, kissing his soft tummy as he angled his hard cock against his hole, rubbing the wet tip against the tight entrance.

Micha nodded, drenched in sweat and flushed all over his face and chest. He looked beyond beautiful. "Like that," he rasped. "Just push, slowly. I can take it."

Swift nodded. "I know you can, gorgeous."

Even just breaching his threshold felt so good. His muscles squeezed Swift's cock deliciously, forcing him to catch his breath. He could see Micha gritting his teeth and taking steady breaths, but when Swift reached up to cup his face, he nodded.

"I'm okay," he said, his voice hoarse. Then he moved his mouth, capturing Swift's thumb to suck it, hard.

"Fuck," said Swift as he breathed out, his throat suddenly dry and his cock throbbing even more. "Yes, baby, so good."

Gradually, Swift slid as far as he could inside Micha, who was now panting so much Swift pulled his thumb away. Instead, he held his weight up with one hand and gripped Micha's hip with the other. Micha wrapped his legs around Swift's waist, then reached up to hold Swift's neck and torso.

"Move, please," Micha hissed, leaning up to kiss Swift on

the mouth. Perspiration ran down Swift's arms and dripped from his forehead. He felt completely free and almost like he was on fire.

"Fuck, baby," he moaned, and he slowly retracted, then drove his cock back into Micha's hot body. "You feel amazing, so perfect."

Micha nodded frantically. "Faster, Swift. Touch my cock. Make me come."

Swift tried to keep his eyes on Micha as he began to thrust in earnest, his hand wrapped around his hot, wet dick. But their foreheads naturally came to rest together as they gyrated, Swift's eyelids dropping as his climax began to build.

"Feels so good," Micha murmured. "Like that, don't stop." He jerked and gasped, digging his fingers into Swift's arms, making Swift hope he was hitting his prostate. It felt amazing knowing he was doing this right for Micha. Not that he would ever judge Swift, he was sure, but he took a certain amount of pride at making his boyfriend happy on the first attempt.

Was that what they were? Boyfriends?

His thoughts were pulled back into the moment as Micha buckled and started to come all over his chest. Swift had seen him come twice before, but there was something so much more primal about witnessing it while Swift was connected deep inside him. Swift sped up, no longer holding anything back, but seeing Micha climax had been enough to tip him over the edge. Within seconds, he was also coming hard, filling the condom as he gathered Micha into his arms and clutched him tightly.

It took several moments to come down from his high. The room was pungent with the smell of their cum and sweat, the tang revitalizing Swift as he inhaled deeply, snapping back to his senses. It was like the air was thick with the care and affection between him and Micha.

There was no hurry to pull out. As he softened, Swift kissed the side of Micha's neck and rubbed his arm. "That was so good," he murmured.

Micha hummed, trailing his fingers lazily along Swift's back as his ankles fell heavily on either side of them. "It was *amazing*," he said sleepily. "I call bullshit, though. That was never your first time."

Swift snorted and gently eased himself out. Really, they should probably have a quick wash, but he was overcome with exhaustion, and Micha looked even worse. So Swift carefully pinched the condom and slid it and its contents off to discard it in a ball of tissue, then handed a couple to Micha so he could mop up a little for comfort. It wasn't that Swift wanted to rub all signs of their glorious tryst off himself right away. He just wanted to be slightly less sticky for when he scooped Micha up in his arms.

Which was exactly what he did next, yanking the comforter over their legs as they spooned together. "Sex is sex, babe," Swift mumbled into Micha's hair. "Apparently, the parts don't matter to me. But the *person* matters very much. And you are wonderful. Perfect."

Micha looked over his shoulder, and they shared a chaste kiss. *"You're* wonderful," he mumbled, his eyelids already drooping. But Swift had one last thing to say before they slept.

"Hey, Micha? Hon?" He slowly blinked his eyes open again. Swift smiled at him. "Whatever happens with your old housemate, we'll work things out together. I've got your back. You can always talk to me about anything, okay?"

Micha smiled drunkenly, patting Swift's arm. "Yes, Swift, okay," he slurred.

Within twenty seconds, he was gently snoring.

Swift didn't mind, though. In fact, he loved that Micha felt confident enough to be that relaxed around him. So he snuggled up next to his damp, naked, slightly sticky man, hugging him close as sleep finally claimed him in a deeply contented stupor.

20

MICHA

"So, do you understand what we're saying, Imogen?" Swift asked as he and Micha sat with Imogen at the kitchen table. Micha was glad Swift was doing all the talking. He wasn't sure he could say a word with his heart lodged in his throat like it was.

Swift was holding Micha's hand, their fingers threaded together and resting on top of the table where Imogen could clearly see them.

That was sort of the point.

"That Micha is your special friend, Daddy?" she seemed confused, and Micha thought he might be sick. He didn't know what he would do if their coming out upset Imogen. She was just a child, but Micha was embarrassed to admit how much her approval mattered to him. They could always help to educate her, but she was frowning at them, and he thought his heart might break. But then she blinked and pushed her glasses up her nose to peer at them harder. "I know that," she said almost scornfully. "You said we love Uncle Micha, and he loves us, and he's going to stay living here, like me."

"Well, uh..." Micha said. They hadn't discussed permanent living arrangements. That seemed *way* too fast for him to officially move in. But Swift just beamed at his daughter and squeezed Micha's hand.

"That's right, little bit. We do love Uncle Micha. So you might see Daddy and him cuddling or holding hands or even a kiss here and there."

"Eww!" she cried with a giggle. "Mushy, mushy!"

"Yeah, mushy, mushy," Swift said, rolling his eyes as he reached over to tickle her side. She shrieked and wriggled.

Micha watched on in a sort of daze. He knew Swift was just repeating Imogen's word, but had he really just said 'love'?

"So Uncle Micha is your boyfriend?" Imogen said, swinging her legs where she was sitting on the slightly too high chair. She was ready for school with her backpack already on. Micha had wanted to wait when they had more time to talk, but Swift had begged him while using his magic hands and lips. He said he didn't want to wait a second more, and Micha had never been so flattered in his life.

But 'boyfriend'? *Crap*, they really hadn't thought this through at all.

"Maybe, hon," Swift said calmly. "Right now, we're special friends, and we wanted you to be the first to know."

Imogen laughed. "Daddy? I already knew. And so does Grandma, and my friend, Cathy, and Lonnie on the bus..." She jumped down from the table and skipped over to the hallway. "Come on! We're going to be late!"

"Did she-" Micha spluttered. "What?"

Swift looked mildly horrified. Then he laughed and kissed Micha's cheek. "I guess that's that," he said as he also stood.

"That's what? Swift?"

He grinned and cupped Micha's face to kiss him on the

lips. "I'll see you after work, sweetheart. Have a good day."

Micha managed to gather his wits together to walk to the door in order to wave Swift and Imogen off. Then it was just him, left to his own thoughts.

He giggled in the quiet, then clamped his hand over his mouth.

This didn't mean he was no longer worried sick about Dale and what he might try and pull. But it had been a couple of days since the incident at the door, and Micha hadn't heard a peep. He had messaged Brie a couple of times with no response, and while he wasn't giving up on her, he couldn't deny the relief he felt at no further nastiness from Dale.

It was unfair to say this was the first time he'd had support in his life. Eventually, he'd come to accept his parents' and siblings' love and care. But it would be forever tainted by the truly awful beginning they'd had as a family thanks to Micha's behavior. With Swift, it felt like a clean slate, a fresh start. Swift's life had been completely turned upside down by the arrival of Imogen, but instead of everything falling apart, Swift had gravitated toward Micha and together, all three of them had begun to bloom.

After her first week at school, Swift had met with Imogen's teacher, who had assured him that she was settling in well, working hard, and making friends. Basically, exactly what any parent wanted to hear. Micha was getting into a routine at the diner, even making friends with some of the staff he wasn't related to. And Swift was getting better at leaving toys out on the floor and not tidying them away the second Imogen wasn't looking. He'd even left Legos out in the living room the other day…unfortunately Micha had realized that the hard way, but after he'd finished cussing, he was oddly proud of Swift.

Their little…unit, would that be the best word? Anyway,

the three of them were getting along swimmingly, and Micha might even argue they were thriving.

It was what gave him the motivation to get his crappy but still functioning laptop out and set himself up in the kitchen for the day. He didn't have a shift later, so he wanted to take the chance to spend some productive hours researching. If he was going to apply to community college, he needed to brush up on some things and take a hard look at what classes he might want to enroll in. Because the more he thought about it, the stronger he felt this was what he wanted for himself.

He wanted more. And until now, he'd been too afraid to ask for it.

A couple of hours passed as he lost himself in an online course on improving his grammar. He was also looking into brushing up on his ALS, as, incredibly, Penny Falls offered a qualification in signing. He thought about all the times Carlee could have benefited from an interpreter. The college also offered an art class he reckoned he might do okay in, as well as a course on early childhood development and education.

It was almost unbelievable that he was really considering these things for himself. When was the last time he took a step back and asked himself what he thought he was good at? Maybe never. But thanks to Swift's never-wavering support and confidence in him, there he was, giving serious consideration to his future.

In between, he fed both Butter and the washing machine, rearranged some of the dishes in the cupboards, then even managed a bit of vacuuming. That ginger hair got everywhere, but after the other day, Micha didn't mind so much.

He was just starting to think about signing up for an online math refresher course before he'd need to walk down to the bus stop to greet Imogen when there was a knock at the door. Fear flashed through him as his mind instantly replayed who'd knocked last time and what had happened. But there was no reason to believe Dale would come back, especially not in broad daylight. Who knew? Maybe it was early trick-or-treaters? The 31st was a few days off still, but it could well be.

As Micha shook himself and finally answered the door, he discovered it was neither a blast from his past nor children seeking candy.

It was a police officer.

Two, actually. A man in uniform and a woman in a pants suit who Micha guessed was a detective.

If he'd thought his blood had run cold before, it was nothing compared to now.

Sweat broke out all over his body, his vision swam, and he thought he might throw up. For real, not like when he'd been anxious over Imogen's response to his and Swift's news.

This was in a 'is my life over?' sort of way.

His first, awful thought was that there had been an accident involving either Swift or Imogen. His second awful thought was that they were here to cart him back off to jail after all.

He'd take prison in a heartbeat. *Please,* he begged silently as he took in the badges before him, *don't let anything have happened to my family.* Oh, fuck! That was the other possibility! Were his folks and siblings okay?

"H-hello?" he stammered.

The woman smiled. "Hi, there," she said in a formal but not aggressive tone. "We're here to speak with a Micha Perkins?"

"T-that's me." She was smiling. It wasn't reaching her eyes, but if she had really bad news, she wouldn't be smiling, surely? Micha cleared his throat. "How can I help?"

"Mr. Perkins," said the woman with a nod. She was maybe

late-thirties, slim, with her brown hair slicked into a ponytail and bangs swept to the side. She hooked her thumbs into her pants' pockets and leaned back into the heels of her boots. "I'm Detective Padilla. This is Officer Wynn. We're here to ask you a few questions, if you don't mind?"

"Sure," Micha said. He resisted the urge to fold his arms over his chest. Instead he copied Padilla and slipped his hands into his jeans' pockets. He needed something to quell his anxiety. "Is everything okay? No one's, um, hurt, are they?"

"Oh, no," Padilla frowned, but the way she shook her head was deeply assuring. "Nothing like that.

"Can you account for your whereabouts last night, Mr. Perkins?" Officer Wynn asked gruffly. He was blond and muscular but in a stone statue sort of way. Completely different to warm and cheerful Swift. His hand rested on the handle of his gun. It might have been holstered, but just seeing it made Micha's stomach flip. "Between the hours of ten p.m. and midnight?"

"Uh..." Micha was completely thrown by the question. "Last night? I was here."

"Can anyone verify that, sir?" Wynn all but sneered.

It was subtle, but Micha caught Padilla roll her eyes. "Officer Wynn, I believe I've got this in hand. Can you wait by the car?"

From the tightness of his jaw, Micha wondered if Wynn maybe wasn't particularly happy that his superior officer was a woman. But he swaggered back to the patrol car that was parked on the curb in front of Swift's house.

Micha spotted a curtain twitch from the other side of the road. *Oh, shit.* Who knew what people might be saying already?

Padilla turned back to Micha. "Okay. Neat. Uhh...so, last night. You were home?"

Micha released a deep breath. He *had* been home. He had nothing to hide! "Yes, I was here. With my, um, friend. We just watched some TV." He shrugged, embarrassed. "Boring."

Padilla rubbed the bridge of her nose. "Oh, better than filling out paperwork, trust me. Well, Mr. Perkins, at approximately eleven o'clock last night, the Farm Fresh grocery store was robbed at gunpoint just as they were closing up. No one was hurt," Padilla said hastily before Micha could interject, "but they emptied the cash register. Eyewitnesses report a man and a young woman." Padilla pointedly licked her lips and fixed Micha with a stare. "Then we got an anonymous phone call not long ago naming you as a potential suspect."

A wave of dizziness washed through Micha, but he clung to the door frame and kept his eyes on Padilla. "Oh, right." He couldn't think what else to say.

Padilla shook her head. "I took this position to get *out* of Seattle and away from violent crime, you know? Now, it's just…" She shook her head. "Anyway. You were here, and you have witnesses, yes?"

"Yes, ma'am," Micha said sincerely.

Padilla clicked her tongue and gave him half a smile. "Don't call me ma'am. It's…stuffy. Okay. Look, between you and me, some folks hear a whiff of gossip, and they haven't got anything else better to do than whip themselves into a frenzy. I'm aware of the situation with your recent arrest, but I trust you're being careful while you're on your suspended sentence?"

"Oh, yes, ma-Detective," Micha stuttered. "Not even jaywalking, I swear. I don't want any trouble."

Padilla nodded, then jerked her chin toward Swift's house. "Then you might want to inform your probation officer of your change of address. We went to your folks' place first."

Icy dread flushed through Micha. He hadn't even thought of that, but of course he had to let them know he'd moved. Initially, he had only intended on staying here for a night or two, so it had totally slipped his mind. Holy shit, that could be considered a violation!

"Of course," he said, his voice sounding strangled in his panic. "I didn't...I mean-"

Padilla arched an eyebrow and shook her head once. "It's okay. You only moved here yesterday, didn't you?"

Micha stared at her for a second. "Y-yes," he stammered. Technically, they'd only just discussed any kind of long-term living arrangement that morning. So it wasn't a *total* lie.

"Thought so," said Padilla, a smile playing on her lips. "Also, I couldn't help but notice that a Mr. Coal notified the department just yesterday regarding an individual connected to your case in Seattle. He reported that you'd had to ask him to leave the premises. This is Mr. Coal's house, correct?"

Micha bit his lip and nodded. "Uh, yeah," he admitted. "It's been a weird few days."

Padilla narrowed her eyes. Then she hummed and nodded. "All right, then. Well, I have to say 'don't leave town.'" She huffed and began walking down the porch steps. "And if there's anything else that comes to mind that you'd like to discuss, you just call the department and ask for me. Anything at all. In the meantime..." She narrowed her eyes at him.

"Stay out of trouble," Micha blurted, nodding. "I promise."

Padilla saluted, turned, and strode toward the patrol car, where Wynn was leaning, waiting for her. He glowered in Micha's direction before yanking open the passenger side door and dropping into the car.

Micha waited until they'd driven out of sight before angrily slamming the front door shut and grabbing his hair with his hands. He let out a primal sort of scream and stomped his foot.

The general store had been robbed by a masked man and young woman, and then someone had anonymously suggested it had been Micha behind it?

It didn't take a genius to smell Dale's dirty fingers all over that.

The *bastard*. When bullying Micha back to him had failed, Dale had turned his hand to framing him. What the hell had Micha ever done to him to deserve that? He'd even protected his worthless ass when he'd been arrested, swearing blind that he hadn't seen him with any iPads.

Now it seemed Dale was determined to stay in town as long as it took to ruin Micha's life for good. Well, fuck that shit, quite frankly. Micha was squeaky clean, and he wasn't leaving Pine Cove.

It struck him like a blow from a baseball bat that for the first time ever he had a life worth fighting for here. He had a budding relationship with a gorgeous, kind, hot-as-hell man. He had a kid who he adored that looked up to him. He had a semi-regular paycheck. He was slowly…*very* slowly… building a better relationship with his parents and siblings.

Hopefully Padilla would catch Dale. Perhaps Micha could do some digging and call in an anonymous tip of his own? That would certainly get Dale away from Brie and stop him dragging her into another fucking felony. But Micha wasn't going to be cowed. He wasn't going to run back to Dale and beg his forgiveness. He certainly wasn't going to go back to Seattle with him. No way.

What he was going to do was take a deep breath, splash some cold water on his face, then walk down the road to wait for Imogen at the bus stop. For the first time in possibly forever, he was in charge of his own destiny.

Or so he thought.

21

SWIFT

"Babe, you have nothing to hide," Swift said firmly as he hugged Micha tightly that night. "It sounds like Padilla knows that too. She handled that incident with Scout and Emery a couple of months ago and seemed on the level."

Micha sighed and nodded against his chest. "I know, thank you. It just seems like I'm always coming to you with problems."

"That's what couples do," Swift said, kissing the top of his head. "We're really good at working together on things. I don't want you to bottle this up."

They were lying on the sofa with some documentary playing quietly on the TV. Imogen was already in bed, and they probably wouldn't stay up much longer. But Swift was grateful Micha had told him about the police at the door. Unlike hearing about Dale and his threat – which had seriously upset Swift, more than he'd let Micha know – this break-in thing was just a misunderstanding.

As much as Swift loved his hometown, he knew it was just like anywhere else and had its fair share of close-minded people. Micha seemed to think it had been Dale who had phoned in the anonymous tip. But it wasn't exactly a secret that Micha had spent a couple of months in jail, especially with him working at his folks' diner. People liked to gossip. It was just human nature. So probably someone thought they were very clever in suggesting Micha could have been the one to rob Farm Fresh. But he'd been at home with Swift, and Swift would have zero problem standing up and testifying to that fact.

He looked down at Micha, who appeared lost in thought as he played with the material of Swift's T-shirt. He was so beautiful. Swift was amazed he'd ever thought he could keep his hands off him. Knowing Micha had held a torch for him all these years was kind of as sad as it was flattering, but at least Swift had realized in time. It would have been beyond tragic if he'd lived his life never knowing what it was like to hold Micha Perkins in his arms.

"What are you thinking about, baby?" he asked.

Micha bit his lip and peeked up through his eyelashes. "Are we a couple?" he asked.

A smile crept over Swift's mouth. "Well…I'm not seeing anyone else. I don't intend to, either. And the sex is fucking spectacular."

"Swift, shush!" Micha hissed with a giggle.

But Swift kissed his lips instead. "What? Imogen's asleep."

Micha prodded his chest. "I know, but…"

"Be my boyfriend," Swift blurted out.

Micha froze, then turned his eyes up to Swift's. "Huh?"

Swift licked his lips and rubbed Micha's arm. "You don't seem all that comfortable with me talking about us out loud. Like you don't really believe it. I promised not to take things too fast, but the fact is that I do feel like we are a couple. We're having great sex, exclusively. You're living here. I'm so happy. So…if it's too fast to do the label thing, I understand.

But if it's not too fast...do you want to be my boyfriend, Micha Perkins?"

"Officially?" Micha squeaked.

Swift nodded. "Whenever you're ready, I'm happy to start coming out to friends and family. I told Rhett I was bi, and he might have guessed who I had feelings for-"

"Oh, god." Micha laughed and covered his face with his hands.

"-but I'm sure both our families will be very happy for us. And our friends." Swift brushed Micha's dark hair back. "How could they not be?"

Micha's smile became bigger as he dropped his hands and stared at Swift's chest in thought. Then he looked him in the eye.

"I'd love to be your boyfriend," he whispered.

Swift felt fit to burst he was so happy. He cupped either side of Micha's face, kissing him eagerly. Micha's hands swept over his chest and arms, digging into his back as he rolled on top of Swift. He'd been getting more confident in the bedroom, and Swift had to admit it was one hell of a turn-on.

"Come here, *boyfriend*," Swift said with a grin, pulling him off the sofa and toward the bedroom. "I want you on top of me where we won't be interrupted."

Micha laughed and covered his mouth like he was scandalized, but there was a sparkle in his eyes. Swift quietly closed his bedroom door and tugged at Micha's Henley.

It didn't take long for them to get naked and pull back the covers. Swift fell backward onto the mattress, hauling Micha up to straddle his hips, their straining junk rubbing together. Micha blushed as Swift ran his hands up his thighs, drinking in every inch of his beautiful body.

"You're perfect," he murmured, reaching up for a kiss. Micha obediently leaned down to meet him halfway.

"You're perfect," he insisted.

Micha had been showing Swift different ways to have sex that didn't involve penetration. So Swift didn't hesitate to wrap his fingers around both their cocks and start jerking them off. Micha rocked into his touch, panting against Swift's mouth. But Swift had been enjoying watching his lover – his *boyfriend.*

"Lean back, baby," he rasped. "Put your hands behind your head."

Micha breathed deeply, then kissed the corner of Swift's mouth. Their eyes locked, he leaned back, interlinking his fingers behind his head, exposing his slim torso with all his stunning tattoos, just for Swift's pleasure.

"Fuck, you're gorgeous. *So* gorgeous."

"Swift," Micha whispered, biting his lip as he twitched involuntarily at Swift's touch. Swift reached up to grab his hip and hold him steady as he jerked them both harder.

"I want you to come all over me, baby. You're mine, and you're so precious."

Micha's chest was rising and falling as he gasped for breath. *"Swift."*

It didn't take much longer. It seemed Micha enjoyed squirming under Swift's gaze as much as Swift loved watching him. He was beautiful as he arched his back and began squirting his load all up Swift's chest. Swift groaned at the delicious sight, feeling his own orgasm build. Before he could jerk himself to completion, Micha took a breath, dropped his hands, then scrambled down the bed, swallowing Swift's cock with gusto.

Swift had to stuff his fist into his mouth to stop from crying out. But he was close and Micha's throat felt so incredible as he bobbed up and down. Within seconds, Swift was coming hard, gripping on to Micha's hair as he did.

A few moments later his senses came back to him and he

started to soften. Micha licked and kissed his sensitive cock, then crawled back up the bed with a grin like the cat who'd smashed the crystal vase.

"How was that, *boyfriend?*"

Swift snorted and pulled Micha down to him for a filthy kiss, tasting himself on his tongue. "I could tease you and say I wasn't sure and that we needed to do it several more times. But I can't lie. That was spectacular."

Micha blushed, nuzzling his nose. "And the good news is that I really like you, so we can do that anytime you like."

"Oh, really?" Swift asked suggestively.

"In fact," Micha said, swirling his finger through the cum on Swift's chest, "I think it's only fair if I help you clean up, too. Do you think two people can fit under your shower?"

Swift waggled his eyebrows. "Only one way to find out."

"And then the ponies climbed the mountain because the bad fairy was chasing them," Imogen was telling Swift at a million miles an hour. "But they had the magic leaf! So they were able to turn invisible!"

Swift honestly wasn't sure if she was describing a TV show she'd watched, a game she'd been playing, or a dream she'd had. But seeing as for once they were early to the bus stop and she was clearly excited, Swift smiled and listened earnestly, happy that she was happy.

He had been wondering more and more what the hell he'd done to fill his days before Imogen had come along and filled his life with so much joy. He'd gone to the gym more, but now Micha was around, helping him get a different kind of workout in. Those PT sessions were far more fun than a stupid run.

Swift knew he was lucky. It was like he'd had no clue

what he'd been missing out on, but it had fallen into his lap anyway.

He should have known it couldn't be that simple.

"Excuse me," a chipper voice said, interrupting Imogen's pony story and causing both her and Swift to look over. A slim, blonde woman in a pink jacket had approached them. Next to her was a boy who looked to be Imogen's age. Sure enough, Imogen smiled at him.

"Hi, Jake!"

Jake didn't even bother looking up from the game he was playing on a cell phone. Swift frowned, thinking maybe he was shy. Or maybe he was just rude.

"I'm Mrs. Clarissa McGill," said the blonde woman with a big smile that didn't reach her eyes. She was pretty, but Swift didn't like the way her gaze was narrowing at him. There was something harsh about her that made the back of his neck tingle. "I've seen you dropping off your daughter a few times."

By 'dropping off,' Swift could tell she meant sprinting to reach the stop just as the doors open. He'd probably seen her too, along with a couple of other kids and parents who sometimes used this stop. It seemed Imogen was the only regular who was there every day.

Swift didn't want to jump to conclusions, so he smiled and nodded, offering out his hand for her to shake. "I'm Swift, Imogen's daddy. Nice to meet you, Clarissa."

She laughed and placed her hand on her chest, ignoring Swift's offer to shake, so he withdrew it. "Oh, I know that. And it's Mrs. McGill."

"Sure," Swift said, still smiling and trying not to feel riled. He glanced at Imogen, who was gaping at the woman with her glasses halfway down her nose. "Is there something I can help you with?"

"Look, I don't want to cause any trouble," Mrs. McGill

said, rolling her eyes and waving her hand. "It's just I wanted to clear something up. I've heard a little thing or two that I'm not very comfortable with, so I just thought I'd check, you know. Clear the air." She wrinkled her nose and fixed Swift with her eyes as she continued with her humorless smile.

But Swift was still determined not to get rattled. "Of course, ask away."

Mrs. McGill twisted her big diamond engagement ring and platinum wedding band. "It's just about the other man who sometimes drops your daughter off. I've been informed that he's a criminal."

Swift worked very hard to school his expression. But his blood felt like it reached boiling point within less than a second. "Then you heard incorrectly. My friend was cleared of all charges."

Mrs. McGill scrunched her nose again, tittering. "Yes, but isn't he being investigated for that break-in?"

"No," said Swift firmly. "I don't know what you've heard, but I'm sorry, you're mistaken. He was with me all night when the robbery occurred."

Mrs. McGill stopped smiling. Good, Swift had no patience for bullshit. "That's the other thing," she said brazenly, raising an eyebrow at him. "Jake said Imogen drew a family picture, and that this man was on it as well as your wife."

"Mommy and Daddy aren't married," Imogen said hotly, reaching up to grab Swift's hand tightly. "Mommy is sick, so I'm living with Daddy and Uncle Micha right now. We *love* Uncle Micha."

Mrs. McGill looked smugly from Imogen to Swift. "Now, I don't think this Micha is anyone's brother, is he?"

Swift looked down, overflowing with pride as his daughter openly glared at this silly woman.

"No," he said calmly. "He's my boyfriend."

Mrs. McGill looked like she'd swallowed a lemon. "This is a *nice* neighborhood," she spat out. "My husband remembers this Micha person from his days at school. *He* says he was nothing but trouble, and it looks as if that hasn't changed."

"Then you're not listening properly," Swift replied. "Micha has done nothing wrong, and I'm not sure what any of this has got to do with you."

Mrs. McGill spluttered indignantly. "This is my community. My family. I have a right to keep them safe from any kind of *deviants*. I don't want to hear of that man being anywhere near this bus stop or my son again, or I'll call the police."

Swift's stomach dropped, and fury flared through him. "On what grounds?" he growled.

Mrs. McGill laughed hollowly. "Child endangerment," she snarled. "Kindly keep your own perverted behavior away from him and us."

"Stop shouting at my daddy!" Imogen cried, bursting into tears. "Don't be a bully! It's not nice!"

As proud as he was of her, he hated seeing her distressed. Swift scooped her up in his arms and glared at Mrs. McGill. "There is nothing wrong with my relationship, and Micha is innocent. I suggest it's you that needs to keep your awful prejudices away from *us.*"

Mrs. McGill flared her nostrils. "We'll see about that," she hissed. "I'm not done here. It is my right as an *American* to protect my child. We don't want your kind around here. I'll be speaking to the police *and* the school. Good day to you." She grabbed Jake by the arm. He didn't even seem to notice as she pulled him along the sidewalk, still playing his game. "Come along, darling. Mommy will be *driving* you to school until we get this sorted."

Swift didn't realize he was shaking with rage until

Imogen rested her head on his shoulder. "That was a mean lady," she said.

"She was," Swift said, rubbing her back. The school bus appeared at the end of the street, so they didn't have long. "But she was also *wrong*, okay? There's nothing bad about Uncle Micha being Daddy's special friend. He's Daddy's boyfriend, and he's a good person."

Imogen sniffed and rubbed her eyes under her glasses. "He reads *all* the different voices in my books," she agreed, which was clearly the highest praise she could bestow.

Swift smiled and kissed her cheek. "We love Uncle Micha. And who does Daddy and Uncle Micha love the most?"

"Me!" Imogen declared proudly, patting her chest.

"That's right, little bit." He placed her back on the sidewalk. "Now, you go and have a *great* day at school. When you get home, you can tell us what new things you learned, okay?"

She nodded. "I promise, Daddy."

Lonnie greeted her as usual. By the time she hopped onto the bus, Imogen's tears were gone, and she was smiling at the other kids again as she took her seat. But Lonnie didn't take off immediately. Instead, she leaned on the steering wheel and arched an eyebrow at Swift. "Everything okay there, Mr. Coal?" she asked.

Swift blinked and managed a smile at her. "Oh, yes. Thank you. Just – uh – speaking with another parent about something."

Lonnie hummed, looking concerned. "Is that so? Well, I hope you have a *great* day." She gave him a firm stare that he couldn't help but read as supportive before she nodded and closed the doors to the bus.

Swift stood by the stop for a while after they departed, acid washing around in his gut. He knew prejudice existed, and some people were awful and narrow-minded. But that was the first time he'd experienced anything like that for himself, and the unfairness was bitter to take. At least Lonnie had appeared supportive, he was almost certain.

Mrs. McGill had no idea who Micha was. She had no clue of the abuse he'd suffered, the burden he'd placed on himself. She also had no idea how sweet Micha was when he wrapped sandwiches up for Swift to find in the fridge. The patient way he brushed Imogen's hair. The adorable way his eyes fluttered when Swift kissed and caressed him.

He was a whole, complex, wonderful person.

But would the police see it like that? Would the school?

With a twist in his gut, Swift realized they would just have to wait and see if the people there were open-minded or if they were poisonous like Mrs. McGill. And there was nothing Swift could do either way to change that.

22

MICHA

Taking out the trash wasn't Micha's idea of glamorous. He was pretty sure it was a chore that no one found pleasure in. But Micha didn't mind it so much as some of the other staff at Sunny Side Up. He'd since discovered, though, that because he *was* willing to take on the task, it had earned him a mild hero status.

"I'd unblock a toilet any day of the week over dealing with those dumpsters," his niece, Rona, said. She patted him on the back while he wrestled with the bags. "Thanks, Uncle Micha."

"Thanks, Micha!"

"You're the best!"

"Don't be telling him that," his dad grumbled as he flipped some burgers. "He'll get a big head." But he winked at Micha all the same.

That morning he'd told Micha he was doing a good job. His dad wasn't always the best at expressing his feelings with his words, but the fact that he'd talked about watching some football together sometime soon meant the world to Micha. He'd always said he was too busy as a teenager, worried about feeling awkward around his dad and not understanding the rules of the game fully. He still didn't really follow football, but that wasn't the point. The point was to do something with his dad that he loved.

It was good to know he was getting something right. Swift had told him about the other mom from Imogen's school who'd said all those terrible things. Micha wasn't even that surprised. He'd been expecting something like that. The worst part was seeing how upset Swift had been about the whole thing. He hadn't had much experience with prejudice during his life. Being with Micha was giving him a crash course.

Micha had almost fallen into bad habits and gotten upset about 'ruining' Swift's life. But something about being in this relationship was giving him strength he'd never had before. It was people like Clarissa McGill who were in the wrong. Micha had just been unlucky in life. He hadn't asked to be adopted or gay. But he was starting to see those two things for the blessings they actually were.

He loved his family. And he couldn't imagine being with anyone he liked more than Swift Coal. It was like he'd been walking around as just a half, and now he was whole for the first time.

Maybe 'half' wasn't the right word. Because Imogen gave him fulfillment in a way he'd never dreamed of. Being her 'Uncle Micha' was one of the best joys he'd ever experienced in his twenty-five years.

He was lost in thought as he threw the trash bags into the dumpster that evening. It wasn't the worst out there, but it did smell faintly of urine and rotting food. There was some sort of leak coming from the roof, causing a persistent *drip – drip – drip –* onto the dumpster lid. Eager to get back inside, Micha brushed his hands on a napkin he'd brought with him for that purpose, thinking about what he'd do if he saw Mrs. McGill at the bus stop in the future. He was so preoccupied he startled badly at the voice that suddenly spoke.

"Hello, Perkins."

Micha dropped the scrunched-up napkin and took a step back as Dale emerged from the shadows behind the dumpster. It was already dark, and Micha hadn't realized anyone was there. But after his initial surprise, anger washed over him.

"Oh my god," he spat, snatching up the napkin from the ground and thrusting it into his apron pocket. "Have you seriously been lurking out here waiting for me to show up so you could make a creepy villain entrance? You need to get a hobby! Rock collecting, bird watching, button making – anything!"

Dale laughed humorously, his eyes darting from left to right. It was the first time Micha had seen him without Brie by his side in months. Rather than reassure him, though, Micha was worrying where she was and if she was okay.

"You always were a funny one, Perkins," he said, licking his lips. "That's why we miss you."

"Oh, give it a rest," Micha snapped. "I'm sorry you're mad one of your little minions got away from your clutches. But I'm a person, not a pawn, and I'm not going back to that house – or that city – with you. I'm staying here."

Dale scoffed. "Don't flatter yourself. This isn't about me owning or controlling you. It actually isn't even about whether or not I like you." He looked Micha up and down in a way that suggested he was undressing him with his eyes. "Although I do, believe it or not with the way you've been treating me."

Dale slipped a packet of cigarettes out of his jacket pocket and made a show of lighting one up. There was just a single light above the dumpsters so employees could see what they were doing in the dark, and the tip of Dale's cigarette glowed against his face.

"This is about what you *owe* me."

A chill rushed over Micha. The slow but steady drip of water was grating on his frayed nerves. He glanced at the diner's back door, wondering if anyone was going to come looking for him. "I don't owe you anything," he said, proud of keeping the tremble out of his voice. "You almost ruined my life. I got *arrested,* and I didn't snitch, even though you set me up."

"You knew what you were getting into." Dale rolled his eyes. Were his hands slightly shaking? "Don't be such a baby. You always blame everyone else for your mistakes."

Micha balled up his fists. "I'm at work. I'm not on a break, so they're going to be wondering what the hell I'm doing out here."

"Stargazing," Dale said deadpan, not missing a beat. "And you'll stand there and listen to me if you know what's good for you." A cruel smile spread over Dale's face as he took a drag on his cigarette. "Or I might have to go see that *adorable* little girl you're living with. Imogen, was it?"

All the blood rushed from Micha's head, and for a second he was fearful he might pass out. But he took a deep breath and steadied his feet. "You *stay away* from her," he snarled, jabbing a finger at Dale's face. "How *dare* you threaten her."

Dale held up his hands, ash drifting down from the cigarette. "Hey, nothing's going to happen to her. *Certainly* not while she's out trick-or-treating. Not if you do as I say."

"And what's to stop me from going straight to the cops?" Micha bit out, still pointing his fingers. "You can't just go around threatening kids."

Oh god, he felt sick. It didn't matter what Swift said. This was absolutely putting Imogen in danger, and it was directly linked to Micha's presence in her life. Micha wanted to believe that Dale wasn't so bad he would really hurt a child... but how well did Micha really know him?

Dale smirked. "The police, yeah. They actually seemed to have their shit together in this podunk, ass-end of nowhere town. Poor little Brie. She did forget to put gloves on when we raided that grocery store. It'd be a shame if someone gave her name to the police. They'd probably link her to those iPads too. That red hair is *so* distinctive, after all."

Micha couldn't believe what he was hearing. "You'd ruin her life," he croaked.

Dale shrugged. "I didn't *make* her come along with me either time."

"Bullshit!" Micha yelled. "You'd have kicked her out the house if she didn't, and you've tricked her into believing she has nowhere else to go! Fucking hell, you're a piece of work. Threatening homeless teenagers and little girls. What the hell did I ever do to you that you'd stoop so low?"

Finally, Dale dropped the friendly act. He slammed a shaking hand onto the top of the dumpster, creating a loud bang. "You disrespected me," he growled. "After everything I've done for you, you little shit. So now you're going to do this for me because you *owe* me. Then we can part ways, no harm done."

"Too late," Micha snapped. He was breathing hard, and his heartbeat had sped up at the noise, but he was determined to keep his shit together. "All you've done is harm. And I don't owe you anything! I never snitched on you about those iPads!"

"Yeah?" snarled Dale, his eyes bulging out of his head. "But then I couldn't shift them to my usual guy. There were other repercussions. I got late on some payments, and these are *not* people you want to piss off, Perkins! They have your name, you know? They know it was you that fucked us over. So if you aren't getting that you should be scared of me right now, at least have the fucking brains to be afraid of them!"

Jesus. The desperation in his eyes wasn't funny. His gaze was darting from side to side again as he flexed the trembling fingers not gripping the cigarette. Micha wasn't sure he believed that anyone other than Dale was interested in him in that moment. He was a nobody that didn't know anything.

But he one hundred percent believed that Dale was terrified of whoever these people were. He sniffed loudly as he paced back and forth. If Micha had to guess, he'd say some bad business deals had gone worse, Dale had turned back to his old favorite habit of snorting coke, flushing even more money down the drain, and now he was in serious shit.

Threatening Micha if he didn't help him.

No, not Micha. Brie and Imogen.

Nausea rolled over him. He was truly powerless to this sub-human bastard.

Micha glowered at him, weighing his options. "Fine. What am I going to do for you?"

He wanted to tell Dale to go to hell, that he wasn't going to prison for him. But the sick fuck knew that Micha *would* serve time to protect Brie and Imogen. Dale had him over a barrel.

"Good boy," Dale murmured, breathing hard. "I knew you'd come to your senses. There's no need for us to fight. I just need help on a little job. Then we can go our separate paths as friends."

The fuck they would. But Micha wasn't rising to that bait. "Go on then. Spit it out. I have to get back to work."

"Well, that's just it," Dale said, feigning cheerfulness. "You do."

He looked pointedly at the back of the diner.

Micha's blood ran cold for the second time in as many minutes. "No," he rasped.

"Why not?" Dale took a final drag on his cigarette before dropping it and grinding it into the alleyway. "You already know the building inside and out. I've cased the joint several times when you haven't been working. It brings in a hell of a lot of cash. You either already have the safe combination or the means to get it. One last clean job when no one's around. Then you'll never hear from me again." He ground his teeth and attempted to smile. "I promise."

The hell he wouldn't. Dale held power over Micha while he could threaten Brie and Imogen. He wasn't going to give that up. This was a complete disaster.

"They'll know it's an inside job," said Micha weakly. "If whoever does it knows the safe combination and the alarm code."

Dale scoffed. "That sounds like a 'you' problem. Besides, as long as we're careful, it'll be *fine.* You'll have nothing to worry about."

He'd never be able to look his parents in the eye again.

But really, what were his options here? He'd put Imogen in danger. The person he'd do anything in the world to protect.

Including sacrifice his own happiness.

If he had to stay away from her to keep her safe, he needed to move out of Swift's place. And if he couldn't be with Swift, he couldn't stay in Pine Cove. If he screwed his parents over after all the unconditional love and support they'd given him, he wouldn't want to stay around them, either. Whatever way he looked at it, his days in this town were over. He'd always been on borrowed time, he figured. He *didn't* belong in a nice place like this. Dale knew it, Mrs. McGill knew it, and deep down, Micha knew it too.

It didn't stop his heart from breaking any less.

"Nothing to worry about," he repeated faintly, knowing he was backed well and truly into a corner. His eyes burned, but he was *not* going to let Dale see him cry. "So, when do you want to do this?"

Dale's smile was like a shark. "Good boy," he snarled. "Tomorrow night. Halloween. It'll be busy on the streets with plenty of other petty crime going on to keep the cops busy."

Micha clicked his teeth. "Just you and me," he insisted. "Not Brie. I'm not budging on that."

Dale rolled his eyes. "Fine, then she doesn't get a cut. More for us." He grinned, but Micha spluttered.

"I'm not taking a cent, you asshole. Keep it all. It'll be dirty money, and I don't want any part of it. I'm doing this to keep you from hurting anyone else. If you don't stick to the rules, I'll just turn myself in and you for the robberies and do my best to make sure they understand that Brie was acting under duress."

"There's a fancy word," Dale said, unamused. "Did you pick that up in *jail?*"

"Do we have a deal?" Micha asked bluntly. "Brie stays at home, and you never, *ever* go *anywhere* near Imogen ever again."

Dale huffed. "You're such a fucking drama queen, you know that? It's embarrassing. Yeah, yeah, the girls will be fine. So long as you don't fuck up again." He began walking down the alleyway. "I'll meet you right here, tomorrow at midnight. Got it?"

"Got it," Micha mumbled.

He waited until Dale vanished onto the boardwalk. Then Micha hugged himself and collapsed against the wall as the sobs racked his chest.

He should have known he'd never get to have this life. He didn't deserve it. Karma remembered the terrible way he'd behaved when he'd come to this town, and was punishing him for being selfish and trying to have exactly what he'd hated so much as a child. Micha didn't deserve a family – not with his parents, not with Swift. He didn't get to be gay. He couldn't outrun the decisions he'd made in Seattle.

It would be best to cut and run now. But after he'd done what Dale wanted. That way there was a chance he wouldn't throw Brie under the bus for the previous robberies, and he wouldn't touch a hair on Imogen's hair.

Nausea rolled over him again, but this time, he retched by the dumpster, his mind going to the most disturbing, wicked, repulsive places. If sacrificing himself satisfied Dale's twisted superiority complex, Micha would do it if there was even a chance it would keep Imogen safe.

The door opened, making him startle. Rona leaned out into the alley, looking confused. "Everything okay, Uncle Micha?" she asked. "We were getting worried."

Micha wiped the back of his hand over his mouth, and Rona's gaze landed on his puke. "I'm not feeling so great," he admitted truthfully.

Her eyes went wide. "Oh, no! I'm sure Grandad will let you go home early. Oh, you poor thing."

He didn't deserve his family's sympathy, but he took it. He couldn't look them square in the eye, knowing what he had to do.

Besides, he needed to get back to Swift's house as fast as he could.

He had to pack.

23

SWIFT

It hadn't been the best day.

During Swift's morning shift, a woman had pulled her hamstring in his spin class. It wasn't anyone's fault. She'd stretched, just like Swift had instructed everybody, but sometimes all it took was a sudden movement in the wrong direction, and someone was lying on the floor with an ice pack, trying not to cry. She'd been pretty cool, laughing through the pain, but Swift still felt awful.

Then Imogen had been grouchy getting off the school bus. Swift couldn't work out if it had been caused by Jake or his mom or another kid or even a teacher. But he wasn't used to Imogen acting out, so when her grumpiness turned into a tantrum, he didn't know how to handle it. She'd insisted on cartwheeling inside the house, even though he'd told her to take it outside. When she'd caught her foot on the living room table, he'd done his best not to lose his temper, but she'd gone into full meltdown.

Eventually, he'd sent her to her room to calm down, intending to let her out for dinner, but she'd fallen asleep. So he'd left a sandwich and some grapes by her bed, leaving the door ajar to listen for her waking up, but it seemed like she'd passed out after expelling all that energy.

He felt wretched. Like he'd totally fucked up. He was anxiously watching the door for Micha to come home so they could talk it through. Even if Swift had handled it badly, he was pretty sure Micha wouldn't be mean about it. He'd just help him with what to maybe do next time. Swift had talked with his mom a little, at least. She'd assured him that kids just got mad sometimes, and he'd done fine. But Swift wouldn't rest easy until he had Micha's input.

He'd almost caught himself thinking that she was Micha's daughter just as much as Swift's, but he'd brought himself up short. Even if he hadn't said it out loud, and there hadn't been anyone around to hear if he had, it still seemed a lot to place on Micha. Yes, he was amazing with Imogen and clearly loved her to pieces, but it was way too much pressure to be thinking of him as any kind of co-parent.

At least not yet.

Swift had shaken himself out of that line of thinking. This whole arrangement was little more than three weeks old. It was tempting to feel like it had been more than that because it had been so intense and they'd been living together, but that was way too fast to be thinking of that kind of commitment or that far down the line. Swift was going to scare Micha off if he wasn't careful.

So he'd kept himself busy by going through some boring bill stuff for the house that he'd been meaning to take a look at. Then he'd folded some laundry. It never seemed to end these days, but Swift didn't really mind. He smiled to himself as he shook out one of Imogen's little T-shirts which Robin and Dair had bought her. It had some video game characters on that Swift didn't know, but Imogen had been delighted by it.

It was easy to think when she was screaming and crying

that it was the end of the world, but the truth was they were probably going to have a million little fights over the years. Swift was her daddy, and like it or not, that didn't always mean they'd be friends. Relationships were built on trust and boundaries, not on always telling the other person what they wanted to hear.

Saying that, he couldn't help but take a moment to bury his face in one of Micha's sweaters and inhale. It smelled like him, even though it had just been through the wash. Swift hoped they would always be friends. That their relationship was just getting going and had years to grow and evolve and flourish.

Even though he'd been anxiously watching the door, when Swift did finally hear a key in the lock, a glance at the clock told him Micha was a couple of hours early. Swift frowned, hoping everything was okay. As eager as he'd been to have his boyfriend home, it wasn't like Micha to bail on work.

"Hey, hon," Swift said softly, dropping the shirt he'd been about to fold back into the laundry basket. "You're home early. Is everything-?"

Everything was clearly not okay. Micha gave Swift a guilty, stricken look down the corridor, then dashed into the living room. Swift frowned and stepped through from the kitchen to the hallway…but not before Micha could march back out again from the living room into their bedroom.

With his backpack.

"Micha," Swift said in growing concern. "What's going on?" He walked into the bedroom to discover with horror that Micha was frantically stuffing clothes into the bag.

"I'm sorry," he whispered. "I put you in danger. I never should have stayed here but certainly not after Dale showed up. I was selfish. I-"

"Micha, stop!" Swift cried in alarm, forgetting to keep his voice down. "We agreed to tackle anything like this together."

But Micha shook his head, grabbing a pair of jeans and angrily trying to shove them into the already pretty full bag. "There is no tackling this, Swift. It was nice to pretend for a while, but I'm no good. I've put you in danger. I've put *Imogen* in danger. I may not be worth a damn, but she is. I won't see her get hurt."

Icy coldness washed over Swift. "Why would Imogen be in danger? Micha-?"

"Dale *threatened* her," Micha snarled. Then his face fell as tears spilled from his eyes. "I'd never, *ever* forgive myself if anything happened to her, so I need to go. I need to go." He shook his head as he whispered the last words, fumbling to pack more socks.

Imogen always said you needed lots of socks for a long journey.

"We need to go to the police," Swift said in horror. "If you're saying he said something – what? Tonight?"

"No police," Micha hissed. His face was blotchy as he gave up on the packing and just grabbed the bag as it was. Before Swift knew what was happening, Micha side-stepped him to go back out into the hallway. "You can't go to the police. Look, everything will be fine. I'm handling it."

"'Handling it'? Micha, what does that mean? Micha, stop and talk to me!" He was now in the bathroom, determinedly shoving his toiletries into the sad little plastic bag which he'd moved them into the house with. Swift didn't understand what was happening. "Where are you going?"

"Away!" Micha cried, sounding broken. "Somewhere I can't hurt you guys, okay? It isn't what I want, but that doesn't matter. Nothing matters when Dale holds all the cards."

"You're not making any sense," Swift said, getting scared.

"Are you going back to stay with your folks? Micha, stop this! We'll call the cops and get Dale to back off, or even better, have him arrested!"

"You don't know all the facts!" Micha yelled back. "It's not just you guys he's threatening. I can't have him hurt people because of me. I'll fix it. Just let me *fix it.*"

"By leaving? No," Swift barked. "You can't just keep running away, Micha. Tell me what facts I don't know. You have to be an adult about this!"

"I'm sorry I can't be who you want me to be!" Micha exploded, tears streaming down his red face as he bit his lip. "I wish I could, believe me! But that person doesn't exist. I'm just a no-good piece of trash. I bring trouble with me wherever I go!"

"You're being ridiculous!" Swift could feel his fear was making him angry. But he was also desperate. How could this be happening?

"No, *you're* being ridiculous," Micha shot back, rubbing his damp face and sniffing as he stormed back into the hall. "You made up this person I could be, but you're better off without me, all right? You deserve someone better."

Revulsion filled Swift's chest. "Are you breaking up with me?" he rasped in disbelief. "Baby, no, stop this! Let's sit! Talk!"

Micha dropped his backpack and grabbed his hair with both hands. "I don't want this," he uttered, clearly distressed. "But – welcome to my life. I don't have a choice. You'll get over me, I promise."

"I disagree!" Swift argued. "Strongly! Micha, please, *I love you!*"

Micha dropped his hands, and his jaw fell open. "That's not fair," he whispered.

Swift covered his mouth, desperately trying not to break down completely. "But it's true," he said thickly, lowering his hands and taking a step toward Micha. "You're so important to me. You light up the room when you walk in. You're sweet and funny and cute and clever, and I *don't want you to leave!*"

Micha sobbed, hugging himself. "I can't, Swift. He's got all the cards. Please don't make this any harder than it already is. I have to do what he says, and I'll never be able to look you or my family in the eye again! I wish it was different. I truly do, but-"

"Daddy?"

Swift snapped his head around to see a very small-looking Imogen clinging to her bedroom door. She'd put her glasses back on where he'd slipped them off earlier, but was still dressed in her school clothes after he hadn't wanted to wake her by putting her in her pajamas. Half her hair had come out of its long braid, and she looked scared.

"It's okay, little bit," he croaked. "Go back to bed."

"But there's shouting. Uncle Micha's crying!"

Micha hastily wiped his face and swallowed. When he spoke, his voice was hoarse. "It's okay, darling. You go on back to bed now."

"No!" she shouted at him and stamped her foot. "Daddy said you're leaving, but he promised you'd stay! I heard! You can't leave! You can't! Mommy already left!"

Swift thought his heart might break as he scooped her into his arms. "It's okay, hon. Daddy and Uncle Micha are a bit upset. But that's what grown-ups do. We talk it out. Everything will be okay."

"No, Swift," said Micha in a broken voice. "There is no talking this through. I'm *sorry*. I wish there's something I could do, but it's out of my hands. I-"

The words died in his throat as a ginger streak shot across the hall, landing on top of Micha's bulging backpack. He blinked his wet eyes and inhaled as Butter swished his tail, looking up menacingly at Micha.

"Butter, shoo," he said weakly.

Naturally, that did nothing at all to shift the furious-looking ginger cat.

"See! Butter doesn't want you to go!" Imogen balled up her fists. Swift could feel her pulse racing through her clothes.

"Micha, this is madness. Please, we can work this out."

But to his utter dismay, Micha's face crumpled and he yanked his car keys out of his pocket. "This is my fault. I have to fix it. I'm sorry. I…I never meant to hurt either of you." He reached down to try and get his bag. However, Butter hissed and swiped out with his clawed paw. "Butter," he pleaded.

Butter hissed, his ears almost flat they were drawn so far back on his head. Swift could cry. The little asshole was holding Micha's stuff hostage, trying to get him to stay.

But it didn't work.

Micha tried again to grab the top of the backpack. But this time, Butter got him good, leaving four bright red streaks on the back of Micha's hand, which he snatched back with a sob. He shook his head, glancing one last time at Swift and Imogen. "I'm sorry."

He pulled his front door key off the bunch, dropping it in the little bowl on the side table. Then he yanked the door open, walking into the night without any of his things, letting the door slam closed behind him.

"No," Swift whispered, but it felt futile to try and go after him when he'd clearly made up his mind.

Imogen burst into tears as Swift sunk to the ground, hugging her tightly. "I'm so sorry, baby," he whispered to her as tears spilled from his own eyes. "Daddy will try and make it right." Because he wasn't giving up yet. Micha clearly felt like he had no choice, but he did. Swift would find out what was going on and help him. He'd forgive him for walking out because Micha wasn't used to life giving him second chances. But that was what Swift would do.

He wasn't giving up without a fight.

His eyes were closed as he rubbed Imogen's back, so he couldn't see what bumped against his leg until he opened them.

It was Butter.

He bashed his head against Swift's shin again, then hopped up to force himself in between Imogen and Swift to curl into a ball, purring. "Good Butter," Imogen said between sobs, petting his back. Very carefully, Swift brushed the cat's fur with his knuckles.

Butter let him.

Somehow, this triumph was what really broke Swift. Butter knew things were so bad he'd let down his walls and was comforting Swift as well as Imogen.

"Good Butter," Swift whispered.

He wasn't sure how long the three of them sat there in the hall, grieving what they'd just lost. Micha's backpack also sat alongside them, like it was haunting them. However, it did give Swift some hope he might come back for it, even if he had to knock to get in.

Swift would welcome him back in a heartbeat.

But for now, Micha was gone, and in his wake, he'd left the shattered pieces of Swift's broken heart. It would be a while before he or Imogen could get to sleep. For once, Swift let Imogen stay in his room.

Butter slept at the end of the bed by their feet.

24

MICHA

It had been a long time since Micha had slept in his backseat. Considering all he'd lost, even that felt like a luxury.

Pops' old car was almost all he had to his name now. At least his wallet had been in his pocket. The few clothes and toiletries he'd owned he'd had to abandon thanks to that damn cat. Micha rubbed the surprisingly sore cuts that Butter had given him. Talk about literally adding insult to injury. He didn't even have a clean T-shirt to wear for his last day as a free man.

The more he thought about it, the more he was convinced Dale was going to set him up. At the very least, he didn't care if Micha came out of this okay. He'd probably see it as a bonus if he got arrested. Micha didn't want that – down to his *bones* he didn't want to go to prison – but if it was a choice between him or Brie serving time, he'd pick himself. If that happened, hopefully Dale wouldn't see any need to go anywhere near Imogen, Swift, or any of Micha's family, especially if he got the money to pay whoever he owed.

God, how did this get so badly fucked up?

Micha bit his thumb, calculating how much money he theoretically had in the bank. Swift hadn't let him pay for anything really while he'd been living with him, arguing he was still getting back on his feet and shouldn't be wasting his first paycheck on groceries or cat food. So he should have a few hundred bucks, at least. That wouldn't last long. But if he was going to end up behind bars, what did it really matter, anyway?

Making a snap decision, Micha drove over to the Walmart in Penny Falls where no one would recognize him. He splurged out on a toothbrush and toothpaste, deodorant, a fresh T-shirt to go under his shirt, and new underwear. Having a quick wash in the store's public bathroom and getting changed made him feel slightly less grimy. Then he bought some food to eat in the parking lot.

He still had over twelve hours until he needed to meet Dale in the alleyway, so for a while, he just watched the stream of people going in and out of the large store. Mostly, he saw a lot of parents, kids, and adult friends stocking up on Halloween supplies. Micha thought of all the parties that would be happening in Pine Cove that night. Normal people having normal fun.

He sighed. He and Swift had spent several days putting together Imogen's pirate fairy costume. She couldn't decide between the two ideas, so they'd decided she could be both. Why not?

Micha stifled a sob and rubbed his mouth, thinking how he'd never get to see her wear that outfit.

He'd never see her again.

Swift must be so angry with him. Micha slumped down in the car and hugged his chest, trying to numb himself to the pain of knowing that wherever he was in the world, Swift would be thinking less of him. Micha was used to being looked down on by people. When it was the likes of Mrs.

McGill, he didn't care so much. But if Swift didn't hate him now, he would after tonight.

And, god…Dad and Pops. Rhett, Hudson, Darcy, and Logan. All their kids. It had baffled Micha they'd always been so understanding of his many screw-ups.

Not anymore. He'd be dead to them.

Fuck Dale for being so cruel. He couldn't have just let Micha live his life, could he?

Not knowing what else to do to pass the time, Micha found a place to park on the way back to Pine Cove. It was a little dirt track somewhere around the outskirts of the lake. He stopped in a small alcove off the road, then cracked the window an inch so he could smell the rich scent of pine trees all around him. Fuck, he was going to miss this.

It was kind of ironic that he'd spent all this time avoiding home, and now he'd give anything to stay. Well, not quite anything. Dale knew that. But if he could do it all again, Micha knew this was where he'd want to lay his hat. Damn, he'd been *this close* to applying for a course at the community college in Penny Falls. He'd been daydreaming about Thanksgiving and Christmas with Swift and Imogen, as well as their big crazy families. *Finally,* Micha had been feeling like he belonged.

Now he had to leave it all behind.

Micha made sure the car doors were locked, then crawled into the car's back seat to curl up and lie down. His thoughts were tumultuous, but eventually, he dozed off into an uneasy sleep for a few hours. If he could just hover in this numb sort of limbo where he only had to get through the job tonight, he could pretend his future might not consist of an orange jumpsuit and little else for the next few years. But who was he kidding?

And then what? Once he did his time, who would hire him? Where would he go?

Urgh, these were exactly the kinds of thoughts he'd been trying to avoid by falling asleep. But it now appeared he was awake and not drifting off again.

So he decided to torture himself by taking a drive around Pine Cove, getting one last look at the home he'd never appreciated enough. He started with the high school, which had been a pretty tough few years for Micha, but damn it, he'd made it. He'd scraped by to get his diploma, and even though that wasn't much, it was at least something he could say he'd done with his life.

Micha bought a cookie from the Rise and Shine bakery, then went to sit and look over the lake for a while. He always found it so calming, watching the ripples lapping at the shore, the gentle breeze ruffling his hair. The sun would set just before six o'clock, so until then, Micha nibbled on his cookie, then wandered along the boardwalk, watching the kids in the arcade. Some were dressed in their trick-or-treating outfits as they played air hockey and Skee-Ball, ready to go door-to-door once the younger kids had gone around right after they'd gotten out of school. Micha checked his watch, wondering how Imogen was getting along.

He'd never wanted to go when he was a teenager, saying it was for babies. Rhett was closest in age to him, but even then, he was seven years older. Micha fondly remembered one year where they'd watched some scary movies at home and eaten Halloween-themed candies until they'd wanted to be sick.

Holy shit. Swift had been there that night. Micha remembered the way his stomach had twisted with every word Swift had said. They'd laughed and joked and yelled at the people in the movies not to go down into the basement. It had been a rare night of just *fun* for Micha.

Micha brushed the cookie crumbs from his hands and

began walking along the street again. If that teenage Micha had any idea he'd get to spend even just a few weeks with Swift Coal, he'd lose his shit. It would have been like winning the lottery. This wasn't how Micha had wanted it to end – he didn't think he'd ever wanted it to end, he realized sadly – but if nothing else, he should appreciate that short time they'd had together.

Micha had understood what it felt like to be wanted and desired by a man. A man he…

Loved?

Jesus. Swift had really said that, hadn't he? That he loved Micha. That couldn't be right. And Micha *certainly* couldn't love him. Swift was just being emotional because Micha had pulled the rug out from under him by leaving. They'd only just decided to officially be boyfriends.

Remembering that perfect moment brought a lump to Micha's throat. It seemed like a million years ago now, even though it was just a couple of days. He'd felt so special and cherished. He wondered if he'd ever be anyone's boyfriend again.

It was too painful to even think about being with anyone else other than Swift. It was probably partially to do with sleeping twice in the car, but the fact that every part of Micha was aching, inside and out wasn't just physical. He didn't know it was possible to hurt this much from sadness. He wanted to make it stop, but had the feeling it was most likely going to get worse before it got better.

He was overwhelmed by the sudden urge to see his folks. He knew it was stupid and might only add suspicion for later, but his feet were walking to Sunny Side Up before he could stop them. As he pushed through the door, hearing the tinkle of the bell, he was suddenly that small boy again, so desperate to be loved but terrified that love was coming from 'bad' people.

Pops and Dad could never be bad. How had his childhood self ever thought that? Even though the diner was packed, Pops spotted Micha enter immediately, giving him a big smile from where he was working on something at the server station. As the door swung slowly shut behind Micha, Pops came around the desk, walking over with Peri the mountain dog ambling by his feet. An enormous fluffy cloud with a lolling pink tongue.

"Micha," said Pops happily. "This is a nice surprise. Are you feeling better?"

"Uh, yeah," Micha lied. "I was just passing by and thought I'd say hi."

Oh, *fuck*. Tears threatened to spill from his eyes where they were welling at an alarming rate. So Micha did the first thing he could think of and threw his arms around Pops' solid form. Even in his mid-sixties, he was still in pretty good shape. He'd always given the best hugs, and Micha didn't feel him hesitate to embrace him back, even though they were in the middle of the packed diner.

"What is it, son?" Pops asked gently, patting Micha's shoulder.

'*Son.*' That was a sucker punch. Micha sniffed and pulled away, swallowing his hiccup as best he could. "Sorry. I, uh, didn't sleep. Because I was sick. I guess I'm tired and worrying about some things."

Pops nodded, then looked down at his faithful dog. "Peri, take Micha in to see Sunny." He winked at Micha. "He'll whip you up one of those peanut butter milkshakes you love."

Micha managed a small smile. They always were his favorites.

Peri knew he wasn't allowed in the kitchen itself, but he bumbled through the diner with Micha next to him, getting fond looks from a lot of the customers. The place had been decked out from floor to ceiling with paper bats, witches, pumpkins, and skeletons. Micha tried to look at every booth, every bit of art on the wall, all the little details he'd miss after he was gone.

After he'd helped Dale rob the place his dad had built up from scratch. The business he grew despite the odds and the prejudice and the hate crimes. People had told him no one would want to eat at a place run by someone like him, especially when Pops had joined him. But they had all been wrong. Sunny Side Up had become the heart of this town.

And Micha was going to betray all that. Defile it.

Of course Dale had chosen this as his target. He loathed seeing other people doing better than him. He probably looked at the loving family and thriving business that Dad and Pops had, and all he could see was *'Why don't I have that?'* It was mean and petty, and Micha couldn't believe he was really going to help him do it.

He had to protect Brie, though. She had no one else in this world looking out for her. And Imogen, oh, god. Who knew what Dale was capable of in his desperation?

So that was that.

"Micha," Dad said as Micha entered the kitchen, hiccuping down a sob and putting on a brave face. "Is everything okay?"

Micha nodded. "I just swung by. Pops said you wouldn't mind making me a peanut butter special."

"Did he now?" Dad grumbled, tossing some spaghetti into a colander, then dumping it into a vat of sauce. "Perhaps Pops would like to come back here and make the damn shake himself?" But a grin was playing at his lips, and Micha couldn't help but notice that Dad handed the spaghetti off immediately to one of the many other kitchen staff. Then he walked over to the freezer, fetching out a tub of ice cream and a jar of peanut butter from one of the cupboards.

Micha leaned against one of the counters out of the way

of the half a dozen people running around, making orders as fast as they could. Despite working around food his whole life, Pops had done a pretty good job of keeping Dad in shape as well. He'd always said that Dad was his 'Robert Redford,' which Micha could sort of see the resemblance to the actor. He was just Dad to him, like Pops was just Pops. But he'd seen photos of when they'd met in their mid-twenties in 1979. They had been quite the lookers.

It was in moments like this Micha appreciated just how fucking brave they'd been to be an out gay couple in a small town. Thanks to their age, they'd both only just avoided doing tours in Vietnam, but they'd seen firsthand the devastation it had wrecked on their generation of men. While Dad had become a social recluse, throwing himself into flipping burgers, Pops had decided nothing was going to hold him back in life. When Dad relented and finally agreed to date, they'd weathered a lot of hate for being gay and a mixed-race couple, not to mention the prejudice around the AIDS crisis of the eighties and nineties. When it had come to adopting Rhett and his siblings, they'd fought the system that said two men couldn't do that, and won. Then they'd taken on Micha, by no means an easy child.

They were made of far stronger stuff than Micha ever would be. They'd not only refused to let the world change them. *They'd changed* the world around them.

If this was the last Micha ever saw of them, he'd always have mad respect for them as well as love. He just wished he could have been a better son.

"What's on your mind?" Dad asked as he handed over the shake in a frosty glass. "We heard some things. People trying to cause trouble."

Micha shrugged as casually as he could, sipping the ice cream drink. But inside, he was panicking. If his parents heard he was gay from the slurs of other people, he'd be devastated after so many years hiding it from them. "About the robbery?" he asked, steering the conversation in that direction and hopefully away from his sexuality. "People talk. They have reason to."

Dad scoffed. "Screw people. Your Pops taught me that. If they want to be unhappy, let them. You can always talk to me and Pops, though. You know that, right?" He was fiddling with a jar of cherries, not looking Micha's way, so he probably didn't see the warm smile Micha gave him.

He did know that, logically. He wished maybe he'd taken them up on that more in the past. It was kind of too late now.

"Ahh, they're my problems. I always have problems. I'll do what I can." He bit his lip, swirling his straw through his shake. "Thank you, Dad," he said stiltedly. "For, um, everything you and Pops did for me. I'm not sure I said that enough. I know I'm a screw-up. But I'd be a hundred times worse in some gutter without everything you guys did."

Dad grunted, picking at the cherry jar label. He opened his mouth but closed it again. Micha knew he was terrible at talking, and didn't really expect much of a reply. It was just something he needed to say.

But then Dad started talking again, his eyes still firmly on the cherries. "You know we got our first dog in eighty-one? We'd gotten a place together. Well, *I'd* gotten a place. No one wanted to rent to two men, let alone a Native American. But Pops was definitely living with me. And he was all 'if we're going to break the lease rules, we might as well break them properly.'"

Dad chuckled and shook his head, getting that wistful look he often did while talking about Pops. Micha couldn't imagine loving someone that much still after forty years.

Well, he could. But it sadly wasn't going to happen for him and Swift.

"So we go see these scrappy mongrel puppies someone

was selling from their house. And the moment we walked in, Pops said 'that one.' And you know which one he pointed to? The runt." Dad shook his head and arched an eyebrow, his eyes a little glassy. "I said, we didn't want the weak and tiny one. We should get the strong one. But your Pops, he told me that I didn't know nothing about nothing."

Micha smiled. Pops always said that to Dad. It was his version of 'I love you, you fool.'

"He told me that the runt of the litter had the hardest start in life, but that made him the toughest. The runt always had to work the most, but that meant he had the best personality, too. The runt of the litter was loyal and fierce." He shrugged. "Every dog we've ever had has been the runt. And as far as I can tell, your Pops' hasn't been wrong."

Micha had those tears in his eyes again and a lump in his throat. He was pretty sure he got what his dad was trying to say about him, in his own dad way. Micha placed the milkshake down, reaching out to hug his old man. Dad let him, resting his head on Micha's shoulder.

"Thanks, Dad," he said thickly.

"You're the runt," Dad said. "In case you missed that."

Micha burst out laughing, wiping his eyes as he pulled away from his dad. He tried to scowl at him, but it came out all wobbly and was most likely ruined by Micha's smile. "Yes, Dad, I got that. Thank you. A lot of kids would take that as an insult. But…thank you."

His dad clapped him on the shoulder. "You're a *good* man, Micha. We believe in you. Whatever's going on, we're here for you. Don't fight alone."

Micha nodded, sobering up again. "Thanks, Dad," he whispered.

It was all pretty clear in that moment.

He couldn't go through with this.

He wasn't sure how the hell he was going to get out of it

without throwing Brie under the bus or endangering Imogen. But there had to be a way. This wasn't the person Dad and Pops had raised him to be.

Who knew…maybe this *was* the person Swift had seen all along? One who finally, for the first time in his life, was going to stand up and say loudly and clearly: *enough.*

He had just over five hours.

He needed to start thinking up a plan.

25

SWIFT

It had been a miserable day. If Swift was honest, he'd been tempted to let Imogen skip school because if she'd been cranky the day before, she was downright distraught that morning. However, Swift knew that wasn't setting a good example of how to deal with things.

"But when is Uncle Micha coming *back?*" she asked for the umpteenth time before he managed to get her out the door.

"I'm not sure, little bit," Swift admitted with a sigh as he tried to wrestle her long hair into a braid. "Daddy will do the best he can."

"Uncle Micha brushes my hair the best," Imogen mumbled sadly.

Swift had to agree. Uncle Micha was the best at a lot of things.

Although there was a part of Swift that was pretty furious with him. Why the hell had he left like that? Swift couldn't be any clearer that he was there to support Micha. That they were a team. And that was *not* how he'd imagined telling Micha he loved him for the first time.

Especially when he hadn't heard the sentiment back. That cut through his heart like a dagger.

He'd been suspecting that was where he'd been heading for a while but honestly the words had escaped his mouth without him meaning them to. Now they were out in the world, though, it was as if they had true power. Of *course* he loved Micha. Everything about him made Swift happy, even the bits Micha thought were broken. Even though Swift was angry and hurt and confused right now, yes, he was madly in love with Micha Perkins.

But was it all too late?

Swift had a pretty full day at work. The plan had been for Micha to pick Imogen up from the bus stop, get her ready in her Halloween outfit. Then they'd both take her trick-or-treating. That couldn't happen now, or at least Swift assumed he wasn't going to magically make everything better in the next several hours, so he needed a Plan B.

Focusing on logistics meant Swift's brain spiraled less. It was so strange. Six weeks ago, Swift would have twitched at any single thing that was out of place in his house. But as he brushed his teeth that morning, his heart ached to see the toothpaste in the holder, like it should have been. Micha was terrible for leaving it on the side of the sink with a cap only half screwed back on.

Swift wanted his chaos back in his life. All the color in his home was because Micha had encouraged Imogen's imagination to fly, and Swift had relaxed about a million times compared to how he'd been before. Swift had finger paintings stuck to his walls, kids' DVDs not even stacked alphabetically, and had swapped potpourri for a dozen photos of his baby girl. Where the crystal vase had once stood before Butter got his paws on it, there was now displayed a papier-mâché monstrosity that Imogen had made and Swift loved more than any expensive artwork.

He'd been hoping to get a photo of him and Micha on the wall soon. Maybe even of the three of them.

As a family.

Mentally, he slapped himself and jumped into the shower, scrubbing himself as fast as he could. He was only going to get hot and sweaty at work again, so he could be hasty. Before he left, though, he wanted to lay out Imogen's costume in full on her bed and write out a few instructions. His parents would normally be ready in a second to step in and take Imogen out, but his mom had thrown her back out and pulled a rib out of place. Although Kestrel would probably be happy to take her niece out trick-or-treating, Swift had to take what Micha had said seriously.

He'd been pretty damn convinced that Dale had made a specific threat against Imogen.

Swift had spent half the night tossing and turning, questioning if he should go speak to Detective Padilla after all. But the way Micha had panicked at the mere mention of involving the cops, then said Swift didn't have all the facts, made him pause. Swift was fully aware he had an automatic trust of authority figures. But sometimes, they didn't always make things better. What if he went blundering in and made things worse?

Swift could maybe take the day off work. It was last minute, but Aspire was usually pretty good about that. However, as he got dressed, he was feeling more and more that the solution was to take Imogen out of the equation.

Jay was already at work, getting ready to teach drama at the high school for the day. Robin was still in Seattle for the next couple of weeks until he and Dair moved. Scout and Emery were on a trip out of state. Rhett had the twins and would already be at the office.

That only left one option. Swift had never been sure that kids were Ava's forte, but he didn't have a choice.

"Yo," her low voice said after a couple of rings. Swift always got the impression his sister was in the middle of a hostage negotiation or in the process of ordering coffee and was aware of holding up the line. To his mind, there didn't seem to be any in between. In reality, she was probably at work at the activity center on the outskirts of town, doing admin work while school was in session. But her tone always suggested an international life of mystery.

That was right. She taught a lot of kids archery. Okay, maybe if she was given the opportunity to (safely) teach Imogen how to use some sort of weapon, this would be fine.

"Oh, hey, sis," Swift said, rubbing the back of his head. "Are you busy? I have a favor to ask. A really big one. Huge."

"Shoot," she said simply.

"Okay, here's the thing." Swift did his best to explain that Micha had fallen in with a bad crowd who was trying to stir up some shit again, and he was worried about Imogen. "I don't get off work until later, so I was wondering, uh…"

"I can take the rug-rat trick-or-treating," Ava cut in. "Oh. Unless she has a lame costume. You didn't get her some dumb store-bought crap, did you?"

"She's a fairy pirate," Swift said apprehensively. "Homemade."

"Outstanding," Ava said matter-of-factly. "I know the dope neighborhoods with the expensive candy. We'll make a killing."

Swift blinked. "That's – are you sure you're okay with that?"

There was a slight pause. "You said this douchebag made a direct threat against my niece, correct?"

Swift swallowed. "Yes," he croaked.

Ava sniffed. "Then Imogen's going to have a night out at the lake cabin with Auntie Ava and Uncle Jay. We'll do the stupid s'mores thing and, I dunno, read her a story. That's what you do with kids, right?"

"Uh, yeah," said Swift, slightly bewildered that she'd be willing to take her all the way up to the family cabin. Imogen would really be safe there. "Did you already have plans with Jay?"

"Nope," said Ava. He could hear the grin over the phone. "I'm recruiting him. He just doesn't know it. Leave all the little bit's stuff out, and I'll come collect it. Then you go find your boyfriend and talk some sense into him. By which, I mean go visit the cops."

Swift spluttered. "Micha's not – I mean – uh…"

Ava snorted. "Yeah, yeah. Text me any parent crap I should know. I'm guessing she won't want to drink whiskey, so I guess I'll go buy juice."

Swift knew he was tired and emotional, but he could have cried. "Are you *sure* this isn't asking too much? It's just with Mom's back-"

"Someone threatened my niece," said Ava with a scoff. "Of course this isn't too much. Don't be a dumbass."

She hung up.

Having known his sister her whole life, Swift could read between the lines. She was almost certainly thrilled to have been asked. He hugged his phone to his chest and considered himself lucky to have been born into such an awesome family.

He hurried to pack Imogen's overnight stuff into the tattered pink suitcase with the mermaid keyring, keeping an eye on the time. Butter was watching his every move, his eyes narrowed and his tail swishing.

"I know," Swift said placatingly. "I'm doing my best to get everybody back home, okay? We're gonna keep you indoors tonight. It's Halloween, anyway. You wouldn't like all that madness. Then I'll get Imogen and Uncle Micha back to us as soon as I can."

Butter lifted his head, like that wasn't what he wanted to hear, but it would have to do. He dropped silently to the floor and stalked off, no doubt to find something to destroy in Swift's room or maybe pee on something.

Swift would just have to find out what that delight was later. He'd already put Butter's food down and cleaned his litter box, so fingers crossed that was enough to keep them civil. For now, he had just enough time before he left for his shift to do what he'd been putting off.

Go through Micha's bag.

It felt like a violation, but Swift wasn't sure he had any choice. He'd tried dialing Micha's phone several times. The first few calls had rung out, but then they'd started going straight to voicemail. Sure enough, there in the bag was Micha's phone charger. It had probably died on him.

Swift pressed the flat side to his forehead and let out a shaky breath. Until that moment, he hadn't really allowed himself to acknowledge that among all his other emotions, he was also *terrified* for Micha's safety. Sure, he was a grown man, but for some reason Dale had power over him and he'd chosen to leave all his stuff here. Where had he slept last night? Was he okay?

He decided to text Rhett. He didn't want to cause alarm, so he was as casual as he could be.

Hey! Micha's left his phone charger here. You haven't heard from him, have you?

Rhett's response was pretty typical. *Lol, if his phone's dead, how would I have heard from him?*

Jerk, Swift texted back. He smiled at his best friend's humor, but that didn't make him feel any better about what the hell Micha was up to.

The way he'd been talking had made it sound like Dale

was forcing him to do something. Considering the last time when he'd involved him in a robbery without his consent, that didn't bode well as far as Swift was concerned.

Swift didn't find anything unusual until he got to the bottom of the backpack. Once he'd pulled out the crumpled clothes he'd seen Micha packing the night before, he found an even more screwed-up paper napkin. The stamp on it showed it was from Sunny Side Up, unsurprisingly. Swift recognized Micha's handwriting. He'd scribbled down a four-digit code, then some kind of rough map. There was a hallway with a couple of doorways off it, but only one room added on. It was a simple square box with an arrow pointing at one of the walls.

Swift's insides dropped.

Dale's MO was burglaries. He'd tricked Micha into one, and they were certain he'd pulled one off at gunpoint here in town. Was he planning another? Was that what Micha had been talking about? Was this a code and location for a safe?

The fact that it was written on a Sunny Side Up napkin sank in.

"I'll never be able to look you or my family in the eye again!" That was what Micha had said to him.

"Oh...*no*," Swift moaned out loud to himself. Was Dale making Micha rob the diner? Why in the hell would Micha agree to that? Swift thought of the young girl Micha had mentioned several times. Did she have something to do with it?

Swift was out of time. He pocketed the napkin, deposited all of Micha's stuff back in their room (where he *would* be back to claim it, soon), then grabbed his gear for work.

It was a tortuously long day. Technically, he had a manager, but really, Swift was his own boss. So he kept his phone on him at all times, getting updates from his sister and then his brother. Once he got over his confusion, Jay was delighted to have an impromptu adventure with his niece. As per Swift's instructions, he and Ava had explained that Swift was helping Uncle Micha, which Imogen was apparently totally on board with.

Getting many, many photos and videos of Imogen in her Halloween costume kept Swift going through the last few hours of his shift. But he was completely distracted and quite frankly lucky that no one dropped a dumbbell on their head on his watch. But the second he could, he was into the showers, then out the door, heading for Sunny Side Up.

It was a terrible plan, but Swift didn't want to put his foot in it with Micha's family if he didn't have to. If possible, they never needed to know what Micha had been planning, or rather, what Dale was strong-arming him into.

So he wouldn't go to them. He would wait.

In TV and movies, they made stakeouts look kind of glamorous. That was a total lie. Thankfully, having watched enough media over the years, Swift had thought to get some dinner and bottles of water before he settled in. He risked putting some music on quietly, but apart from that, once his Chinese food was gone, he had nothing to do but watch the comings and goings of the diner.

After a couple of hours, he thought he was going to lose his mind.

At least to start with, he saw a lot of trick-or-treaters. As the evening drew on, those in costumes got older. But then people were mostly at the places they wanted to be for the night, and Swift was just left squinting at the patrons of the diner.

This was crazy. He didn't really know anything. *If* Micha and Dale were going to try robbing the place, who was to say it was going to be tonight? Yes, Micha might have made this drawing on a napkin from his folks' place, but what if it was for somewhere in Seattle? They'd have had plenty of time last night and today to make the drive. They could be sitting outside some random building in the city right now.

But Swift couldn't bring himself to quit. His gut was telling him to stick it out. If there was even a chance Micha would be here, that he could help him out, Swift was going to take it.

It was all he had right now.

It was difficult, sitting there alone in the dark, not to churn himself into a mild frenzy of worry. Thank fuck his siblings knew him far too well. He just felt calmer when he knew things were taken care of and he had some kind of control.

So they messaged non-stop not only throughout Imogen's trick-or-treating but through dinner and bath time and story time and bedtime. She was a bit worried that Butter was lonely, but apparently Auntie Ava had utterly convinced her that Butter had invited all his cat friends around for a party where they were going to drink milk and dance to Taylor Swift.

Knowing his little girl was safe meant Swift could focus on the man he loved. He'd stay here all night if he had to. He was on his third coffee of the evening and had even been really bad by dashing out to take a leak down a nearby alleyway. But he couldn't risk taking his eyes off the diner on the other side of the road for long.

At just before midnight, everything paid off.

He was struggling against dozing off, chewing gum, and humming along with some Creedence Clearwater Revival when a shadow crossed in front of the diner. The lights had been out for half an hour, the last customer having left at eleven and the staff clearing off as soon as they could after that. Swift probably wouldn't have noticed anything if he hadn't been staring avidly at the diner. More importantly, he never would have recognized the person's gait if he wasn't so in love he even knew how Micha fucking walked.

It was him. Oh, *god,* it was him. He was still in town. He was still *alive.* That was probably a complete over-reaction, but Swift had pictured himself several times during the day identifying Micha's cold body in a police morgue, so his relief made him gasp out a sob.

Before he could stop himself, Swift had deposited his gum and was scrambling out of the car. He closed the door as quietly as he could, then jogged across the dark and empty road, silent in his sneakers. Micha had hurried around the building and down the alleyway in between Sunny's and the building next door. As Swift got closer to the diner, he slowed.

He could hear voices.

"What the *fuck* are you talking about, Perkins? We had an agreement!"

That had to be Dale. Swift felt his lip curl and his fists clench. He crept along the storefront, holding his breath.

"Dale, listen to me." Micha's voice was firm, but Swift knew him too well. He caught that slight crack in the last word. He was begging. "This is *everything* I have. Seven hundred dollars. And I'll send you more when I have it. But I can't do this. They're my *parents.* Please, please don't hand Brie to the cops. I'm fucking indentured to you, okay? I'll" - his voice really did crack- "I'll come back to the house, do whatever you want. Or I'll keep working here and send you my paychecks. Just *don't* destroy Brie's life and *stay away from Imogen.*"

At the mention of his daughter's name, Swift almost tripped over his own feet. But he kept silent. He was just about at the corner of the diner now. Once he saw what was happening, maybe he could intervene. Or maybe Dale would listen to Micha' ridiculously generous offer. It was obvious

Dale had something on the Brie girl, probably implicating her in the previous robberies. That was why Micha had refused to go to the police.

But of course Dale wasn't open to being reasonable. Swift didn't even know him but was fully aware of how much of an asshole he was.

"Are you fucking unstable?" Dale snarled incredulously. "These aren't the kind of people you pay in installments! Quit fucking around! Were you dropped on your head as a child? Oh, I don't suppose you'd know. Let's call the group home and find out."

Swift's rage flared, and he silently dashed the last couple of feet to look around the corner. Dale was backing Micha up against the wall by the dumpster, his shaking finger jabbing into his face. There was a single lamp pointed down off the wall, illuminating them. With most of the boardwalk street lights turned off, that meant Swift was probably in the shadows for them. Largely invisible.

"*ALL* you had to do was get me in. Alarm and safe codes. *Baby's* work. But no, you had to go and be a little bitch about it. *Again.*"

"I'm not robbing from my folks!" Micha shouted. "I don't expect a piece of shit like you to understand loyalty. But I'm not doing it!"

"Is that so?" Dale said nastily.

He pulled a gun from the back of his pants and pointed it at Micha.

Swift didn't know he was running until it was too late.

26

MICHA

ALL MICHA COULD SEE WAS THE DARK BARREL OF THE GUN pointed at his face. It was like everything else turned to molasses around him. There was nothing else that mattered but the black hole and the bullet that could shoot out of it in a split second.

His knees threatened to buckle, but he was too frozen to even move that much.

He was going to die.

This idea had been dumb with only a slim chance of success. But he'd had to try. If this was it, at least he still had his fucking dignity. Or so he'd hoped. Right then, there was every chance he was going to pass out or puke. He couldn't even force a sound from his throat, let alone speak. He was barely breathing.

Regret consumed him. Not for defying Dale but for every other fuckup that had led him to this point.

And for every moment he'd never get to spend with Swift now.

But he hadn't betrayed his parents. He'd kept Imogen and

Brie safe. *Dear god*, even if he died tonight, he prayed Dale would have the humanity to leave them alone.

Swift probably hated him, but Micha hoped that some power out there led Swift to discover the truth. That Micha loved him too – he had since forever, if he was being honest – and he'd given his last breath to try and do right by him.

The air was damp from earlier rain. The persistent dripping from the roof was faintly breaking through the fog of Micha's all-consuming panic. *Drip – drip – drip.* He couldn't get enough oxygen into his lungs, and his mouth tasted like acid.

The gun was too close to try and do anything. Dale had it right up in his face. Micha supposed his only hope now was to play along and do what he said, then take the first chance he could to run or push him away or hide. None of those situations seemed like they would really work, but Micha wasn't going to just give up.

"Let me in, *now,"* Dale yelled. His eyes were blown, no doubt from whatever he was on, and they darted frantically from Micha to the door, over and over. "You don't know what these guys will do, Perkins! But I swear to fucking god if you don't let me in right now, I'll do twice as bad to you, Brie, that kid – you'll regret *ever* fucking me over!" He shoved Micha into the wet wall with his free arm, then grabbed the gun with both hands again, trying to stop it from shaking. "Just deactivate the alarm, and-"

His arms went suddenly upward, the gun flying out of his hands, clattering somewhere in the shadows of the alleyway. In a blur, someone grabbed Dale by his scruff, spun him around, and slammed him next to Micha against the wall.

Micha scrambled away in shock, unable to believe his eyes. *"Swift?"*

Swift was breathing heavily. "It's okay, baby. Find that gun, *but don't touch it.* Kick it under the dumpster."

"Who the *fuck* are you?" Dale screamed, slamming at Swift's arms.

Swift. *Swift was here.* Micha could have burst into tears, but he didn't. For the first time in a long time, he didn't want to cry. He was angry, but the power he felt from knowing he could *do something about it* gave him strength. So he edged around where Dale was trying to skirmish with Swift, looking desperately for where the gun had fallen.

"This is none of your business!" Dale spat. "Just carry on walking! Perkins! *What the fuck?* You heard what I said about that kid-"

Micha stumbled over his feet, horror washing over him. But Swift twisted Dale around, getting him into a choke hold. "Mention my daughter again, asshole," he snarled in a tone Micha had *never* heard him use before.

Micha realized that aside from getting the gun away, Swift hadn't hit Dale once. He was just restraining him. It was better than he deserved, but it made Micha oddly proud of Swift for not dropping down to Dale's level. Micha had almost forgotten that Swift taught self-defense. Dale was thrashing and trying to kick out, but Swift swiped his legs from under him and pinned him to the floor.

"Baby?" Swift said. His voice was strained, but Micha could tell he was trying to stay calm. "Any luck with that gun?"

Oh, god. Swift was probably so mad at him! He'd caused such a mess and now he couldn't find the gun!

"Swift, I'm so sorry-" he croaked.

But Swift shook his head as Dale wrenched from his grasp, but Swift slammed him back down again.

"It's okay," Swift rasped, sweat running down his neck. "It's going to be okay, baby. Just find that gun, kick it away. Then we can call the cops. We're a team, remember? You can do this."

"Fuck you!" Dale howled. *"Fuck you, Perkins, I'm taking you down with me!"*

But Micha ignored him. As petrified as he was, he looked into Swift's beautiful sky-blue eyes. He'd said they were a team. He smiled at Micha despite everything going on.

Maybe he didn't hate him.

Then god fucking damn it, Micha was going to do him proud now. Adrenaline rushed through him, clearing some of the fog. He latched onto the sound of the dripping water and felt the icy breeze cut down the alleyway, touching his damp skin and making him shiver.

The gun. Find the gun.

"I'm on it, Swift." He couldn't see shit in the dark, but if he stopped looking back into the light, his night vision would get better.

His attention was now almost fully focused on searching for the weapon. However, he couldn't help but take a tiny fraction of his mind to totally marvel that Swift was calling him 'baby.' Not only was he here – a miracle in its own right – but he was using pet names for Micha.

Something Dale hadn't missed, either.

"Baby, baby, baby," he snarled with a mocking laugh. "Holy fuck, Perkins. Who's the Captain America boy scout you've enthralled with your cock-sucking abilities? Although if that's the case, you must have vastly improved since-"

"Since what?" Micha bellowed, seeing red. He spun around, his fists balled. He hadn't found the gun yet, but Swift was practically sitting on the bastard. "Since you bullied me into letting you fuck me? Since you threatened to kick me out if I didn't suck you off? You evil, twisted-!"

"Micha!" The voice that rang out was Swift's.

And he looked like he was about to cry.

Fuck. Yeah. Micha hadn't exactly told him about that awful part of his time in Seattle. To be fair, at the time, Micha had convinced himself that was what he wanted. But listening to his words like Swift was probably hearing them, he heard them for how bad he knew they truly were all along.

"Have you found that gun?" Swift said, his voice strained but not angry. With Micha, anyway. He looked down at Dale with pure, unadulterated fury.

If he was honest, Micha was finally feeling some of that anger too. But he didn't just want to scream and shout.

He wanted justice.

"I'm looking, baby," he said pointedly for both Swift's and Dale's benefit. Dale snarled in disgust, but Swift's expression softened. He smiled warmly at Micha in the glow of the pathetic light above the dumpster.

It was enough for Micha to hope that Swift didn't hate him, though. So he dropped to the grimy floor, looking for anything unlevel with the alleyway. Bingo.

He didn't want to touch the gun, terrified it would go off with the simplest nudge. But he was almost certain Dale hadn't pulled the safety back. So he dashed over to where the thing was lying, then tapped it with the toe of his sneaker.

Nothing.

Tap – tap – tap. Then Micha whacked it like Megan Rapinoe hitting the ball into the back of the net, sliding the ugly bit of metal out of sight under the dumpster.

Micha jogged back over. Swift was sweating profusely, but his hold on Dale was thoroughly impressive. He was sitting on his legs with his arms twisted behind his back. "What can I do?" Micha asked. "Do you have a phone to call the cops? Mine's dead."

"Back pocket," Swift grunted. But he winked at Micha before focusing all his energy on Dale once more.

Dale, however, wasn't giving up without a fight.

"You're calling the cops?" he screamed, then laughed like a

maniac. *"You?* Excellent. Kiss your probation goodbye and Brie's entire future. What do you think these guys are going to do if we don't pay them?"

Micha crouched down to look Dale in the eye. "Not 'we' – *you,*" he spat. *"I'm* going to call the police. And you're going to admit to those robberies. You were the one holding the gun at Farm Fresh as well. If Brie gets dragged into it, I'll testify you made her do it."

They stared at each other. For the first time ever, Micha saw Dale flinch. But Micha had Swift by his side, so he dug deep and refused to bow down. Dale ground his teeth, his eyes glassy.

"Why would I do that?" he demanded. But the bravado was fading.

"Because it's the right thing to do," said Micha. "I'm *done.* I tried to give you an out, but you wouldn't listen. You pushed and you pushed and you *pushed.* I have to trust that the system will be fair. And if it's not…" Micha swallowed, trying not to let his fear get the better of him. "I hope at least you'll go down and they'll let Brie off with a warning, like they did me."

And if he went to prison this time, so be it.

"Micha," Swift said, his blue eyes wide and fearful. "Just… just go. I'll handle this. Don't be here."

Micha felt like his heart might break. He knew Swift was trying to protect him – and his offer was certainly tempting. But he couldn't do it.

"It's okay," Micha whispered. He got up and walked around to retrieve Swift's cell from his jeans pocket. "I'm done hiding and lying. If it gets this creep off the streets, then I'm willing to gamble and let the chips fall where they may."

"Perkins!" Dale screeched. "Don't be a fucking moron! We can all still walk away from this!"

Micha clutched the phone to his chest. He hadn't realized

how cold it had gotten. His breath came out as little clouds of smoke. "And let you trick other people? Let you send more people to prison? No, Dale. It's over."

It felt like it took forever for the call to go through, for Micha to hurriedly ask for the police, all the while Swift was straining against Dale's efforts to wriggle free. Swift was a machine, though, not budging until the wail of sirens pierced the night and flashing blue and red lights crept closer.

"Micha, please," Swift begged in the last few seconds they had. "You can still go. You haven't done anything wrong! What if they say it violated your probation just by being here?"

Micha had spent the few minutes waiting for the cops, awkwardly pacing the alley with the phone gripped in his hands. But now he hurried back over to Swift. Dale had finally gone limp, accepting the inevitable. So Micha stood by Swift and slipped his arm over his back, kissing his hair.

"It's okay – no, Swift – *listen.* None of that matters right now, okay?" The sirens were getting closer. Swift looked up at Micha with scared eyes, so Micha cupped the side of his face. He felt light-headed and heartbroken and so, so relieved, all at once. "I fucked up a lot. But you helped me forgive myself. I…I love you too, Swift. I have for ten years. Being with you has been a gift. I never wanted to leave. *Please* believe me on that. Whatever happens, I love you."

"Micha," Swift said weakly.

Micha quickly slipped Swift's phone back into his jeans pocket, walked to the middle of the alleyway, then put his hands behind his head.

It didn't take long.

"Police! Don't move!" a male voice bellowed down the alleyway. Officer Wynn. *Shit.* Micha's heart was hammering in his chest. His knees wanted to buckle as he remembered

what had happened last time he'd been arrested. He wanted to shake and cry, but he held as steady as he could.

"I'm not armed!" he cried back.

"I have the suspect here!" Swift screamed. "Don't shoot! *Don't shoot!*"

"Get down on your knees!" Wynn screamed. Micha dropped like a stone, his fingers digging into the back of his head.

"I'm not armed!" he repeated.

"Wynn!" a female voice hollered, a pair of boots stomping down the alley. Micha didn't dare look up higher than the knees, but he saw a fitted pants suit and couldn't help but feel a thrill of hope. "Officer Wynn, stand down. Somebody tell me what's going on here."

"I apprehended this man trying to rob the diner!" Swift cried out. "The man on his knees is my boyfriend. He called it in. He was trying to stop the robbery too. We believe this man held up the grocery store at gunpoint. Please, ma'am."

Micha dared to glance up as Padilla waved her hands up in the air. "Okay! Everybody *stand down.* None of these men are armed! Wynn, secure the suspect."

"I kicked the gun under the dumpster," Micha said, loud and clear.

"He threatened my boyfriend with it," Swift snarled. "I knocked it out of his hands."

Dale whimpered, his face smooshed into the asphalt. Swift finally got off him, but several armed officers descended instead, cuffing him and hauling him to his feet.

Padilla waved her hands again with an impatient look. Micha said about a million prayers as the officers not apprehending Dale lowered their guns. Micha was sure the rest of Pine Cove's police were hard-working, upstanding officers. But he couldn't deny he breathed a massive sigh of relief again as half a dozen firearms were lowered. Wynn was glaring at him like he'd love nothing more than to cuff Micha too, but he was busy dragging Dale toward the cop car parked outside the diner.

Padilla marched over to the dumpster and shined her flashlight underneath. "Oh, yeah. Will you look at that? A gun. Neat. Let's, you know, bag that shit up and maybe read that gentleman his rights." She nodded at Micha and Swift. "We'll need to ask you boys some questions if that's okay?"

"Yes," – "Of course," said Micha and Swift in unison.

Padilla let slip half a smile, then schooled her face back to an almost scowl. "All right, team! Let's go!"

Micha didn't dare move, though. It was as if he was frozen on his knees with his hands behind his head. Until a big pair of warm arms slipped around him. "It's okay," Swift whispered. "I've got you. It's over. You were amazing, baby. I'm so proud of you."

He probably said more, but Micha only caught half the words. All he could hear was Swift's rumbling voice and feel his tight embrace.

"Hey, boys." Micha blinked and peeked over Swift's bicep to see Padilla with her hands on her hips. "This is very sweet and all, but how about we get off our asses and take a quick statement so your friendly neighborhood Padilla doesn't lose her job, hmm?"

Micha laughed and wiped his eyes. "Absolutely, ma-" He pulled himself up and met her gaze. *"Detective.* I'll tell you everything you want to hear."

Padilla's mouth did that thing again where it wanted to smile, but she wouldn't let it. Instead, she extended her arm out toward the boardwalk. Micha felt so grateful he almost couldn't stand.

He wasn't being cuffed.

In fact, Swift wrapped his arm around him, practically lifting him off the ground as he walked him toward Padilla's car. Then he perched next to Micha against the hood as they were given those tin foil blankets that marathon runners got.

Oh, right. He was probably in shock.

But it was partly his fault that he was.

Except…Padilla waved her hands and narrowed her eyes at Micha halfway through his story. "So this Dale guy we have in the back of the car pressured your friend in both incidents? That's coercion. Not to mention breaking and entering, armed robbery, illegal possession of a deadly weapon, unregistered gun, and brandishing a weapon. Harassment of you. *And* multiple accounts of sexual assault."

Micha balked. It sounded so bad all strung together like that. "I mean, I-"

Padilla did the hand wave thing. Micha got the impression she didn't always have the patience for talking. "No, Mr. Perkins, this is more than enough to go on." She flipped her little notebook shut and jabbed it toward Micha's nose. "Although you know you should have told me half this stuff when I came to your house, right?"

Micha's stomach flipped with fear. "I was worried about my friend."

Padilla hummed and flipped her notebook back open. "Yeah, that's not great. But I think she's got a good case for coercion. Do you think you could maybe get her a good lawyer?"

"Yes," cried Micha and Swift at the same time.

Padilla held up her hands and chuckled. "Okay, it's not a competition. But the sooner she comes in for questioning, the better. And, Mr. Perkins, you know what I'm going to say to you and Mr. Coal, right?"

Micha wanted to pass out. He still wasn't in handcuffs. Swift's arm was *still* around his waist. "Don't leave town," he said quickly.

She winked at him. "Good boy. Now, skedaddle. I'll call

you both tomorrow or…" She wrinkled her lip and checked her phone. "Monday. Probably Monday. You look like you need to sleep for several days. I'll call to arrange another interview. Make sure we've dotted all the t's and crossed the i's." She kissed her teeth and rubbed her eyes. "I hate Halloween, but thanks for giving me an actual collar. This guy's rap sheet has already pinged up over a dozen different reports." She dropped her head back and grinned to the sky. "I can think of at least three guys who'll now owe me a beer."

Micha was too afraid to move, but Swift's arm was still around his waist. So when he stood, Micha did too. "Thank you, ma'am," Swift said.

Micha squeezed his hand. "Detective," he corrected in a whisper.

Padilla scoffed. "You can call me 'mother' at this point. Just leave. Go home. Get off my crime scene." She grinned, then snorted as she walked off. "Okay, who has my coffee?" she called out to the uniforms around her.

Micha felt like he was floating in another body. But Swift squeezed him tight. "What do you say?" he asked, concern weighing down his words. "Can we go home?"

The sob that Micha had managed to cling on to for the last couple of hours finally escaped. He flung himself at Swift, hugging his firm chest as tightly as he could. "If you'll have me?"

Swift laughed. It sounded a bit wet, like he might have been crying.

"Oh, sweetheart. You never even left."

27

SWIFT

Logically, Swift knew that Micha needed to drive his own car back to the house. Emotionally, he'd had to bite his tongue to make himself let go of him. Then he'd driven at the maximum speed limit to get himself back home as fast as he could. He'd run inside, lit several candles, and started a bubble bath running.

Because he was so horrified by what had happened, his only response was to fill his and Micha's world with things that were warm and comforting and beautiful.

While the tub was filling, he dashed out to check Micha hadn't pulled up yet, before running back into the kitchen to find that ridiculous hot chocolate kit Imogen had insisted they get with mini-marshmallows and tiny white chocolate stars in each packet. If he started heating a pot of milk now, maybe he'd get two cups made by the time Micha got home.

Home.

After stopping the hot water overflowing in the bath, Swift rubbed the heels of his palms into his eyes and let out a shaky growl that sort of became a laugh.

Everything was going to be okay. Micha was coming home to him and Imogen.

Micha loved him.

Dale was out of their lives, and Micha's friend Brie would hopefully be okay if Padilla was to be believed. Micha had stood up to the asshole who had been controlling him, and now they could move on with their lives. Together. Suddenly, it was as if the future was open and full of countless possibilities.

There was a part of him that wanted to dwell on what Micha had said about Dale pressuring him to sleep with him. That was important. But Swift sensed it would be as much a can of worms as Micha's confession about his slipper-wielding, homophobic foster dad. So maybe not tonight. Tonight, Swift just wanted to wrap his baby up in his arms and hold him tightly, protect him from the rest of the world.

He was lost in thought as the pot of cocoa began bubbling, so he hastily stirred it some more. It was important not to lose sight of the most important fact. There was nothing standing in their way.

He and Micha loved each other.

The headlights swinging into the drive alerted Swift that Micha was almost at the door, so Swift busied himself pouring out mugs of hot chocolate and adding the whipped cream on top to hold the marshmallows and sprinkle stars. He just made it to the door in time to place one mug on the table, next to the bowl with the key that Micha would hopefully, surely, be accepting back. Before Micha could knock, Swift opened the door for him.

He looked tired and disheveled and like he might burst into tears, but he was here.

"Baby," Swift murmured, pulling him in for a hug across the threshold with his free arm. Micha groaned and leaned into him, clutching onto his sweater tightly. "Come inside. Let me take care of you. Come on."

After shutting the door and bolting it to keep the rest of the world well and truly away, Swift picked up the key, holding it up for Micha. He was about to say something sweet about not rushing into anything when Micha let out a sob, fumbled to snatch the key from Swift's grasp, then shoved it back onto his set of keys with fierce determination.

Swift figured that was all they needed to say about that, then.

"I've run a bath," he said instead, gently pressing the mug of hot chocolate into Micha's hands once he dropped the full set of keys into the bowl. "But let's just go sit for a minute, okay?"

Micha nodded, leaning in as Swift wrapped his arm around his back. Swift picked up his own mug, then gently steered them into their bedroom.

Where Butter was curled up on the comforter.

But Swift had decided he was no longer going to treat the cranky cat like an enemy. He was a part of this family, just the same as any of them.

"Look, Butter," he said cheerfully. "Look who's home."

"Um, Swift?" Micha tensed up beside him. However, Butter unfurled from his position on the mattress, yawned so wide it looked like his head was going to split in two, licked his paw, then hopped off the bed. Swift and Micha watched as he crossed the floor…then bashed his head straight into Micha's shin, purring as he entwined himself between their legs.

Micha looked at Swift with a stunned expression. Then very carefully, Micha leaned down and offered Butter the backs of his fingers.

Butter rubbed his head on them once, then sauntered off into the hallway, still purring.

"Is he possessed?" Micha asked, standing back up.

Swift laughed and kissed Micha's temple. "I just think he knows he's got a good thing when he sees it. Come on, into bed. And where's your phone? Let's get it charging."

Micha pulled it out of his pocket and handed it to Swift… then paused. "Hang on. You unpacked my things?"

Swift placed his drink down, then plugged the phone into the charger that was attached to the wall on Micha's side of the bed. He turned to encircle Micha in his arms. "I hoped you'd come home."

"I never should have left," said Micha thickly.

"Shh, it's okay now. Come cuddle with me."

They curled next to each other on the bed, sitting up just enough that they could sip their drinks. Swift felt it warming him through his bones. It had been pretty cold out there.

"Look at this," Swift said happily after they'd reached the bottom of their mugs. He pulled up the many photos of Imogen from that evening. "Ava and Jay took her out trick-or-treating."

"She looked amazing," Micha said, cradling the phone in his hands. "God, I'm so sad I missed it. And you missed it too?"

Swift shook his head. "There'll be plenty of other Halloweens. Other costumes. I think tonight was something that had to happen so we could move forward."

"Yeah?" said Micha. "How so?"

Swift smiled and placed their mugs down so they could snuggle more. "Actually, by kind of staying the same. Micha, please stay living here. Please un-break up with me."

Micha snorted and buried his face into Swift's chest. "I never really broke up with you. Not in my heart."

"Well then, that part's easy, isn't it?" said Swift flippantly, but inside, his own heart was doing backflips. He'd been pretty sure with the whole 'I love you' that they were back together, but it was even better to hear it confirmed out loud. "And you'll stay? With us?"

Micha nodded, looking up with big brown eyes. "Was Imogen very upset?"

Swift debated downplaying it. However, he decided the truth might hurt for a second, but it would also prove something to Micha. "Yes," said Swift. "She was distraught. But I promised her you'd come home, and you have. She loves the crap out of you, hon. You are more important to us both than I think you truly realize."

He expected Micha to get upset, but instead, he smiled. "I'm starting to get that, yeah," he admitted with a sniff. "So… uh." He bit his lip and looked at Swift for several seconds. "If we're going to be together and live together…I was thinking…maybe it's time for me to come out. If you're ready to come out too?"

Swift felt like songbirds burst into chorus inside his chest. "More than ready, baby," he said, cupping his boyfriend's face to kiss him lovingly. "What about something crazy? A party, here, on Saturday. Halloween 2.0 so Imogen can wear her costume again, and we can invite all of our family."

Micha spluttered. "Oh, god. You don't do things by halves, do you?" He considered a moment. "Um, there's no ramp for Darcy's chair."

"I'll get one installed tomorrow," Swift said. "I think we can both take the day off work after everything. We'll get this place ready to welcome the hundred people we're related to and then some. If that's a yes?"

He held his breath as Micha looked at him. Then a smile illuminated his face, making Swift grin too. "That's a yes," said Micha.

Swift kissed him. Then he kissed him again. Then he sighed, happiness filling him like he'd never known. "I love you, baby. So much. Just so you know."

Micha laughed and rubbed his wet eyes. "I love you, too. I feel so lucky. Teenage me doesn't know what's hit him."

Swift waggled his eyebrows. "I'm actually more interested in the grown-up you, thank you very much. Can I tempt him into the tub? I lit candles and everything. It's romantic as fuck."

Micha chuckled as Swift pulled him to his feet. "You lit candles?" he asked incredulously. "But what about the mess they'll make?"

Swift turned and picked him up to cradle him in his arms, causing him to squeal delightfully. "Before you and Imogen, my life was all boring and orderly. Now I have mess and chaos and *love,* and I wouldn't have it any other way."

Micha kissed him hard as they stumbled against the wall. "I think I swapped some of my mess for your stability, and, baby, it feels so good."

"You feel good," Swift murmured into his mouth, letting him back down to the floor.

He wasn't sure when the relief of having Micha back for good was going to wear off, but for now, Swift was going to indulge in it. He kissed Micha's neck as he slipped off his shirt, then pulled back long enough to remove his T-shirt as well, leaving a trail along the hall as they stumbled into the bathroom. Swift leaned over to run some more hot water into the tub full of suds. The only light was coming from the candles he'd hastily lit. He didn't want to tell Micha just yet and spoil their mess analogy, but they were actually battery ones that he'd simply switched on. In his defense, that had been faster than messing around with matches.

Next time he'd light a hundred real wax ones, just for Micha.

Swift ran his hands over Micha's inked arms, loving every artistic inch of him. He touched the thorny rose over his heart, then kissed it. That was his Micha, all right. Beautiful but difficult to nurture and with the potential for pain. But also representing so much love and joy.

Micha rested his palms on Swift's shoulders, like they were anchoring him while Swift undid his belt and pulled it free. Micha's eyes drifted closed as Swift made short work of his jeans and underwear, leaving him beautifully naked.

"Step in, sweetheart," Swift said, stopping the water and offering Micha a steadying hand to get into the tub. Micha sat in the middle, facing the taps with his elbows on his raised knees and his head resting on his folded arms. He groaned, presumably as the hot water soaked into his skin.

Swift stripped in seconds, then carefully lowered himself behind Micha, pulling him in between his open legs so they could hug, chest to back. Micha let his head fall onto Swift's shoulder, turning so he could gently kiss the side of Swift's throat.

"I think I'm in heaven," he murmured.

Swift closed his eyes as he rested his cheek against Micha's damp hair, inhaling the spicy bubble bath, the warm steam from the water, and a scent that was just Micha. "Me too, baby."

Micha took a deep breath. "It doesn't seem right I should get to be this happy," he said with a sigh. "But I'm done second-guessing every good thing that comes into my life. I *choose* to be this happy."

"Yes," Swift hissed, hugging him tighter across his chest. "That's what I want to hear."

"I...I..." Micha stammered. *"I want to go to college,"* he blurted out. "Just the community one in Penny Falls. I thought...if I can appeal my time served and get it expunged from my record...I thought I could look into becoming a teacher. Or some sort of childcare. Or an ASL interpreter. I want to give back with a job I really care about. Does that sound dumb?"

Swift realized a lump had risen in his throat. "That sounds incredible," he said as he tried to swallow. "I think you'd be amazing at that. I'd support you one hundred percent."

Micha let out a shaky laugh and looked at Swift over his shoulder. "You would?"

"Without a doubt." Swift leaned down to kiss Micha's gorgeous lips, his heart thumping from excitement. "I keep telling you you're amazing, Micha Perkins. The whole world should know it too."

Micha moaned, taking Swift's hand and placing it on his soft belly, under the water and just above where his hardening cock was bobbing in the water.

"Show me I'm yours," he begged in little more than a whisper.

Swift groaned, slipping his hand around his length. "I'll show you *every day*, baby. I promise."

He took his time, teasing Micha's shaft and playing with his hard nipples. Micha had said he was lucky, but Swift knew he was just as fortunate. This incredible human being wanted to be with him, to stay and build a life together. It was more than Swift could ever have hoped for.

When the water started cooling and Swift had gotten himself rock hard rubbing his cock against Micha's perfect ass, he pulled Micha from the tub so they could quickly dry off. Then Swift picked Micha up once more so he could wrap his legs around Swift's waist.

He couldn't help but notice how close that put his hard, weeping cock to Micha's waiting hole.

In a moment of madness, Swift swept all the plastic bottles and jars off the bathroom counter, along with the toothbrushes and toothpaste. Everything went clattering to the floor where he'd dropped their damp towels. "Swift!"

Micha squeaked in shock as Swift dumped him onto the counter, still with his legs around Swift's waist.

Swift grinned, and Micha giggled, incredulous at the mess. "I told you," Swift growled as he reached up for a fresh bottle of lube from the cabinet. "I'm embracing the chaos."

"Oh my god," Micha said breathlessly, stroking his length. "Are you going to fuck me right here, Swift? Can I have your cock like this?"

Swift captured his mouth for a filthy kiss, tipping Micha slightly back so he could push his slippery fingers inside him. "You can have whatever you want, baby," he rasped, managing to pull a condom on despite his wet fingers. He pressed his tip against Micha's entrance, causing him to moan and cling on to Swift's back. "I want to fuck you every way. You're mine, Micha. I love you."

Micha choked as he leaned back, taking Swift's length all the way. It didn't take long before they were rocking back and forth, staring into each other's eyes in the steamy bathroom. Swift thought maybe it was the adrenaline's doing, but he was going to come pretty damn soon.

"Touch yourself, darling," he moaned between kisses. "I want to see you come."

Micha bit his lip, bracing one hand on the counter as he met Swift thrust for thrust, jerking off for Swift's pleasure. "Baby," he was whimpering. "Baby, yes, so good."

They gained speed, chasing their climaxes as their motions became more and more frantic until they were both coming as they dug their fingers into the other's flesh.

Swift gradually regained his senses, pulling Micha in for a loving hug. "Holy fuck, you're incredible," he mumbled against his neck.

"So are you," Micha said tiredly.

For once, Swift didn't feel guilty about leaving all the mess until the morning. He grabbed a washcloth to wipe them both down after disposing of the condom, then led Micha to their bedroom.

Tomorrow they would collect their little girl and set about fixing the house. The day after, they would welcome all the most important people into their home to officially announce they were a couple. Then after that, they would start building the rest of their lives together.

But for tonight, it was just the two of them. They belonged to each other's hearts now, and Swift couldn't imagine anything more perfect in all its messy, flawed glory.

28

MICHA

After the craziness of the past few days, that Friday was refreshingly calm in comparison. As promised, Swift took the day off from work. Micha hadn't been scheduled to go into the diner even before the almost robbery. His folks had been stunned to get a second visit from Detective Padilla that morning in so many days, but when Micha spoke to them over the phone, he assured them he'd explain more in person the next day at their little get-together.

As he'd spoken to Pops, Micha wasn't surprised when he'd simply accepted this. But he was sure his dad would have more to say. He'd decided to be as honest as he could. That Dale had tried to blackmail him, but ultimately Micha had tried to stop him, succeeding with Swift's help. He wasn't going to lie, though. He was going to admit he'd almost done it in order to protect the people he loved. He was done hiding. It wasn't going to be easy, but he was determined.

Swift drove them both to the hardware store in town, simply called 'Dave's.' It had been in Pine Cove longer than Micha could remember. Together, they'd researched and watched some online videos, then managed to put together temporary ramps in front of Swift's front porch and out the back so Darcy would be as welcome as everyone else. Swift fretted, promising to install better permanent ones, but Micha assured him that for now, it was totally fine.

Of course Swift knew Rhett really well, but it made Micha's heart flutter how eager Swift was to accommodate his family. Swift never made him feel like they were weird like other people had. They were just different, and different was good.

And in between driving and DIY, there were all the little kisses. The touches to Micha's back and arms and neck. The light pressing of lips to hair. All the teeny tiny ways that added up to leave Micha in no doubt that he was loved in spite of everything that had happened. Adored, in fact.

Just how Micha felt about Swift.

There was a lot to process from the night before, and Micha knew he'd have to unravel that in time. Someone had dropped a wooden board in the hardware store, and for a second, he was right back there in the dark, damp alleyway with a gun in his face. Swift had patiently rubbed his arm and waited for the adrenaline to fade and for Micha to come back to his senses. He was sure this wouldn't be the last time he'd freak out, but knowing that Swift had his back meant he felt he could face that during the coming weeks and months.

Auntie Ava and Uncle Jay had gotten Imogen to school just fine. So that afternoon, Micha and Swift walked down to the school bus stop hand in hand, eager to see her again. Micha felt horribly guilty for what he'd put her through, even though he'd been trying to protect her. Swift had said she would absolutely forgive him, and when she was older, they could explain what had really happened better to her. Micha hoped so.

Sure enough, the bus had hardly even stopped before the

pair of sparkly pink glasses that had been pressed up to the window disappeared. *"Uncle Micha!"* Imogen screeched as she all but flew off the bus and into his arms, bursting into tears and dropping her tattered pink suitcase on the sidewalk. "Uncle Jay and Auntie Ava said you'd be here, but I wasn't sure!"

Micha did his best not to cry as well, stroking her messily braided hair. "I'm *so* sorry, little bit. I promise to never scare you like that again, okay?"

"Has the bad man gone away?" she asked into his neck. Micha looked up at Swift, his eyebrows raised. But she was a smart cookie, and she'd probably picked up on what people had said.

"Yes," Micha said firmly. "He's gone away forever."

Dale had already been charged, according to the brief phone call he'd received earlier from Padilla. Micha didn't wish any harm on him, so he hoped whoever he was afraid of would leave him alone in prison. But honestly, it wasn't Micha's concern anymore.

What he was deeply concerned about was Brie, but she'd walked into the station that morning, insisting she went alone, and confessed to everything. She was a minor, and this was her first offense, so there was every chance she'd be let off with a warning. Micha hoped so and would do everything he could to help her get back on her feet. Swift had a lawyer friend, one of his PT clients called Elias, who was taking care of her. He seemed pretty confident.

Imogen sniffed as she let Micha go, then turned to Swift. "He came back!" she announced proudly, as if Swift didn't know. He laughed and hugged her.

"Yes, he did."

It was only then did Micha realize that the bus was still there, its doors open. One other kid had gotten off, totally and completely absorbed in a game on his phone.

"Jake?" Swift asked, having just spotted him too. Oh, this was the kid of that woman who'd had a lot to say about Micha. He'd seen her around before that incident. But right now, Clarissa McGill was nowhere in sight.

Micha leaned in to see Lonnie frowning at the kid, who seemed totally oblivious that he was standing alone on the sidewalk.

"Was he supposed to get off here?" Micha asked.

Lonnie shrugged, tapping her hands on the steering wheel. "He said so. But I don't like leaving kids alone, not when I know they're a good few blocks from home."

Micha looked down, but Jake was still fighting zombie chickens or something. "We'll wait with him and call his mom," he said before he really thought it through.

Lonnie sighed and gave him a grateful look. "Are you sure? I have a responsibility to get these other kids back on time, too."

Micha nodded. "It's no problem, ma'am."

Lonnie preened. "Ma'am," she repeated quietly to herself as she closed the doors and drove away.

Micha looked at Swift and Imogen before crouching down in front of the little boy. "Hi, Jake," Micha said. "Is your mommy on her way?" Jake shrugged, not looking up as his thumbs whizzed over the screen. "Hey – do you have her number on your phone?" He nodded, still playing. "Great! I tell you what. When you finish that level, can you give her a call for me? I'd do it, but I don't know how."

Jake looked up and frowned. "It's easy. A baby could do it. I can pause the game and show you?"

Micha chose not to be insulted by the bluntness of a five-year-old and instead gasped. "Could you? That would be so cool."

"Daddy," Imogen whispered, dancing from foot to foot. "I really gotta go to the bathroom."

Swift's mouth dropped open as he looked between her and Micha. "It's okay," Micha said. "I've got this. You get her home."

Swift didn't look sure, but Micha was. Jake's safety was more important than Mrs. McGill's opinions. After almost doing several very bad things yesterday, Micha felt strongly about doing something right and getting this kid home.

Swift nodded, leaned down to peck a kiss on his cheek, then took Imogen's hand along with her suitcase to hurry her home.

Micha turned back to Jake, who was waiting with his phone held out. "I'm ready to show you," he said. So Micha nodded and hummed while Jake talked him through making the call, then got him to put it on speaker in case he needed to interject.

"Jake!" Mrs. McGill's voice practically screamed through the receiver. "Where are you?"

"I got off the bus," Jake said, sounding confused. "Where are you? The man said I should call you."

There was a pause. "What man?" Mrs. McGill asked.

"One of Imogen's daddies," said Jake without missing a beat. Micha's heart contracted, delighted, even though he was technically wrong. "Can you come get me? I paused my game."

Another beat of silence. "It's okay, Mrs. McGill," Micha said tentatively. "I'm happy to wait with him."

"Oh-okay," she stammered. It sounded like she was running. "I-I'll be *right* there. Don't move, Jake!"

"Bye, Mommy." He closed the call, then immediately began killing his zombie chickens again.

Micha crossed his legs and sat on the curb. Jake seemed happy to stand and play the game, so Micha didn't interrupt him. Within ten minutes, a red Porsche screamed up to the curb, and a frantic Clarissa McGill came running out, almost tripping over her black pumps.

"Jake!" she cried tearfully. "You were supposed to get off at your father's stop today!"

"No," said Jake calmly as she threw her arms around him. "You said 'see you later,' and that means this stop."

Mrs. McGill looked like she wanted to argue with him, but Micha decided that was probably a good time to get back up to his feet. Mrs. McGill looked guiltily at him as she pulled Jake to her side. "You," she uttered.

"Hi," Micha said, brushing his hands on his jeans. "It's okay. Luckily, Jake was able to show me how to use his phone to call you. He's just been playing his game since. He's very good at it."

Surprisingly, Jake looked up from the screen at that, blinking owlishly. "Thank you. I'm on level fifty-seven, and it's my most all-time favorite."

Micha smiled. "You're welcome." Then he looked back at Mrs. McGill, not seeing someone who had called him terrible names. He just saw a scared mom.

Mrs. McGill looked between him and her son. "Jake is just a – a little different, that's all," she said defensively. Micha had already guessed Jake was probably somewhere on the spectrum. He hoped Mrs. McGill wouldn't be the kind of parent who saw that as a problem.

He smiled warmly at her. "Different is good," he said, thinking of his family. "What is 'normal,' anyway?"

With that, he nodded, then turned to walk back home.

Home. That had become his new favorite word.

Ensuring Jake had gotten back to his mom safe made him feel like some balance had been returned to the universe. Micha knew he had a lot of atoning to do still. But as he made them all pancakes and eggs for dinner, he hoped he,

Swift, Imogen, and even Butter were on their way to a better life.

That night, all of them (including Butter) slept in the big bed together. It was one of the best night's sleep Micha had ever had, even with small feet and paws in his face.

The party the next day was a roaring success, although Micha and Swift's announcement that they were dating didn't go quite as they'd planned.

"Oh my god, no way," said Kestrel in full deadpan sarcasm mode.

"Tell us something we don't know," Rhett heckled.

"Duh," Ava chimed in.

"Well, I think it's just *wonderful*," Swift's mom, Deb, said with a tut as she dabbed her eyes with her sleeves.

"Yes, good for you, baby bro," said Darcy, who also looked a little glassy-eyed.

Pops came over to them. They'd decided to have another cookout in the back yard to fit everyone in despite the slightly chilly temperatures. Swift's place wasn't half the size of his folks', but they all managed to fit just fine. (Not that Butter would agree, as he spent the whole party under Imogen's bed, making himself scarce from the many strange children and the curious Peri and Smudge.)

Pops wrapped his arms around Micha as everyone began talking and helping themselves to more food that, despite her sore back, Deb had whipped up with almost no notice. Pops looked Micha in the eye. "I know why you thought you couldn't tell us," he said, cradling the back of Micha's head and patting his back. "But we always suspected, and we never once minded. You're our son, no matter what."

Micha didn't even try not to cry at that, but at least he was still smiling. "I love you all so much," he mumbled through his happy tears. His parents knew he was gay, and he'd also confessed to the details of the almost robbery to them.

And of course, they still loved him.

It was probably one of the most wonderful days he'd had in his whole life as both families (and a few friends) mingled and got to know one another. The kids tore through the house, and Swift didn't twitch once about mud on the floorboards or knocking anything over or letting the central heating out. Almost. Anytime he looked like he might be getting distressed, Micha kissed his cheek and rubbed his back, calming him down.

They could clean the floors and replace or glue back together anything that got damaged. But the sounds of all the children's laughter as they played was priceless.

Micha introduced Swift to his niece, thirteen-year-old Carlee. Swift had been working all morning on how to sign 'Hello, my name is S-W-I-F-T. Nice to meet you.' Carlee beamed at his clumsy but pretty coherent effort.

"Nice to meet you, too," she said out loud as she also signed, then winked. "Don't worry. Uncle Micha will teach you more."

Swift had beamed at Micha with such love. "Yes, he will," he agreed.

The most surprising moment of the day, though, came a little later. Micha almost missed the knock at the door, as everyone was already there, so they weren't expecting anyone else. Wondering if it could be Padilla (again), he slipped away from the party to answer it alone.

However, it wasn't the police or anyone unsavory from his past.

It was Clarissa McGill with Jake by her side, and she was holding a bunch of flowers.

Her smile was fixed, and she looked more afraid than she did happy as she thrust the bouquet at Micha. "Thank you," she blurted out. "You didn't have to wait with Jake yesterday. He wouldn't stop talking about how nice you were, and he, um, doesn't do that. He doesn't really like new people. I said some things about you, and I think maybe I was, uh, wrong. I was wrong. So, thank you."

Jake was engrossed in his game as usual. But then he looked up and raised his eyebrows. "Oh, hello, Mr. Perkins. I'm on level fifty-*eight* now."

"Wow, really?" said Micha. "That's amazing!" Then he looked back up at Mrs. McGill and nodded toward his flowers. "I really appreciate these, thank you. And we're all learning new things all the time. It's okay. Hey – do you want to come in? We're having a little late Halloween thing."

"Oh, no," Mrs. McGill stammered.

"Is there cake?" Jake asked, looking up from his game for the second time in a minute.

Micha smiled at him. "It's vegan, but yeah, there's cake."

Jake nodded and turned his game off. "Cathy at school says we should all be vegan," he said as he wiped his feet on the mat, then marched on in.

Micha bit back a laugh. "So I've heard," he murmured, then extended his arm out. "What do you say, Mrs. McGill?"

She licked her lips and seemed to think it over. "You can call me Clarissa," she said with a twitch of a smile.

Swift was the only one surprised by her entrance. Everyone else greeted her warmly. But Swift made a point of coming over to Micha and hugging his side. "You *amaze* me," he said softly into his ear, sending a shiver down Micha's spine.

Their guests stayed long into the night, but as tired as he was, Micha almost didn't want them to leave. Swift assured him in the end that they'd be doing it all again for Thanksgiving, and Micha was able to relax. This wasn't a one-time event. This was just the start of a lifetime of a big, happy, messy family.

With the party done and an all-around success, life returned to what had become normal before the incident at the diner. They had several days of work and school and chores and meals. It was delightfully boring, and Micha loved every second of it.

Then the next Saturday rolled around, bringing with it a new chapter in their lives.

"Don't be nervous," Swift murmured as they left the car after their two-hour drive. Imogen had her very best pink overalls on with her Avengers jacket, clutching her pirate ship.

"I'm not nervous," Micha said as they each took one of Imogen's hands in the parking lot, ready to walk into the diner that didn't look all that dissimilar from Sunny Side Up, and yet it was completely different.

As much as Micha had finally come to a point in his life where he embraced that different was good, right now, he didn't want things to change. He wanted them to stay the same.

"Okay, I'm a little nervous," he muttered.

Swift gave him a sympathetic smile. "It's going to be okay, baby. I promise."

"Come *on*," Imogen cried, straining against their hands, her pirate ship gripped precariously between her and Swift's fingers.

Micha reminded himself he was a guest here. This wasn't about him, not really. And if Swift said it was going to be okay, he needed to believe him. Micha still held his breath, though, as they stepped inside the diner. Swift looked around expectantly, but Imogen yanked both her hands free to throw them up in the air.

And screamed.

Not a little shriek. A full-blown beyond excited scream. *"MOMMY!"*

Micha couldn't help it. As he watched her expertly sprint down half the length of the diner, dodging servers and patrons like flags on a skiing slalom, tears sprung in his eyes. The woman who rose from the booth clapped her hands over her mouth and looked to be struggling with tears of her own.

"Is that Amy?" Micha whispered. Swift nodded, his expression tense but not quite readable. So Micha took his hand and squeezed it. He was still getting used to that in public spaces, but in that moment, he didn't hesitate. Swift turned to look at him, his eyebrows raised. Micha smiled. "It's going to be okay, baby."

Swift rubbed his mouth with his free hand, nodded, then managed a small smile. "Yes, it is," he said determinedly.

Imogen was already babbling nonstop at her mom by the time Micha and Swift reached the booth. Amy was a woman of average height with soft brown hair, green eyes, and glasses, although hers were less sparkly than Imogen's. She pushed them up her nose as Micha and Swift approached, and Micha almost had to stop in his tracks at the sudden family resemblance. But he kept on walking by Swift's side, letting his hand go as they reached the table.

"Amy," Swift said as she turned to embrace him. Imogen paused in the middle of whatever story she'd been telling, and Micha realized with a jolt that this would be the first time she'd ever seen her parents together. "It's so good to see you."

"Oh, Swift," Amy said with a tremble, clinging to the back of his jacket. Then she took a deep breath and let go. "And you must be Micha?" She held her hand out, and they shook. "I'm pleased to meet you."

"And you," Micha said genuinely.

They all took their seats and pulled their jackets off. Imogen was looking between her folks with an open mouth, pulling absently at the pirate ship's cannons.

Amy swallowed and placed a red poker chip on the table. Micha frowned, not understanding what she was doing until she spoke. "Thirty days sober," she said, her voice only wavering a little. Then she managed a timid smile. "It's actually more like thirty-five days now, but you don't get chips for that. I have to wait for two months now."

Swift was sitting on one side of the booth next to Micha with Amy and Imogen on the other. Swift reached out and grabbed her hand, squeezing it with a sincere smile. "Well done. I'm *so* proud of you."

"What's that?" Imogen asked, pointed at the chip. Amy picked it up, offering it to her.

"It's like a special coin that says Mommy is getting better. She's going to get more of them, so she was wondering if you could keep them very safe for her?"

Imogen's eyes went wide. "Like a pirate debroom?"

"Doubloon," Micha whispered to Amy.

She caught his eye and smiled. Really smiled. "Yes! Oh my goodness, exactly like a doubloon. And look." She fished a silver chip out of her purse too. "Here's another one. Do you have somewhere safe you can put them?"

Imogen put on her pensive face. "Maybe in my cookie tin that looks like a mermaid, Uncle Micha?"

He realized it had been posited as a question to him. "Oh, yes," he stammered. "That sounds like a great idea."

Amy looked between him and Swift for a second with a smile, then pointed to what was on the table. "Hey, little one.

I got you a pack of crayons and a picture from the nice waitress to color. Do you want to?"

Imogen squealed and got to work right away, soon totally absorbed in her work.

Swift puffed out his cheeks, then smiled. "We call her 'little bit.' That's kind of crazy."

Amy stared at him for a second with a wry smile. "She puffs her cheeks out, just like that. I'd forgotten you did it too."

Swift beamed, looking at Imogen. "Two peas in a pod," he said affectionately.

Amy swallowed and toyed with her water glass. Micha tried not to panic she was about to say something bad about them. "I mentioned to the waitress that we needed to talk for a minute, so I hope that's okay," Amy began. Swift nodded, so Micha did too. Amy inhaled slowly. "I'm sorry. I'm *so* sorry I never told you, Swift. I convinced myself you wouldn't want a part of" -she glanced at Imogen, but she wasn't listening- "our lives. That I was on my own. But it sounds like you've been doing a beyond incredible job as Imogen's daddy, and Micha, I hear that's in no small part to you."

Micha blinked as the attention was suddenly turned to him. "Oh, no," he spluttered. "Swift has...I mean he..."

Swift took his hand and gave him The Stare. The one that meant Micha was supposed to stop being hard on himself any second now. "He's been fantastic," Swift agreed.

"I had no idea, you know?" Amy said, looking between them. "That, um, you swung both ways."

Swift gave a light chuckle. "I only sort of knew. It took meeting Micha to find out for sure."

Amy bit her thumbnail and grinned. It looked like relief more than anything. "I know you said you're bi, but seeing you with a guy...Swift, it just makes sense. Maybe it makes sense with *this* guy in particular. But...well, I'm worried it'll make me a terrible person to admit this, but I'm trying to be really honest with everything since going into rehab. It's much easier to see you so happy with a guy rather than another woman. It makes me feel like I failed less, which is dumb, I know. But I'm going to run with anything that helps and makes me feel better right now."

Swift reached over to also take her hand. "You're not a failure. We've got some pretty solid proof to that fact right there." They all glanced at Imogen, still coloring with her tongue poking out between her teeth. "But you're right. Micha and I are *so* happy. And it means a lot to know you're okay with that."

Amy sighed and visibly squeezed Swift's hand, looking at Micha. "I know I got messed up on some things, but I've known love is love for a damn long time. You guys make a great couple, and there's nothing I can ever really do to repay the fact that you took care of my baby girl when she needed you most." Amy took a deep breath. *"Our* baby girl."

Swift glanced at Micha, then Amy. This was what he'd been most worried about. "Yes," he agreed. "Imogen has become an essential part of my life. I'd have supported you before if I'd known. But now…I was really hoping you'd consider joint custody."

To Micha's surprise, and he was guessing Swift's, too, Amy laughed loudly, then slapped her hand over her mouth. "Swift, hon," she said, shaking her head with a crooked eyebrow. "I came here today to beg *you* for joint custody. Of course we can work out something. Actually, I…" She took a deep breath and looked around the diner. "I think I have too many bad memories here in Olympia. I pretended to be someone I wasn't here. I told myself…I told myself I was *never meant to be a mom,*" she whispered so quietly Micha almost didn't catch it. However, that meant Imogen didn't either. "But as soon as we were apart, I knew that wasn't the truth." She sighed and rolled her neck, making it click. "I partied so much because I was lost. But this is a fresh start. So I was thinking I might...well, that I might move to your little town. Pine Cove, was it? Then we could both see Imogen all the time."

Swift let out a little cry that was almost a sob. Micha reached over and squeezed his thigh with his free hand. He felt like this had to be a dream. No one was this lucky.

"You'd really do that?" Swift asked.

Amy nodded. "It might take a while. But I already checked. They have several AA groups there. And one of my old school friends said I could sublet from her. I'd need to find a job, but yeah. I'll make it work. Imogen deserves her mommy and her daddy." Amy smiled over the table. "And her Uncle Micha."

"Are you talking about me?" Imogen demanded, looking up from her enthusiastic coloring.

"Always," said Amy, brushing back her wayward bangs. "Hey, who did your braid? It's beautiful."

"Uncle Micha," said Imogen proudly.

Amy laughed. "Of course he did." She pinched Imogen's cheek, making her giggle, then reached her hand over the table, offering it to Micha. For a second, Micha didn't know what to do. Then he placed his palm against hers. "You're important to my child as well as the father of my child. So I'd really like to be friends, Micha. And I'd be honored if you'd like to keep co-parenting with Swift."

"Oh, no," Micha spluttered. "I wouldn't want to step on anyone's toes."

Amy squeezed his hand and winked. "You're not. It's the twenty-first century. There's no such thing as a 'normal' family anymore, am I right?"

Micha felt a little light-headed, but he managed to nod. "I couldn't agree more."

"Okay," Amy announced a little brashly. She sniffed as she let Micha and Swift go, rubbing her eyes under her glasses, then picked up her menu. "Who wants ice cream?"

"Mommy," Imogen said with a giggle as she rolled her eyes. "You can't have ice cream for lunch! You can have it – like – like – *after*. But not *for* lunch."

Amy scoffed. "I don't know about that. Shall we ask Daddy?"

It was as if his whole life Micha had been looking in one of those mirrors with all the lightbulbs around the edges. Except several of the bulbs had always been blown and dark. But in that moment, they all suddenly came on for the very first time.

Some women didn't plan on being moms. Some women – or *girls* – were never meant to be moms. They either coped the best they could…or they tried to give their kid the best chance they could by wrapping them up in a sweater and leaving them on the doorstep of a police station.

Some people didn't get the best start in life, and sometimes that meant they lost their way.

But they could always find their way back.

Micha looked at Amy, and he saw parts of himself, but he also saw a lot of his own biological mom. Maybe she'd desperately wanted to keep him, but didn't know how. Maybe she'd been terrified and had just been trying to do the best she could. He might never know. But for the first time in his whole life…he let that anger toward her, that resentment, just float away. He hadn't even realized how heavy that disappointment in her had been on his shoulders. But it wasn't fair, and in setting it free, he felt almost reborn.

He *had* parents who deeply loved and cherished him. He had the best brothers and sister anyone could wish for. And now, not only did their partners and children also count as his family, but he had Swift and his brood too. All *his* siblings, friends, doting mom and dad, and now the mother of his child, too.

And what could he even say about Imogen? His precious pirate fairy, whose mom had just so unbelievably generously agreed to share a little bit of parenting with him.

She was right. What was a 'normal' family these days, anyway? They'd find a way to split the days between them, raising Imogen together, Micha was sure. Why couldn't he be on Imogen's family portrait, the one that was now stuck to their fridge with a cat magnet?

That made him think of something.

"Uh, we were wondering," he said, pulling Amy's attention from her menu. "Why is Butter called Butter?"

Amy snorted and glanced at both their hands. Micha's scratches were still four pink healing lines. "Oh no! I'm so sorry. Has he been a nightmare?"

"We're doing okay," said Swift fondly.

"Well," said Amy with a chuckle. "You'll know you're doing *good* when he head-butts you. That's why he has the name. He's a head-butter. When – *if* – he decides he likes you, he'll bash his head right on into your legs. But don't hold your breath. He kind of likes me and loves Imogen, but aside from that…" She sucked her teeth and laughed. "He's a meanie, that kitty cat."

Micha turned to Swift, who beamed at him.

Micha hoped Swift was thinking what he was thinking. If they'd already conquered the evil cat, was there anything they couldn't do together? After all, parenting was *easy*.

Well, even Micha couldn't claim it was 'easy.' But they were pulling it off together, as a team. And their team was going to grow. And all together, maybe they had a real shot at building a family in Pine Cove. New lives, for all.

Never in a million years would Micha have believed he could have been this happy. Even the situation with Dale was close to being fixed. Dale was on his way to prison, and despite Brie currently being in custody, Padilla was convinced she would be let off with a warning, just like Micha had been.

She even seemed to think that Micha could apply for expungement now, not wait until his suspended sentence was done. That *might* mean he could apply for college courses in the new year rather than having to wait until next fall.

And above it all, he came home every night and shared a bed with the man he'd been in love with for what felt like his whole life. The man responsible for his sexual awakening. The man he'd carried a torch for all these years.

Nobody was that lucky. Nobody got to be with the person they fantasized about as a teenager.

Except for the second time in his life, it seemed the universe had smiled on Micha. The first time had been when it had brought him to Dad and Pops. The second was when it had brought him back to Swift and his daughter.

And now Micha was happier than he ever could have imagined.

So he ate ice cream for lunch with his not-so-normal family, keeping one hand on Swift's thigh pretty much the whole time.

Just because he could.

EPILOGUE

Eighteen Months Later
Micha

"Imogen, can you come here, please?"

It was a gorgeous summer day and a Saturday afternoon, which was all the excuse they really needed to have a little party outside. It helped they had a couple of other reasons, though, for a small family affair.

Swift and Micha's house had become the central hub for all the Perkinses and the Coals. Today it was just a small affair with both their parents, Rhett, Louella, and their twins, Amy, and her new boyfriend, Skip. They'd been dating for a few months now. However, Butter still wasn't very sure about him. He was currently scowling from under one of the shrubs, no doubt lying in wait for the perfect time to assault poor Skip's ankles.

Micha had wanted to invite Brie as well, but she was touring with a local band, living her dream of becoming a singer. She'd lived with them for a month after the nastiness

EPILOGUE

with Dale, but she was a city girl through and through. This time, though, she'd moved in with that nice girl she'd taken to the ice-cream parlor, who turned out to be the guitarist of this band. Micha was extremely happy they were still together and living their best lives.

It was a good-sized group of people in the yard. They had enough folding chairs for everyone, and it wasn't too overwhelming. One of the reasons they'd decided to get together was to start introducing Skip to some of Amy and Imogen's family. They'd met at AA, and Micha was proud not one person had even mentioned the fact that they'd kept it a sober gathering, let alone caused a fuss. Amy was thriving in her new life, and both the Coals and the Perkinses supported that.

The other reason they were celebrating was that Micha had finished his first full year at college. It had taken him a while to enroll to start with, but now he was balancing a pretty full class load with part-time work at the diner. It was enough of an income to keep him going through his studies, with Swift's support, of course. He hoped that within another year or two he'd be able to start work on a teaching qualification. It was his dream to teach kindergarten or one of the other earlier grades.

But they weren't doing much celebrating without cake. Imogen had run off, saying that she and Swift were going to go fetch it along with paper plates and a knife to cut it with. They'd picked it up from Rise and Shine that morning, but Micha hadn't even seen it since it had entered the house. It was vegan, of course. Imogen had been very passionate about that ever since the first day in the bakery. Micha and Swift were proud to support her, often eating what she did.

If the cake ever made it outside. Oh, god. Micha hoped no one had dropped it or that Butter hadn't gotten his claws on it. He was a much nicer cat these days, but he still had his moments.

"Imogen?" Micha called into the house again. He was getting slightly concerned, but just as he was going to get up to investigate, Imogen's panicked voice came shrilly from the kitchen.

"No, Micha! Stay there! We're coming now!"

Micha glanced at his brother, who shrugged. Except... why was he smiling like that? "Rhett?"

"What?" he said innocently. "Aww, look. Cake!"

Micha turned along with everyone else in the garden. But Micha was the only one who gasped. No one else seemed surprised by the two-foot-wide monstrosity or by the crazy number of candles on the top.

Swift was helping Imogen to carry it, who looked like she was going to pass out from the stress of keeping the damn thing level. "Oh," Micha cried as he stood. "You should have asked for help! What's all this?"

"No!" Swift and Imogen yelled together.

"Sit *down,* Uncle Micha!" Imogen said firmly.

Micha laughed and waved his hands. "Okay, okay," he said playfully. "At least let me clear some of the table. You can put it here." He shook his head as he moved some of the plates and bowls of food. Honestly, this was a lot of fuss for his school stuff. He wouldn't even graduate for another couple of years.

However, when they finally set the cake down, he realized it wasn't anything to do with school.

He managed to read the swirly frosting written on the cake just before his eyes filled with tears. "Wha-?" he said faintly.

The cake read *'Will you be my step-daddy?'*

Imogen slipped her hand into Micha's. He blinked,

EPILOGUE

making the tears roll down his face. When he could see again, he realized Swift was kneeling beside them both.

On one knee.

"Oh my god," Micha whispered, aware every single person in the yard was watching, holding their breath. Even the toddler twins were being quiet.

Swift grinned, and it was only then that Micha realized he was holding a ring box up. "Micha," he said thickly, his eyes shiny but his grin lighting up his whole face. "You make this family complete. Will you make it official and be my husband?"

Micha hiccuped, tears streaming down his face.

He was the little boy nobody had wanted. How could he grow up to be somebody that felt so loved?

"Yes," he managed to utter. "Yes, Swift, yes."

The yard erupted into riotous cheers that got Peri barking and sent Butter streaking back into the house. But Micha hardly noticed as Swift and Imogen swept him up for a crushing hug.

"I *told* you so, Daddy," Imogen gloated, wriggling free after a few seconds. "Of course he'd say yes!"

Swift apparently hadn't been so sure, as he and Micha continued to hug and Micha felt his chest shake. "I just had to check, little bit," Swift said.

Eventually, after Rhett told them to quit it and Imogen blew out the melting candles, they laughed and separated. Swift showed Micha the ring box. Inside was a platinum band, intricately molded with roses on a thorny ring. Swift touched the spot on Micha's chest where the similar tattoo rested.

"Because you stole my heart," he said emotionally.

Micha grinned, gently easing the ring from where it was nestled. It was slightly too big on his finger, but that was okay. They'd get it resized. Lots of things took a little work to make them perfect.

"Funny," he said as he beamed over at Swift. "You always had mine."

"Eww!" Imogen cried in over-exaggerated exasperation. "Mushy, mushy!"

"Mushy, mushy!" the twins repeated, running around the lawn.

But Micha didn't care. In fact, he was sure there was going to be a lot more 'mushy, mushy' in their futures.

Swift kept his arm around his waist as they stood and hugged everybody one by one. Pops cried, naturally, but Dad produced a card of congratulations from nowhere, the smug bastard.

"How did you know I was going to say yes?" Micha protested with a laugh.

Pops scoffed. "Because we didn't raise an idiot! Honestly," he added with a tut.

It turned out everyone had known what was going to happen. Micha loved that they'd gone to such an effort to surprise him as a family. Pops and Deb were already scheming on a big, official engagement party that they were planning at Sunny Side Up. Amy had a present for them all booked up: a spa weekend for two over in a fancy lodge near Penny Falls. "I'm so happy for you," she said sincerely as she hugged Micha tightly. "This family wouldn't be what it is without you."

"Thank you," Micha managed to mumble, threatening to cry again. "Thank you, everyone," he said louder. "I...I started out in life with no family. It took me a very long time to realize that word doesn't just mean who you share a blood relation with. It's who you share your heart with. So, thank you."

"Less crying, more cake," Rhett demanded, dabbing his

EPILOGUE

eyes. The party laughed, and they dutifully got to cutting up slices for them all to share.

Micha wasn't hungry, though. He was too full of happiness to eat, staring at his almost perfect ring, watching some of the people he loved celebrate on his and Swift's behalf, knowing there were even more people out there to keep celebrating with later.

He was aware that life was unpredictable, but sometimes when it turned everything upside down, it gave you what you never knew you were missing. Or in Micha's case, the person he'd been yearning for since he knew what love was.

He was sure now that whatever the universe threw at him, he'd be ready. Because he had Swift by his side, and the best pirate captain step-daughter he could ever hope to wish for.

Life was truly perfect, made better by all its mess and flaws.

Thank you for reading Micha and Swift's story! The next Pine Cove book will be coming out on November 15th, 2019. To pre-order right now, click here! getbook.at/PineCoveBrightHorizon

If you would like to be the first to know when my new releases are available, as well as read several awesome and totally FREE stories, please sign up to my newsletter! Emails will only be sent occasionally and you can unsubscribe at any time.

If you enjoyed reading Homeward Bound, I would very much appreciate it if you could share your experience with others online. Reviews, recommendations, fan works and general love is the best way for me to reach new readers. For giveaways, sneak peeks, ARC opportunities and general fun times, please join my Facebook group! Helen Juliet Books. We're very friendly!

Thank you to: my beta reader, Mum; editors Meg and Tanja; cover artist AngstyG; cheerleaders John, Ed, Amelia, Cara, Lucy, Susi and Piper; loving husband; and fur babies Arya and Tyrion.

Helen xxx

NEXT IN PINE COVE

Ben Turner is besotted with the handsome older man who's always in his bakery. They have nothing in common…until one day Ben discovers he's an overnight millionaire, and his customer could become his protector. But they hardly know each other. He'd be crazy to accept his help, right?

Lawyer Elias Solomon knows his crush on the beautiful young baker is ridiculous, however when he suspects Ben is being taken advantage of, he can't help but step in. Elias's upcoming fortieth birthday has made him adventurous, but he never imagined he'd accompany Ben all the way to England.

Ben has never even heard of Great Aunt Nancy, his corrupt and bitter English family, their enormous home and orchard grounds, or the business they run from it. All of which he now apparently owns. It's up to Ben to save the estate with Elias's help, but does he want the responsibility? All he *really* wants is to fall into Elias's bed and never leave, and soon the chemistry is too much to ignore.

Elias can't see how they'll make it work when they're from different generations. But when old rivalries take a dangerous turn, he soon realizes he'll do anything to keep Ben safe from harm…and in his arms.

Book Four of Pine Cove. Bright Horizon is a steamy, standalone MM romance novel with a guaranteed HEA and absolutely no cliffhanger.

Click here to pre-order Bright Horizon on Amazon today!

PREVIOUSLY IN PINE COVE

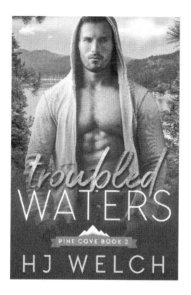

Scout Duffy doesn't know what's worse. The fact that his scorching one-night-stand is his bratty new client, or the fact that he doesn't even remember Scout. But beneath all the bravado, Scout can see Emery is terrified, and he'll do anything to protect him from his attacker. If only he would lower his walls and let Scout into his heart as easily as he lets him dominate in the bedroom.

Being out and proud his whole life means Emery Klein has never been safe. But now his charity work and social media fame have put a target on his back from bigots, and his friends force him to hire a private bodyguard. Emery doesn't need to be judged by some straight former-boxer, but his attraction to the gorgeous hunk is insatiable. When Emery finally recognizes Scout, they can't keep their damn hands off one another, if only for as long as Scout's in town.

There's a reason Emery never looks too closely at the men he sleeps with, just like there's a reason Scout lives out of a suitcase in motel rooms. Will two men hiding from hurt realize the love that could heal them both is right in front of them? Or will Emery's attacker take everything before they have the chance?

Troubled Waters is a steamy, standalone MM romance novel with a guaranteed HEA and absolutely no cliffhanger.

Click here to get Troubled Waters on Amazon today!

PREVIOUSLY IN PINE COVE

Robin Coal wonders if asking his straight housemate Dair to be his fake boyfriend for his high school reunion will be the worst thing he's ever done…or the best. But there's no way he's going home to face his abusive ex alone, and former Marine Dair is just the protection he needs. So long as he doesn't find out about Robin's secret crush, everything will be fine.

Mechanic Dair Epping never expected to spend a week sharing a bed with his adorable friend, however pretending to be bi is easier than he imagined. He knows he'll do anything to keep Robin safe from his ex-boyfriend, but as the chemistry between them grows, the line between fake and reality begins to blur.

Could Dair actually be bi? Even if he was, would an ex-Marine really be interested in a computer geek like Robin? When his ex's intentions turn dangerous, how far will Dair go to protect the man he's falling for?

Safe Harbor is a steamy, standalone MM romance novel with a guaranteed HEA and absolutely no cliffhanger.

Click here to get Safe Harbor on Amazon today!

ABOUT THE AUTHOR

HJ Welch is a contemporary MM romance author living in London with her husband and two balls of fluff that occasionally pretend to be cats. She began writing at an early age, later honing her craft online in the world of fanfiction on sites like Wattpad. Fifteen years and over a million words later, she sought out original MM novels to read. She never thought she would be any good at romance, but once she turned her hand to it she discovered she in fact adored it. By the end of 2016 she had written her first book of her own, and in 2017 she fulfilled her lifelong dream of becoming a fulltime author.

She also writes contemporary British MM romance as Helen Juliet.

You can contact HJ Welch via social media:
Newsletter (with FREE Homecoming Hearts material and original stories) – https://www.subscribepage.com/helenjuliet
Facebook Group – Helen Juliet Books
Facebook Page – @HJWelchAuthor
Email – helenjulietauthor@gmail.com
Instagram – @helenjwrites
Twitter – @helenjwrites

ALSO AVAILABLE

Scorch – Homecoming Hearts #1

Blake has never had a boyfriend before. Because he isn't gay. Until recently, he was part of one of America's most successful boy bands. After their record label ruthlessly dropped Below Zero, Blake has no choice but to head back to his hometown with his overbearing family.

Elion never thought he'd get another chance with his high school crush, the pop star hunk Blake Jackson. Not when his life is the opposite of exciting, stuck as a barista in the town he grew up in. When Blake walks back into his world though, Elion feels like there might be something between them after all.

All Blake wants is to pursue his first love of dance again. But in order to do that, he finds himself the star of a reality TV show, and the producers are determined to spice things up. They don't care that Blake isn't gay, not when Elion makes such a cute boyfriend. The pair send the ratings through the roof and find themselves forced to continue the charade. At least for the time being.

As reality and fiction begin to blur, falling in love becomes a tantalizingly possibility. Dangerously so, as a real-life superfan decides that Blake belongs to him and will do anything to claim him.

Elion will have to fight if he's to keep the man who has fallen into his arms. But Blake will also have to fight to keep Elion safe from harm.

Spark – Homecoming Hearts #2

Joey Sullivan is hurting. All he ever wanted was to escape his homophobic family. For a time, his dreams of being a popstar succeeded with Below Zero. But when the record label throws the band aside, Joey ultimately has to face the shame of returning home.

Gabe Robinson loves his town. As a firefighter, he'd do anything to protect it. He even tries to help the prickly, fallen-from-grace Joey Sullivan. Gabe is nursing his own broken heart though, so his immediate attraction to Joey can't be anything other than a rebound.

An unexpected road trip forces Joey and Gabe together and the sparks fly between them, but it can't last. Their worlds are too different. Joey plans to get as far away from home as soon as he can, yet Gabe can't imagine any other life. But when Joey hits rock bottom, Gabe is the only one who can save him. Protect him. Keep him warm.

Gabe's saved lives before. But can he rescue hearts?

Burn – Homecoming Hearts #3

Raiden Jones never thought he'd need a bodyguard. His life as a songwriter has been tame to the point of boring compared to his popstar days. But when a malicious hacker starts destroying his career and threatening his life, he finds himself desperately in need of protection.

After leaving the Marines, Levi Patterson takes a place with his uncle's private security firm. The last thing he expected was a dumb babysitting job for the bratty, privileged Raiden. However, the two men have no choice but to get to know each other as they are forced on tour with one of Raiden's remaining clients.

Levi has never told anyone of his secret, occasional hook-ups with guys from his unit, and Raiden's never thought about going with another man before. But it's obvious the increasing chemistry between them is becoming more than physical, and there's only so long they can resist.

As the hacker becomes bolder, Levi finds himself in a race against time before Raiden is taken from him forever. He's no stranger to combat, but with his heart on the line, he finds himself in the fight of both their lives.

Steam – Homecoming Hearts #4

Bad boy movie star Trent Charles is more famous for his outrageous behavior than he is for his acting these days. After one scandal too many, his manager sends him home to the snowy ski slopes of Wyoming to get his life together. No parties, no fast cars, and certainly no women.

Ashby Wilcott is done with bad boys. His heart is broken from his last relationship disaster. A few weeks of peace and quiet in the mountains is just what he needs. He is absolutely not interested in moody Trent Charles, even if he is hot enough to melt snow with his rippling muscles and mysterious ways. Good thing Trent is straight.

But the two men can't seem to stay apart. Trent finds himself pretending to be Ashby's boyfriend, a lie that gets Ashby invited to a wedding as Trent's guest. Regardless of Trent's protests that he's not interested in the beautiful Ashby in that way, the chemistry between the two steams up. With only a few weeks together, what harm can they do having a little fun?

As outside forces threaten to tear them apart, Trent realizes Ashby means more to him than just a fling. In fact, he'll do anything to protect him.

Blaze – Homecoming Hearts #5

International pop sensation Reyse Hickson has it all. Or so it seems. Thanks to his homophobic label, he never expects to find love. But when he's saved from a mugging by a gorgeous stranger, the chemistry between them is undeniable. Reyse can't help but fall into his savior's arms…and his bed.

Corey Sheppard is nobody's hero. He got himself out of the foster system and stands on his own two feet. He could never be anyone's closeted lover. But there's so much more to Reyse Hickson than the world sees. Corey just can't stay away.

When Reyse's dad suffers a stroke, Reyse insists on going home. In desperate need of a friend, he asks Corey to join him. A short time together is better than none. With Reyse's lifestyle, they know it's the best they can manage.

But for the first time in his life, Corey finds a family with Reyse. And Reyse doesn't think he can hide how feels for Corey, even though his label threatens to drop him if he ever comes out. Can Reyse and Corey walk away from the best thing that's ever happened to either of them? Or is this love worth going down in a blaze of glory?

ALSO AVAILABLE

Storm – Men of Hidden Creek

"I can't do this without you"

Chase Williamson was never meant to be a dad. Like it or not, though, he's now the sole guardian of five-year-old Lyla and terrified of messing it up. He needs help, but who wants to rescue a high school dropout? Certainly not the gorgeous newcomer in town, even if he is an ex-Marine.

Hunter Duke is looking forward to a small-town life to drive away his demons. Maybe meet a nice girl? Adopting a puppy begins to fill the hole in his heart, but it's an unlikely friendship with Chase and his daughter that really starts to make Hidden Creek feel like home.

When social services threaten to take Lyla away, Hunter knows he'll do anything to prove that this town is wrong about Chase. Could it be that this is the family he was searching for all along?

Welcome to Hidden Creek, Texas, where the heart knows what it wants, and where true love lives happily ever after. Every Men of Hidden Creek novel can be read on its own, but keep an eye out for familiar faces around town! This book contains a three-legged puppy with attitude, a long-awaited comeuppance, and enough kisses to mend any broken heart.

Ashes – Men of Hidden Creek

"It's always been you."

Kris Novak pours his heart and soul into his job at Hidden Creek's only gay bar. When an arsonist burns the place to the ground, his whole life goes up in smoke and only his long-time crush can save him.

Firefighter Remi Washington never told anyone he's bi, let alone acted on it. But when he temporarily offers his spare room to his best friend's younger brother, he's drawn to the twinky, beautiful Kris in a way he can't ignore. How long before he gives in to this temptation?

Soon Kris stands accused of having started the fire and he has to fight with all his strength to clear his own name. Will Remi risk outing himself to stand by Kris's side, or will that closet door remain closed forever?

Welcome to Hidden Creek, Texas, where the heart knows what it wants, and where true love lives happily ever after. Every Men of Hidden Creek novel can be read on its own, but keep an eye out for familiar faces around town! This book contains a daring rescue, a meddling mommy matchmaker, and enough sparks to start a wildfire.

Masterpiece – Men of Hidden Creek

"I want to trust you."

Koby Duvall always knew his place at school. Art nerds like him were just target practice for guys on the football team. NFL star Vince Russo may never have bullied him, but the two men are still nothing alike. Except when Koby is asked to create a sculpture of Russo, they find themselves stuck together.

Vince is only home for a few weeks over the holidays while he recovers from a head injury. Face to face with his former classmate, he finally has a chance to prove to Koby that he's more than just a dumb jock.

However, sparks fly and Vince realizes he and Koby may have more in common than they thought. But all Vince knows is football, and coming out in the NFL is career suicide. When a violent grudge comes back to terrorize Koby, though, Vince knows he'll do anything to protect the man he loves.

Welcome to Hidden Creek, Texas, where the heart knows what it wants, and where true love lives happily ever after. Every Men of Hidden Creek novel can be read on its own, but keep an eye out for familiar faces around town! This book contains a steamy modeling session, big families with even bigger food portions, and enough chemistry to melt steel.

Printed in Great Britain
by Amazon